MW00529209

Olena Nikitin

Amber Legends

CONTENTS

Copyright © 2023 by Olena Nikitin

Published by Viper Dawn Press

eBook ISBN: 978-1-7394473-3-5

Paperback ISBN: 978-1-7394473-4-2

Hardback ISBN: 978-1-7394473-5-9

All rights reserved. No part of this publication may be reproduced, stored or transmitted in any form or by any means, electronic, mechanical, photocopying, recording, scanning, or otherwise, without written permission from the publisher. It is illegal to copy this book, post it to a website, or distribute it by any other means without permission. Olena Nikitin asserts the moral right to be identified as the author of this work.

Editing: Sally Altass

Cover: GhostArt_Dx

Illustrations: GhostArt_Dx

Chapter Header: Reina Diaz

This novel is entirely a work of fiction. Although you can find here geographical and urban characteristics of Gdansk, Tricity and the Polish Pomeranian region, the names, characters and incidents portrayed in it are the work of the author's imagination. Any resemblance to actual persons, living or dead, events or localities is entirely coincidental.

External content

Olena Nikitin has no responsibility for the persistence or accuracy of URLs for external or third-party Internet Websites referred to in this publication and does not guarantee that any content on such Websites is, or will remain, accurate or appropriate.

Content Warning:

Dear Reader, we appreciate that everyone has a different level of sensitivity and may be triggered by different topics. It is up to your discretion whether you can handle the content in our books.

The book is intended for a mature audience of particular interests and contains a certain amount of coarse language, graphic sex scenes as well as sexual innuendo. You can also find scenes of death, and physical violence also some mentions of animal cruelty.

It is a work of fiction. Any resemblance to actual persons, living or dead, events or localities is entirely coincidental, and the names, characters and incidents portrayed in it are the work of the author's imagination.

Chapter One

No good deeds go unpunished, and looking at the clock, I wondered what sort of brain fart made me agree to swap tonight's shift with Tony.

The day had started badly and turned even worse, with my head pounding hard enough that my brain must have been trying to escape. Pouring enough painkillers down my throat to stun whatever creature was driving a spike into my eyes was my first mistake. The reaction of my liver was slow, but it was evident the cocktail of coffee and paracetamol wasn't appreciated. Now, I was nauseous and clutching my side like a victim of a vicious hen-do.

As I prepared for this evening's shift, the music from the radio faded into the latest news report. An outraged reporter talking about the missing tourists and the spate of knife crime in the docklands area. Still, the shiver running down my spine had nothing to do with the statement from an officious commissioner, dismissing the violence as gang warfare or unruly youths acting out, his disdain showing how little the man cared as long as no one rich was hurt. No, this was another of my hunches. My famous sixth-sense, which my medical team often relied on, told me the violence would escalate into something frightening if not addressed in time. I fought the temptation to call the police, realising that while the staff in my department followed my instincts, no sensible officer would listen to nebulous premonitions from a local doctor.

It didn't take long to organise myself, and my recovery was well on the way when mistake number two was made. A second cup of coffee made me jittery, unable to sit still, and my reaction to the cat jumping onto the kitchen counter left me staring down at the broken shards of a mirror on the floor.

As I grumbled about superstitions and seven years of bad luck, I noticed a minor cut from the mishap along my forearm and decided something had to change. Maybe I'd reached my burnout point, or my luck had nose-dived, but my *little problem* had worsened in the last few months. My mother had called it my *little problem*, as if ignoring the nightmares and uncanny knowledge could fix it. However, my visions, hunches, and occasionally seeing invisible people never improved. The older I became, the more shadows moved as if alive, but I learned how to live with it. What other choice did I have? Sometimes, I even saw the mirage of another city in all its medieval glory, fused but separated from my beloved Gdansk. I tested my eyes and scanned my brain, but my health was perfect. It was all in my mind, so I kept quiet and carried on, hoping no one would notice the lead doctor wasn't the most sane.

Today felt different, with an atmosphere I was too tired to analyse. Maybe tired was the wrong word. When you work in the Emergency Department, tiredness becomes as close a friend as any human, but this time, I felt worn down to the bone. When I started my career as a doctor, everything was exciting, and the adrenaline rush could keep me going for days. Now, ten years later, I was just worn out. Same shit, day in, day out, with different and often hostile faces, and a failing social system that brought us all to our knees. Maybe that was why I sensed death, or perhaps it was just a skill that comes with experience.

I held to this thought because what was the alternative? I was not fucking psychic, or worse, teetering on the edge of a mental breakdown. *No, Sara, you are simply brilliant at your job, with vast experience and knowledge that gives you insight into what is wrong with your patients. Oh, and you are bloody good at pep talks and denial.*

It was true. I may be an unbreakable doctor at work, but in my private life, I ran away and hid each time I felt threatened, hoping my friends would come and dig me out of Sara's Den, as they call my apartment. My smirk echoed my feelings on that thought as I leaned down to pick up the broken glass from the floor.

I left the car at home, the warm autumn sun easing the tension between my shoulders as I strode confidently to work. Autumn had always been my favourite time of year; especially September when it had just begun, the cooler air reducing the summer's unrelenting heat and the trees slowly changing their finery to the rich golds and russets that felt like a hug for the soul.

The city was bustling as the evening's entertainment warmed up, with restaurants and bars opening to encourage those eager to enjoy the nightlife. Young men and women, dressed to impress, rushing to the next experience. While the unfortunate few, like myself, jostled each other on the tram toward another night of blood and catastrophe.

I wonder if they will bring another one from the notorious Anchor, I laughed out loud at my absurd thoughts provoking disapproving stares from the other tram users. Of course, we would receive a victim of a brawl or lover's squabble. The Anchor never failed to deliver clients to the hospital.

I wished it were different, that it was possible to see the world with the fresh eyes of a medical student. Now, the expectations were low; all the cards were marked, and I always knew whether I would win or lose. Still, I had to go; I was good at my job, and maybe, if I were lucky, there would be lives saved by my stubbornness today. That had to be enough to keep me going.

'Hey, boss, beautiful day, hmm?' Tom, our porter, welcomed me at the entrance, making me smile with genuine affection, and I nodded in reply. The evening was warm, with birds softly singing in the background. It was indeed lovely.

'Hello, Tom, yes, it's a beautiful day. Let's hope for a good night, too.' He laughed as we both knew there would be nothing good about it, and I slipped through the automatic doors, a feeling of dread settling into my bones.

Pale pink in the sunset, the full moon had just begun rising, and my instincts told me tonight's shift would be a nightmare. Worse, I still had this bloody headache to deal with. So, I crossed my fingers, hoping Nina, my best friend and the best nurse I knew, would be on shift to save my sanity.

As expected, the sad, lonely, and hopeless stormed our defences together with an obscene amount of drunks. Now and again, we had a genuine emergency, and I would be called to assist my staff. Thankfully, most of the time, I could sit in my office nursing my coffee, organising the steady flow of patients in and out of the department.

It was well past midnight when the phone rang, and a panicked intern informed me we had a stabbing inbound, a cardiac arrest with the knife still in the wound, coming through our front doors. My Gdansk delivered on its reputation, I guessed, eyes rolling at my thoughts as I reassured the intern in a quiet, professional manner.

'Calm down, prep the team and ensure we have plenty of blood on hand. I will be there in five.' I said, and somehow, this message made me smile. At least the night wouldn't be so dull now, even if it was another stabbing to add to my recent collection.

Despite Nina's absence, the resuscitation room was prepared just as I liked it, and a quick team briefing showed me everyone knew their individual roles. It wasn't long before the doors burst open, and the paramedics came in with... a corpse on their stretcher. Yup, a corpse. There's cardiac arrest, and then there's a body so dead I couldn't even feel the shadow of a soul. Unfortunately, this was definitely the second.

The knife had penetrated his chest to its hilt, and while the paramedics were desperately trying to save him, I knew this one was long gone. The grey cloud of death covered him, the soulless body bouncing rhythmically during the chest compressions. He had no chance, but I couldn't tell my team their efforts were pointless. There was no science to back up my claim, so medical training kicked in and, taking a deep breath, I issued the order.

'Stop chest compressions.'

'No, he has no pulse.' The paramedic tried to argue, instantly making me wish Damian and Rysiek were here, but one look at my face and his voice faltered.

'He's running on empty. How do you plan on restarting an engine without fuel?' I said and turned to the team. 'Secure the airway, prepare O neg and get me a thoracotomy set. We need to crack him open to plug this hole in his heart.'

Like a Formula One pit crew, my team was ready in less than a minute. Pride surged at their response as I bent over to start the incision when the patient's bright blue eyes snapped open in surprise, and a cold, male hand grabbed my wrist in a vice-like grip.

'Oh, hell no, you are not doing that.' His voice was cold and commanding, and the man, about to be opened up like a giant clamshell, sat up, the dagger still fully embedded in his chest. *What the actual fuck*, I thought, looking at him in shock. It is one thing to feel like there is more to the world than science can explain and a whole other one to stare at this discovery in its smugly amused face.

'Did you just pull a Lazarus on me?' I heard myself saying, despite my voice being drowned out by screams of terror and the clattering of fallen medical equipment. I didn't care. Why would my attention be anywhere other than the talking corpse before me? Maybe years of conditioning, medical missions to war-torn countries and stories my grandmother told me; stories that had suddenly become very real prepared me for it because I was as calm as he was dead. *I will never break a fucking mirror on the full moon again,* I thought, observing him as he looked around, his gaze eventually falling on me.

'Pulled a what?' He asked, still holding tight to my wrist, and for no apparent reason, I reached out with my free hand, pulling the knife from his chest. Some say emergency people are built differently, and while I still could barely believe what just happened, part of me methodically analysed the situation. This man was definitely alive, yet no blood escaped the wound, and I bit my lip, trying to comprehend the insanity. He didn't even wince when I examined the gaping hole, poking it with an inquisitive finger. He just looked on with impatient annoyance, utterly unphased, before asking again.

'I pulled a what?'

The knife in my hand looked odd. I'd seen my fair share of weapons, combat, folding, and kitchen knives, but this was different. It was vibrating... no. Looking carefully, it didn't move, but something felt... tension. That was it. It felt as if it were under tension, like the cable on a bridge or, more accurately, a string on a bow, ready to release its murderous power, aimed at this man before me. In fact, it refused to be pointed anywhere else. Nothing about this blade was normal. Ornate Slavic engravings adorned the metal that, whilst bright and clean, felt like it belonged in a museum. I had to resist the urge to stab it back into the gaping hole in the man's chest. I wasn't sure whether the knife was driving the desire or my curiosity at seeing the strange man's reaction. Then, the real, screaming, noisy world crashed into my consciousness, and I focused on answering his question.

'Did you just resurrect on me, like Lazarus, or maybe Jesus would be more accurate as nobody here helped you? What the fuck are you, a zombie, vampire, or something else that sparkles?' My rambling question made the very alive man laugh.

'Yeah, or something. Now, be a darling and give me the dagger. It still wants my life, and I see you are keen to give in to the temptation.' He commanded, looking into my eyes as if trying to reach into the depths of my soul, but his five minutes were gone. My anger broke through the shock of the situation. Now he faced a very focused woman with a powerful urge to tear him a new one... newer than the one that brought him here, anyway.

'Pack it in, Romeo. First, the dagger is evidence, and second, I'm not your darling, so you can stop trying to make puppy eyes at me. I've seen this constipated look far too many times. That is borderline creepy. Who, or should I say, what, are you?'

One thing I was sure of was that he looked human, but apart from his looks, there was nothing human about him, and even this external glamour faded when I looked closely. Besides, no one called me darling or tried flirting when I was poking a gaping hole in their chest. The conclusion was simple. Either he wasn't human, and all the strange things I saw in the shadows were real, or I'd been hauled to the psych ward and pumped full of powerful drugs. The reasonable part of my brain would bet on the latter, but everything felt so incredibly real. When my shift finished, I would be searching for answers. Proper answers to the questions I had blissfully ignored for years, but now was not the time. He was still staring at me, and I'd read too many awful romances to fall for the charm of a wounded stranger.

I knew I was rambling, but I had to stall for time. I couldn't stab him. That clearly wasn't viable from a doctor's perspective, not to mention it hadn't killed him the last time it was used. Hope that my staff was calling for help started fading as the lack of alarms or codes called over the tannoy system began sinking in. This strange calm left a chill running down my spine, kicking my body into action. I hit the stranger's hand with the hilt of the dagger, freeing myself from his grasp. Jumping back, I tried to bolt through the doors just as they opened, and my body bounced off something... someone, who grabbed my arms, saving me from falling unceremoniously to the floor, his large frame not even affected by the impact.

When I looked up and saw my saviour's face, I must have been gaping like an idiot, as a man I could only wish lived in my wet dreams held me tight to his chest. With a slightly annoyed grimace, he released me, and I staggered back, trying to regain my balance.

'Who... who are you?' I stuttered, but he didn't even look in my direction, his gaze fixed on my miraculous patient. It reminded me of Kosovo when a warring party came to the hospital to finish the job. My instincts kicked in, and, like the last idiot, I positioned myself between the arsehole on my table and the coiled danger in front of him.

'Whatever you came here for, you won't finish it here. He may piss you off, and I'm betting that's what happened, but he is still my patient. You will not fight on hospital grounds. Leave before I call the police.' I said, pointing the dagger in his direction.

I attempted to look in control of the situation, ignoring the part of me screaming in terror, berating me for making a terrible mistake. The careless arrogance of the man before me didn't change, even when I pointed a deadly weapon at his chest.

Instead, the corner of his lips lifted in smug amusement as I pointed the eager dagger at his heart. His green eyes lit up with swirling gold, and a tingle of power washed over my skin. For a second, I didn't see a man standing there dressed in a tailored three-piece suit but something monstrous, barely clad in breeches, with a golden torque around his neck and smoky tattoos that glinted with burnt umber and gold over his skin while fireflies danced between his antlers.

Antlers? The vision was gone as soon as I concentrated, but my yearning for the beast remained, and with it, the electrifying feeling that washed over my skin with the tidal wave of power. Whatever I believed didn't matter anymore, the damage was done. I was afraid. No, I was terrified by the strangeness appearing in my life. My scientific, ordered world creaked and shattered, and just like the mirror earlier, I was left to collect the pieces. The pragmatic part of me realised the life I knew and loved had ended, but under the fear was something more. *What did it mean for me if these monsters existed, if corpses could rise from the trolley and a man with antlers could walk into my Emergency Room?*

My heart was pounding because, deep down, I wanted this to be real. I wanted my nan's stories to be authentic. I wanted this beautiful savage monster to be real. My bedtime stories and lullabies that soothed a child terrified of shadows were so vivid when she weaved them. My crazy, scorned grandmother talking about the magical guardians and lurking monsters, who I now realised must have seen them, too. Relief washed over me. I was not crazy, but what the fuck was I and why was I the only one seeing this?

Chapter Two

'Surrender.' The simple, softly spoken word carried so much power that my hand lowered, and the sudden urge to stab him disappeared. The dagger lay dormant, its tension subdued. Then, as if it was the most natural thing to do, I handed it over to the stranger. *What the actual fuck*, I thought, but without the burning need to kill, it was easier to reassess my situation.

The raven-haired man on the gurney, handsome as he was, paled in comparison to the work of art that commanded my compliance. He looked close to forty, tall at just over six feet, with broad shoulders, a short beard, and rich auburn brown hair with hints of the burnt umber of his imaginary tattoos, but what made him stand out from the crowd was the aura of command. This man was born to lead, and I could easily see him in a general's uniform. *Maybe he is an undercover police officer?* As soon as this thought flashed through my mind, I dismissed it. He was a leader, but I doubt he ever followed an order. He was precisely the type I always fell for, and after the initial fascination was gone, that left me bruised and hurt, searching for a more docile lover. The man in front of me was perfect, or, I should say, perfectly intimidating. His strength spoke to me on a visceral level, and he clearly knew some... magic?

As I stood there appraising him like a prime side of beef, for a split second considering asking him for help with my visions, the object of my unwanted desires opened his mouth, and all my physical and scholarly interest departed to where the sun didn't shine.

'Adam, really? Out of all of them, you got yourself loaded into the ambulance? And then you let this woman get hold of Czernobog's dagger? Did you lose your mind completely, or did it temporarily land in your pants?' He said, and just like that, my interest nosedived. He might be handsome and have the knowledge I needed, but I wouldn't fall for this honey trap again.

Too often, I fell for men who made my pants wet and messed with my head, and after my fling with Kamil in Kosovo, I promised myself the next man who walked into my life would be different. I was attracted to danger, and the man before me was a walking red flag summarising all my lousy relationship choices. Whatever he did prevented me from doing something I would later regret, but this idiot talked over my head, and nothing cooled hot flushes better than misogynistic bullshit.

I huffed angrily, finally gaining his attention, but not for long.

'Get yourself off this thing. The rest of the hospital is clear. There's only this one to bespell, and we can leave.' He said, and his dark green eyes dismissed my presence like a stubborn cockroach.

'I tried,' said Adam, his voice sparkling with amusement, 'but she resisted my compulsion, then ripped the dagger from my chest. You can sort this one out yourself. Forest magic might work better on the stubborn wench, especially since you've already broken through Czernobog's spell.'

'No one will *sort me out*, and if you've hurt any of my team, I will have you dragged into court and hung out to dry.' I said as the tall man approached. I took a few steps back, but the resuscitation table blocked my escape. Without a word, he grabbed my arm and sank his gaze into my eyes, whispering something. A peculiar feeling spread through my body. Time felt like molasses. I wanted to please him. I tried to forget like he wanted me to. Instead, the touch of his mind awakened a strange, untamable desire. I knew I wanted him, but why did I feel I belonged to him? I stroked his beard impulsively, trailing my hand along his neck. His skin was warm and surprisingly soft, and I pinched it gently, enjoying the texture between my fingers.

'You have such a beautiful vein. I'd love to touch it,' the words escaped before I realised, my other hand joining the mutiny and playing with his jugular. My voice dropped to a breathless purr, but part of me resisted. *What the fuck am I saying? His vein?* Suspicion rose in my mind, shielding it like a fortress. It wasn't right. I never flirted in the workplace, not even facing the man who spoke to the very depths of my soul. I shook my head, then jerked in his grip, and he stepped back with a shocked expression. Whatever he was trying to do hadn't worked as planned. I knew the moment he finally looked at me properly when his lips twitched, and the narrowing of his eyes told me he was confused and curious.

'What the hell was that? Hypnosis? If you were hoping a smouldering glance would earn you a kiss, your technique needs work.' I said, hoping they couldn't see my embarrassment, and Adam started laughing.

'I didn't think it would work on her, but seeing the great Forest Lord fail was funny.'

His mocking was a catalyst, and the man he called the Forest Lord grabbed my arm harder, a mask of anger replacing the curiosity.

'What are you?'

His grip on my arm made me hiss in pain, and I punched him, or I would have if he hadn't grabbed my fist and pulled me closer. His pupils widened when he pressed me to his body. I could feel his breath quicken,

'Fuck. What are you, woman?' he murmured, inhaling deeply. I knew my arm would bruise, but the worst part was the feeling that he saw me and he liked what he saw. Atavistic fear returned and burned inside my chest, giving me the strength to break free from his hold. He released me when I jerked backwards. I was free, but

I'd had enough of my mixed reactions and their attitude, so I hit the panic button on the wall for the first time in my life.

'I'm the doctor that will kick your arse so hard you'll never be able to find it. Now get the fuck out of my E.R. before the police arrive. I don't know what happened here, but I have a department to run, and you just made my life more difficult. So off you go before I rip that dagger from your hand and put it back where it came from.'

I counted the seconds it should take for security to arrive. I knew these men should be detained, but I was too freaked out to deal with this, and as time passed and no one turned up, I looked outside. Life on the other side of the glass door appeared normal as if nothing was happening. Like we hadn't just reanimated a corpse, and I wasn't standing between two men who looked ready to kidnap me, leaving my body to float down the Motlawa.

I'm so fucked. I thought, trying to find a solution to my predicament. It was time to be wise, not brave, and make sure I didn't end up with the dagger in my chest, but suddenly, the tension washed away, and the green-eyed man looked at the name tag on my chest with a lazy smile.

'So you don't know yourself. We will fix that. I will come back for you, Sara. We should have a friendly chat about today's events. Till then, please, no gossiping. No one will remember, and they won't believe a word you say. You should keep quiet for your own good unless you plan on spending the rest of your life in a mental institution.' He stroked my cheek with a finger and left the resus room, undisturbed by the passing staff.

The rest of the shift passed by in a haze of surreal normality with no reanimated corpses or luscious, annoying Forest Lords wandering around. Not a single person mentioned a patient with a knife in his chest, but I couldn't stop my hands from shaking. We had a few routine cases, cardiac arrests, and the usual drunken calamities, but I was surrounded by blank stares with each mention of the evening's strange events. By the end of the shift, I was sure it was a side-effect of too much coffee and the usual burnout. That, or the years of fighting impending death, pretending I didn't know the strange voices or creatures I sometimes saw meant a mental breakdown had finally happened, and I was medicated and on the bus to the asylum.

When I finally escaped the hospital in the morning, thick fog from the river obscured the quiet streets. I felt the other town on the edge of my consciousness hidden in this milky veil, and I had to remind myself the silence was due to it being Sunday, not thanks to a sudden world catastrophe. Still, such condensation was unusual for this time of year, and the Motława didn't produce this much murkiness even on its worst days.

I could have taken a tram, I should have taken a tram, but I had to reconnect with the world, and like a fool, I wandered through the old town, where the city I lived and the one I sensed felt almost the same, and strolled along the riverbank. Water birds called, their haunting song drifting over the water, breaking the peace of this surreal moment, but that was precisely what I needed, giving me some normality and the opportunity to think. Now all I wished for was the morning sun to dispel this dreadful feeling I had been carrying in my chest since encountering that infuriating, fascinating arse of a man.

The patient, Adam, was handsome with his dark hair and blue eyes, in a rakishly polished way, if you liked that type of thing; but no one could compare to his compatriot, whose green irises seemed to have engraved themselves onto my soul. It was interesting how standing beside his boss made him so easily forgettable despite his unique injury. I suspected that the fascinating man had done something to me as each time I closed my eyes, I could see him looking at me with an intensity that burned like the sun while I stroked his neck, praising his vein.

'Vein, out of all the things, a vein ... oh, for fuck's sake.' I said, chuckling and cursing softly, lost in thought and secondary embarrassment. *It had to be some kind of hypnosis.* I tried to rationalise. How else could I explain my reactions and how I felt about the man who invaded my workspace, threatened me but left me feeling needy and helpless in a way that I should, but didn't hate?

Out of anger, I kicked at an uneven cobblestone, but the slippery bastard left me scrambling to keep my balance. I tried to regain my equilibrium, not wanting my day to end as badly as it started, broken mirror be damned.

A powerful arm encircled my waist, pulling me against a firm, muscular body. 'Well, fucking you can certainly be part of our negotiations, but for now, let's talk about our encounter.'

The familiar voice sent a shiver down my spine. My curves pressed against a body that I couldn't help but be vividly aware of. *No, no, no, not Mr. Vein man.* I instantly recognised the timbre. The soft baritone caressing my senses could belong only to one man. Smoky Eyes stood behind me, rescuing the poor damsel in distress from the evil cobblestones. Much to my shame, he must have heard me, and now I leant against his chest, my thoughts racing so hard that it was a struggle to listen to his words.

How was it happening again? Usually, a strange man grabbing me would earn a black eye or ruptured balls, but I couldn't help myself around this arrogant bastard. *There goes my feminist membership card, along with a pair of wet panties,* I thought as I extricated myself from his embrace.

'Thank you and goodbye,' I blurted. My decision to move away made him frown, and he looked at his now empty hands for a moment. The confusion in his eyes should not have been cute, so I quickly scowled to cover up my reaction when he stepped in front of me.

'Good morning, Sara. You should be more careful on these quiet streets. You don't want to fall through the rabbit hole and wake up in a completely different world. It would displease me greatly if I had to search for you there. Now, how do you like your coffee?'

'My what?' *Who cares if he was displeased or not?* I thought, trying to wrap my head around what had just happened.

His casual question left me flustered and confused. First, what was he doing here? Second, where did he expect to find an open coffee shop Sunday morning in Gdansk?

'Your coffee? The scent of it was all over you, even in a sterile hospital setting, giving me the impression you liked it.' He smiled, and when I still didn't answer, his smile turned into a frown. 'We need to talk, and you look tired. I thought coffee would help you focus. There is a nice little coffee shop around the corner, already open. Unless you prefer a more civilised drink, I can find a nice herbal tea to help with your exhaustion.'

'Coffee is fine. I don't like to drink chopped grass.' I muttered. My response raised the corner of his mouth in a smouldering version of a mischievous smile.

'Oh, my lovely Sara, but you haven't tried mine. When I make you herbal tea, you will taste pure bliss, not chopped grass.' His voice held delicious promise, and I wasn't sure we were talking about tea any more. Before I could even respond, his mouth tightened slightly. 'We will have time for that later. Let's get you that coffee. So... shall we?' He offered me his arm as if this were perfectly natural, and I accepted because I was an idiot fascinated by dangerous men.

We must have looked like a Victorian couple wandering along the riverside, passing the few unfortunates forced at work on a Sunday morning. I could not believe what I was doing. This man, everything about him, screamed danger, yet I let him lead me wherever he wanted, like a lamb to the slaughter.

When a sudden breeze threw dry leaves and debris in our direction, he raised his hand, sheltering my eyes in an old-fashioned gentlemanly gesture, and whatever the wind carried slid down along the invisible wall.

'Thank you, but what do you want from me?'

'Don't overthink it, Sara. Today, we will just talk. If we come to an agreement, I will explain more about your situation, and maybe we will even see about any other benefits you may like.' He said, and my hand on his arm curled into a fist. How could I let this man take control of the situation so quickly?

'I don't even know your name.' My voice was pleading, and I straightened in disgust when I heard myself covering my embarrassment with a cough. 'So what is your name?' This time, it sounded more like old me.

He smiled and led me to a table in an open but deserted restaurant.

'Leszek Borowy, but you can call me Leszek, so how do you like your coffee?'

'Latte with caramel.' My answer seemed to amuse him as the corner of his lip rose in a mischievous half-smile again before he left to place the order.

At this point, I should have been halfway across Gdansk, running away from him, but no, the feeling of safety and home kept my rear in the seat as I watched this strange, hypnotic man with a curiosity that any cat would be proud of. *He found me here, so he will find me anywhere. I must know what he wants and who he is*, I thought, convincing myself to stay. Besides, it was better to talk in public than be cornered in a dark alley because I was sure Leszek wanted this conversation, whether I cared or not.

When he returned from the counter, the aroma of fresh caramel goodness hit my senses, helping me settle back into the normality of coffee with a handsome stranger.

'What do you want to talk about?' I asked, avoiding his eyes to stop making a fool of myself again.

He chuckled quietly, amused somehow by my question, but the sound was thick, sweet molasses trailing down my spine with slow, delicious progress.

'I want to offer you a job, Doctor,' He said, and when I frowned and shifted on the chair, he added. 'Last night was a revelation for both of us, and I rarely encounter something that can surprise me. I genuinely don't want to kill you, but I can't let a seer run around unchecked. In exchange for your doctor's skills and, more importantly, your silence, I intend to offer you a rather generous remuneration. All you have to do is call me if you encounter any more unusual patients or strange items like the dagger last night.'

The coffee suddenly lost its taste. What Leszek was offering was essentially a mob job, even if this mob appeared to be supernatural, and I wanted nothing to do with it. I wanted to know more about this world, but there must have been other ways than getting myself entangled in with this man and whatever crime syndicate he was dealing with.

'And if I refuse?' I asked, although I knew the answer before I spoke.

The velvet softness of his eyes hardened into ice-cold steel, and Leszek leant closer.

'Your unique abilities, including the resistance to my magic, make you my problem, Sara, and if I can't solve my problems, I bury them.'

I swallowed hard, knowing deep down he was speaking the truth. He called me a seer, and something inside my chest felt the rightness of his words, which made this experience even more terrifying.

'What guarantee can you give you won't bury me, anyway?'

'None. Still, you amuse me, little seer, and I like your confidence. That is more than many of my problems can attest to. Let me show you some perks of working for me.'

He reached out, tucking a stray wisp of hair behind my ear. His hand landed on my cheek, and I froze, unsure where this was heading. The warmth flowing from his touch was invigorating, washing away the tiredness of the night and the need for sleep. My muscles relaxed, and I melted against him, exhaling slowly. Something inside me recognised a power I couldn't comprehend. I felt synergy, like whatever he was completed what I am. This restorative magic and his touch weakened my will and made me want to crawl over and curl up on his lap.

'Stop, please.' I whispered, and he took his hand away with a hint of surprise.

'You appeared to be enjoying it, though.' There was no shame in his voice, more disappointment that I told him to stop. His reaction firmed my resolve to stay away from him. I couldn't let a stranger manipulate me like this, so I jerked back to avoid his touch and looked at him with a hostile grimace.

'You didn't leave me much choice, but I want more than immunity. Give me your phone number, then find someone to teach me what a seer does and how. I will call you if I encounter a strange patient, but please don't contact me otherwise.'

My words felt like shards of glass as I spoke them, but determined to avoid this stranger's allure, I forced them past my lips. When he passed me his business card, I didn't even look as I grabbed it and my purse off the table.

'Thank you for the coffee, goodbye.' I called out, rushing toward the tram stop.

'See you again soon, my lovely Sara.' I heard but tried to ignore it. His touch had invigorated me, and now, like a graceful doe, I jumped up the curb toward the safety of my home and far away from the strange man whose verdant eyes made my heart flutter.

Chapter Three

I blinked at the flickering computer screen, wondering why everything my befuddled mind had typed into the weekly Emergency Department shift report looked like the ramblings of a lovesick teen writing fanfic. With a sigh worthy of the aforementioned story, I gave up. I had to skip it. There was no way to explain my strange patient. People didn't sit up with no blood or pulse and start talking, and that was without having a strange dagger sticking out of their hearts, a blade that encouraged the urge to stab the nearest hot-blooded male.

My frustration at the inability to complete a cogent document ended with the bang of the laptop's lid as I slammed it closed. Why would I even bother? No one would believe it. No one ever did. I remember trying to tell my teachers about the shadows and creatures I was seeing or telling my friends what questions would be on the test. All that happened was me becoming an outcast, with other children mocking me and calling me a witch. So I stopped talking, and now, when I finally had proof, this handsome arsehole made sure no one would remember it, and once again, I had to keep my silence.

Handsome arsehole. Leszek held answers to so many of my questions, but he was precisely the type of man I'd promised to avoid. Yet, for the last few days, I seemed unable to focus on anything else. I worked hard, taking on my junior duties and even exercised to eliminate this weird tension in my body, but nothing helped; I kept daydreaming about the sensual touch of a man with fireflies in his antlers.

A glance at the clock told me it was less than an hour from midnight, with the day wasted on restless activities and pointless paperwork. I considered going back to bed. I would soon be starting a day shift, and it was better to get back into a reasonable sleep pattern, but once under the covers, my thoughts drifted to him again. My imagination ran wild, and I stroked the sensitive skin of my thighs, wondering how his strong, masculine hands would feel as he looked deep into my eyes. It didn't take much effort to ignore Leszek's threats and dismissive manner, the need for a release overriding the little common sense I had left. Besides, even if I didn't want to be near him, it didn't mean I couldn't find pleasure while thinking of him. It helped that he would never know, and with this final justification, I allowed myself the indulgence of fantasising about that firm body while I stroked mine.

The feeling was so delicious it took me a moment to register the sound of knocking at my front door.

'Oh, for fuck's sake!'

It was one thing to disturb a woman this late at night; it was another to disturb one close to the best climax she'd had in weeks. I was ready to tear my visitor a brand new orifice and shove their interruption right up it. So, grabbing a robe, I stomped to the front door, throwing it wide open to confront whichever idiot was knocking, only to encounter my Lazarus impersonator, flanked by two human walls that could have been extras from a gangster movie. To make the situation even more confusing, he held a cup of what my nose identified as liquid gold, A.K.A. caramel latte.

'You are needed, woman. Dress and come with us. Oh, and Leszek said to give you this to avoid being punched.'

He pushed into my apartment as if he owned it, leaving his escort standing in front of the doors like obedient guard dogs, and looked at me.

'So are you going dress, or should I throw you over my shoulder as you are?' He was clearly angry at something, maybe at being a messenger or, worse, a courier, but his arrogance awakened my mean streak, and I answered with a snarl.

'Woman? Where did they dig you up from? The middle-ages? I see why you ended up on my table. I don't have a dagger, but my kitchen knives are sharp, and I know anatomy better than whoever put that blade in your chest. I should have left it there or pushed it deeper to pierce your rotten heart.'

'Czernobog's dagger can't hurt my kind, and I was not its target, but you are welcome to try. Oh, and after we find out you can't stake me, I will stake you, and I'm sure you will love it.' He said with laughter as he followed me to the bedroom.

Interesting euphemism. I don't know where the idiot got the idea I would enjoy myself staked on his cock, so I did my best to ignore his presence while I dived into a pile of washed, unfolded clothes, trying to find something suitable for a late-night, probably bloody trip. Unfortunately, the annoying idiot spent his time looming over me, and I had to admit to feeling intimidated.

I couldn't overpower him, and even if I managed it by sheer luck, what next? A bare-knuckle fight with the men he brought with him. No, this time, I had to comply. Of course, having a stranger in my personal space in such a manner fuelled the anger bubbling up inside, and I couldn't help but give in to its urging. Standing up suddenly with my least wrinkly top raised in triumph, my elbow shot back, catching his stomach with all the force I could muster. The painful "umph" that followed pleased me greatly.

'I'm sorry. I didn't know you would come here to watch. Or maybe you're into lace panties? Out of professional curiosity, tell me, did it hurt a lot? Does paracetamol work on your kind?' My sweetly saccharine voice conveyed my anger as clearly as the assault on his person, and with a vicious sneer promising retribution, Adam forced the cooling coffee into my hand.

'If you weren't under his protection, this would play out differently.' The fangs suddenly on display were clearly meant as a warning, but I was too angry to care.

'If you weren't under his protection, my elbow would be aimed at your bollocks. Now get out of my bedroom before I change my mind and find something silver to stake you with.'

'Silver is for werewolves, you idiot.' He said, muttering curses as he left the room.

Alone, I looked at the coffee and took a sip. Velvety, caramel goodness flowed over my tongue, and I sighed softly. *Beware of Greeks bearing gifts*, my distracted thoughts reminding me of the old saying as I pulled on jeans and a simple jumper. I just wished this gift could be refused, along with its demands. On returning to the living room, Adam was unfortunately still there, arms crossed over his chest, looking like fury incarnate as he attempted to win a staring contest with my cat.

'Leszek called. We need to hurry.'

With this renewed sense of urgency, the doors were barely closed before the two goons flanked me, their broad shoulders forcing my feet to move at an uncomfortable speed as they escorted me to a large black Range Rover. 'At least it is not a black Volga. So which one of you boys felt the need to overcompensate?' I said, provoking surprised stares until I felt compelled to explain my remark. 'It's an old joke, you know. There was a rumour the Communists kidnapped children in a black Volga to work in the mines.' I pointed to the car, waiting for their synapses to catch up before adding. 'At least it is not a black Volga.'

Only Adam laughed, but it wasn't at my joke. 'Oh, you think we didn't understand? No, darling, my men simply struggle to comprehend why you think we need to compensate for anything. I'd be happy to prove my point when you're finished with the boss.'

With that statement, I was bundled into the vehicle, an overwhelming smell of wet dog making my eyes water as the two henchmen sat on either side. The entire situation was oppressive, and I decided my unwilling companions should share in my misery, so I blurted out in pure spite.

'Are we there yet?' I said as we passed the first crossroads, and Adam looked at me in the rear-view mirror.

'No,' He answered sharply, tempting me to repeat my question. With each passing junction or red light, I repeated, 'Are we there yet?'

The satisfaction I derived from the slowly tensing shoulders and deepening scowls made my smile grow over the miles of our journey until, at one point, I was sure one of Adam's henchmen's eyes flashed with a golden glow as his head snapped in my direction, and he growled.

'Will you shut up?'

I chuckled, looking at the nameless guard and, led by another self-destructive thought, I sang.

'Oh, Grandma, what big teeth you have!'

The roar that shook the car scared me silent, but moments later, the vehicle came to a screeching halt in front of an old warehouse at the docks. I was pushed out of the car and into the building with a brutal efficiency that proved my captors were eager to get rid of me. At the end of the long, dark corridor, we stopped in front of some rusty doors, and Adam pointed at them with a sarcastic smile.

'Show us you are as good as Leszek thinks, or your screams will entertain me as the boys show you why grandma has such big teeth.'

With a nonchalance I didn't feel, I pushed the door open and smirked.

'Of course, I'm that good. I'm bloody excellent. Why else do you think I'm here?'

I stepped into a dimly lit room, and the view that greeted me made me wish I could turn back time and swallow my words.

Most of the room was drowned in darkness, but one brightly lit area was filled with a metal table upon which some animal was strapped, writhing in pain and howling so pitifully it made my skin crawl. Leszek stood there, calm and composed, but I could see a deep frown on his face as he placed a hand on the animal's head before turning his gaze toward me.

'Thank you for coming. I didn't want to drag you here in the middle of the night, but I had no choice. I encountered a situation only expert hands can help with.'

His apologetic tone didn't calm my anger, and I marched toward him, pointing to what looked like a massive dog.

'What kind of sick experiment is this? I won't take part in anything like this.' I heard the pitch of my voice rising like it always did when I was on the edge of going fully berserk, and I would not calm down this time. Few things truly angered me in life, but animal cruelty... Gods, demons and even the owner of the most mesmerising eyes in Gdansk couldn't make me torture an animal.

Agitated, I gesticulated wildly, trying to unstrap the poor beast, and my hand trailed dangerously close to the creature's head. Before I knew it, Leszek grabbed me, pulling me away from the snapping muzzle.

'Sara, this isn't what you think; he needs your help. Please, I know you are angry, but I don't want to lose this boy.' He said, pressing my hand to his torso before I ripped it from his grasp.

'I won't torture animals, you bloody psycho. Who the fuck do you think I am?.. wait, did you say help?'

I was confused, with rage boiling inside me, ready to explode if he denied me an answer. Instead, Leszek placed his hand on the animal's head. The beast on the table stilled under his touch, panting heavily, its eyes darting between the man who touched him and me.

'Change.'

A sense of déjà vu overtook me as the power in that one word took my breath away, just as it had in resus, but this time, thankfully, it wasn't directed at me. Even so, I felt a slight whimper slip past my lips at its strength. However, the poor animal on the table felt the full force, shuddering and twisting to escape. I couldn't help myself and stepped forward to stop Leszek from torturing the defenceless dog, only to stop as the writhing animal blurred before my eyes, changing, elongating, its fur slowly disappearing. The step backwards was involuntary as my mind struggled to comprehend what it saw. No longer was there a large dog on the table, but a naked young man screaming and cursing in pain. I could see several bullet wounds unevenly spread across his torso, a strange grey smoke rising steadily from each hole. I had minimal experience with this type of wound. Gdansk had violent crime like any city, but gun violence was rare. However, the local mob "families" occasionally clashed, and a body would spend a few moments under my care before heading to the morgue.

Fuck, I was going to lose this boy! I thought frantically, trying to find the best solution to this situation. *Get a grip, Sara!* I mentally smacked myself, thinking that, in all irony, it seemed I was the only one who had some shred of sanity to tackle this situation. So I took a deep breath, and this time, my voice commanded obedience as I donned my professional persona.

'We need to take him to the hospital. Bring some covers, and I will call in a favour from the speciality ambulance team. The guys from S3 won't say a word if I tell them not to; now hurry!' I said in the way I could always command a crowd of medics during the trauma code, and his people twitched to follow my instructions before Leszek's headshake stopped them from complying.

'That's not how things are done here, seer. Our healer will look after him, and his shifter magic will do the rest, but until those bullets are removed, no one can help. Whoever wanted him dead mixed magic, wood, and iron with silver, stopping anyone from getting close.'

'Are you out of your mind?! I'm trying my best here, but you mistake me for a surgeon. I work in the E.D. I can keep him alive till he gets to the theatre, but that's it, so don't be difficult and let me take him. He will die here because I don't have the tools or skills to save him. Fuck it, I'm done with this, and if you can't help, don't disturb me.'

I moved to the table, releasing the leather belts that kept the man's frame tied in place, but Leszek stepped in my way and firmly took my hand. His expression was stony, but I could see sorrow in his eyes when he spoke.

'No, Sara, you help him now, or I put him out of his misery. Choose, Doctor; his fate is in your hands.'

Chapter Four

As if to confirm his words, the metal doors to the room slammed shut with a thud, and a small operating trolley full of tools that reminded me of the Soviet occupation appeared beside the patient.

'I don't care how you do things here. That is not the end of our conversation. I have no anaesthetic or anyone to monitor this boy's vitals. This is cruel, inhuman, and pointless!' At my wit's end, I shouted at Leszek, trying to rip my hand from his grasp. He was visibly tense but waited until I calmed down, then ignored me to position himself by the man's head.

'You are right, but he is not human and will endure it. I will make sure of it.'

As soon as he uttered those words, the patient opened his eyes and protested, his voice hoarse from screaming.

'My Lord, I can do it. I don't want your magic. I'm one of the pack. I'm no weakling.' He complained, but Leszek's hand lowered to his forehead, and again I heard the command in his voice.

'Sleep,'

There was magic in his voice. The order was so powerful I swore we were suddenly in the depths of the Kaszubian forest. The scent of verdant greenery, enticing resin and rain filled the air, and I inhaled deeply, relaxing almost instantly despite still standing in that dark, damp warehouse, but the sensation disappeared as quickly as it appeared. As its calm, supportive presence disappeared, I exhaled slowly, closing my eyes briefly to hold on to this serenity for longer. My moment of indulgence went unnoticed. When I returned to reality, the injured man was unconscious, and Leszek looked at me strangely, clearly impatient for me to begin.

With no other recourse, I mentally prepared myself. I'd wanted to help, but not like this. I was willing to transport this boy to the hospital and lie my way through the documentation and procedures. Instead, I was out of my depth and about to perform surgery only done in theatre.

Improvise, Adapt, Overcome. You are an emergency doctor who won't wimp out in the face of adversity. My simple mantra enabled me to calm down, steadying my hand, and when I was ready, my anger was replaced by crystal clear focus. Following my instincts, I took a scalpel from the pile of random tools before me and trailed it along the skin, making the first cut. My patient didn't flinch, but Leszek, whose hands were still on the patient's temples, hissed quietly, distracting me.

'What the fuck?' My question was to no one in particular, but the woman who brought the tray emerged from the shadows and answered.

'The Master is experiencing the child's pain and shielding him from it, so hurry, we don't have all day. Take out the bullets so I can start the real healing.'

I found her tone amusing, even as I was scolded. 'Fine, I will hurry. It's not like this is someone's life here.' I sneered, high on adrenaline, before removing the first bullet lodged in the man's shoulder muscles. The next one was tricky as I moved to the abdomen, carefully cutting through the layers and trying to recall all my anatomy classes. I was so focused on my work that I barely noticed the sweat pouring from Leszek's forehead. Cutting and tying bleeding vessels, then suturing the wounds, I worked like a robot until I reached the last hole where the bullet had entered right under the clavicle.

My steady hands began trembling as I thought about cutting near the subclavian artery. 'I can't do it. I ... there are too many structures here. It will kill him if I slice through the wrong one.' I said, trying to calm my nerves.

'Feel it, Sara, use your magic. It will guide you to the bullet. You are doing great; I trust your skills.' The husky voice averted my attention from the fearful wound, and I looked at Leszek.

His face was ashen, and I gasped, seeing the dark circles under his eyes, yet he encouraged me to continue. I bit my lip, sliding my hand over the wound. Again, it was nothing but a hunch, but I knew what to do, and with a determination I hadn't felt since my student days, I slowly peeled back the layers of flesh till I retrieved the last bullet. Suddenly, it felt like time sped up, and the wound bled profusely, expelling dark plasma before the flesh regained a healthy colour and knitted itself before my eyes. Whatever was in the projectiles stopped shifter healing, and once I'd removed the cause, his natural abilities returned with a vengeance, speeding the regeneration.

The healer woman pushed me aside, her hands working swiftly, pressing some green paste over and into the wounds while cooing over the youngster like a mother hen. I staggered away, dizzy, exhausted, and relieved I didn't kill the boy. All I wanted was to sit on the floor, but that wasn't an option as my chest was encircled by a pair of muscular arms that held me up, pressed to a body with zero softness. I refused to look up at Leszek, afraid of what I would see, instead choosing to watch the healer chant as she scattered more herbal concoctions over my patient's body, my eyes widening at the changes happening before my eyes. The man who should be dead from his injuries, gaining a healthy colour, wounds that would take weeks to heal already scabbing over.

'You were amazing, my Firefly. I never thought I would see a human fighting so hard for one of the Nether. Yet here you are.

My miracle doctor.' The quiet voice whispering in my ear sent shivers down my spine. He was still holding me, his nose trailing slowly over the curve of my neck, praising my skills. His voice was so sensual that my thoughts drifted to the vision of the forest. To make matters worse, my fingers softly stroked his forearms as my body melted against him.

It appeared my reaction to his embrace was more than welcome, his softening expression in perfect counterpoint to the hardening elsewhere on his body, and, as a blush spread over my cheeks, his fingers stroked under my chin, tipping it up for a kiss.

'Sara?' Desire burned in Leszek's voice. He wanted this, and as his gaze drifted to my lips, I swallowed hard as my earlier fantasies suddenly came true.

He is not for you. Think Sara, you can't do this again. I'd only met him a few days ago, but it was clear the pull drawing me to him also affected this powerful man. I loved the thrill of danger and was no stranger to one-night stands, but my relationship history was a string of failures, and I always fell for the same type. Powerful and dominant with a streak of violence in their blood. Still, all the others had let me go when I ended it. With Leszek, I couldn't even say no to illegal surgery. He was my fantasy, but it didn't mean I should act on it. We weren't friends; in fact, we were adversaries. This gangster had dragged me here to do his bidding. So, fighting my body's desire, I pulled away, staring into his eyes with all the outrage I could muster.

'That was not part of our agreement and must never happen again. What were you thinking, forcing me to operate in the warehouse with tools from a museum?'

I was practically shouting, and my voice drew Adam's goons inside. They stood in the open doorway, looking at the scene. Their eyes narrowed, observing me until a gesture from Leszek sent them away. Only Adam remained, looking at me with a knowing smirk.

'If you're finished, I will drive this shrew back. That's if you really are done and don't intend to use her services in your bedroom. You have been very tense lately.' The vampire said before he turned his attention to the table. 'What do you think about the wolf? Will he live?' I saw anger flash over Leszek's expression, although I couldn't understand what caused it until he answered.

'Tone down your insolence. Yes, he will live, and as soon as he is properly awake, you will investigate who shot him. You can start cleaning up here; I will drive her home.'

They talked over my head again, ignoring me as if we were living in the last century. I should have interrupted their little game of coddling the helpless woman, but I didn't have the energy to fight. I was tired, dirty, and not in the mood for their testosterone-fuelled display.

'*She* can take herself home, and you two should refrain from contacting me ever again. But who am I talking to? I told you this last time I saw you, and here I am doing your dirty work. I'm breaking our agreement, and frankly, I don't care if you bury me.'

I said, marching toward the door, followed by Adam's laugh and Leszek's angry commands for his subordinate.

Sunlight blinded me as I left the warehouse, and I cursed the loss of another night's sleep. Before they could adjust to the brightness, I closed my eyes, feeling the comforting embrace of the forest, Leszek's voice deepening the connection despite his words.

'Sara, we need to talk.'

I turned around and looked at him, sheltering my eyes from the rising sun.

'We've talked a lot recently, and you forced me into doing this. That boy could have died. I'm not a surgeon, and you forced me to operate....' I stopped, swallowing back tears. There was no point in explaining that I would be shattered if this young wolf died under my care. Instead, I sniffled, clenching my fists.

'So what do you want to talk about now? How you forced me to perform surgery in filthy conditions, or how could I lose my licence for operating outside my scope of practice? Oh, no, wait, maybe you wanted to talk about how you did something to me in the hospital, and now all I can think of is how to make you touch me. So, what is it? What you want to talk about, oh mighty Forest Lord?'

The concern etched on Leszek's face when he approached me further infuriated me, so I held my hand out to stop him before the compassion in his eyes could melt my defences. I needed the anger to stop this madness and time to process what happened. *He ma-*

nipulated you to do his bidding, I thought. Luckily, it was enough to bolster the fury inside. I'd hated being surprised and treated like a puppet my entire life, and I was confronted by an abundance of both tonight. He made me feel vulnerable and unsure of my skills, not to mention stripped of choice, because I couldn't let the man on the table die, and Leszek somehow knew it.

When he finally stopped, the distance seemed too far and not far enough, his frowning eyes more confused than upset. I watched as his hand lifted toward me, only to fall, fingers clutching for something neither of us understood. I longed for a comforting embrace, but the fact I was longing for his touch made me want to slap him.

Leszek was the one who turned me into this emotional wreck, disrupting my life with the force of a tornado, and now I wanted him to be the one who took all my worries away? *Get a fucking grip, Sara, or pay an escort if you're that desperate for male attention.* I scorned my weakness, annoyed that I wanted to hurt this green-eyed demon for what he did and kiss him for what he was. Even if I didn't know who or what he was. Instead, I clenched my teeth, calming my racing heart and acted like a reasonable adult.

'I know you have secrets, and I understand the circles you move in, whatever you call them, differ from mine. I agreed to help by contacting you about any "special" arrivals to the hospital, but that's it. I'm not a mob doctor, supernatural or not, and I refuse to be put into a situation like this again. Do I make myself clear?'

A light smile played over his lips before he nodded and pointed to the car. 'Yes, you made yourself perfectly clear, my Lady. Please allow me to drive you home.'

'I told you I can get myself home. I don't need a lift.' My outburst didn't discourage him. Instead, he opened the car door and gestured inside. When I didn't move, he came and gently placed his hand on the small of my back, barely touching it.

'Sara, please. You are tired and have had no sleep, so please let me take you home. I owe you this and much more for what you did. Let me look after you.'

'... and whose fault is that?' I asked, but he was right, and I didn't want to spend an hour on the tram trying to stay awake, so I let him lead me to the car. His smile was as radiant as the morning sun when I settled in the seat, and I involuntarily smiled back. It had been so long since someone wanted to look after me. *He also looked after the injured teen, yet he would let him die if I refused to help.* This thought sobered me up. I was another pet project to the man who seemed to work in some weird, magical underworld.

I turned to the window when the door closed, confused by conflicting emotions. Leszek must have sensed my mood, and we drove silently for a moment before the infuriating man broke the silence.

'I have done nothing to make you want to touch me. In fact, I'm as surprised as you are that you react this way.' He said, and I rolled my eyes. There was no better place to discuss my body's weird attraction than being locked in a car with a handsome stranger.

'Fine! It is my fault, then. You are handsome, and I'm horny, but I see no problem with it, as we'll never meet again. Right? And as soon as you disappear from my life, I will easily find a replacement.' I said, inhaling deeply when the car filled with his earthy forest scent and the vehicle's speed increased to dangerous levels.

'No, it is not fine, and you'll never find a replacement because I'm going nowhere.' His voice was quiet, the answer spoken after a terse silence, and my eye gravitated to his tight, angry lips.

'That is my decision about who I met and how. What right do you have, telling me what I can do?'

'Power, little seer, that is my right. Whatever fate put you in my path, you are mine now. I won't risk anyone using you to discover my secrets or expose my people. Still, I would happily oblige if you so desperately need comforting.'

'You must be fucking joking.' I said, overwhelmed by his statement. Suddenly, he turned to look at me.

'No, I'm not fucking joking. I'm deadly serious. I am the only man who will touch you until I figure out who you are and why my magic affects you so strangely.'

'Look out!' I shouted when the car swerved across the carriageway in front of an oncoming truck. Leszek snapped his fingers, and with a bang, the truck's tyre exploded, sending the lorry into the roadside ditch.

'Fine, no one will touch me. I get the message.' I answered quickly, holding the seatbelt for dear life while Leszek moved the car back to the correct side of the road.

My whole body shook as I stared at the wreck, not realising I held my breath until the lorry door crashed open, and the driver climbed out, shaking a fist at our disappearing vehicle. 'He is fine. I'm not a monster.' Leszek said, as if my opinion of him mattered.

I slumped in the chair. The adrenaline rush left me weak with a pounding heart, a foul taste in my mouth and more questions than I could express. Leszek might not consider himself a monster, but a man willing to cause a crash to prove a point was not a good man, either.

'I'm sorry for your distress, but there will be no arguments until I know what to do with you. You will follow my instructions.' As he finished, Leszek lay his free hand on my knee, squeezing it lightly. I wanted to protest, but a quick look at his face and I choked back my words. It must have been tiredness rather than his strangely soothing touch because before I knew it, my eyes were fluttering closed as I leaned against the passenger door, an E.R. doctor's ability to rest when needed kicking in. I vaguely remember a gentle rocking when he lifted me from the car, and softly spoken words intruded on my dreams as I embraced his neck instinctively.

'I'm sorry. I keep forgetting how fragile humans are.'

'Yeah, we are all wilting roses.' My words were garbled but must have amused him because I felt a soft chuckle when he lowered my feet to the floor.

'You are anything but a wilting rose or any other flower. Now give me your keys,' he said, still embracing me.

I blinked several times, trying to focus my eyes, only to notice we stood in front of my apartment.

'You wish. What next, a toothbrush in the bathroom and a drawer for your boxers?' I said, patting my trousers till I pulled the keys from the back pocket. It took a while to slot the key into place, and with each moment, I felt his gaze following my every movement. When the door finally opened, Leszek pressed his hand to the door frame, locking me between the wall and his body. 'I don't invite you in. You can't cross my threshold.' I said and saw his body shake with a quiet chuckle.

'I'm not a vampire, and I don't need a toothbrush... yet, but I will visit you tomorrow evening around six o'clock. Your life is changing, Sara. Whether or not you like it, you are part of my world now, but I promise to make this transition as easy as possible for you.'

'The hell it will; I like my life just the way it is.' My chin lifted defiantly, but looking at him from such an angle was difficult. I was going to say more, but as soon as my lips parted, he inhaled sharply, looking down at me.

'Yes, you will. Now go to bed before you tempt me too much.' His words were harsh, but the hand trailing along my neck in a soft caress sent a different message, and I shivered, leaning closer. *What the hell is happening to me?* I saw his pupils widen and his body press closer the more I leaned toward him.

'Go!' Leszek pushed me inside and shut the door behind me. The loud thud and sudden space around me shocked my thoughts awake, stripping all the charm from the encounter.

'What in the ever living fuck was that?!' I asked, turning back toward the door, only to be met by solid wood and silence. Why he can't be normal? Why my life can't be normal? A few days ago, my only problem was worrying about slowly getting crazy. Now, I suddenly advanced to become a gangster trophy, isolated and untouchable, and I couldn't even talk to my best friend, Nina, for fear of retribution. After shaking my head in disbelief, I picked up my cat, who'd strolled from the bedroom and was now rubbing himself against my shin. I needed to sleep it off, but didn't want to be alone in an empty bed. In his strange demand for my chastity, Leszek didn't mention the cat, and it was about time my furball earned his keep. My world had imploded, and I was very much in the mood for a little cry.

Chapter Five

Magic danced around my fingertips as I stood there like a fool, looking at Sara's closed door, wondering what was wrong with me after pushing the confusing woman into the apartment, slamming the door closed to avoid surrendering to the strange craving burning inside my body.

I'd almost crashed the car when she mentioned letting another man touch her, the mere thought of it causing me to lash out like a child. Sara was a seer, which should have been reason enough to avoid her, as my relationship with the Tricity Coven was strenuous at best. Those damn women blamed me for everything in this region, but there was something. Her mere presence expanded my perception of magic, her touch... embracing her. I felt like I'd never tied my magic to the Gates of the Nether, and that disturbed me, as no mortal was supposed to have such power. She couldn't bespell me, and I was sure she was as annoyed by our mutual attraction as I was. *Damn woman is up to something; she must be.* The thought eased my disquiet, but the image of her during that first meeting swept aside my calm as I remembered foolishly trying to coerce her mind into forgetting me, only to falter at the fierce magic burning in her soul, its fragile beauty belying the strength hidden in its depths. Her magic, her beauty, but most of all, the bold defiance she showed defending Adam, knowing I could destroy her, had awakened something I'd buried in the past. A need to care for someone who would fill the loneliness of my soul, someone who wouldn't be afraid or subservient to me. A need for a companion.

I rarely paid attention to humans. After a thousand years, you learned to keep a distance from such a foolish, short-lived species even while protecting the land from their wasteful habits, but something about this one, as fierce and blond as a Valkyrie, had forged a connection I didn't want to deny, awakening a possessiveness that surprised me.

It didn't make sense. Even if she was willing, her life would be just a grain in the sands of time marking the trail of my life, yet the thoughts of seducing the alluring woman elicited a groan of desire. The visions of her naked body, lost in passion, sent a shiver down my spine, but now wasn't the time for frivolities. An unknown enemy threatened the balance between Gdansk and Gedania, and I needed to discover a way to free us both before my cravings destroyed everything I had built. *Sara is human. She will fade and die like all the rest.* I repeated the mantra because even the strongest seer's life was a blink of an eye in the Forest God's lifetime. *What if she was put on my path by my enemy?* A sweet little morsel to distract me. Was that why Adam landed in the human hospital with Czernobog's knife in his chest? This thought was disturbing, but even worse was that it was working, and even with such suspicion, I barely cared. The desire to rip her from the concrete cage and make love to her in the glory of Mother Earth was undeniable, and whoever chose her did it well.

You are mine, Sara. You may not know it yet, but you are mine. My hand pressed against the dead wood of Sara's door, and green tendrils of ancient magic carved intricate patterns on its surface, sigils of protection and possession, a stern warning for those with the wit to see that the woman who lived here was inviolate and protected. That was the best I could offer her, especially as the recent attacks left me little time to deal with... this.

Whatever I felt had to cease, even if I couldn't stop thinking about the raw hunger on her face at my touch, my fierce little seer. As soon as I sorted out whatever was causing problems in my city, I would return to her, even if only to find out why this fierce doctor was so alluring.

The journey home was the perfect time to mull over the situation, and I couldn't help but smile at the realisation that Sara's magic placed her firmly within my jurisdiction, along with the other supernatural communities within Gdansk. The forest and the sea had divided this territory hundreds of years ago when it was still a fishing village with barely a few citizens. Jurata never disputed this. It felt natural, as she preferred her ports and sailors while I presided over the verdant forest and inland dwellings.

Then came the split, and the magic that freely coursed in those lands was locked in the Nether, with old gods and beings that could not live without it, leaving those too human to survive behind. That also left us, the guardians of the order and keepers of the Gates to the Nether, the gods and spirits willing to sacrifice their power to help those we were forced to abandon in the human world. We kept ourselves and our people hidden in plain sight, but with modern technology impacting every piece of life, more and more ordinary people knew of our existence. The bullets Sara removed from the shifter were evidence of that, man-made and created to kill those of the elder races.

The plans I'd made to insert a mole in the hospital were now superfluous, the opportunity Sara had presented too good to pass up. Watching her perform surgery she insisted was beyond her was a revelation. She was so innocent and unaware of her magic that I realised we had gained an asset worth keeping. It also made me wonder if there were more ordinary people who lived their lives unaware of the gifts they carried. All because of one woman who resisted my compulsion. If she was my enemy's gift, I had to monitor her, but if not, I had already decided to use her to further my plans, but now new possibilities presented themselves. I had to create a place where she could thrive, expanding her skills without worry or hesitation. *I will build an Emergency Room of her very own, a safe space for her and my people.* I thought, remembering how repulsed she was by the ancient tools she'd had to use.

The laughter that escaped my lips was unaffected by recent events, and I almost crashed a second time that day as my car danced on the road, imagining how surprised she would be when I showed her a brand new workplace, which would be very close to my office. I reached for the phone and rang Adam.

'Find me a small empty warehouse, preferably close to our main building, and contract our builders to renovate it.'

'What for?' Adam's voice was surprised, and I didn't blame him. That purchase would be a significant investment, and I was always prudent with money.

'We need our own treatment facility, especially now with these recent attacks and having careless men show up in the hospital with knives in their chests.' That was partially true. Lately, more of my soldiers returned injured from their guarding duties, and it was time for me to do something about it.

'Of course, blame it on me. I'm betting it has more to do with our latest acquisition.' Adam's sarcasm was palpable but not without its merits. Still, discussing my decisions about Sara's future was not his place.

'Keep your thoughts to yourself, bloodsucker, and find me somewhere.'

The laughter on the other side of the call annoyed me enough to schedule an extra weapons training session. Adam clearly needed a reminder of who was in charge. I'd allowed the vampire to get away with far too much over the years, but I couldn't help seeing him as the young man who'd awoken irrevocably changed after overindulging at a wedding, the desperate craving for blood making him dangerous. With no one from the local nest claiming him, I was tasked with this burden, and through the years, his charm had grown on me, like mould. If nothing else, he was entertaining and loyal, which eternity knew, I needed.

The car came to a stop with the tyres protesting loudly, the gravel still scattering as I walked into my house. White walls contrasted nicely with the vivid green overabundance of plants filling every corner. I chose this oasis of calm when the small island was still covered with forest, its temple filled with tribute to the Horned God, and I used some of my power to cloak this place, discouraging most visitors.

Human progress had barely touched this pristine land, as I only allowed the elder races to settle here, giving them refuge from persecution and intolerance. It was not isolated from humanity, but I restricted how much technology encroached on the sanctuary, allowing only a superficial environmental impact.

As I settled in my favourite chair, I released the magic that hid my form from human sight, the Chesterfield creaking as it accommodated my primal form. I allowed my thoughts to drift to the past, to the last time I allowed love into my life, committing everything to a woman as capricious and wild as the sea. My sight drifted to the desk holding a statue of a woman painstakingly carved in glowing amber.

Eyes trailing over the beautiful form encapsulated by the magical amber, nostalgia and bitterness fought as memories played out in my mind. *Why do I still keep you here, little warrior? You chose the Nether while I remained here.* I knew why, despite the passage of time, it was both a warning and punishment for the betrayal that only a loved one can inflict. Now, there was another form eclipsing that of the Warrior Queen from my past, Sara's determined expression battling past her doubts as she fought to save a stranger.

Was this determination the trait that attracted me? The first memory of my golden warrior was seeing her face down the raiding party that had killed her siblings, spear and buckler a blur as she danced through their ranks, merciless and deadly until staggering from exhaustion and blood loss, she pierced the leader's chest, ending the battle, and leaving them to rot on the ground as she fulfilled the funeral rites for her kin.

I looked at the statue one last time, then locked it away in a drawer. *I won't poison my mind with those thoughts anymore. What will be will be, and fate weaves the fabric of our lives. It is time to focus on the things I can control.*

That focus needed to be aimed at the cause of the latest attacks. There had been no warning, no demands, nothing to hint at the vaguest clue as to why my people kept disappearing. Like the teenager riddled with arcane bullets, their bodies turned up days later, desecrated and lifeless, the wolf being the first to be found alive. I withdrew my phone from its protective case and called the pack leader. It took several rings before a rough, wary voice answered, and I hoped he was not playing pissy dominance games because I needed his cooperation.

'Hello?'

It may have been framed as a question, but there was no way Tomasz didn't know who was calling and why. I was sure he wanted to be anywhere else than on a call with me, but he wouldn't dare to refuse me, knowing I could destroy his pack if challenged.

'I'm glad you picked up Tomasz, your young wolf. How is he?'

'Licking his wounds and singing the praises of the beautiful human doctor that saved his arse. Is it true? You letting humans into the fold now?'

His accusation irked me, but I understood his reasons. Tomasz had to care for the entire pack, but the disinterest in his voice when talking about the pup's life made me think we might need a new pack leader soon.

'Send him to me. I need answers, and yes, a human doctor is in my service. It is time we expand the business, and unless you think you can challenge for my position, I suggest you remove that tone from your voice.' I knew I was goading him, but finding out how he felt was useful and hopefully would help me decide whether he could be saved. 'Her name is Sara. She is skilled in medicine, not fazed by fur and fangs, and knows how to be discrete. She is just an associate, but if any of your pack thinks to lean on her, I will hold you personally responsible. I hope I'm making myself clear?' I didn't realise my magic infused my voice until I heard Tomasz's muffled whimpering.

I was about to add something to lessen the impact, but there was a strange choking noise before I could, and the pack leader spoke, compliant and reverential. 'Yes, Master, no one will touch her. As for the pup, he will be on his way in a minute.'

I put the phone down, cursing my lack of control. Fear had never been a favoured tool while overseeing the magical world. I preferred respect and common accord, which allowed our community in Gdansk to flourish. However, after only knowing Sara for two days, here I was, subduing a respected leader for showing contempt for her species. I needed to bed the wench or figure out what was fuelling this fascination. Otherwise, I would quickly lose the esteem of my subordinates over this obsession with a human.

The thought of taking the seer to my bed was appealing, but I was too old to give in to my baser instincts. No, I would investigate why Sara affected me this way before anything else happened. *My delicious doctor, let's see what difference time and distance make to this feeling,* I thought, stretching out like a cat before scrolling through the news, waiting for the young werewolf to arrive.

The light doze I awoke from reminded me why I paid for an accountant. Financial reports could send me into a coma, and the one open on the laptop was no exception. It took a moment for me to wonder what had awoken me, but a hesitant knock reminded me of the visitor I was expecting.

When I let him in, the werewolf pup staggered as he entered the room, desperately trying to look unaffected by his injuries and turning bright red as he failed to hide his body's need to transform and complete the healing process. With an assessing gaze, I forced the teen to wait longer than necessary, giving his bravado the respect he desired before gesturing to the seat next to mine.

'Sit down, lad; you don't have to pretend here.' I nodded toward the chair, and when he hesitated, I projected the forest's calming aura. The comforting scent of the sacred grove filled the room as the boy shuffled to his seat. Dejected, the poor soul hung his head, and I felt the need to reassure him.

'Just sit. I dislike having people towering over me during a conversation,' I said, trying to inject a little friendliness into my tone, smiling when it appeared to improve his mood. 'Tell me what happened. How did you get captured?'

'We were unloading a shipment of amber for artisans and artefacts for Gedania at the docks when it happened. We were... what... can you tell me what happened to my friends? Two members of my pack were with me, but nobody wants to tell me what happened to them.'

'We haven't found them yet. Adam and his people only found you when they checked the warehouse.'

I watched him crumble, a short sob escaping his lips as uncontrolled shakes wracked his body, but I had to continue, even as I increased the strength of my calming aura, knowing it was the only way we'd find the other members of his pack. 'I'm sorry, but I need to know what happened if we're to have any chance of finding your friends.'

'They shot us with some bizarre-looking weapon that shot bullets of sunlight, and when they hit, it was... it was the worst pain I've ever felt, and the bleeding wouldn't stop. I think I passed out 'cause next thing I know, I'd fallen between two crates, and there was shouting all around.'

Bullets of light? Were those strange projectiles bespelled as well as constructed of cursed materials? It would explain the overpowering of Tomasz's shifters and how so many people had disappeared so easily. I looked at the boy, hoping he would recall more about that night when he blurted out.

'Oh, the shouting; they spoke Russian, but I couldn't tell exactly what they said. It sounded like the old stuff you talk to Adam in sometimes, the same words, but different.'

'And what did you hear?' The human government had ongoing issues with Russian mobsters, but the elder races never dared to encroach on my territory. *There's always a first time, and with Czernobog's dagger being used on Adam, it could be a neighbouring Guardian too bored with the current status quo.* This thought was intriguing and worrying, especially regarding unearthing a weapon designed to kill my kind.

'I don't know, I could barely understand them, but I think it has something to do with your business. They mentioned amber a lot and mentioned summoning the old master.'

'Tell me what happened to you. Why weren't you killed?'

The haunted look the werewolf gave me pricked my conscience, but I couldn't afford to ignore the issue. I had to have an answer. There were more important matters than looking after fragile feelings, but the pup remained silent despite my stare pinning him to the chair.

'Make a guess if you're unsure. What do you think they were doing?' I added when he didn't respond.

'I think they were testing it, Sir. They must have forgotten about me or thought I was dead, but the others were still alive when I awoke, and the shooting hadn't stopped, only slowed down, one or two shots, then more talking. I wanted to help, my Lord, but

I was in so much pain and... I'm sorry, but the screaming, I was scared and... I'm sorry, I should have tried....'

'Could you see what was happening or just hear it?' The need to know who or what had carried out the attack was starting to frustrate me, and the wolf's reaction affected my demeanour.

'Sir, I couldn't see, but they were close enough for me to catch their scents. The shooters, well, they were wolves like me and the boys, but whoever they were talking to was human, no doubt in my mind, and I think they feared him; the wolves, that is.'

This situation was becoming more and more complicated. Amber technically belonged to Jurata. She had created the substance from the resin of my trees aeons ago, back when we hoped she would be able to remain in the human realm with me. The creation of the amber into reservoirs of time depleted most of her power, but even this was not enough to bring her true form from behind the Gates. Since she departed for the Nether, trade in that commodity belonged to anyone powerful enough to take it, and as it was the best material to store magic, I made sure to seize control of the local business. It didn't hurt that humans coveted amber, and the supernatural community was more prosperous because of it. However, it now seemed someone wasn't satisfied with their market share and was trying to muscle into my business, which would take money and power, especially when it was well known I was happy to kill in order to maintain control. Could this be a power play by Czernobog's followers? The appearance of their weapon suggested that, but it would take a visit to the Nether to find out.

Gdansk's mirror city in the Nether, Gedania, housed the council of Guardians; only they would have the information needed to avoid an all-out war with an enemy I had only just learned existed, but the very thought of contacting those arrogant pricks and the possibility of meeting with Jurata made my skin crawl.

Lost in thought, pondering the implications of the recent attacks and travelling to Gedania to find out who was responsible, I almost forgot about my visitor until the surprisingly patient werewolf cleared his throat self-consciously before speaking.

'My pack leader said I was saved by a human, Sir, that she's one of your protected.' The way the pup worded his statement made my hackles rise, and I wondered if I would end up punishing him for disrespect.

'And what it is to you, pup?' He flinched at my word choice, upset that I didn't see him as the adult he considered himself to be, one capable of fighting for a place in pack hierarchy.

'She helped me. I know it was on your command, Sir, but she didn't flinch, and I know I wouldn't be here now without her. I want to repay her kindness. I... all I know is fighting. If that... I would be her Guardian in our world, plenty of my kind; they don't like humans....'

My interruption was harsher than intended, as I reacted as if this boy was questioning my abilities, 'You can barely walk, and it will take too long to regain your strength. How do you intend to protect Sara? By bleeding on her carpets?'

'I can tail her when she goes out and make sure no one is after her. I can...'

'No, Adam already has his men monitoring the situation. I don't want you getting in their way. If you must express your gratitude, send her flowers or chocolates. Women are supposed to like such things. Now, go rest, or you'll never heal.'

The young wolf leant forward, intending to protest, but with one raised eyebrow, I suppressed his desire, and he bowed before exiting the room. *I wouldn't be surprised if he curses my name all the way to the pack's safe house. Still, he is too young and inexperienced to be anyone's protector, let alone a woman who I ... who I what exactly? Have known for less than two days and crave with a desperation that borders on obsession?* My thoughts drifted to her surprised face when I pushed her into her apartment and slammed the door behind her. I'd subdued a faction leader because he mentioned her name. Maybe I should take myself the advice I gave the wolf pup. Perhaps I should back off, send her flowers and forget about the situation. But there was a slight problem; I didn't know what flowers she liked.

'For fuck's sake, I'm losing my mind!' I slammed my fist on the table, the wood protesting at the impact, bringing my assistant rushing into the room at the noise, only to look at me in shock when he saw my expression.

'Inform Adam to assemble a small team for an assignment tonight. We need to increase surveillance at the docks, especially near the Gates to Gedania, and ensure everyone wears a bulletproof vest. I want no more surprises. Then ensure our people in the police avoid the area tonight... Oh, and find out what flowers Sara likes and send her a bouquet.'

'Yes, Sir... wait, what? Who is Sara?'

'What didn't you understand? I know Adam thinks he is indestructible, but tell him it's my order, and if the police oppose, remind them what happened the last time they interfered with otherworldly affairs. Sara is the human doctor I have recruited recently. She helped me with a minor crisis. Adam's driver will know the address for the delivery.'

'No, I know all this... but Sara? And flowers?'

Michal, the burly bear shifter who worked as my assistant, looked at me as if I'd lost my mind, and I didn't blame him. Maybe I had, but something deep inside me wanted to remind that stubborn woman of my presence. I couldn't visit her tonight, but I wanted her to know she was in my thoughts. I removed my jacket and rubbed my neck. Tonight's excursion needed careful planning and increased security near the Gates, but before I turned my attention to the laptop screen, I looked at my assistant and added, with a hint of mischief.

'You're right. Flowers are not enough. Ensure they are delivered with freshly baked cinnamon buns and a caramel latte.' As an afterthought, I added. 'Oh, and send a letter to the Coven requesting a meeting. They have a stray lamb in desperate need of training.'

'The Coven, Sir. You are not on friendly terms with them. Is that wise?'

'They will listen, and whatever illusionary power they think they have, I can remind them of their place if they step out of line. Please handle my requests with care and no more questions. I have repeated myself enough today.'

The disapproving grunt my assistant produced as he exited the room made me chuckle, but as soon as my gaze fell on the scout's reports, I knew it was time to focus on the problems I'd neglected in my hubris and defend the little empire I had built before these latest challenges threatened to tear it apart.

Chapter Six

Of course, I was not watching the clock and hadn't noticed that six p.m. had come and gone without Leszek turning up. To make a point, proving he meant nothing to me, I had resisted the urge to dress up and was lounging in my house clothes, a comfortable set of mismatched sweats, and while these clothes had a lack of holes in them, it wasn't to impress the annoying mobster and my rear didn't look amazing in them. Well, Okay, that last sentence was a lie, but a woman has to have standards. Scarface, my feline partner-in-crime, was sitting on the other end of the sofa, his disfigured muzzle and single fang pointedly looking at the pristine litter box in disgust, clearly still upset that his territory now smelled of fresh daisies. An innocent victim of my need to keep busy as I waited on Leszek's visit.

My imagination ran wild, picturing his expression when he saw my dishevelled appearance, and I smiled in satisfaction, even though the spotless apartment was a clearer sign of how I felt about all of this.

With the newly discovered world of magic, my mind recalled the dozens of fantasy books on my shelves, with their fascination with fated mates. It was easy to believe this strange attraction was a product of subconscious wish fulfilment or possibly Leszek's weird mojo messing with my brain chemistry because every time I remembered his voice, it felt like thick molasses was sliding down my spine.

Working in the E.R. had cured me of such naivete, and over the last few hours, I had analysed my feelings to death and knew the real reason for my attraction was my inability to intimidate him or dominate the terms of our interaction. After years of failed relationships, I craved a man who challenged me and didn't meekly follow my lead, so despite telling myself I didn't want to see him, I was angry when he didn't show up. The mess I made tearing up the napkin was a stark reminder that I had been stood up by a man who looked at me like a starving beast would his next meal, and he didn't even have the time to grace me with a message.

'Well, fuck you, too.' I said to the ceiling, angry that he made me feel disposable, the flavour of a moment, good while it lasted, forgotten when it was out of sight. *His loss; at least I didn't waste my time doing my makeup. Besides, there's no situation a cat, wine, and a good book can't fix.*

Halfway through preparing a hot, relaxing bath designed to put me in a better mood, I heard a knock on the door. The temptation to pretend I wasn't home was powerful and very immature. *I will politely listen to his excuse and then tell him to return home.* I didn't care, was barely dressed, and as my bathrobe covered everything necessary, he didn't deserve further effort.

It was too late for a date, and I wasn't interested in hearing if he had another emergency. *I'm not his booty call or a mob doctor*, I thought, marching toward the doors, ready to give Leszek an earful and slam the door in his face. The bouquet thrust in my direction took me by surprise, and judging by the round eyes of the messenger, he was just as astonished to see a scantily dressed woman answering the door.

'Iyyy... delivery for Sara Wilska?'

His shocked stutter earned him a curt nod as I tried to hold back my laughter, watching his valiant effort to avoid looking at my cleavage. I still wore a bra and panties, but the poor boy's imagination had obviously run away with his ability to think. While I observed him trying not to look at me, I almost missed his attempts to give me the massive bouquet of freesias till he pushed it in my face.

With a cough designed to hide the breaking of his voice, the messenger launched into a spontaneous speech.

'I apologise for tonight. There are matters requiring my attention that can't be postponed, even for the pleasure of your company. Please enjoy my little gifts. I didn't forget about you, Sara, and I never will.'

'You what? Boy, I don't know you, and I'm way beyond your age group. What nonsense are you spouting?'

What the hell is going on with my life? My thoughts were racing when, shocked speechless, I tried to collect my jaw from the floor. Why was an unknown teenager offering me such a passionate speech? I saw the bright red blush crawling up his neck when I finally took the flowers, and he reached into his bag to pull out a warm paper bag that smelled like cinnamon rolls and coffee.

'Eww. You're way too old for me. That was the message, Master... I mean, Mr Borowy asked me to tell you.' He put the bag next to me on the floor, turned and left while I stood there, not believing what had just happened.

The coffee and rolls smelled divine, and freesias were my favourite flowers. Even if the boy's remark offended me slightly, I took the gifts and quietly closed the doors.

'Too old, really? I'm barely over thirty, not some old prune.' I said, conveniently forgetting I pointed out the age gap in the first place. I put everything on the kitchen table before going to the bathroom to turn off the water.

There wasn't much to unpack: a coffee, two sweet buns and the flowers. As the messenger said, they were little gifts, a cheap trick to gain favour. My mind knew it, but something deep inside warmed, looking at those trinkets. I saw the honey trap and was waltzing into it with a cheerful smile. *He is smoking hot and is clever enough to find your favourite everyday pleasures to keep you pliant, so try acting like an adult and don't fall for his pretence of caring.* My common sense fought hard with my feelings until I finally stopped grinning like an idiot.

The old practical Sara soon reminded me of the injured boy Leszek had forced me to save in such terrible conditions, so I ate, drank, took my now tepid bath and went to bed. Whether I could sleep was another matter, but I was determined to forget the Forest Lord. *The further we stay away from each other, the better,* I thought, quietly blessing whatever kept him busy. I closed my eyes. *After all, there's work tomorrow, and that is my priority.*

Chapter Seven

If anything else went wrong today, someone would bleed, heavily. My frustration stemmed from the dockland trip to sniff out the Russians who attacked the werewolves. It was a monumental waste of time and resources as, despite using my best trackers, there appeared to be no evidence that anyone had even been ambushed there. Next, while trudging through warehouses, shipping berths and containers, I received a mental call from the Council of Gedania. I'd stood in some foul-smelling building as they demanded to know why ordinary humans seemed to have found the Gates of the Nether and were trying to breach the barrier despite the added security.

Gedania, the Nether's version of the Tricity area, Gdansk, Gdynia, and Sopot, existed in a separate reality, one that lay so close to this one that it overlapped in places, making it possible to travel between realms at these, as we called them, Gates, but only if you had the magic to see them. It hadn't always been like this, but when humanity drove the elder races close to extinction, each race's great and powerful came together to perform a spell so immense it stripped them of much of their magic. The result, however, had been worth the cost, providing a home for those that iron, silver and rowan could kill.

Many cities like this existed worldwide, the strange magic of the Gates attracting both humans and the elder races. Despite this attraction, the Nether races, whose existence heavily depended on magic, could only visit the mortal world, not remain in it, just as anyone with human blood could cross to the Nether but be unable to stay. However, without magical blood running through your veins, seeing or passing through the Gates without assistance was impossible.

The one exception to this were the guardians, those who sacrificed their power to the great endeavour, forever tied to the mortal world as anchors and protectors of the descendants of magic. Guardians, like me.

The Council took great delight in mentioning the Dark Arcana, but I didn't know anyone in the city who chose this path. Not that anyone would dare to dabble into a blood sacrifice, death magic and time and continuum shifting spells that could rip reality apart. Especially knowing the punishment for such hideous magic was death. I didn't need a crazed mage running around murdering humans to fuel their spells.

Still, during our search of the docks, I sensed something strange. There was a hint, a lingering afterglow of magic, but the signature was unusual, and I couldn't pinpoint the source. Just as I decided to call off the search, leaving a regular if slightly larger presence patrolling the gate area, one of the pack whined after coming into contact with the warehouse wall closest to the waterfront, and that's where I found traces of silver and some unknown substance that burnt my fingers.

My magic, born of the forest and wild places, reacted to the unusual substance, burning brighter as it instinctively protected me from further injury. It was as dangerous to me as it had been to the werewolves, and I understood the unit leader's reluctance to comply when I ordered him to track the deadly material. The wolf looked at me in disgust but didn't argue against my decision, knowing how important this was, leading us onward with his superior senses to the old dock master's building.

The structure was old and imposing, even in its state of disrepair, with faded white numbers over the portcullis indicating it was built before the First World War during Prussia's rule. Its walls were decorated in the old Germanic style, its clean lines and thick walls constructed with warfare in mind. Inside, darkness wrapped around us like a soft blanket, and I saw several wolves' eyes flashing green as they caught the moon's faint glow.

The scent we'd been following grew strong enough for me to discern, and the gathered men growled in unison. I silenced them with a raised hand, but their muffled snarls had already awakened something in the basement. At the sound of shuffling feet and a faint cry, I gestured for someone to investigate. The stench of rotten fish hit my nostrils as soon as the enforcer opened the basement doors. The noise grew louder as he entered, and I heard a woman's voice between the vile sounds of torture.

'Please, no more. I told you everything I know. I can't open the gate, not the one you want to enter.'

The lilting call of a siren suddenly filled the room, awakening a soul-deep longing and sadness in the hearts of the gathered men. If not for my hastily cast spell to stifle its effect, the despair and yearning would have led them to a watery grave.

I gestured for the team to hold their positions and went downstairs. The sight confronting me lit a fury within my soul that was difficult to control. Two Sirens were held in this disgusting pig sty, one already dead, the other....

I couldn't look away from the sight, no matter that she was a denizen of the sea, one of Jurata's children. Since the goddess escaped to Gedania, I cared for her people as best I could, and this act I would never forgive.

'Your song does not affect me, daughter of the sea.' I said, approaching the siren pinned to the wall, held up by two blood-encrusted bolts. 'Tell me, who did this to you?' Her eyes were full of pain and disbelief as she looked at me.

'My Lord, you found us. We hoped you might, but why did you come so late? When I heard... I sent him to the sea with the last of my strength... My sister... they refused to give her water, laughing as she begged for her life. She sang the song of the sea, but our Lady didn't save us. Why did she abandon us?' The resignation and betrayal in her voice tore at my heart with vicious claws. I knew she wasn't using her gift consciously, but even in this state, she still affected my emotions, opening old wounds. Jurata didn't just betray her people when she left but shattered my heart with her decision.

Without realising it, my hands had grasped the bolts, ablaze with pain from its vile touch, as I applied all my strength to pull them from the wall. They were well secured, but I refused to stop, my magic flaring to life, green tendrils spreading over the concrete, weakening its hold before I ripped the bolts out of the wall. If the alloy composition hurt me this much, I couldn't imagine the agony it caused to the abused siren.

'Shh, little Delphine, tell me who did this to you,' I said, gathering her helpless body in my arms, her quiet sobs the only sound in the darkness. She was so delicate, yet someone tortured her brutally, and my blood boiled for revenge. She shivered in my embrace, pressing her face into my chest as a muffled cry tore through her.

She was not a creature of the land, and my magic could only help a little, but I let it coat the girl, muting the pain as much as possible.

'We shouldn't have listened, should have trusted you, but when the men turned up, offering us more money for amber, the elders didn't hesitate to make a deal. At first, everything went well. It was when their leaders turned up that things started going wrong. They renegotiated the deal with promises of returning dominion of the seas to us, saying they needed our help to lure in people, especially those frequenting the Anchor and other brothels. The elders didn't care; the disgusting filth deserved whatever happened to them, so they agreed, and my sisters were taken. When I objected, they took me and Laura and brought us here to...,' the sentence ended with a sob, and I used the last of my power to help numb her pain.

She started talking again as I carried her outside. When we emerged from the basement, the pack sent me a questioning look, and one werewolf pointed to the dark entrance of the basement.

'What do you want to do with it?'

'Treat the body respectfully and give it back to the sea.' I answered, trying to restrain the anger those words awakened, and despite their usual brash attitude, the pack completed the task with surprising sensitivity.

'There are more girls in the Anchor. They don't want to be there, but those bastards have a means of controlling them. Please, help them like you helped me. I swear we didn't want to do it. Our

Lady abandoned us, but you came for me. Only you guard this place now, and we have no one else to turn to.'

The siren sagged in my arms, finally succumbing to exhaustion, and I passed her to a waiting wolf. 'Make sure she reaches her kin, no, find a pod outside the city, grant them a favour if they take her in, they will know how to help her, then inform your Alpha we are visiting the Anchor.'

The man nodded, carrying his precious cargo, and I strode back to the basement for another look. There wasn't much evidence except for a few cages and the siren's blood. It looked like our enemies used it as a convenient location rather than a permanent base. I turned to the leader of the wolves.

'Call Adam, tell him I need surveillance on this location. I want him to check the security cameras and registration plates of all the cars in this warehouse zone. He must inform me immediately should he find something suspicious. Whoever looks out of place must be followed. I need to find their base, not their dumping ground.'

I dismissed the unit and headed to my car. It was too late to visit Sara. For a moment, I weighed driving to her house just to see the symbol I carved on her doorway, but ultimately, I decided against it. Still, the visceral need for her presence didn't help to calm my senses. I hoped she enjoyed the flowers at least. Thinking how surprised she must have been brought a smile to my face. I would rearrange my visit for another night, as tomorrow I would be going to the Anchor. If Nadolny was cooperating with the trespassers, I had a bigger problem than I initially surmised. However, if they were using his club without his knowledge, he could be a valuable ally, especially since he was one of the few humans who knew about the existence of the Nether and Gedania.

Something in the siren's words gnawed at my subconscious, warning me something was off, wrong, but try as I might, I couldn't identify the issue. I decided it was more important to discover why someone was trying to enter the Nether and who these Russians encroaching on my territory were because the coincidence of their presence was too obvious to ignore.

As I drove through Gdansk, I allowed my mind to drift, mulling over the recent problems and concocting a plan of attack for the next day. With the streets still busy, despite the late hour, I focused on the siren's words, feeling the return of my magic as they repeated in my mind. *Only you guard this place now.* She was correct; this domain was mine, and whoever encroached upon it would face the consequences.

I pressed the speed dial button on my steering wheel and rang my assistant. I knew he wouldn't be happy, but I was past caring about his beauty sleep.

'Call the Coven. I want to see their mistress in my office tomorrow.' I said as soon as I heard the click of the open connection.

'What? Who is it?' The sleepy voice from the other side told me Michal wasn't fully awake, not just yet.

'Who would call you at three in the morning with orders to fulfil? Get me the Coven Mistress, and if she makes excuses, tell her she comes to me, and we talk in peace, or I visit her precious little villa in Sopot and ensure her cooperation by other means.'

'Yes, of course. Is there anything else you need, Sire?'

I raked a hand through my hair before answering.

'Do you remember what Adam said about the woman who stabbed him in that brothel?' I should have looked into it earlier, but so many things had diverted my attention, and it wasn't the first time a scorned lover treated my unruly vampire to a blade. However, this was the first time they'd used something as deadly as Czernobog's dagger.

'Well, he said she had a beautiful voice, a good pair of tits, and he was so enchanted he didn't notice when she stopped reciprocating his interest.'

'Enchanted...'

'What?'

'Nothing. I just realised why he acted like an idiot that night. It pains me to say it, but it may not be entirely his fault this time. Tell him to come by later, then you can go back to sleep. I can hear it in your voice. You will be unbearable tomorrow.'

'And whose fault is that?' I heard him grumble before I ended the call.

The warm embrace of my estate wrapped me up in a welcoming cocoon of love as soon as I drove through the gates, the tranquillity of the setting loosening the tight knot that surrounded my heart. However, for once, it could not ease the fury ignited by the scene earlier that evening, so instead of resting, I went to my grove to train, hoping to direct the anger into something useful. As I moved into position, I almost smiled, recalling my contempt for the old man who taught me this fighting style. He came from the east, and with a skill I'd never seen before, it took less than a moment to put the mighty Leszek on his arse without seeming to move.

Our friendship had been a beacon of hope and light in what had become the lonely fog of my existence, but as all mortals do, the man had died, leaving behind a legacy of brotherly love that still lingered despite the realities of the world.

As the first rays of dawn were turning the sky a beautiful soft pink, my kata came to a close, and, breathing slowly, I finally felt ready to rest.

Whoever knocked on my bedroom must have decided they no longer wanted to live, but when the door opened and my assistant strode in to rip open the curtains, I realised this was his version of payback.

'Rise and shine, boss! What a wonderful day to finally wake up,' he roared, an evil grin on his face. With one look through the window, I realised the sun was past its zenith, and it was already the afternoon.

'The Coven?' I asked, voice croaking until I cleared my throat. 'Did you arrange a meeting?'

'Yes, they will be here in an hour,' he answered, his smug smile reminding me of the first rule of leadership; *Don't piss off your assistant.*

'Why didn't you wake me earlier?' I said, grumbling even as he put a breakfast tray on the bed, but he only shook his head.

'Because I wanted to live? I haven't seen you dance with a sword since I was a cub, and my predecessor told me to keep my distance if such an event occurs.'

I didn't bother hiding my smirk. Michal was right. I hadn't used a sword in a long time, preferring to perform the unique kata bare-handed. Still, whenever I was overcome with rage, the days of blood and steel would call, and my blade would appear. My body became death incarnate until the meditation of the stylised forms calmed my mind. I could use guns, but I didn't like them, and they didn't like me. Something with my magic disrupted the combustion inside the cartridge, causing misfires, so if I ever needed to fight, it was with my hands or a blade, their simplicity suiting me better. *The poor man must have thought I was preparing for war,* but after remembering last night, he might be right. Turning to Michal, the last of my meal put aside, I asked.

'What matters need addressing today? Any news from Tomasz or Adam? Did the wolves extend my request to the owner of the Anchor? I would hate to drop in unannounced, but I will if my hand is forced.'

'Yes, an invitation came earlier, very polite and well written, if I do say so myself. The owner of the Anchor not only invited you but also mentioned some special event to be held in your honour.'

That was most inconvenient, and I sighed, getting more than I expected. Not only would the underbelly of the Tricity area know that the Forest Lord visited the local mobster, but they would also assume we are on friendly terms. That was the problem with hastily executed plans, but looking at my assistant, I realised it wasn't the only one.

'Anything else?'

'The young wolf, the injured one, came earlier, saying Sara had some trouble at work. One of Nadolny's bouncers took in an injured girl, and then he overheard the nurses saying she was reckless because the man almost hit her. The pup was concerned, so he said he would keep an eye on her.'

My hand clenched around the cup with a force that shattered the ceramic into pieces, splashing hot tea onto the floor, but I barely felt it. I knew where she worked and that unpleasant patients caused problems now and then, but the thought that someone might hurt Sara, my Sara, made my voice savage.

'Find out who he is and make him disappear.' I heard myself saying, and despite my usual care with local politics, I didn't care how this person disappeared. He dared to threaten my woman, and I was not in the mood to let it slide. *My woman*, that thought drove away the remnants of sleep as I wondered at the strange idea. The voice in my head tried to reason with my feelings, but I shook it off, getting dressed. I had to be ready before the Coven Mistress arrived and in apparel that would still be suitable for that den of iniquity, the Anchor. That required I abandon my usual style. I mentioned it to Michal, and after he dived into my closet, I accepted the clothes he prepared. Still, I almost snapped at him when he came and ruffled my hair.

'What the hell are you doing?' I asked quietly, looking in the mirror.

'The newest trend on the internet. Now you look like one of those fantasy book boys my daughter loves so much. All hot, bothered and roughened. You are only missing wings.' He answered with a smirk. I was lost for words, but my expression showed the full extent of my discontent. Still, the person looking back at me from the mirror appeared much younger and ruggedly handsome. My hair was naturally wavy, but now it was artfully laying in random directions as if I'd just left my lover's bed. Somehow, my thoughts drifted to the doctor, imagining her hand causing this silky mess, and I had to chastise myself again before I could focus on the problem.

'Tell the men to be ready, choose the best fighters and... give them the benefit of your hair expertise. All weapons must be concealed, but don't let them come unarmed. I don't know what Nadolny has prepared or whether he is working with our enemy. Oh, and let the Coven Mistress in as soon as she arrives,' I said, dismissing him to focus on strengthening the wards around my property. It was always better to be prepared if the witches were coming.

Chapter Eight

The Emergency Department was as hectic as ever, but its chaotic nature centred me, and thoughts of my recent troubles disappeared. You have no time to brood over a new, magical reality when patients are shouting, crying, and bleeding for attention, or you are in your latest battle with a bureaucracy seemingly designed to make you grey at thirty. Still, the hospital didn't feel the same anymore; its corridors filled with the shadows that had plagued me since childhood.

I tried not to act skittish, but the telltale sign of the imminent death of the patient we were resuscitating left me distracted, and when a wailing voice echoed in the corridor outside, I nearly dropped the ultrasound probe.

If this kept up, it wouldn't be long before someone noticed me staring at things that weren't there, or worse, saw me treating a patient I knew had died differently than others. Surprisingly, thinking about Leszek's gifts stopped me from worrying about the surrounding strangeness, making it easier to accept that weird occurrences were a regular part of my new life. He was also the only person I knew who could tell me what these shadows were and what seeing them meant for me.

When I overheard two nurses whispering in a corner, looking around furtively, my internal alarm screamed at me to investigate.

'Did you see those Russian goons? They were so suspicious, and saying those bites were from a dog? Who did they think they were fooling? Idiots. Do you think they have a fighting ring? Maybe they have bears or something?' Ewa always had a theory about everything, and almost everything led to the conclusion the government was misleading us.

'What Russians?' I asked, goading her into sharing the latest conspiracy, hoping for some light entertainment despite my foreboding.

'Limb injuries, Sara. Your junior took care of it as there was nothing that serious we needed to concern your ladyship about.' A grin and a wink offset her teasing. 'Your new intern handled it well, but it was weird. Those men, all dressed in black like gangsters out of the movies, came with a skinny guy with a weird tattoo that spoke Polish, claiming that there was a mishap with a guard dog because, yeah, a dog has the strength to break the femoral bone of a grown man. I don't think so, but that's what they said before ortho took them to theatre.'

She dragged over the work tablet and typed something quickly. 'Look, do you think a dog did that?'

The pictorial record taken before the surgery showed the full extent of the damage. I felt a chill run down my spine, remembering the young man who had been an overgrown wolf before his transformation. *Fuck, I need to talk to Leszek.* We can't have someone running around biting people. I covered my dread with a pleasant smile, joking about Himalayan mountain dogs and other large breeds.

I left to find somewhere quiet to call Leszek when the doors to our staff room opened, and a handsome male face smiled in my direction.

'Sara, could you help me with something if you're free?'

The voice belonged to the new intern, a heartthrob that the nurses gushed over. Even the older, married psychoanalyst always smiled whenever he walked into the room, and I had to admit that he was pretty, if a little too meek for my tastes. Noticing my interest, he continued. 'We have a young lady who requests a female doctor, and unfortunately, you're the only one on shift. I'm afraid it's a Chippendale lineup out there.'

The phone call would have to wait. As he mentioned, there was an overabundance of men on shift today, but that happened sometimes. In this department, requests for female doctors meant one of two things: domestic violence or sexual assault. This always brought flashbacks I didn't want to remember. I'm notorious for falling for the wrong men. Handsome devils who like violence a bit too much, and it was only a matter of time before one of my powerful, domineering boyfriends hit me. The memory flooded me of the stunned betrayal I felt when a man I thought I loved so carelessly hurt me because I preferred studying for my anatomy exam rather than attending one of his flashy parties. Good old uni times. Still, I was raised by spirited women who taught me no one could lay a hand on me and walk away without consequences, so I grabbed the pan soaking in the sink and smacked him with it before kicking him out of my life. I might have nursed my black eye for a week, but it was worth it. Thankfully, I was not raised to be a victim, but how many women had the example of my grandma, a war orphan who built a life for herself or my mother who continued her pregnancy despite a broken spine and a husband killed in the motorbike crash that almost claimed her life?

I shook my head to banish those thoughts. The helplessness of these situations always brought out the worst in me, and facing a crisis where I couldn't help except to collect evidence set me on edge. *Training this week will be interesting*, I thought. My weekly Krav Maga practice sometimes became the only outlet for the violence I wanted to use on the culprit after hearing of their brutality.

'I wish these were medieval times.'

'What?' my junior asked, hearing my murmur.

'Nothing, I just need to remove my shining armour and stop charging on an empty field,' I said, chuckling slightly, observing his confused expression. I couldn't change the world. Kosovo taught me that much, yet I had this stupid need to try every now and again.

'We love you, Sara. You're a great boss, but you are so weird sometimes,' he said, shaking his head, and I laughed harder, observing another shadow. A slim silhouette of a man whose gaunt face looked at me without recognition hung in the air before slowly disappearing into the wall.

'You don't know how right you are.' I said, determined to talk with Leszek later. If there was any way he could help me control what I was seeing, I would beg him to help, even if this cost me an arm and a leg.

'What can you tell me about our new patient?' I asked instead.

Despite her injuries, the woman in the examination cubicle was breathtakingly beautiful, also very young, with her hair styled and coloured in the manner typical of students wishing to express their personalities. The moment she noticed my presence, her head snapped round before, equally fast, it dropped into a pose of fearful submission.

'Wait outside.' I told my colleague, who frowned at my wilful dismissal of chaperone protocol but kept his silence and left. I sat down, waiting for the click of the door, quietly assessing the young lady's body language and visible injuries.

The bruise under the left eye, more covering her neck in the telltale shape of a hand, and swollen, split lip left little to the imagination. The fearful, hesitant flinching told me there would be more injuries, her attitude one of long-term abuse.

Giving her a moment to get used to my presence before introducing myself, I used the time to control my breathing and purge my anger, knowing how little use it would be in this situation.

'Hi, I'm Sara. I will be your doctor, and who you might be?'

'My name is Ilona. I... can you help me? I need to work, but no one will look at me like this,' she said, and I gasped at the entrancing undertone in her voice. The timbre was deeper than expected, but even those few simple sentences carried a quality that spoke straight to my soul, almost compelling me to do her bidding.

'I will try my best, Ilona, but I need to know what happened to you before I can help you. I can see you were beaten, and it was likely not the first time?' I watched the girl's eyes fill with tears and knew my answer. 'Let me examine you and ensure none of the injuries are dangerous. Everything I see or find will remain confidential unless you want me to alert the police.'

As usual, I couldn't do anything unless my patient wanted to cooperate with the authorities, but when she pulled her jumper up, I wished I could lay my hands on whoever hurt her. The black, green and yellow bruises all over her torso fanning the flames of my fury.

'Can you tell me who did this, Ilona? If you can, I promise to make sure this never happens again, and there won't be any mention of your name.' *Fuck, I did it again!* I thought, chastising myself. I knew better than to make such a promise, but my instincts were screaming at me that this was the right thing to say, and for once, I didn't want to ignore them.

Gently touching her rib cage to assess if there were any fractures, my eyesight blurred, and something inside flared to life, showing me the image of a figure from legends that looked remarkably like the girl before me.

'You are a siren. Is this related to Leszek and his men?'

Ilona flinched, trying to avoid my hands before hastily straightening her clothes. 'He would never....You are insane. There are no such things as sirens. Nobody hurt me; I simply fell. Get another doctor.' The panic in her voice made Ilona difficult to understand, but I caught her outrage at my accusing Leszek and knew he needed to know what happened here, his instruction to call if I saw anything unusual finally proving useful to me.

'You are not the first non-human that I've treated. I know things... I know...' *fuck, what did vampire boy call him.* 'I know the Lord of the Forest.' I said, desperately trying to reassure the woman, urging her to trust me. I knew if she left this room, I would never see her again, and it wouldn't be long before my paramedic friends would be gossiping about another woman's corpse pulled from the Motlawa River.

Ilona gasped, grabbed my hand, and looked me in the eye for the first time.

'That man, I can't... Stay away from this for your own sake. Even the Forest Lord can't help, but please tell him we don't want a war, that my sister is sorry for killing the vampire.' I couldn't help my dumbfounded expression. *Her sister... vampire... fuck, does she mean Adam?* I was still trying to make sense of her words when the doors burst in and a burly man entered. He gave Ilona one look, and the woman's posture crumpled, the colour draining from her face.

'We are going back, the boss called, and he is unhappy with you.' His voice and slightly crooked nose told me he had seen a fight or two. I didn't recognise him, which was a surprise as I'd stitched up almost every local troublemaker at one time or another.

Something made me step between the injured girl and the stranger, his reaching hand knocked aside by my raised arm. I could easily see my younger self in her. A uni student, a strange bird in the flock of hens with no one to turn to. Her abuse hit me hard, even harder, because she was one of them, and just like that wolf kid, she was injured by the brutal world. I needed to protect her. Common sense be dammed. I couldn't unsee it. I couldn't close my eyes, pretending she was just another patient because now I knew things were not always as they seemed. I wished I had met someone in the past who would step in to protect me.

'Your boss can wait. I haven't finished the examination, which means my patient is going nowhere,' I said, pushing every ounce of my authority and anger into the statement. The door was open now, and anyone in the corridor, as well as the security cameras, could see if he threatened me or, even better, attempted an attack. I could feel myself begging for him to get violent, knowing that if he laid a finger on me, I could retaliate, and he would be locked away, and I would have the chance to ask more questions.

For a moment, it looked as if it would work as he assessed the situation with a hostile glare, and I saw his jaw muscles pulsing when he clenched his teeth, but Ilona slipped past me and nodded to him meekly.

'It's Okay; I'm finished here. Please give me a moment to collect my things.' She moved back toward me, reaching for the bag still on the chair, and as she picked it up, I heard a soft whisper.

'I will be in the Anchor tonight, where he makes us work. Tell the Leshy he is in danger.'

Ilona left, and it took all my energy not to scream my frustration at the world. I knew the place she was talking about; the Anchor was the most infamous nightclub in Gdansk, known for a willingness to host every vice money could buy. Their customers often frequented our department on Saturday nights, telling stories of overpriced drinks containing more drugs than alcohol and how they woke up in a ditch with empty pockets and painful heads. It took great strength of will not to congratulate them for still having their kidneys, the lucky bastards. On the other hand, those who frequented that establishment were unlikely to have healthy organs to harvest. Still, my frustration aside, who was this Leshy that was in danger? It couldn't be Leszek, could it? Had the girl misspoken in her haste to escape?

For a moment, I thought of asking my uniformed friends for help. The police often raided the place, finding nothing, almost as if the owner knew they were coming, so it would be best not to leave it in the hands of the law. Ilona was a siren, or at least I suspected she was because she never confirmed it, but that gave me leverage. Leszek wanted a mob doctor, so if I kept to the original agreement, he would need to persuade me in other ways, like helping me save an abused girl and her sister and a little assistance with the damn shadows.

I pulled out my phone, searching for his business card simultaneously. Maybe I was making a mistake, but the desperation in Ilona's voice told me I had little time. I needed to find her before whatever war she mentioned left the hospital full of innocent bystanders caught in the crossfire.

My hands were shaking as I typed a brief message.

'We need to talk. Meet me at the Anchor at eight pm. It's urgent. Sara.'

Chapter Nine

Veronica Sandow, the current Mistress of the Gdansk Coven, barged in without knocking, though thankfully, I heard the witch's angry footsteps long before she reached my study and opened the protective wards, avoiding the unpleasant mess her body would have made on the carpet.

'What is the meaning of this? I'm not some errand girl to be called in the middle of the night by your assistant, no less, and summoned to your office without explanation, Leshy.' Her raised voice annoyed me immensely, but I held back the cutting remark that came to my lips and gestured to the comfortable chair by the fireplace.

'Please, take a seat. Would you care for some tea? Our discussion may take some time.'

'Discussion? What do we have to discuss? After all the times you've taken such pleasure in reminding me who rules this land, oh mighty Leshy, now you want to be civil?' she asked, and I closed my eyes for a second, taking a calming breath. That's why I avoided the Coven. Their current leader was an air witch as unstable as her element, but I needed the woman's cooperation to train Sara and to help trace those experimenting on our people.

'Sit down.' I ordered, saturating my words with power, and the woman dropped on the chair with an annoyed huff. 'Thank you. As much as I appreciate that the name the humans worshipped me by is still remembered, please call me Leszek. I need your help, and I will pay whatever price you think the service deserves, but remember to be mindful of what you ask.'

'My... help?' She said, her eyebrows climbing so high they left her looking comically naïve.

'Yes, I found a seer in Gdansk. Untrained and unaware of her powers. I need her trained and protected from malicious magic. Can you do this for me?' I made sure my voice was devoid of emotion, one leader making an agreement with another. Earlier, I thought about how much to disclose of what Adam learned about Sara whilst studying her family tree but decided against it. The less she knew about my interest in Sara, the better. Also, giving the Coven Mistress information that Sara's bloodline came from a long line of mountain witches would give them the idea they could take my seer away from me. So I kept to myself the knowledge that her grandmother was a war orphan, the lost child their Coven had searched for over several years. She had been relocated to the north of Poland with her adoptive family, essentially cutting the magical child off not only from her land and Coven but also from her past. No wonder Sara didn't know about her magic.

'You found a seer? What, she fell from the world tree into your lap? Or maybe you captured and imprisoned one of my Coven?'

'I found her in the hospital. Her name is Sara Wilska; she is a doctor, not one of your witches. She belongs to no one, and up until recently, she was unaware of what she is. You could even say she is one of mine, as her discovery was my achievement. Finders keepers, as the young like to say. Besides, I hired her and I need to have her trained. Preferably as soon as possible.'

'Then train her yourself. Why should I waste my time with some ignorant, non-believer you want to fuck?'

'We both know my power is of the forest, and if that were where her talents lay, I wouldn't need your help. As for her talent, she resisted a vampire's compulsion... and mine, so she's strong enough to face down the gods. That should tell you something.' I probably shouldn't have revealed that part, but the sudden pallor on Veronica's face made it all worthwhile. I saw her swallow; the knowledge she couldn't match such power must have been galling to the strongest witch in Poland.

'Fine! We will train her under one condition. If she decides to join the Tricity Coven, you won't object. Tell me, what else can she do?' She said, and I saw calculation and greed in her eager posture. A witch that could resist my magic would give them an advantage that would change the balance of power in the Tricity area. Still, I could agree to this and then make sure Sara chose me, especially after taking steps to befriend the stubborn doctor. The strange attraction between us could only help.

'Of course, I won't stop her. I believe in freedom of choice, but you must also respect her decision without trying to indoctrinate her. As for the rest, I don't know what she can do. She resisted compulsion and has a gift for healing. I watched as she operated on a shifter with antiquated equipment and no help, yet she still saved him. I don't think her medical skills are entirely learned knowledge.'

'That sounds fair. We have a deal, Forest Lord. I will phone you when I have her teacher ready or train her myself. Is this all?' Veronica stood up, but I gestured for her to wait.

'One last thing. Someone, possibly a Warlock, is encroaching on my territory. There have also been several attempts to breach Gedania's Gates, and people from the elder races were wounded. I found the seer thanks to someone using Czernobog's dagger to stab Adam. Please verify none of your flock is experimenting with the Dark Arcana, and if there is, I want their head on a silver plate. If no one with you is involved with the Dark Arts, I would appreciate your Coven's help to find out who it is. Contact Adam or Michal if you have any news.' I said, noticing her hands grasp the chair rim harder.

'And you are telling me this, why?'

'Because I am not apportioning blame and prefer to warn a potential ally before your Coven is attacked. I also want to know where you stand in all this. Whilst not asking for support, even though it would be appreciated, I strongly suspect that if you don't join forces with me, there won't be a Coven left to lead when this is ended.' The warning was probably too dire, but I needed to clarify the situation.

'Better the devil you know,' she said with a smile. 'We won't stand by you, but we won't stand against you. We may not see eye to eye, but I appreciate your keeping things in order here. As a gesture of goodwill, I will tell you this. About three months ago, we sensed the presence of a Warlock. It didn't last long, but those more aligned with the spirits claim he is still here, maybe in Gedania, as he is masking his magic. It is possible, but he would have to use Dark Arcana to hide from us, and we both know such magic requires a blood sacrifice. Maybe she can find him for you after we train your seer.' As she finished her statement, I felt my phone vibrate.

I'd ignored it when it vibrated during the meeting, seeing Sara's name flash on my watch's screen. Explaining everything to her would likely involve being insulted, but once we sorted this mess out, I would take her to the best restaurant. However, I now had to focus on the issue at hand.

Adam sauntered into the room with a cocksure swagger and the stench of too much aftershave.

'Leszek, we have to go. You wouldn't want to miss another delightful party. Oh, hello, Veronica. Are you joining us?' Adam sounded as provocative as always, his fingers trailing over the arm of Veronica's chair, lightly brushing against her arm.

'No, I'm leaving, and it is Mistress Veronica to you, you damn blood-sucking Lothario.' She said, marching to the door before I could ask for more information. Besides, as Adam said, it was time to go. I looked at him, groaning slightly at his choice of clothing.

'Tone it down. We are supposed to blend in, not attract attention.' I taunted him, but he only threw me a mischievous grin.

'Look who's talking, or maybe you plan to visit Sara after the debauchery in the Anchor? Messy hair, open shirt. Oozing Alpha charm? I thought you disliked showing off.'

'Keep your ridiculous speculation to yourself and your dick in your pants. This is about information gathering, not pleasure. I want to know whether Nadolny is collaborating with whoever is attacking us and what the sirens are doing in the Anchor. A word of warning: as much as I value your talent, one more word about Sara, and I'll rip out your fangs.' Adam looked at me momentarily, his eyes flashing briefly with concern before the jester's mask returned.

'I'll do my best to ferret out every little tidbit; just don't blame me if they ask for a bite or two. You know how they struggle to resist the charms of a handsome vampire.'

'Whatever, as long as you don't hurt or kill them, their charitable blood donations are none of my concern.' I said, taking my coat off the armchair and pointing toward the door. 'Shall we? As you said, we can't keep the King of the Tricity Underworld waiting too long.'

Chapter Ten

After the incident with the battered girl, the rest of my shift dragged worse than a department meeting discussing hospital policies. I checked my phone several times, but the newest bane of my existence conveniently ignored my text. I even tried to call, but there was no answer.

The moment the evening shift arrived for the handover felt like Liberation Day, and the door was still swinging long after I left. With barely enough time to change, I chose an outfit that wouldn't stand out but not make me look like I was there touting for business or be an easy mark for the drug dealers.

The pair of leatherette trousers and a silk tank top gave me a relaxed but sexy look whilst also allowing me to move well if I needed to fight or run if things got complicated. I smiled at my reflection, liking how the black lace bra peaked out from under the blouse, making my cleavage noticeable enough to distract any man's gaze from my face. To finish the ensemble, I added a short cardigan to ward off the chill night air and a pair of simple pumps to make it less likely to turn my ankle in an emergency. Opening the jewellery box, I put on all my heavy rings, transforming my hand into a knuckle duster and wrapped my hair in a tight, sleek bun.

The woman that looked back at me from the mirror looked dangerous in a dark, sultry way, and I felt adrenaline cursing through my arteries, readying me for the challenge.

I barely remember the drive, but I made sure to park my car two streets from the Anchor. The anonymity should provide me with enough protection if things went south, and the last thing I needed was a street camera to record my number plate. It took only a couple of minutes to arrive at the club entrance. I didn't expect it to be so crowded, but those gathered seemed annoyed, partying on the street rather than inside the club. Watching the muscular men posing in front of women in revealing clothes was entertaining, and I congratulated myself on my outfit choice. With a bit of luck, the dim lighting and a confident swing of my hips, I think I could pass for someone in their late twenties.

I looked at my watch, worrying when I saw it was already eight, with Leszek nowhere to be seen. His absence crushed my hopes that he saw my message and couldn't reply, but I decided I didn't need a knight in shining armour. Still, this was the infamous Anchor, so I gave him another few minutes in case he'd been stuck in traffic before sighing heavily and walking to the club entrance. The bouncer gave me a measuring look and crossed his arms.

'Private party, sweetheart. Come back tomorrow.' He was shamelessly ogling me, but his statement sounded final. Still, if he was so interested in my cleavage, there was a chance his brain might be suffering from a lack of blood, so I boldly used my charms to encourage his interest, letting my cardigan slip off my shoulder and taking a deep, dramatic breath, practically forcing the girls out of their supportive covering.

'But Ilona asked me to come. Zbyszek... I mean, the boss told her to bring more girls tonight, so here I am. She told me it would be a special night and I should meet her inside so she can disclose the details.' I improvised, pretending to be a performer, lying smoothly to get my way while batting my eyelashes at the frowning bouncer.

Zbigniew Nadolny, known by the working girls as Zbyszek, owned the Anchor, and the man had a reputation. I hadn't met him personally, but my colleagues in the police cursed his name with frustration and professional respect. Prostitution, extortion, handling stolen goods, he did it all without a hint of shame, but they never had successfully prosecuted him for anything.

Officially, he was a philanthropist who owned a nightclub on the edge of the latest area to see urban renewal, thanks to an influx of lawyers and architects determined to rescue the beautiful pre-war buildings, but despite these upright citizens, crime was still relatively high, and it all seemed centred around Zbyszek's club, without ever happening inside. That was the official version, but those working in the emergency services knew he was merciless to his enemies, and the latest rumour was the drug dealers that sold their produce to a school in Sopot disappeared, courtesy of his influence. Even I was surprised by that information. To think there was such a thing as a Crime Lord with honour.

Knowing all this, I still stood there using his name whilst thrusting my breasts in a man's face to gain entry into this infamous club. *I must be mad putting my neck in the noose for a stranger,* I thought, but I wanted to talk to Ilona and maybe, if lucky, find out what was happening in my city.

I knew Zbyszek didn't beat his prostitutes, or at least none of them came to my emergency room. I even heard he only took a small cut of their earnings and even set them up with official employment as hostesses so they could have health insurance, but someone had hurt Ilona, and not just once, and it appeared her boss was sweeping it under the carpet. *Was he the man who ordered the siren to stab Adam, or was he someone else's lackey and was ordered to cover up the problem?* I felt the need to find out and help this poor woman before it was too late, but I admitted to myself this was frightening and, standing before the bouncer, I second-guessed my plan and intentions.

Leszek said magic was his domain. This story had plenty of magic, so I hoped seeing the damaged siren would force his hand, but my plan had backfired. My grumpy hero was nowhere to be seen, the club was closed to the public, and I was now standing here sincerely hoping I would be refused entry. When I turned to walk away, the cogs in the bouncer's brain finally skipped a notch, and he grabbed my arm.

'Fine, let's go. Ilona isn't working today, but I'll take you to the boss and see what he says.'

Bloody hell, I thought, mind racing as I bit my lip, trying to think of an excuse. Using Nadolny's pet name made everything so much worse, and now I was stuck. The bouncer held my arm with a firm but surprisingly respectful grip as he escorted me inside. *Fuck, what now? I didn't plan this.* I ran through as many scenarios as possible whilst stumbling slightly to slow our progress. The place was almost empty. I could see Nadolny's goons scattered about and pay-per-hour girls dancing lazily around the metal poles. With blaring music and skittish waitresses serving drinks, it was a sad attempt at a party, the atmosphere heavy with tension. As we moved to the VIP area, the number of heavyset men grew, and my nervousness worsened. When one of them brushed his hand over my exposed skin, my forearm prickled with goosebumps, and the realisation that I was in deep trouble settled into my soul.

I could play stupid, which was most likely my best choice and be a bimbo for the night, hoping no one noticed the real me under all this heavy makeup and distracting clothing. The plan was good until the bouncer pulled aside the heavy curtains to the room set aside for Mr. Nadolny's special guests.

FUUCK!

The voice screaming in my mind knew how much trouble I was in, but with the bouncer behind me, my escape route was blocked. I had never thought I'd be grateful to be confronted by two naked women kissing passionately, their display partially shielding me from the eyes of the stranger hiding in the shadow.

'Boss, this woman claims Ilona told her there was work for her tonight. Is she a new one for the collection?' His question gave me a new idea. Playing stupid could work, especially since Nadolny was famous and rich enough that I could pretend to be a gangster groupie who craved his attention and lied to get it.

I intended to put my heart and soul into the performance, but when I looked up to begin, my fears of being exposed vanished, replaced by shock and anger. The gangster's guest had shifted slightly, and it was his face emerging from the shadow that triggered my outrage.

'And what the hell are you doing here?!' I asked, my eyes widening in shock as I wrecked my own plan.

Next to Zbyszek, lounging indolently and looking like the personification of lust itself, was Leszek. I couldn't tear my eyes from his collar that was open too low to hide his delicious chest hair, the rumpled fabric a victim of the roaming hands of the barely clad woman perched on his lap, while his rolled-up sleeves exposed muscled forearms that held the female in place and I swear Leszek flexed them when he noticed me staring.

'Do you know her?' Nadolny looked at me with unbridled curiosity, pushing a lock of dark hair behind his ear. There was no malice in his grey eyes, more barely restrained amusement and interest, but in desperation, I wracked my brain for an explanation for my presence, nearly stumbling backwards when Leszek pushed his entertainment away and pulled me onto his lap.

The movement was so sudden I gasped, unable to protest, before he grabbed my neck from behind and pressed his lips to mine in a long, devouring kiss.

He tasted as good as I'd imagined, and I couldn't prevent moaning in response, barely registering his whisper. 'Play along if you want to live.' He said, shifting his kiss to my earlobe before turning to the other man as if nothing had happened.

'Forgive this intrusion. It appears I wasn't explicit enough in my instructions when she was informed no other man could touch her. Yet she let your guard lead her here like a common whore. Her nosiness and jealousy will get her in trouble, but if you're willing to forgive her intrusion, I warrant she will furnish me with the reason.' He smirked when Nadolny burst out laughing.

Leszek instantly returned his attention to me. 'Did you miss me, my Firefly? Or maybe you came to find some entertainment of your own despite my explicit warning? Judging by how you are dressed and the fact I like your hair loose, I would say it was the latter, so tell me, which is it?' He pulled the pins from my bun, and my hair fell over my shoulders in a cascade of honey-coloured softness. Brushing it with his fingers, he gave me a warning squeeze when I tried to pull away.

A sudden wave of heat washed through my body. I knew it was role-play to protect me, but I enjoyed Leszek's bossy attitude far too much despite knowing that I shouldn't. I needed to talk to him and gain his help in finding Ilona and getting out of this place unscathed, so I had no choice but to play along, and part of me rejoiced at the idea making it easier to slip into a gangster girlfriend persona.

'You know how I miss your presence. I wanted to stay home, but when your men joked about where you were going in front of me... Well, I hate when you are with other women,' I said, swallowing hard and pausing before leaning against Leszek's chest, my hand stroking over the impressive muscles, sliding into the open collar.

'I decided to find you, even if you were rutting in the Anchor. I knew Mr Nadolny would help. He has an excellent reputation, and you once said he is an honourable man. So I took the risk because I needed a powerful man to help me find you. If I knew you were too busy sticking your dick in the local whores, I would have done things differently, but you should have at least plucked up the courage to break up with me.'

I knew I was rambling and that my story made little sense, my words and actions contradicting each other, but I put my heart into this performance. My chin shot up when I stood up, blinking several times, hoping to shed some tears. After all, this was the best break-up speech I'd made in my entire life. Passionate and full of desperate, broken-hearted love. It was time to leave the scene in a grand finale. I turned to the club owner, looking at him with doe eyes glistening with tears. 'I'm sorry, Sir. I shouldn't have lied, but your club was my best chance at finding him or asking for your help. I know both of you value discretion, and I didn't want to involve anyone else. May I talk to Ilona, please? I didn't realise she wasn't working today, but I really need a friend now. '

I was buttering him up so much that the gangster might slide off the leather sofa if he moved, but when Nadolny tilted his head, his eyes narrowed, it became clear he hadn't fallen for my act. With a calculating look toward Leszek, Nadolny reached over and patted my thigh, his hand lingering a moment longer than was polite.

'I understand, my darling. Your concerns were valid, and I would be more than happy to assist you, but seeing the evidence of his behaviour, perhaps you should change the focus of your affection. After all, as you said, I am an honourable man, and I refrain from tasting the merchandise more than it is absolutely necessary. I would be happy to have such a brave and loyal woman by my side. I could even promise not to stray... too much.'

Panic washed through me. I'd blown it, making the gangster suspicious enough to test Leszek's attachment to me. I smiled, but my mind went blank, lost at how to extricate myself, only hoping Leszek would continue helping me. When the firm grip of my saviour's hand dragged me beyond Nadolny's reach, I collapsed into his embrace in relief, startling slightly as the air filled with the scent of the deep forest, the tension in the room squeezing my chest till it was difficult to breathe.

The world stilled as Leszek focused his icy gaze on the gangster, no longer a demon of sinful decadence but the embodiment of death, as he snarled.

'No one touches what's mine. Including you... *my friend.*'

Chapter Eleven

(an hour earlier)

Zbigniew Nadolny's welcome was surprisingly jovial, as he acted like I was a long-lost brother returning to the fold. However, when I looked around the club, the lack of revellers was telling, especially when dour tattooed men in dark suits replaced the rowdy pleasure-seeking youngsters, not even pretending to flirt with the entertainers and wait staff.

'Leszek, I am honoured that you visited my humble establishment. I do hope you will partake of our unique entertainment this evening, yes?' Nadolny gestured for me to join him, standing up and extending a hand. I almost missed the gesture as I scrutinised the men behind the mob boss, noticing his grimace as I took his hand in a firm but friendly shake.

'Yes, well, I am here to discuss business, the troubles in the docks specifically, but we are both sophisticated men, and there's no reason our meeting cannot be pleasurable.'

I saw the fleeting wariness on his face before he relaxed, nodding to a nameless suit who left the group as Nadolny gestured to the couch.

'We can talk about it later. I have the best wines and women in the Tricity. To my great pleasure, we recently recruited some of your kind if you wish to try. Why not enjoy both while my man checks what we know about the docks?'

I ground my teeth, noticing several men reach for whatever hidden weapons they possessed as soon as I moved. Adam bared his fangs, and although I could easily tear this place down, I sighed, sliding into the seat next to my host. With a new and unknown adversary, I needed information as I sounded out a potential ally. For now, I would do my best to placate my human counterpart.

'If you're offering the best, then how could I refuse? Let's see if your reputation is as impressive as I've heard.'

The subtle insult was met with a stiff smile, the barb merely a reminder that I, too, was a power to be reckoned with. As if on command, a blond girl appeared with two glasses of wine, settling onto my lap with a coquettish smile that had its charms, and I didn't object as her hands moved over my chest, even when her nimble fingers opened my shirt. I knew Nadolny was observing my reaction, and I did my best to pretend I was enjoying myself.

I almost succeeded. I say almost because it wasn't long before another henchman joined us, leading the last person I expected to see here. *Sara! What the hell is she doing here?* I thought, and to my surprise, seeing her in danger awakened the twinge of fear I'd not felt in centuries.

All of my men were selected and trained for close-quarter fighting, and those with me tonight were the best, their unique talents making them difficult to kill, but Sara? Even if I utilised all my power, could I stop every stray bullet if mayhem erupted? *I have to get her out of here, and quickly.* My thoughts were racing, and judging by how her eyes grew, Sara hadn't expected to find me here, either.

The best way to protect her would be to pretend not to know her, but of course, the damn woman had other ideas, asking me why I was there, even though she knew I frequented such lawless places. With my plan in as many pieces as the MS Batory, I rolled my eyes and thought fast, grabbing the annoying woman, displacing the poor entertainer in the process, replacing her with my newest conundrum and kissing her passionately.

Her lips, soft and pliant, melted all thoughts except one. Why hadn't I done this before? She felt divine, reminding me of when the world was new and full of wonder. The magic of my beautiful seer ignited an inferno across my lips and tongue as she teased open my mouth, deepening the kiss. A soft moan escaped her lips, stripping me of reason, yet I was the one who broke away, whispering a warning as our lips parted.

Hoping Sara was as quick on her feet as her job suggested, I released my hold on her neck and slowly stroked a finger down her spine. Despite the quizzical tilt of her head, Sara remained seated, pressing a hand to my chest and pouting prettily. Now, we could rescue the situation without Nadolny seeing the seer as a threat or a weakness to be exploited. All it required was a lecherous mobster to see what he expected: the jaded Forest Lord and his latest distraction.

As I continued stroking Sara's back, hoping to reassure her that I had the situation under control, her mood switched, and with righteous indignation, she angrily tore into my character. Every inch the spurned lover, appealing to the mobster next to me when my response failed to satisfy her fake outrage, simultaneously charming Nadolny whilst distancing herself from me.

It might have worked, but ever the shrewd entrepreneur, Nadolny distrusted the coincidence, deciding to test me and proposing a deal. He knew he was balancing on a knife's edge, but finding a weakness of the Forest Lord was worth the risk. Unfortunately, when he suggested Sara become his, the thought of this man laying a hand on her body ignited a rage that had me pressing her back against my chest, magic surrounding us in a green mist as I warned the gangster off.

'No one touches what's mine. Including you... *my friend*,' I said. Sara's head snapped around, her eyes searching mine. A confused frown marred her forehead, announcing her desire to contradict me, but when Nadolny pulled away, uncomfortable in the presence of my power, something in Sara's posture changed. A hint of mischief danced in her eyes as she slid her hands under my shirt again and pouted in mock outrage.

'What if I want to? Why can you play with other women, but I can't touch another man?' She asked, painfully pulling the hair beneath her fingers.

'Because you are mine, Firefly.' I said with finality, refusing to flinch as she continued to pinch my skin under the pretence of playful stroking. Playing much? I thought, trying hard to resist the urge to flip her body over and spank the mischievous minx. The way she wriggled in my lap, never losing eye contact, fanned the flames of my desire, and Sara knew it, her hand placed directly over my heart. The shock of Nadolny laughing broke the spell of our exchange, and we both turned to look in his direction.

'Yes, why don't you let your Lady play a little, especially with her temporary replacement at your feet?' Belatedly remembering the waitress, I looked down, the poor girl staring up in abject terror. I waved her away, and she moved back, scrambling past the surrounding henchmen, but before she could escape, one of them grabbed her arm, making the woman whimper in pain.

'Nobody will touch my woman, as she well knows, so I will make sure to punish her later.' I swatted Sara's bottom lightly, smiling when she bit her lip. 'As for your little gift, I may let her join us, so tell your men she is not to be touched.'

I saw Nadolny gesture to his assistant, who released the girl, letting her retreat to the dancefloor, and without a word, a brunette scurried over to sit with the mobster. With no hesitation, Nadolny leaned over to run a hand roughly over the female's breast, her wince almost imperceptible. In response, Sara quickly returned to character, shifting and seating herself on my lap, her thighs pressing against my waist.

What the hell is she doing? I felt my trousers tighten as the reckless woman kissed and bit my neck. I could not push her away or end this without compromising the deception, but she was dangerously close to being ravaged by the primaeval demon that ruled the forest, and I was almost past caring who saw.

Sara's teeth nipped at my earlobe as she spoke, the words splashing ice-cold water on my libido. 'I came here to talk to Ilona. She is one of the sirens. They are working for Nadolny, but not voluntarily. Help me get them out, please.'

Did she come for the sirens? But why, and how was the woman who barely knew about the Nether, already risking her life coming here asking to help the merfolk? My mind raced as I wondered how she knew about the sirens, especially so soon after my encounter with one of them during the raid on the dockyard. I wish I could ask, but with her message passed on, she returned to her ministrations, and I couldn't help the groan that slipped past my lips as the woman drove me wild with the touch of her body, eliciting a passion I thought lost to the ages.

With desire came clarity, and the perfect idea came to mind: an opportunity to keep Sara close, ensuring her recent entanglement in the siren's problem was only a coincidence and protecting her from the Coven's influence.

As the breath within my chest escaped, its sound formed into words. 'I will, but only if you agree to live with me.' I reached up, my fingers entangling in her hair, and forced her lips to mine, claiming them with fervent passion, breaking away only to complete my demand. 'Three months, Sara, that's all I ask. This pretence you started must run its course, or we will both be in danger.' It was a partial lie, but I was learning what motivated this force of nature and knew she would ignore any threat to herself.

Sara's body stilled, and I saw the hesitation in her eyes before she looked at Nadolny, who, oblivious to the world, enjoyed the ministrations of the brunette. I followed her eyes and gently took her chin, directing her attention back to me.

'I'm not him. I won't force or coerce you into sex, but freeing the sirens could cause a war. You've already declared yourself to be my woman. Keep up the pretence and give me three months so I can protect you.' From the corner of my eyes, I saw Nadolny open his eyes, observing us, and I leaned closer, cupping her face in my hands.

I saw the decision in her eyes before she closed them,

'Yes,' her answer was barely audible, but it was enough for me. Sara agreed to the deal, and magic, old as the world itself, bound us together. Something inside me roared in triumph, and I leaned forward and sealed the deal with a kiss that tasted much sweeter, given willingly. Three months was time aplenty to woo this delicious woman, and I intended to use every second to my advantage.

'Remember your promise when I fulfil mine.' I said, turning toward Nadolny. It was time to go back to business. Even if this wasn't my original intention, to keep Sara, I was ready to challenge not just one human gangster but the world.

Chapter Twelve

To say things hadn't gone as planned was an understatement of epic proportions. I came to talk with Ilona and ended up sitting on Leszek's lap, enjoying his touch in public while he caressed my back with slow, reassuring strokes. Nadolny observed us closely, pretending to be focused on the brunette that pleasured him, and as much as it pained me to admit, I knew that after my outburst, I had to play the pretty, but not necessarily intelligent, girlfriend.

Should I try to leave the club and ignore what's happening around me? The thought was tempting, and I would be doing exactly that in any normal situation, but here, there were no casual bystanders to provide disapproval or protection, just dour henchmen and studiously oblivious entertainers, none of whom would lift a finger to help if Nadolny decided on violence. I enjoyed a good adrenaline rush as much as anyone, but this was a whole new level of crazy, and I didn't know how to navigate these dangerous waters.

My instincts said to trust Leszek, and despite my past, I always followed my gut. I wouldn't say I liked it, but I had to rely on the only person who might know what was going on here. The one man who could protect me if things went sideways in this viper's den. Besides, we both knew it was just pretend, right? At least, that's what he'd said.

I shouldn't be reassured to be held by a stranger who looked at me as if I were prey, but something about Leszek encouraged me to relax, and as I lay my head on his shoulder, I could feel the tension magically drain away. I could look after myself in most circumstances, but just this once, I allowed him to take control, caring for my safety. I liked how he pressed me to his body, the sensation dulling the fear whilst awakening all my senses. I could blame the predicament, but I was old enough to know better.

I'd felt attracted to him from the beginning, and now, facing danger together, I was acutely aware of every part of his body: the firm muscles, the heartbeat, fast and slightly unsteady, and then there was the hard length pressed against my thigh as, unable to resist, I nibbled his earlobe, asking for his help with the sirens. He'd agreed, but the condition he set for his assistance gave me pause, even through the haze of arousal that seemed to control my every action. *It is just a game, and we both know it.* Men like him knew only two forms of commitment. A trophy girlfriend or the always forgiving wife. I could pretend to be the former but would never agree to be the latter, and by now, he should know it. Three months of being this gorgeous man's arm candy, it is, then.

Despite my protestations of pretence, I could not meet Leszek's intense regard and closed my eyes, but the infuriating man took that as an invitation to kiss me again, shocking me with how demanding such a gentle kiss could be. I could feel his longing through the trembling fingers cupping my face, his other hand sliding through my hair to clasp the back of my head, holding me in place. His beard tickled, and I chuckled slightly. He used this opportunity to deepen the kiss, tongue slipping inside to taste me, and I wondered what his senses told him about me.

Heat pooled inside me while my heart hammered out its beat at the speed of a freight train, drowning out all thought. My hands again found their way under his shirt, revelling in the lush hair. He ticked every box of my little kink, or as my friend Nina called it, my bad boy obsession, but I couldn't help it; I liked them hairy, masculine and dominant. Sophisticated, clean-shaven men didn't do it for me. Now, feeling the soft pelt on Leszek's chest, I realised this man had all three of those traits, and I prayed to any listening deities that he wasn't an arsehole as well. I moaned, scraping my nails against his skin. We were in public, but my inhibitions had disappeared when his rich scent enveloped me. He could bend me over and fuck me right there on the table, and I wouldn't care less about other people watching.

Has my drink been spiked? The fleeting thought worried me until I realised I hadn't touched a drop tonight. *Leszek's magic, he is using it to make this believable.* I thought, desperately needing something to explain my behaviour at his touch, my abandonment of decorum in the face of danger.

Why do I want him so much? The sensible question broke the spell of our passion, allowing panic to wash away the pleasure. Leszek must have sensed my reaction, withdrawing from the kiss immediately, releasing his hold. Maybe he wasn't an overbearing brute after all, but he was sure as hell eager to enjoy a willing partner's desire.

Only now did I hear the slow clapping of our host, Nadolny, looking me in the eye as I turned my head, the predatory grimace on his face instantly disturbing me.

'That was an entertaining display. Let me know if you ever tire of your latest pet. I would like to enjoy such receptive passion.'

I felt Leszek's hand tighten its grip on my thigh, but before he could respond, we were interrupted by an employee's arrival. I observed the gangster's face change during the course of their whispered conversation, the convivial mask dropping as fury overtook him.

'It appears you were right. We recently had a security breach, and one of my warehouses was, let's say, repurposed for a different function. It also appears some of my... clients went missing. Nobody of consequence, but rumours of such things happening would create difficulties for business relations. Thank you for bringing the issue to my attention. What would you like for such a... favour?'

A laugh escaped my lips, more a snort of derision. Regardless of the danger, I couldn't help thinking the reputation of the Anchor and its boss couldn't get much worse, though it was good to know Nadolny wasn't involved with his client's troubles. I opened my mouth to ask about his staff, but Leszek wrapped my hair around his hand, tilting my head back and trailing his fingers along my throat. He was silent, ignoring the question. It felt like he was making a point, asserting his dominance. Only I wasn't sure if it was over me or Nadolny. Still, when he spoke, his intentions became apparent.

'I came here to warn you as we share this territory, and I believe Tricity is crowded enough without a third player. I also have a request that may help curtail further disappearances.' I watched him pause for effect, and when Nadolny nodded, acknowledging his words, Leszek continued.

'Monitor the docks. Warn off anyone your people don't recognise; I will instruct my staff to do the same. Also, this new player may be responsible for your missing clientele. Some of my people were forced to spy on you. The sirens you are so proud to have acquired are not here by choice, and I want them back, unharmed.'

'We both know I don't force women, and my employees are treated better than any similar establishments. Do not question my integrity or honour. However, for the sake of this discussion, let us assume what you say is true. What if I choose to punish them? After all, their actions threatened my business, so how can I let them walk away unharmed?' Nadolny stood up, ready to challenge Leszek, but the Forest Lord simply raised an eyebrow.

'Adam, take my woman outside. It is time for the men to talk business.'

I watched as the arrogant vampire approached, and Leszek handed me to him, not once looking away from Nadolny. When I tried to protest, Adam squeezed my elbow. 'Not now, please,' he said, and the fact he was so polite gave me a pause.

Are they going to fight now? Panicking, I turned toward Nadolny. *And the Oscar for today's performance goes to...* I thought, pulling out my sweetest smile whilst disentangling myself from Adam's grasp.

'My friend, the one I asked about earlier - Ilona - she told me you've never raised your hand to a woman who works for you. I know she works here, and I know someone hurt her recently. Could it be the men you're both talking about? Please, don't fight - not when I can clear this up by speaking to Ilona. Just, please, let me talk to her. I would be very grateful.'

My strange act left both men frowning, the unexpected interruption confusing them, and Adam groaned quietly.

'I'm sorry, boss, I will take her out.' He said, but Nadolny stopped him.

'It didn't take you long to drop the act and reveal why you came here. That is interesting, but I'm more curious about how grateful you could be, girl.' He smirked, and instantly Leszek moved in my direction.

'Very?' I answered, unsure where this was headed.

'Kiss me like you kissed him, and I will let the sirens go. No questions asked, no hard feelings. Pour your heart into it and let your kiss soothe away any animosity. After all, as you said, I must uphold my impeccable reputation, and having a taste of the Forest Lord's woman will satisfy my pride. So what will it be? Your touch for their freedom?'

'You are crossing the line. No one can have her but me. I told you, Sara is mine.' Leszek moved to grab me, but I darted toward Nadolny before latching onto the surprised gangster's mouth.

He tasted of alcohol, but I didn't care, thinking of it as a disinfectant when I pushed my tongue between his lips. Still, I knew he told me the truth from the first touch. He wasn't interested in me, but Leszek's revelation made him look weak; now, he had to re-establish his position in front of his men, which was exactly what I hoped for. We could leave here without casualties if I used this ego-driven dominance battle. Now I only needed to fake an orgasm or similar nonsense, and we would be done here.

Before I could vocalise my fake pleasure, Leszek's hand grabbed me by the scruff of the neck, pulling me away from Nadolny.

'You got what you wanted. I expect the sirens to have their contracts torn up and released from your employment by the morning at the latest.' He said through clenched teeth, pulling me behind him.

'Not a word, Sara. Not a fucking word. We are going home,' he added, squeezing my arm so tight I couldn't even dream of escaping his grip.

I could see he was fuming, but I couldn't understand why. *Did my actions ruin his plans? It's not like I could have hurt his feelings.* Yes, we had fun on the couch, and I promised to pretend to be his girlfriend, but surely he wasn't being serious? Besides, I was a bloody hero for ending the confrontation without violence.

Fresh air hit my face as Leszek slammed the front door back on its hinges. I tried to untangle myself from his grip, finally losing my temper, but Leszek pulled me further, right around the corner. He slammed my shoulders against the wall with bruising strength. We were in a dark alley, away from prying eyes, and I was helpless before this raging beast of a man. So vulnerable that my knees buckled.

'When you give me your word, treat it seriously. Do not throw yourself at another man like a wanton,' he snarled, tilting his head. I could see the muscles of his jaw pulsing as he tried to regain control.

'You are mine, Sara, maybe only for a limited time, but you are entirely mine. You gave yourself freely, body and soul; during this time, no one else will touch you.' His voice was low, barely audible, spoken through clenched teeth, but the implication I welcomed Nadolny's touch was unbearable.

'You are nuts if you think I wanted him. I would kiss a pig's bollocks to get us out of there without bloodshed while you wanted to start a fight. We got what we wanted. Those women will be safe. I'm sorry I hurt your precious ego in front of your associates, but you can stop being an arsehole about it. You don't own me.' I said, despite my heart racing from fear.

When he grunted, annoyance at his arrogance replaced my fear. I looked up angrily to confront him, but the green light in his eyes and the power surrounding us caused my certainty to falter.

'Don't you understand, Sara? I do own you, my Firefly. You gave me your consent, your promise, and my magic sealed the pact. I was ready to tear the club to the ground, to destroy the underworld boss of Tricity for this... for you, so yes, I own you. You will not flirt with or touch another man for as long as our contract lasts; get used to it,' he said, and I knew that, entranced by his touch, I may have made a terrible mistake.

His anger didn't subside after he bundled me into the car and silently drove me home. I didn't mind this, as his tantrum allowed me to sort through my feelings. I couldn't lie to myself; we had uncovered an ugly truth tonight. Our characters were incompatible, clashing on every occasion, and I didn't like him or the situations he put me in, but our bodies were another thing entirely.

If only I could forget who he was and what he wanted from me, I could have the best sex of my life. I was sure of it. Still, the pleasure would no doubt come with strings attached. He already thought he owned me, at least for the next three months. The last thing I wanted to do when the three months passed was to become the booty call for a paranormal mobster as well as his illicit surgeon.

Yet I'd landed myself in a situation where I was seen as both, and something in his statement told me he believed every word and would follow our agreement to the letter. *I need to learn more about this world before I get into more trouble,* I thought, stealing a glance at Leszek's profile.

My titular owner was driving with an unyielding expression, making me feel tired just looking at him, the sigh it caused catching his attention, but he didn't utter a word whilst inspecting me. Finally, wheels screeching in the parking lot, we arrived, and I prepared to flee from this uncomfortable situation.

'Pack whatever you'll need for the next few days. I will wait here. You won't need much clothing, just some pyjamas for now. We can buy you the rest tomorrow.' My hand froze on the door handle as I processed his words.

'Sure... wait, what?' I sat back, looking at him wide-eyed, wondering if I'd heard him right. The arsehole was smiling, and I felt like tucking my tail and fleeing from the predatory look.

'You think what you did in the Anchor was clever, right, brave even? No, Sara. You placed a target on your back the size of a house because now, fucking everybody knows that you're more than an empty-headed bimbo. I named you as my woman, and then you spoke out of turn, interrupting my business, yet I didn't punish you. What impression do you think that will give people like Nadolny?' He grimaced, shaking his head.

'I will tell you what that mercenary bastard thinks, what they will all think; I care for you, you have me wrapped around your finger, and if something happens to you, it will be a clear sign I'm not strong enough to protect my woman or that if they threaten to harm you, they can manipulate me. So I will protect you until my enemies leave or they are dead and buried, and for me to do that, you need to live in my house.' Leszek was visibly struggling to hold back his anger, and the steering wheel was bearing the brunt of that fight. I knew I shouldn't, but something deep inside me wanted to soothe this raging male.

'I'm sorry. I have little experience in such situations, but with so many deaths recently, I couldn't face the possibility of you being hurt because of me. I will be fine, I promise. I'm not normally that stupid.' I said, smiling and placing my hand on his face.

His eyes darkened before he closed them, pressing his bearded cheek into my palm.

'Sara... I'm sorry. The way he looked at you, I... when you kissed him, it was too much, and I knew how much danger you were in. I apologise for my words, but they are true. Please grab whatever you need because it is not safe for you to stay here,' he said, and suddenly, his lips were on mine. Hard and unyielding, taking me like he was trying to erase Nadolny's touch from my mind. I gasped when pleasure shot through me, and Leszek used the moment to slide his tongue inside, possessing me completely. When he finally ended the kiss, I was panting desperately, trying to collect my thoughts while he looked at my lips smugly.

'Look, I get it. You, me, we could have *happy, fun times*, but I can't just leave,' I said finally. 'This is my home, and what about my cat? I can look after myself whilst pretending to be your woman. I will attend whatever functions you need me to and climb on your lap for all your men to see who is the boss, even if it costs me every drop of self-respect, but I won't leave my home.' I said, watching warily as his eyes darkened.

'Do you think I want you there simply for sex?' he asked grimly

'Well, if not, you are doing a great job of confusing me.'

'I told you, you need to be somewhere safe,' he said, eyes narrowing with irritation. He huffed, raising his hands. 'If you are so afraid of me, I can promise I won't touch you unless you ask for it,' he said, and I snapped, rolling my eyes.

'It's not that! I never said I didn't like your touch. I like it way too much for my own good. That's the problem! That and the fact that once you shift my sorry arse to whatever place you deem safe, I'd be dependent on you. Can't you see where this is going? So no, I won't leave my home,' I said, crossing my arms on my chest, wondering what patron saint of stupid and demented ideas made me shout all this in his face.

I'd said a lot but couldn't tell him the real reason. I didn't want this fascination to become something more. I wasn't ready for that, not with Leszek. Whatever drew us together made things too complicated.

'It was not a question. Please pack yourself and your cat or parrot or stamp collection. Take whatever you feel is important, but pack yourself and return to the car. I will wait here.'

Here we go. Leszek's appeal nosedived every time he bossed me around. He was calm again as he raised my hand, kissing my fingertips like this could soothe my anger, but I needed to leave the car before I choked him. I rushed inside my apartment, slamming the door behind me, listening for a moment to check if he'd followed me up, looking at Scarface, whose unblinking stare silently judged me as I turned the lock.

'What? I can't go with him. I'm my own woman with friends, a job and sanity, the last still mainly intact. I can't live with a man who makes me feel like a horny teenager. You know it will end up exploding in my face. He isn't the sort of man I can sample, then toss him out of the door with his cab fare as a thank you.' I swore I heard the cat snort as I picked him up, but it was probably just wind.

Half an hour later, Leszek's car was still in the parking lot. I was standing at the window wondering how long it would take till he lost the last of his patience and left, so the knock on the door took me by surprise. I hadn't seen him exit his car, but the unmistakable scent of the forest told me who was on the other side.

'Sara, are you ready? Do you need any help?' his deep baritone sent shivers down my spine. I walked over, stood behind the door, looked at the handle, and braced myself to answer.

'I'm not going anywhere. Please leave.'

His fist hammered the door with such strength that I worried the composite miracle of modern carpentry wouldn't withstand the force. I stumbled backwards, my heart pounding in my chest. *Is he going to break in and take me by force?* I wondered, trying to calm my fears. Silence descended the moment I moved, and I couldn't help but hold my breath in anticipation.

'Sara, don't be stubborn. I only want to protect you. When I told you your actions planted a target on your back, I left out a few details. The siren you encountered is involved in something dangerous, something that's already left some of our brethren dead, and after tonight, the same people who wounded the wolf pup will be after you. All I want is to make sure you are safe. I won't touch you. I won't even come close unless you ask, but I must ensure you are safe.' Leszek's voice was quiet, yet the tension within its soft tones drew me closer till I lay my forehead against the solid barrier.

'I will be safe. Please, please go home. I have to work tomorrow.'

'Sara...'

'No, moving in with you would strip away my freedom. Arrange a date or call me if you need my services, but I won't move to your house tonight.' I cursed myself for saying tonight as if he could persuade me any other day, but my answer seemed to satisfy him.

'Fine, have it your way for tonight. I will see you tomorrow, but please think about it. Despite the circumstances, I really enjoyed this evening. If you fear I would impose myself upon you, invite a friend to keep me honest, but on my honour, I would never force you.'

I placed a hand on the door, stroking it, remembering the feel of Leszek's chest. My breathing deepened when I sensed his presence, forcing me to step away and shake my head before I submitted to my cravings.

'All right. I will think about it, but please leave now. I need to rest, and so do you.' My words were almost a sob, and moments later, Leszek's departing footsteps told me I was alone.

Chapter Thirteen

I moved to the couch and sat down, feeling numb after Leszek's departure. Even cushioned by the soft fabric, I couldn't relax a single tense muscle or ease the turmoil in my mind. My plan had backfired so badly that I failed to wrap my head around the enormity of my fuck up. So I grabbed Scarface, placed him on my lap, and gently stroked his soft, luxurious fur while I thought about it.

One day, I'm going about my own business, patching up the residents of Gdansk; the next, I'm pulling a dagger from a vampire's chest. Then, after catching my breath, with unimaginable stupidity and bravado, I became a mobster's girlfriend. I knew Leszek was some sort of local boss. What else did I know about him? Although I hadn't heard of Leszek and his kind until recently, Nadolny acted as if they were old comrades and respected him, which begged the question. If he knew, who else did? I thought I was the odd one, the outcast who saw shadow monsters on every corner, mentally unstable, but with Adam and Leszek's appearance, it now became evident magic was real, and I was part of a whole new world. One filled with dangerous creatures and the humans that knew of them, which, according to Leszek, instantly put me in danger. That and the fact I was now associated with him.

I snorted at this thought. Associated with him? If you called climbing the man like a tree could be considered associating, then I was definitely that. Maybe I should consider shares in liquorice in order to lower my libido around that damn man.

I had learned something new tonight, though, a new perspective even. Despite both men's ruthless involvement in criminality, I suspected Leszek and Nadolny contributed to making Tricity's crime rate lower than the surrounding areas. Their willingness to talk and cooperate, after the usual male posturing, was surprising. Not that I condoned crime, but I wasn't some naïve youngster and knew how bad the violence would be if no one controlled the streets, as was clear with the recent spate of stabbings.

Were the attacks a result of whatever had caused the two gangsters to meet? Some new player disrupting the established order, or perhaps internal disruption from an ambitious underling? I liked my city and enjoyed the freedom to walk unmolested on its streets, but there was no telling what would happen if the situation escalated. The crime here was... orderly, and I knew who I had to thank for this.

A hollow laugh shook my body, and I buried my face in cat fur.

'Now I'm defending the criminal underworld, but it is my city, my home. What should I do, fluffball? Help them? Call the police?' I asked, scratching the cat's chin.

'What am I even saying? There's not a shred of evidence they've done anything wrong. Can you imagine me going to the police and telling them what I've seen these last few days? Even Kamil would laugh me out of the station, and he's known me for years.'

As I stared into Scarface's inscrutable gaze, there was a flash of something at the corner of my eye, and as I turned, a face appeared from the shadows outside my window, looking directly at me before fading away once more. *Fuck, I need to get my imagination under control.* I closed my eyes, letting the cat's purring calm my racing thoughts, but as I relaxed, my mind connected with something: an awareness, hungry and annoyed that the stroking had stopped, the realisation that my imagination wasn't creating this phenomenon left me gaping.

I sat there, mouth open, as my cat nonchalantly jumped off my lap and walked over to the cupboard that held his food.

'Scarface... how?' I asked, utterly baffled by this latest development, seriously worried that I'd lost what little sense I had left and could now talk to my feline companion. Not that I hadn't been talking to him before, but never with the expectation he'd answer. Finally closing my mouth, I pinched the bridge of my nose, massaging the frown I knew would be there, hoping to make everything disappear.

'Finally, I thought I'd have to bond with a witch if you didn't figure out your magic. Feed me, woman. You can brood over your gentleman caller later. Why you'd chase after the Leshy without feeding me first, I don't know. Seers! Almost as bad as witches, always forgetting what's important when something pretty distracts them. Come on; this bowl won't fill itself.'

I walked to the kitchen, looked at my cat, and seriously considered getting an MRI. I filled both bowls without once looking away from Scarface.

'Who? What are you?' I asked when he snapped at the food, devouring it with gusto.

'Did your eyes stop working? I am a cat, and a very frustrated one at that. Do you know how long I've waited for you to hear me? How can I guide you if you never listen? I'd be better off as a familiar to those ignorant witches than a guide for a deaf seer. Never mind, you are listening now, and I am too comfortable to leave. If you haven't already worked it out, my job is to guide and protect you through the dangers of the sight and trust me, it is not easy; you are barely home, you don't have wards, and you have no idea who you are or what you're doing. What a nightmare. Now pack your bags. You are going with the Leshy tomorrow.'

'Leshy?' I asked, because why not? Why not sit in the middle of the kitchen floor talking to a cat that scolds you worse than your grandma?

'Leshy, Leszek, Forest Lord, Beast Master, it's all the same, but he's taken an interest in you, so use him. That being has power knowledge and can teach you about the sight.'

'Right, and that's your best advice? I'd rather eat a bowl of your food, but I will pack a bloody bag, just in case,' I said, laughter escaping my control. 'I can't believe I'm taking orders from a cat.'

I ignored the feline's mocking snort and poured a large glass of cucumber water before pulling a travel bag from storage. I started with the essentials like cat food, then moved to the bathroom, adding a few necessary cosmetics and a suture kit.

In the end, I picked two practical outfits and some light cotton pyjamas, somehow finding myself holding up a mossy-coloured satin camisole finished with golden trim as I stood before the open bag.

I looked at the delicate fabric shimmering lightly in my hands. I'd bought it impulsively, but it had been sitting at the bottom of my drawer, unused and forgotten for longer than I wanted to admit. A useless waste of money, but I wanted to put it in the bag. I just didn't know why.

'Good choice. The Leshy will enjoy seeing you wear his colours.' I heard Scarface's voice and nearly dropped the satin.

'Will you shut up? Leszek won't be seeing anything,' I said, unsure if I was trying to convince the cat or myself, but I put the shimmering beauty in the bag anyway, pretending not to see Scarface giving me the side-eye as I did. Tired as a dog, I threw myself on the bed, unable to object as my feline overlord sat on my chest, curling up to sleep as usual.

'You are fat,' I said when he finally settled.

'And you snore, but I never complain.' The voice in my head made me smile. Apparently, all the men in my life were pompous arseholes. Still, I couldn't raise the energy to care, and, exhaling slowly, I closed my eyes. There were many things to consider, but whatever the future threw at me, I would think about it tomorrow.

The adrenaline from the evening's adventures slowly wore off and wrapped in a soft, thick blanket, I drifted off, determined to catch a few hours of sleep before the morning. However, I was wrong if I thought I'd sleep peacefully. Like many other nights, my dreams were filled with shadows trying to get into my thoughts. That was before Scarface rubbed his nose against my cheek, curling his tail around my neck, speaking reassuringly in my mind, the words softened by his purring.

'Sleep, little witch. You're safe with me.'

I wouldn't curse the morning I wouldn't, but the headache and familiar taste of cat hair were gleefully cavorting with the singing birds and bright sunlight that refused to stop shining in my eyes, making me wish I could ignore reality. A reality I soon realised included a car parked halfway across the city in a street near the Anchor. I would have to walk to work or, more likely, take a tram, as my body had lost its youthful ability to recover from a night out. If I had been drinking, that would be the perfect excuse for this feeling, but I didn't even have that. So, with only a few minutes to make myself presentable, I stretched, only for Scarface to interrupt, begging for food.

'Come on, monster, let's feed you,' I said, forgetting my late-night conversation with the feline wasn't a dream, and headed to the kitchen, following the dramatic display of feline hunger. The tin I chose resisted my desire to open it, the ring breaking off and flying across the apartment, but with the help of a paramedic's knife and fierce determination, the lid gave up the fight just as a loud banging on the door startled me into releasing my grip. The can fell to the floor, spilling its contents in a gloopy mess.

'What in the living fuck?' I cursed, breathing deeply to calm my racing heart. It was seven in the morning. My neighbours would curse my name if visits at such ungodly hours and late-night arguments became my new routine. No one with any common sense would visit me at this time, not before coffee, not before my brain remembered that I was supposed to heal, not kill, humankind.

I waited a moment longer, my heartbeat almost normal, before I opened the door with a mighty yank. The corridor was empty. I expected at least the echo of steps fading into the distance, but all was quiet, like no one had tried to break down my door moments ago.

Well, not entirely empty, I thought as my gaze drifted toward the floor and noticed a brown paper bag.

'If it is another coffee and cinnamon roll, I will kill him.' I shouted, hoping that whoever delivered the package was listening.

I suspected Leszek intended to court me to make the pretence of a relationship believable, and as sweet as the gesture was, it was more of a nuisance this early. I wiped the silly grin from my face and tried thinking of a way to untangle myself from the mess I'd found myself in because I wasn't sure how long I could endure Leszek's courting, especially if it continued to cause this much disruption before work.

I picked up the bag, carrying it to the kitchen. It was light, with only one item, and my curiosity was piqued when I noticed the velvet box inside.

I held the gift box up to the light, hesitating to open it as I didn't recognise the name on the top. The black velvet covering felt sophisticated, a small decorative hook holding the lid in place. It slid easily from the loop, and I gasped when I saw what was inside.

The padded interior held a silver necklace with a pendant in the form of an ancient rune that shimmered softly under the pale light of the morning sun. It was beautiful, but far too expensive for me. Where would I wear it, anyway? To the hospital? I was so enamoured by the beauty of the gift that my fingers were reaching for it without realising until a sharp mental command froze me.

'Don't touch it!'

'What? Why?' I asked, staring at Scarface as he jumped on the table, hackles raised.

'That is Czernobog's rune, a dark gift, one hexed to cause harm. Pour salt over the cursed object to dispel its evil intent.'

'Czernobog? Like Czernobog's dagger. Like this...' I snapped my fingers, trying to recall the correct information. 'Like this eastern deity of death, darkness, and something else, you know... evil.'

'Gods give me strength with this one. Yes, Sara, something evil. So will you finally purify it?'

'Fine, but what's it supposed to do?' I asked, grabbing a jar of salt from the cupboard, bemused by the situation, but I followed the cat's directions, dutifully burying the object under a small mountain of white.

'Enthral you, force you to fulfil every wish, every command of its creator. It will give you nightmares that trigger insanity. This is very bad, Sara, and whoever gave it to you knows you are vulnerable.'

My worst fear was not being in control of my actions, and I focused on ensuring every part of the rune was covered in white and half of the table with it. Busy with my task, it took me a moment to notice the note attached to the inside of the lid.

I prised it out with a butter knife, frowning, unsure what to expect, barely breathing until I saw the small, neat writing.

'Fuck... I mean, what the fuck is this, and how? What should I do now?' I shouted, rubbing my forehead, but I could not erase the foreboding that flooded me when I glanced at the note. It had only been a few hours; I hadn't even had the time to process it myself, let alone act on the danger.

The game had changed, and not in my favour. I looked at it again, hoping it might disappear, but no, on the exquisite white vellum, more suitable as a wedding invitation than a threatening note, were words that froze the blood in my veins.

My beautiful Lady Sara,

Your willingness to play with fire is commendable. I wish I could have observed how you manipulated those two fools, but unfortunately, my business called me away. I would ask you to consider a proposal, one that will set us all free. Wear my gift and learn of your power.

I look forward to meeting you, Soul Shepherd.

N.

N? Who the hell was N. N as in Nadolny? No, he mentioned manipulating two men. It must be someone else. I couldn't think clearly, but the danger was obvious. Somehow, this N. was aware of my presence and already knew what happened in the meeting between Leszek and Zbigniew Nadolny. I looked at the bag I packed yesterday and once again at the letter, and I sat heavily on the couch, looking at my cat.

'We are so fucked, Scarface. So very, very fucked,' I murmured, the cat nodding sagely in agreement.

My gaze gravitated toward two words in the note, Soul Shepherd. Was that my power or some weird title? If not for the bloody cat, I'd have touched the rune, possibly giving that arsehole control of whatever magic I possessed. Leszek was a dangerous man, but he was honourable in his own manner. I was sure he'd never hurt me, well, almost sure, and now, despite my protestations, it looked like I needed to move in with him.

'I will end up sleeping with him, you know. I act like a horny teen whenever he's around.' Saying it out loud helped me to centre my thoughts, even if I was grimacing with every word. Still, part of me wondered if yielding to temptation and tasting this forbidden fruit wouldn't be all bad.

'If you think sleeping with a powerful male willing to bend over backwards to please you, even knowing the danger you put yourself in, is the worst that could happen, then adjust your priorities.' The voice in my head was the stark reminder that this furry bastard was my guide, but strangely, his voicing my concern put the whole thing into perspective.

'If I agree to this with open eyes, I may get something out of this strange arrangement. It wouldn't just be sex, albeit bloody good sex, but I could get Leszek to teach me about my magic.'

Chapter Fourteen

A quick look in the mirror proved the lack of sleep had left me with nothing besides messy hair, and although my beard was longer than I liked, it would be fine for a few more days.

However, the reason for my restless night would need my immediate attention, and it had very little to do with the tentative alliance with Nadolny. After last night's events, it was clear Sara and my reaction to her presence was the problem. She haunted my dreams before I'd gotten to know her, ripping me from sleep with unfulfilled desires that even I didn't fully understand. The one image I couldn't forget was the image of a woman's eyes, my soul lost in their depths.

I never saw my dream lover's face, but I couldn't forget that sensation, and ever since Sara had crash-landed in my world, the echoes of my dreams flared to life, making me wonder if there was more to our attraction than I wanted to admit.

A derisive snort escaped my lips at that thought. I knew better than most the fleeting existence of humans, so the idea of finding a soulmate amongst their kind? Ridiculous, I thought, even as I remembered the moment I first used magic on Sara, compelling forgetfulness. How completely overwhelmed I'd been when her power embraced my being, coaxing it back to life. For the first time in millennia, I experienced limitless power, not the carefully hoarded scraps remaining after the Nether's creation, but the primordial forest's true essence.

One taste of it might have been coincidental, a reaction to the seer's magic, but when Sara kissed me last night, I'd done more than experience my magic; I had used it, and that should be impossible.

I looked down as the chair creaked ominously, realising my grip on the armrest was causing the noise. My brows arched in disapproval when I saw my nails tearing through the tough leather. *Damn that woman, why did I lose control whenever I thought of her?* A seer was an incredible prize, but it didn't explain how she affected me. In her presence, my magic felt vital, but there was more. Sara's intelligent and passionate nature spoke to the savage in me. Her touch lit up my body like no mortal woman ever could.

The last time I felt that alive, that myself, was when I was with Jurata governing these lands. Sara was perfect for me, and I wanted her by my side for as long as her short mortal life allowed.

An urgent knocking on the door interrupted my reverie, and my snarling command was answered by the entry of my newest millstone, the injured wolf pup whose cowering submission sobered my anger better than any bucket of water.

'What brings you back to my office so soon, boy?' The petty address revealing my anger was not entirely under control. I sighed, straightening and gesturing to the nearest seat.

'Sir, the doctor, Sara. Someone brought her a gift today. I thought it was one of Nadolny's people, but now I'm not so sure. He smelled human, but the scent was off, like rotten meat. He left a bag, fleeing before she answered the door. Sara seemed surprised but still took it, and I thought you'd like to know. I... it's probably nothing but...' He stuttered, and I snarled in irritation.

'Just say it!'

'It felt wrong. It smelled like the people that shot me.'

I leapt to my feet, and the pup staggered back, putting his hands up in a defensive gesture.

'Sir, she went to work after this. Completely unharmed, with no weird smell on her.'

The calming breaths I took made no difference to the desire to rush out and check Sara was safe, but gods damn it, I refused to give in to my urges, so instead, I forced my body to sit back in the chair and smiled at the terrified werewolf. The smile was a bad idea as the teenager paled and desperately looked toward the door. It looked like Nadolny, or our newest player, knew about Sara and was testing the waters. I had underestimated the wolf and was grateful for his courage in sharing this information. I looked at the decanter next to me and poured myself a small measure of whisky, offering the other glass to the boy. A gesture of acknowledgement that didn't go unnoticed, the teen's eyes widening as he sat down.

'You did well bringing this to me. What is your name? I forgot to ask last time.'

'Jarek, Sir. Thank you, Sir. I want you to know I will guard her. I know you think a young wolf can't do much, but I can. I can be your eyes and ears because no one ever notices me. Sir, she saved my life, and keeping Sara safe would go some way to paying her back, this man...' His voice trailed off, and he gulped back the whisky. Jarek started coughing as soon as the fiery liquid hit his throat, and I struggled to restrain my smile, especially when his features firmed into determination.

I couldn't help it. I liked this bold youngster, barely nineteen and still finding his way, who was so angry at the threat to his saviour and incredibly protective of her. Even with my thoughts focusing on Sara, I appreciated her young guardian's determination and dedication to helping.

'I will take care of this matter, but you have permission to guard her. Be discrete because she won't appreciate being watched and avoid getting involved if something happens. Call your pack or Michal for backup. From tomorrow, you will start training with Adam and Tomasz. You are too smart to be a simple pack soldier, and once you are ready, I may have a position for you.'

Joy, pure and innocent, blossomed on his face. He looked at me like I'd handed his dreams to him on a silver platter. I thought he would cry for a second, but he reined himself in and bowed to me.

'You won't regret it, Sir. May I talk to her? Please.' Jarek's request surprised me. Now, he was pushing boundaries, and I frowned, hoping I hadn't mistaken his loyalty for a teenage crush.

'Why? There'd best be no thoughts of romance in that head of yours. The doctor has already agreed to my claim, and anyone who contests it will die.' I said it so calmly, but surprisingly, I meant every word. I had intended to give the wolf a healthy reminder of the age difference. Instead, I threatened his life. Then a chuckle escaped me, startling poor Jarek as I realised the hypocrisy of my thoughts. Age gap, really? What was going on in my head at the moment?

'No, I just wanted to thank her. Also, guarding her will be easier if I can earn her trust; that way, I can warn her of any danger while calling for help. She is nice but way too old for me, anyway.' Jarek blurted out uncomfortably, and I burst out laughing.

Jarek was too smart for his own good but knew nothing about women. In my eyes, she shone with a light that would never be dimmed by age. Sara was not too old for anything, even by human standards.

'Yes, you can talk to her. I suggest you choose honesty when you introduce yourself. Just don't call me to save your hide if you tell her she is too old for you.' I said, noticing his face redden as he bowed, and, with a quiet thank you, Jarek left the room.

Once I was alone again, I opened my laptop. It was time to clarify my position. I didn't think Nadolny was responsible for the gift, not after the pup's report, but there was a grain of doubt after her performance with the gangster... I just wanted to make sure, even if marking my territory was ridiculous. My email to him was as short as I could manage.

Someone sent Sarah a gift today. It will not happen again. My woman is off-limits.

L.B.

The tracking software informed me that the email had been seen, but the impersonal method was wholly unfulfilling. I had to talk to Sara. Accepting gifts from strangers could only end in tragedy, especially with our association. If it was Nadolny, I could tackle the issue easily despite the burning jealousy, but if the pup was right... I didn't like the fact that our mysterious trespasser knew about Sara. Another good reason for her to move into my house, if the bloody woman accepted my help, of course.

A glance at the clock told me it was nearly lunchtime, and after a moment of consideration, I changed my plan, postponing a meeting at the docks. I didn't expect the next shipment to be loaded until late afternoon, but with recent events and my merchandise going missing somewhere between our warehouses and the buyer, I wanted to inspect the shipment myself. However, it could be done later, after it was loaded.

An incoherent grunt answered my call, the owner of the bad mood unhappy at such an early call. 'Adam, I will be late for the inspection, so have a beauty nap. Maybe it will help with your pale complexion. I will see you this afternoon,' I said, unable to resist teasing my friend whenever he was irritable.

'You've got to be kidding. You insisted I woke up during the day because I'm your side bitch that needs to go everywhere with you, and now you are telling me you'll be late. Let me guess. Your loyal bloodsucker can wait his turn while you chase after your newest conquest.' He was furious, and I couldn't blame him, but I wasn't interested in dealing with his petulance.

'Mind your words. I saved your depraved arse from the witches, and I'm the only one that'll put up with your antics. You are my bitch, as you eloquently put it, and you will wait as long as I say. Sara is not a conquest. She is... an ally.' I knew it was harsh, but Adam's jealousy would get out of hand if he wasn't reminded of his place. There was a pause before he gave a huff and mumbled a reply.

'What?' I snapped.

'Just tell me one thing, Leszek. Where are you heading if not to the port?' He asked, and I bit back a curse, but I didn't want to lie to my second in command.

'To the hospital.' My answer was met with a single triumphant laugh from the other end of the call.

'You may delude yourself, but not me, my friend. I don't know how it happened, but she has hold of you by the bollocks. Don't forget you have a company to manage, and half the elder races depend on this income. They work for you, respect you and rely on you. You can't be seen as a weakling chasing after a human. Just fuck her and be done with it.' He said, and I closed my eyes, letting the magic in me drain to the ground before it caused damage to my home. *He can't help himself, can he?*

'Adam, I have been too lenient with you because I like you and you are useful, but that ends now. If I dropped everything and walked through the Gates of the Nether, no one could stop me. Jurata would welcome me with open arms in Gedania, and this little empire, built on amber and petty manipulation, would collapse. You all live in relative peace here because I gave up my power for the sake of our people. So if I've found a woman that makes me happy, no one will stand between us. Understood?'

I stopped, shocked silent by my statement, but it was true; Sara made me happy. She didn't fear me, obey me, or worship me. I could be the man I used to be in her company, and when her magic touched me, I felt complete. I wouldn't give that up. After a tense pause, I continued.

'It sounds like you finally understand. What I choose to do with Sara is none of your concern, and if you ever disrespect her again, you and your new seethe will be on the train to the last stop in South Poland.' My voice was glacial when I ushered the threat, but Adam went quiet, and when he spoke this time, his voice held deference and contrite apology.

'My apologies, Sir. I will head toward the harbour and wait for you there. Is there anything else you need me to do?'

'Not for now. Tomorrow, you can present your report on our progress in acquiring a warehouse and repurposing it as a medical unit, and maybe I'll treat you to that new Japanese whisky we were gifted last week,' I heard Adam grunt, and I couldn't help but smile. The cocky vampire found himself on the shitty end of the stick, and he didn't like it. Still, given the task, I trusted Adam to account for every coin.

I ended the call and, choosing a suit good enough to impress Sara, dressed and prepared to surprise her. In a moment of inspiration, I ordered snacks and drinks for her department, and this small kindness left me feeling guilty for scolding Adam like that. I valued his friendship, preferring to work with him instead of over, but I couldn't allow disrespect toward Sara. It would endanger her life and undermine my position in the volatile criminal world.

Chapter Fifteen

I arrived at work a little late, provoking a few surprised glares, especially after I couldn't blame my unusual gift and resorted to the good old-fashioned *'Tram was late'* excuse. Still, the work day carried on until I heard my name.

'Sara, look at this.' The triage nurse called me over, the informality relaxing my suddenly tense shoulders, and I trotted to the window.

'Look at what?' I asked, unsure of what she was looking at. The morning sun brightened a street as busy as usual, enhancing the familiar sight, rays of light filtered by the trees, turning the view magical. The stream of people coming in and out of the hospital didn't pause to admire the dancing shadows, rushing to handle their day-to-day business. Some strode toward the Emergency Department, while others walked past to enter the hospital through the main doors. Nothing looked out of the ordinary, but after my troubling morning, I couldn't help but feel something was amiss.

'At them.' My gaze followed the direction her finger pointed, focusing on two men strolling past nonchalantly. That is until I focused on them, and they turned to look directly at our window as one. You never see people strolling to the hospital; something about the place affects everyone who frequents its corridors, from the worried trot of those facing uncertainty to those dragging their feet facing the certainty of bad news. Even the staff walk differently; each step they take filled with purpose. Seeing two men casually wandering outside, then looking straight at our window, set off every instinct I had, and despite their innocuous appearance, fear skittered down my spine until I shook my head. *Stop thinking everything is related to you, woman,* chastising myself for assuming everyone was out to get me. Paranoid much? I thought, even as I remembered someone else noticed their behaviour first.

A curse slipped out as my pocket vibrated, my phone's timing as perfect as ever, and I pulled out the offending device, looking at the caller display. Only a few people outside my family had this number, and the people calling were so close to being a family that my mother regularly fed them.

'What's up, boys?' I said, happy to hear from Speciality Ambulance Three, my ride or dies, Damian and Rysiek, their distraction cheering me enough to consider inviting them for drinks later.

The two paramedics, or the Dream Team as they like to be called, were my old ambulance crew. The cockiest pair in that uniform, but when you were as good as they were, you had a right to be.

When faced with horrifying injuries and hopeless situations, their barrack's humour saved the sanity of many colleagues, myself included, and they were universally loved because of it.

My boys. I smiled at the thought, remembering our adventures. When I took over the Emergency Department, I had to resign from the ambulance shifts, but seeing those two always brightened my mood no matter what kind of patient they delivered.

'Get ready, vixen. We have incoming for your tender hands only. There was an explosion on a cargo vessel followed by a hold fire. Kris is still there dealing with the mess, and most of the casualties were taken to the port hospital, but they can't deal with this one; he's knocking on heaven's door and needs your special touch. Sixty per cent burns, including airway, tubed; vitals stable at the moment. See you in ten.' It was comprehensive and short, just how I liked my information, especially as they didn't give me much time to prepare. My thoughts drifted toward Kris, another of our little family, a burly firefighter who, in a way, was a father to us all, and I hoped he stayed safe. Then, my thoughts went back to the patient.

Special Touch. As I said, they knew me well. The simple term had become a code Tricity's ambulance crews used when they dragged patients out of their districts to see me. Not because I was the best, but because I had a running competition with death, and sometimes, what those patients needed was hope and a doctor more stubborn than a pack of mules who wouldn't give up if she knew their souls were still there. The tenacious, obstinate, and bold spirits needed me fighting in their corner when Death hadn't called them home.

'Begin the burns protocol. I want the plastic surgeon, critical care, and trauma teams here in five. I'm going to resus to prepare,' I told the triage nurse and turned to Nina, the nurse in charge and my best friend, who was already dressing in a surgical gown to receive the patient, 'Send a porter to storage for all the burns kits he can find.'

'Never a dull moment with you and those two clowns. I'm guessing they expect another of your miracles?' she said, and I smirked. Nina and my boys shared mutual respect, professional courtesy and a complicated love-hate relationship from the moment fate put us together during an expedition to war-torn Kosovo. I didn't fully understand it, but I thoroughly enjoyed the snide comments and mean remarks that made me laugh each time they had another legendary battle.

'If you wanted to have dull shifts, you should have chosen dermatology,' I jested, and she looked at me with a glint in the eye.

'At least, I would have flawless skin, while you will always look like something the cat dragged in. Do you sleep at all, or did you get in the middle of another domestic fight in a bar?' She pointed to my eyes and grabbed my arm when I turned my face away, ignoring her question. The guilt must have been written all over my face because she frowned.

'You answer me when I'm asking, young lady.'

'Yes, ma'am, right away, ma'am.' I said, teasing her, but I knew I was in trouble. Nina had used her matron's voice, and no matter who you were, you listened when you heard that tone asking you a question.

'I was just at a party and came back late. You told me I should start meeting other people, so I'm meeting other people,' I said, watching her eyes narrow in suspicion.

'And you're telling me this now? Five minutes before we're elbows deep in peeling flesh? Just don your gown, Sara; this conversation is not over. For years, I've asked you to crawl out of your shell and trust men a little, but no, you were living for work, books, and your weird fight club. Now you're a party girl all of a sudden? Nope, not buying it.'

'Who knows, maybe I just didn't tell you about my wild side.' I answered, laughing, as we rushed to Resus. My boys gave us enough time to prep the area, briefing the team as everyone got into position before the doors crashed open, the gurney sliding into place carefully despite their haste. Moments later, the room was a hive of organised chaos as the team leapt into action.

The paramedics had done an excellent job intubating such a damaged throat, and I nodded my gratitude as they stepped back, shouting out the medications given and the stats of our patient. The critical team took over airway management while plastics cut long gaping escharotomy lines to open the swollen flesh, preventing further damage.

This patient was determined to live, and I focused on directing the team, ensuring we had enough supplies and everyone concentrated on their task. I missed hands-on work, but someone had to lead, and through the years of experience, I was the best person for the job.

The elbow in the side didn't phase me as Damian decided my stress levels were peaking. 'Stop drooling. I know you would want to be one with the scalpel, but that is a suitable punishment for leaving us.' Rysiek smirked as my toe cracked into his partner's shin, his pen never stopping as he wrote his notes: two peas in a pod and the most unlikely romantic couple. I envied them the comfort of being together while doing what they loved.

With the work almost finished, the man looked like a mummy covered in dressings and bandages, and I turned toward my friends.

'I could never leave you. You're the best men I ever slept with, ' I said, referring to when we'd been forced to share a tent and where the nickname Sara and her boys originated. I elbowed him for laughing, but we both heard the alert from his radio, signalling an upcoming call from the dispatcher.

'Yeah, yeah, just remember, you can always come back. It was good to see you, vixen. Please send our humble regards to this dragoness of yours.' They nodded toward Nina, who, without looking, flipped them off.

I wanted to ask them to pick me up after the shift, but our conversation was interrupted by the critical care doctor who came over, pointing toward the patient.

'Give me fifteen minutes to prepare a bed upstairs, and we'll transfer him. Is it OK if I leave you here?' he asked, and I nodded. Soon, I was left alone in the cubicle while the nurse prepared a transfer kit outside. With a bit of free time, I approached the patient, the poor soul surrounded by cables and tubes, the sight pulling at my heart, pity for the struggles he would now face.

After an event like this, life would never be the same, the pain and scars staying with him forever, and I wished my special touch was more than insight, that the magic I supposedly possessed could heal him. Reaching out, I stroked his forehead with my finger. It made little sense, as he was in a medically induced coma, but I wanted him to know we were here for him and would do our best to help his recovery.

'You are not alone. Have only pleasant dreams,' I whispered before the maelstrom of his memories assaulted me. He was a ship worker, an engineer carrying out minor repairs. Today, he'd crawled under the deck to chase down a weird electrical fault when five men dressed in dark overalls arrived, their faces hidden behind dust masks. He heard them discussing disrupting the next shipment before they were ready to take over. So he challenged their presence, but a deafening bang rang out, and agonising pain blossomed in his belly.

The engineer's pain felt so substantial I screamed, hand pressed to the imagined hole in my abdomen, feeling fresh red blood gushing out. I felt my body balancing at the edge of consciousness, struggling to differentiate between reality and vision. Pale hair caught my attention; the white-blond strands belonging to a man turned toward the bulkhead, drawing a strange symbol dancing with coruscating flame. As I studied this mesmeric person, he sensed my attention, turning to regard me in turn, his eyes briefly revealing a hint of surprise before changing to pure, unbridled satisfaction.

'Soul Shepherd, you found me. How impressive. I cannot wait till we meet in person, my Lady.' his words reverberated in my mind, oily and foul, making me gag and forcing me to break away from the patient.

It is only a vision, only a vision. I repeated the words as a mantra to dispel the memory of the engineer's pain, but even as I gripped the bed's railing, I couldn't forget everything that had happened.

Fuck, he was talking to me, not the engineer; how is that possible? It was the past, a vision... and the bullet wound. Did we miss it? As I stumbled, trying to collect my mind, still feeling my consciousness split between realities, I pressed the alarm button, and the rest of the team came back running. This man was fried to crisp, but it was not an excuse to miss something so significant. Guilt flooded me when I grabbed the phone, dialling the duty surgeon, who, in his infinitive wisdom, wasted time questioning me before he agreed to join us.

Finally, the surgeon and the anaesthetist stood there while I cut away the bandages, showing them the crusted skin flap that overlapped the wound.

'Here, he needs theatre before this perforation causes sepsis.' The longer I talked, the more I felt a headache grow. I had barely slept and hadn't eaten today. I hadn't even had my coffee, and this case made me feel dizzy, especially after the mistake I made. When the theatre nurse took the patient upstairs, I inhaled unsteadily and turned, heading toward the cafeteria.

As I left the resus room, I noticed my colleagues gathered around, looking suspiciously like they were waiting for some juicy gossip, attempting to cover sly smiles as their eyes turned toward me. Fortunately, Nina came to my rescue as I wondered why I'd become the centre of attention.

'A man is waiting for you at the reception. I've never seen someone so out-of-place in all my time at the Emergency Department, so you better hurry before—What the hell is that?' She exclaimed, and I spun around to see what she pointed at. Some idiot had parked in front of the triage, taking up the ambulance space before unloading two crates of what looked like snacks and coffee.

Ready to tear the driver a new orifice, Nina strode over, fists clenched in anger and telling the foolish man off, only to turn around, laughing as she announced.

'Sara, seductress extraordinaire, has charmed a local business owner into providing us with lunch.' She said and grabbed a passing nurse to lead the delivery man to the staff room.

We sometimes received perishable goods, usually pastries and coffee that didn't sell that day, as a gift for the night shift, but it was never for lunchtime, and everything looked deliciously fresh. My stomach rumbled, and I was about to ignore whoever was waiting for me for the appeal of fresh coffee while my attention zeroed in on an apple strudel. I was ready to give in to my precious love of baked goods, but something told me disregarding my visitor would not be the best idea.

Nina was right. The visitor turned out to be Leszek, resplendent in a tailored three-piece suit and more handsome than any rugged movie star. He crouched, entertaining a harried mother's child while three teenagers swooned over him, trying to attract his attention until one gathered the courage to stand up and approach.

'Hi, once our friend has been seen, we were thinking of going to a bar, would you care to join us? I can give you my number.' She said with hope written all over her face, and I saw the amusement in Leszek's eyes.

'You are very kind, but I'm afraid I'm already taken.' He said, and I moved closer, trying to save the day but still avoid my colleagues seeing us together. No such luck as the frustrating man spotted me, calling out across the waiting room.

'Sara, my love, I hope you had a good night. I apologise, but work kept me from your side. An unforgivable sin, but I hope you will allow me to take you for lunch?'

I stood, gaping like a stunned fish as he stalked over, gathering my unresisting body into his arms and claiming my mouth in a deep, possessive kiss before I came to my senses and pulled away as far as his hands allowed me.

'Not here... please,' I whispered, and I felt Leszek's smile against my cheek while the tension seemed to leave his body. His beard brushed my ear when he whispered.

'Yes, here. The more people know you are under my protection, the better, and if they know how much I'm willing to do for you, then even better. You are mine, Sara and I want everybody to know it,' He whispered, taking my hand and lifting it to his lips, kissing it before I could react.

'We can eat in the hospital cafeteria if you're busy, or if you don't have time, I can pick you up after work for a proper meal.' Leszek said this part much louder, and I noticed the waiting room grow quiet, with several heads popping out of the E.R. to eavesdrop on the conversation.

'Fine, let's go,' I said, panicking and dragging him to the staircase. On the lower ground level was a corridor for the storage area that we often use as a route to the cafeteria, its quiet emptiness perfect for avoiding difficult conversations with colleagues and patients, but in my haste, I had forgotten one thing: Leszek and his overwhelming presence. As soon as we disappeared from the line of sight, the impossible man grabbed my shoulder, pressing me against the wall as his lips descended to my neck.

'What are you doing? We are alone; there's no need to pretend.' I said, pushing him away, trying to find an excuse to break from his touch before it went too far. He inhaled deeply, and a shiver ran down his body as his nose trailed over my skin.

'You promised me three months, Sara, and yet only this morning I find out you accepted a gift from someone else. Who was it? Nadolny? He is not for you, my little seer. He may have honour, but he is a dangerous man who would overshadow your light, moulding you to his desire. I cannot let that happen. We will go to your house so that you can pack for your move into my home,' He said, and I found it challenging to focus on his words, his breath giving me goosebumps as it brushed over my neck.

'And you? How are you different? All you can think about is how to lock me up,' I said when he gently stroked my cheek.

'No, Sara. I want to lift you to where your light burns brightest, but for now, you are in danger, and I will do what I must to ensure your safety. Gdansk is not safe for our kind, and until you can protect yourself, it would be suicide to be alone. I would never lock you up, my Firefly. My home is not your cage but your shelter.' His eyes shone with tenderness laced with desire as he spoke, causing my heart to race in response. I wanted to protest and say something clever, push him away and go my own way, but I felt my hands sliding to his shoulders to pull him closer, feeling his heartbeat against mine.

As the tension grew, Leszek suddenly frowned, his magic overpowering my senses, and he lifted my fingers to his nose, inhaling deeply and growling at what he discovered.

'Why do you reek of Czernobog's filth?'

Chapter Sixteen

What do you do when a gorgeous man presents you with a speech that touches your soul, only to stop and look at you with eyes consumed by primordial power, one that has terrified humans for centuries? Well, I lost my temper, grabbed his expensive suit by the lapels, and pushed the arsehole away with all my strength.

'What? I don't reek of anything.' I snapped, outrage overcoming whatever fear I might have felt. 'You mean magic, yes? Whatever! I meant to tell you, anyway. The gift you mentioned? I don't know who sent it, but my cat said not to touch it as it was dangerous.'

Leszek raised an eyebrow, and I realised what I'd said, revealing that my cat could talk, the heat of my cheeks telling me how red they must be.

'Your... cat?' he asked, his amusement at war with the anger in his eyes, but when I tried to push him away, his hand stroked my chin as he forced me to look him in the eyes. 'No, my Firefly, don't hide your face. It is good you've already found your guide, but I should be the one to teach you, not your cat. What exactly was this... gift? Did you open it?'

'Yes, it was just a necklace. I thought you'd sent it as it looked weird and expensive, but a letter told me to choose the third option and wear it. Oh, and it called me a Soul Shepherd, like some priest in a frock. There was no signature, just the letter N.' My explanation was rushed and unclear, but could I swear Leszek paled as he listened.

'Even more reason for you to move in with me. Czernobog's magic, which I can still sense on you, is dangerous. He presides over death, darkness, and all the vile creatures you see in nightmares. Who knows what will be delivered next time or who will visit your dreams? You did well following your guide's advice. Now, it's time to follow mine. I can even change into a cat if that will make you listen.'

You visit my dreams, I almost said before his last sentence hit me. Did he just make a joke? I stared at the man who blasted into my life, disrupting it with his arrogant demands whilst my hormones were voting for me to jump on board and ride him to O Town, and now he had a sense of humour. It felt as if he genuinely cared for my safety, even when I made him growl in frustration, but woe to me, I kind of liked it. A warm, gentle smile bloomed on his lips when he noticed my gaze, and against my better judgment, I smiled back.

'Maybe you should change. I like the feeling of soft fur against my skin.' I teased until a familiar flash of desire instantly sobered me up. *What the fuck am I doing?* Leszek's presence kept distracting me, and the more I resisted, the more I felt attracted. I had already resigned myself to hiding at his home until I knew more about my magic and learned how to protect myself. However, I didn't want him to think he could snap his fingers and get what he wanted.

'What is a Soul Shepherd?' I asked, and he moved closer again.

'It is someone that wields a certain type of magic, usually women, which is why so many humans distrust it, slander and defame its users, but the elder races know better. A Soul Shepherd can see through the veil into the spirit realm and touch the threads of life, connecting them to the physical world. There is no offensive or defensive use for your magic in the physical world, but it can affect those whose existence spans the veil. Why that makes you a target for Czernobog's servant, I don't know, but the consequences will be dire if he takes you. Where I live, he can't reach you. Nobody can, as it is the seat of my power, warded with spells and power older than this city. Please come with me.'

He was very convincing, especially when his thumb trailed over my lips. Maybe because of this and how my body reacted to him, I felt I had to set some boundaries.

'I will consider it, but we will discuss my living arrangements before I decide. I will continue pretending to be your latest fling, but let me be clear, this is just for appearances, despite all the attraction. Also, this stalking me at work has to end. I've never brought my love life to work, and this is no time to start... and I won't be ordered around like one of your goons, either, so that must stop,'

I marked each point, jabbing my finger into Leszek's chest, expressing myself far too harshly when he was trying to be understanding because his expression hardened, and irritated by his lack of answers, I pushed him away. It felt like wrestling with a mountain. Unfortunately, our struggle didn't go unnoticed.

'Sara, is everything all right?' Nina's voice called out at the worst possible moment. When my friend cautiously approached, I stopped my struggle, instead trailing my fingers over his rumpled lapels as I turned and smiled widely.

'Nina, you wanted to know what I was doing last night. Let me introduce Leszek; Leszek, this is my good friend Nina. I made his acquaintance a while ago, and we've been getting to know each other ever since and... he's just asked me to move in with him. You've been nagging me to be more adventurous, so I agreed to take him for a test drive.' I said, seeing her eyes dart from my face to the rugged man pressing me to the wall.

Leszek's eyes lit up at the notion of my agreement, glowing brighter when I mentioned the test drive. Even if it sounded implausible, it was better to convince Nina before she misjudged the situation, dragging half the department into a welfare check and arming them with knuckle dusters. Knowing her, she wouldn't hesitate to call for backup and blow it out of all proportion.

'Bullshit! Get your hands off her, arsehole. Sara, step away while I will call security. I knew something fishy happened when I saw how bad you looked this morning.' Nina barked.

Here we go, I thought, strangely proud of her. My friend, ready to fight whenever family was threatened, and all I could do was widen my smile, hoping for the best. Nina was a human lie detector and could sniff out bullshit from miles away, which was likely why she followed me to the basement. Unfortunately, she was now directing her anger toward Leszek in a mistaken attempt to save me.

'There is no need for security. As you can see, Sara is quite comfortable with me, if only a little tired after last night's adventures.' Leszek eased away from me and approached Nina, who moved a few steps back. Her eyes widened rapidly whilst studying him, trying to assess the danger. The scent of the deep forest filled the small space, its magic making her features slacken while her gaze lost focus, her eyes no longer staring daggers in Leszek's direction.

Whatever he was doing to Nina made my skin crawl. How quickly he took control of her mind and body. Such magic, and what it did, felt obscene, but I was too worried about Nina to care. I grabbed Leszek's arm without a second thought.

'Please don't. She is not your enemy to hurt. You win, I'll go with you, do what I'm fucking told, whatever you want, but please don't hurt her.' I pleaded, unsure what he intended or how to stop him, but the man who could make Nadolny comply with his demands was a man who could do anything he chose in the Tricity.

Leszek's eyes burned with vivid green fire at my capitulation as he turned toward me, visibly angry, so angry that the air crackled with wild magic. I didn't know how to calm him, so I did the only thing that affected his mood. I approached, placing my hands on his chest and stroking over the quivering muscles. He stared into my eyes for what seemed like an eternity, the fire slowly fading as he stood there, silent and unmoving.

'You believe I would hurt your friend? Do you think I am capable of hurting a defenceless human that was trying to help you? All I was intended to do was remove the memory of this moment from her mind to save her from worrying for you. I am delighted to know there are people who would fight to protect you, but I think it's best if she isn't involved with our world right now. So let me erase the memory of us fighting and replace it with something more palatable.'

'Replace with what?' I asked, feeling the atmosphere grow heavy, my breath stolen as Leszek pinned me against the wall, lips descending to mine in a bruising, passionate kiss. Nina gasped as her eyes refocused, her cheeks flaming with embarrassment at catching us embracing. None of that registered in my mind as the world spun on its axis, a moan escaping my lips when his teeth scraped my bottom lip, and the jolt of desire sizzled down my spine. *Was he this good at kissing, or was his mind magic once more at play, manipulating my senses?* I thought when my knees buckled.

'Sara, what are you doing? What if someone else saw you acting like a bloody medical student, getting handsy in the basement? And with... with whoever this is?' Nina's voice trailed off as Leszek stopped kissing me, and we both turned to look at my friend. Gone was the woman who wanted to call security. Instead, Nina looked like she wanted to congratulate me, amusement flashing in her dark brown eyes.

'Helluva replacement,' I muttered under my breath. Leszek lifted a hand, gently stroking a stray lock of hair behind my ear.

'And one I enjoyed immensely,' he said, but I was already straightening up and avoiding Nina's eyes, repeating the explanation from earlier.

This time, she laughed at my half-truth.

'Well, he must have an impressive... point for you to agree so... enthusiastically, Sara,' she said, eyes flicking downwards toward Leszek's trousers in a pronounced manner. 'I'm guessing we have you to thank for lunch today. Interesting strategy, buttering up her people and keeping them busy while you ravage Sara out of sight. Well, you've been caught, so keep it tucked away in the future so you don't tarnish my friend's reputation.' Nina's amusement had disappeared during her lecture, and now she looked at Leszek with all the authority of her position.

'Nina! I'm not a bloody virgin, and you are not my mother.' I said, annoyed that I was blushing again.

'Not that reputation, you silly mare, your professional dignity. You are the doctor in charge, not some junior sneaking off for a quickie at work, no matter how pretty he is,' she answered, turning her matronly disapproval in my direction, leaving me begging for the ground to swallow me whole.

With a respectful nod of his head, Leszek smiled in resignation. 'My apologies, Matron. I didn't intend to cause any difficulties for Sara. I'm glad my show of appreciation was so well received, and I'm reassured that she has such a dedicated friend who cares for her.' The gentle timbre of his voice made me shiver. Just a moment ago, he'd wiped Nina's memory, and now he was playing the charming lover with such ease that it made me doubt if any of my feelings were real.

'Nina, just call me Nina because if you can convince her to go to the basement with you, then we're bound to meet again.' She said, and I had to hold in the urge to punch them for talking over my head, but I sighed dramatically instead.

'If you two have finished, I have patients requiring treatment.' Turning to Leszek, I pasted on my most saccharine smile. 'I'm sorry darling, there will be no lunch date today.' My pet name for him provoked a smile, but I was already looking at Nina.

'Aren't you worried about people wreaking havoc up there? Shouldn't you be somewhere else?' My not-so-gentle hint made her laugh, but my friend knew when to retreat.

'Fine, see you soon, just don't make me come back again,' she said, disappearing up the staircase. I turned toward Leszek, who regarded me with a contented smile. This time, I didn't hold back. The well-aimed punch hit him in the chest, but he didn't even wince.

'I will have to thank her for the opportunity to kiss you. Maybe I should invite her to stay if it encourages such passion unless you want to kiss me of your own volition?' he said with glee, and it took a few calming breaths before I could speak to him without shouting.

'Look, I get it. We both feel this chemistry between us. I agreed on pretending to be a couple, so you're probably thinking, *the hell with it, let's behave like it's real and have some fun.* That does not sit well with me. You're a complete stranger who disrupted my life, revealing a whole new world of magic and danger, so how am I supposed to contend with this without processing the craziness? I have a good life, work I love, and friends who are the only ones who could help me process this much weirdness.' With a headache forming, I closed my eyes. 'I will move in because it seems reasonable to me and important to you, but please, let's try not to do something we'll both regret, no matter how tempting. Teach me about my magic, then, if we haven't killed each other, let's agree to go our separate ways...' My voice trailed off when I opened my eyes to the sight of Leszek's hard, feral smile. He didn't appreciate my speech, and the taut severity of his features told me I wouldn't like his response.

'Sara, for the next three months, I will do what I want with you, and if I decide to treat you like my woman, I will. You swore an oath to the Forest Lord, and no amount of arguing will help you evade payment. I will take you to your apartment after your shift so you may pack, and then you will move into my home. At least then we can avoid receiving gifts meant to harm you.' I drew a breath to argue, but when Leszek sighed, rubbing the bridge of his nose wearily, I backed down, letting him continue. 'Go back to work, little healer, before your friend comes back to berate you,' he said as he leaned over, kissing my cheek tenderly and heading back upstairs.

I looked at his back, too angry to say anything else. He was adamant about ignoring my words, but what was worse, he seemed unable to stop touching me, and I felt so tired fighting it; part of me wishing to go with the flow and see where I took me. I sighed deeply, following him upstairs.

My cheeks flamed as Leszek made a scene of saying goodbye in reception. Only after he was gone did I realise I hadn't told him about my vision from touching the burns victim. I was sure he could help or at least explain why it happened, but, at least for now,

I was determined to find my answers rather than risk deepening my bond with him.

'Nina, I will be in intensive care if anyone needs me,' I said. My friend nodded, busy checking charts as I headed upstairs.

It didn't take me long to find him. The man in question had returned from surgery, still wrapped in burns dressings while his life hung by a thread. Looking at him, I knew he'd taken a turn for the worst as the grey veil of death shrouded him despite the best medical attention.

'At least show me who did this to you,' a deep sadness seeped into my voice, knowing we'd failed to save him, and I lay a hand on his forehead, ready for the pain. The vision replayed as before, the same men and their leader painting flaming symbols on the wall. I clenched my teeth when the man was shot, focusing on the fair-haired leader while he drew the sigils. Finally, my vision darkened when the victim lost consciousness. I memorised the face of the enemy and the symbols he painted. That would have to be enough.

I pulled away from the engineer's memory, panting heavily, but I couldn't leave the room, not just yet. Whatever it meant, I was a Soul Shepherd, and I wanted to help protect his soul or guide it to the afterlife.

'I know the pain is unbearable, and you are scared, but I promise you are not alone. If you wish to fight, I will try to help, but it is okay if you cannot continue; I can ease your journey. I will seek out your murderer and bring him to justice.' As I spoke, my fingers stroked the poor man's forehead, my words a gentle whisper. I didn't need to look up to see his response, the monitors going crazy as his soul flickered before it finally disappeared. *Was that the purpose of my magic? To ease the soul's passage and let my patients feel less alone in their final breath?* I thought, fighting back tears, the moment breaking my heart, even as I felt it, the veil, the afterlife, whatever it was, opening up to gather him to its bosom. When the light was no more, I walked out before the alarms dragged the crash team to his bed for whatever futile efforts they made to save him.

It was such an arrogant promise to make to a dying soul. Now, I was afraid. This new magic, soul guiding or whatever you would call it, felt too grand for me, yet it felt so right. The worst was that a man who didn't hesitate to kill had seen me in the vision. The sensation I'd felt when it happened was similar to the moment I saw Czernobog's necklace, forcing me to come to the only logical conclusion: he already knew where I lived, and I was sure he wanted my magic.

Standing in the corridor, I saw the crash team rush past me, equipment in hand. The last person, the intensive care consultant, a colleague of many years, stopped beside me, placing a hand on my arm.

'Yes?' he asked, hopeful, but I shook my head. We both understood the meaning of this question, the experience of years behind us.

'No,' I said, and he squeezed my arm.

'Alright, at least he didn't suffer for long. Go, I'll take care of him.'

It struck me how easily he accepted my judgment. Maybe I should have realised earlier that my entire career as a prodigy was a lie based on the magic I pretended I didn't have.

Now, I could no longer pretend, but as my grandma said, try the window if the door is blocked. Leszek was my window of opportunity to learn, to be safe, and maybe even smile, as long as I wasn't too eager to rely on him.

'Well, Tree Boy, you got yourself a girlfriend. Hopefully, you don't snore too loudly,' I said. Accepting the inevitable lifted an immense weight from my shoulders. I didn't know what I was, but I was determined to find out and learn to be the best... whatever... I could be.

Chapter Seventeen

After leaving Sara's side, I sat down to dine alone. I couldn't help it. I caught myself smiling each time I remembered the blush on Sara's face when I kissed her fiercely, staking my claim for any prying eyes to see. She would come to my home today, and I couldn't wait to see her reaction when she saw the island. My home, my sanctuary, the one place I never took any of my fleeting romances. *I want to see her walking between my trees, those dainty hands brushing the bark of ancient oaks.* Even thinking about it brought so much contentment that I wished time could flow faster.

For my meal, I chose a cosy little cafe along the banks of the river Motlawa, hoping the calming flow of its deep waters would positively affect my chaotic thoughts. The ships and yachts slowly sailing past, gorgeous boulevards and magnificent granaries always helped remind me why I continued to protect the people under my charge. Here in the centre of the old town, under buildings and mud, beat the heart of Gdansk, a city that had never surrendered its freedom despite being conquered countless times, my home.

Thinking over today's events, I remembered Jarek's desire to protect Sara and wondered if he was already watching her. If he was, then his insistence that no one noticed him was correct; not once had I detected a shapeshifter and with that, my mind inevitably turned to the woman herself, the note she'd received this morning worrying me the most. A Soul Shepherd. If correct, then the situation was becoming more complicated. Sara, who, like the spirit of Gdansk, loved her freedom and was unyielding in the face of any such threat, would not appreciate the measures needed to keep her safe from those wanting to exploit her magic.

I could still taste her on my lips, and I mentally slapped myself for thinking of her and not the problems that needed to be addressed. I did it again, but the lingering scent of her body and the thought of her in my home stripped me of my reason. Damn it, this was going to be trouble. I may have overstepped in the basement, but I'd been worried and angry, which brought out the worst of me. Sara had been attacked after I left her unprotected, Czernobog's magic inflaming every protective instinct, almost unleashing the beast I tried to keep hidden. I didn't want her to fear me or be disgusted by my true nature. I wanted my Firefly to trust me, not just with keeping her safe, but with her heart.

As things were now, she didn't trust me enough to share anything unless I tricked it out of her. It was surprising that Sara had already discovered her spirit guide, but it opened up another source of information. However, with it being a cat, they weren't known to be the most helpful creatures.

'Your coffee, sir.' Allowing her fingers to slide across the back of my hand, an overly familiar waitress placed a large glass before me, falling back as I snapped my head sharply in her direction. 'A caramel latte, just as you ordered. If it's not right, I could always make a new one,' she said with a slight shiver.

I nodded, turning back and ignoring her presence, reaching for the pale concoction. Coffee was not a favourite of mine, but Sara seemed to enjoy it, the sweet taste reminding me of her lips as we kissed. Unfortunately, the vile commercial brew had nothing in common with the tingling spice of the doctor's lips, the overwhelmingly sickening sweetness of the coffee curdling my tastebuds, and I settled for breathing in the aroma to prompt the memory, inspiration flashing before me as I savoured the scent.

As I called Michal, my smile was full and satisfied. 'Install a coffee machine in the kitchen and buy the best roasts available,' I said, not even bothering with a greeting.

'Sir, I have been trying to reach you for the last two hours. There was an incident at the docks, an explosion on the ship due to be loaded today, and something similar happened at Nadolny's warehouse. He's been on the phone ever since, demanding answers, saying he hasn't touched your woman, so why did you attack his property? What should I do?' He asked as I thought about the situation. This must have happened during my visit to the hospital, the last-minute change of plans possibly saving the lives of my men.

'Tell Nadolny I'll be at his office in half an hour, and tell him he has an information leak. I'll explain when I get there. Ensure Adam and his team are alright and secure the shipment if it wasn't on the ship. Oh, and don't forget the damned coffee machine; we'll still be having a guest over later.'

'That woman?'

'Yes, that woman and, if I'm not mistaken, her cat as well,' I said, finishing the conversation. As soon as I put the phone in my pocket, I headed to my car. It would take me about half an hour to drive to the Anchor in the heavy traffic, and that was the meeting I didn't want to be late for.

Nadolny welcomed me with a scowl, surrounded by henchmen who prevented me from approaching him. As I looked at their raised palms, my gaze slid to their free hands, each one disappearing into the open jackets they all wore. With a raised eyebrow, I turned to my host, waiting for his next move, gathering power as I did. As the tension rose, I slowly raised my hands, palms up in a gesture of non-aggression, hoping Nadolny's men wouldn't start shooting.

'You know that won't work, so don't allow anger to cost you the lives of your men. I am here to talk peacefully.' Somehow, I kept the anger from my voice, knowing I still needed this man's resources and not wanting to cause unnecessary bloodshed. Instead, I pushed my magic into the surrounding concrete, the cold dead material sprouting moss and grass at my command.

'Who torched my building? It happened right after you sent me that ridiculous warning. Am I to believe it was a coincidence?' he said, pacing like a caged tiger, but he sent his men out of the room with a wave of his hand.

'I don't know, but if it's any consolation, there was an explosion on a ship I contracted for the amber shipment, and it happened at the same time I was scheduled to inspect the cargo.' I smirked, 'Maybe you are covering your tracks, and you used my email as an excuse for war?'

We both knew he wouldn't hesitate to do precisely that if the circumstances fit, but the gang leader knew I wouldn't be there if I believed he had.

'My apologies, Forest Lord. Please have a seat, and let's discuss our problem. As I'm not tree fertiliser, I'm guessing you think it's this new player.' Nadolny looked far more confident now that the posturing was finished, and smiling, I sat on the nearest chair. He chuckled. 'Yes, I know how you dispose of your enemies.'

'Better than polluting the Motlawa,' I replied, shrugging.

'Fish have to eat, too. So someone wants to kill you and put me out of business, or perhaps set each of us against the other while they wait in the background, ready to collect the spoils of war.' Pouring himself a good measure of whisky, the gangster proffered the bottle, taking it away when I refused.

'It appears so. Not to mention someone dressed like your staff delivered a package to my Sara.'

'That would explain the message, but do you really think me that stupid?'

Alone in the private space of his office, we didn't have to posture, and talking to the man who, in a way, shared my troubles was surprisingly liberating.

'No, you are not that stupid. How else could you learn of the Nether?' I asked because he'd known for decades, and I'd never discovered how. Nadolny brushed his hair away from his ears, and then I saw the slightly pointed tips, easy to hide in the longer style.

'Half of whatever mongrel slummed it with a human prostitute. I am simply a product of the times, as they say.' He said it with a shrug, and I changed the subject.

'Do you have any leads on our adversary?' I asked, and he shook his head.

'If I knew, they would already be feeding the fish. A whole warehouse of alcohol and cigarettes went up in a puff of smoke, almost half a million in goods. It feels like they want control of the docks, and while I can weather such a loss, it is a major inconvenience, but if it happens again, let's say my business may suffer. I'm being honest with you because I appreciate your reasonable, non-aggressive approach, which allows me to pursue my different fields of interest. I doubt your replacement would be as generous.'

'Your first mistake is the assumption there could be a replacement. Second? That you think me malleable.' Was it time to end this business arrangement? I wondered, but Nadolny smirked.

'I kissed your woman and lived.' He said, and I shook my head, hands clenched at the mere reminder he touched her, but my anger was toned down by the following statement. 'I have businesses operating in your territory, and as much as it pains me to admit it, I know they still exist because you allow it. Not that this admission will ever see the light of the day,' he said, and his answer made me return his smirk. Nadolny was as cunning as I thought him to be. He also knew his place in the pecking order, so I was more than willing to keep the pretence going.

'The woman you saw me with, Sara? She was targeted after visiting this club before my men knew of her existence. I want to hear from you she is safe from your men and that you will investigate how our enemy knew her address so quickly.'

'I knew there was more to that woman than a pretty face. You've never once gotten close to a female in all the years I've known you. I understand your feelings, but attachments make you vulnerable. I would advise you to treat her less favourably. Some people don't have my principles and don't know what you really are.' I hid my surprise at Nadolny's advice and readied myself to leave.

'If you hear anything, I trust you'll inform me or take action to eliminate the threat. As for your warning, I will give you one in exchange. Double your guard on any businesses in the harbour. It was an acolyte of Czernobog that threatened Sara, and there is little doubt our adversary is involved. I will let you know as soon as we discover more information and send someone to place wards around your warehouses. It won't help much against physical attacks, but it will help lessen the threat from magic.' I rose quickly, eager to leave.

Nadolny nodded, but I saw the corner of his mouth lift. 'Thank you. You have my word that neither I nor my men touched your precious morsel, but it doesn't mean she is safe. I will investigate any information leaks from my side, but it is more likely they are monitoring our movements, and since the last assassination failed... your Sara might be next. Grieving men have no heart to fight wars.'

'But avenging spirits do. Anyone who harms her will die, and it won't be quick or civilised. Thank you for your advice, though. It is a good start to our new arrangement.'

Without a second glance, I headed back to the car. Sara would finish work in two hours, and I wanted to look at the ship before picking her up.

As I pulled up to the harbour master's office, the poor man was visibly upset, gesticulating wildly in front of Adam. When the distressed official noticed my arrival, the blood drained from his face, his hands dropped to his sides, and he stuttered an apology for wasting my time, assuring me the cargo was safe and stored far from the incident. Once he was finished, I nodded to Adam, watching as a brown envelope changed hands, and we headed toward the ship. My second turned toward me when we were out of earshot, cursing angrily.

'The bastards were trying to kill us, well, you. The hold was engulfed instantly, several explosions cutting off the escape routes simultaneously. No one could have survived that; even you would have struggled, especially so isolated from the earth. There were several victims, all sent to the port hospital. Well, that's what I heard, at least, but I'd have to confirm that, and no one is able to speak. There were no other witnesses, so we're stuck until someone wakes up or the police find something.'

I had to fight the urge to investigate myself. *Fire, out of everything, they chose fire, simultaneously isolating me from my source.* That information was not well known. Only the oldest beings, those involved in creating the Nether, knew how to destroy my physical body. *What the fuck is going on?* I thought, struggling with my temper.

'Who's on the inside?' I asked, knowing Adam must have arranged for someone to be on the investigation team, checking what the local authorities missed.

'One of the wolves is an arson investigator. She knows what's needed and has Michal's number as well as mine, just in case. If Nadolny thinks he can get away with this, I'd happily pay him a visit.' I could hear the bloodlust in Adam's voice and laid a hand on his shoulder.

'Hold your fangs. Nadolny had nothing to do with this,' I said, squeezing his shoulder. The frown Adam gave me after flicking his gaze to my hand made me smile, and it widened as the red hue faded from his eyes.

'I know you are trying to avoid gang warfare, but who else could it be? He is the only one strong enough to attempt a takeover and knows about magic. He even forced Sara to kiss him in front of everyone. Leszek, don't tell me you're letting him get away with this. If you won't confront him, I will. That way, you can blame me for it.'

I knew why Adam was so upset; the organisation was our family, and he was determined to defend it at all costs, but my overzealous protégé still struggled to listen. My hand tightened on his collarbone until it gave a satisfying crunch, and Adam's face contorted in pain. My magic seeped into his skin, immobilising him.

'When I said he had nothing to do with it, it was because his warehouse, full of alcohol worth thousands of dollars, burned to the ground. Also, you forget about our newest enemy. Remember the attackers who captured the merfolk, shot Jarek and most likely coerced a woman to stick Czernobog's dagger in your chest, or maybe you've forgotten the last few weeks? If your brain isn't rotting from the tainted blood you're drinking, you would see someone is trying to set us up, and you're helping them by contradicting me in public.' After releasing my hold, Adam instantly clasped the damaged shoulder, pressing the displaced collarbone back.

'That was fucking unnecessary, and who the hell is Jarek?' He said, using vulgarity to cover the pain.

'And that's the only part you picked up on out of all that? Once again, I had to prevent you from making a reckless decision. Jarek is the wolf pup you saved, and probably have a very complete file on him back at your office. He is Sara's new shadow, as your people weren't keeping a close enough eye on her, letting a stranger leave a package for her that contained a bespelled item. That young man was the only reason I even knew about it.'

The frown Adam gave me when I criticised his team was protective and made me proud, even if his attitude didn't.

'I will look into it, but are we hiring kids now? Leszek, what's going on? Why are you treating this woman so differently?' I didn't blame him for the questions, so I answered his question despite the surge of anger.

'She is a Soul Shepherd.'

'I don't care if she suckles from... she's what?'

'A Soul Shepherd, Soul Stealer, God Killer, whatever you want to call her. Now you know why I have to keep her close.' If I'd been on the ship with Sara acting against me, her magic could easily have tethered my soul to this body, and I would have died a true death, with no escape to the Nether and no afterlife in Nawia. Worse still, it was clear Czernobog's servant knew this and had tried to capture her.

'You could kill her, end of problem.' Adam, it seemed, was back to his pragmatic self as he stepped out of reach, knowing my reaction. 'Fine, you want her by your side? Not your wisest decision, but fine.'

'Don't make me break any more bones,' I said because I couldn't explain my reasoning behind this decision, only knowing that if something happened to her, a part of me would die too.

Even with thoughts of Sara teasing my soul, there was work to be done. After she was safe in my home, I needed to take Czernobog's dagger to the local Coven. Now that we had a tentative understanding, their artefact master might tell me where it came from or at least tell me whether the curse that forced the user to target non-humans was aimed at Adam. The crunching of bone distracted me, and looking over, I watched as the vampire repaired the damage I'd caused.

'I wish you'd find another way to make your point. I may heal easily, but it still hurts. We should ask the paramedics and firefighters if there's any new information. The hold was empty, so with such an intense fire, if it wasn't Nadolny, it was likely caused by someone magical. Your power would be useful for that.'

'Not this time. Use your artefact to check for spells. I have to pick up Sara from the hospital.' I realised my mistake when Adam cursed, shaking his head.

'Of course. I should have known. Since you met Sara, I feel I don't know you anymore. I understand you like her, but do you know what it looks like when you keep running at her beck and call?'

'What is so hard to understand? I protect what is mine, and if she's the only woman to make me feel alive since Jurata, then so much better. You are still young, but after several millennia, you will learn to cherish anyone who brings colours back to your life. Now, please excuse me. I need to pick up my woman before she talks herself out of going with me. I will meet you in a couple of hours. Find out what you can about this incident, and come over later, and you might get some of that whisky I mentioned earlier.' With that last remark, I headed back to the car.

Adam was trustworthy, even if he could barely tame his impetuous nature, but something else made me rush to pick up Sara. The faint charred smell I detected on her. I'd ignored it when we met today, but knowing my luck, she'd encountered a victim from the ship fire, and I was curious if she'd discovered anything.

My finger lifting from the call button, I barked out. 'Buy the best cat food you can find,' I said, hearing my assistant choke in reply.

'Wha...?' I didn't wait to hear his questions, knowing he would fulfil my order. If Sara was anything like the local witches, her ball of fur was as close to her as a child, and I intended to buy myself into its good graces.

Chapter Eighteen

For bribery in the ER, money just won't cut it, so with baked goods, coffee and the promise to return the favour, I persuaded my colleague to come in an hour early so I could sneak out and return home with plenty of time to discuss today's events with Scarface.

A guide. That term still felt weird, even after being confronted by the reality, but thinking it over, even before he talked, Scarface had always been there for me. His grizzled muzzle pushed its way into my hand every time I needed comfort from the stresses of work, especially when the shadowy monsters refused to leave me alone.

After handing over the department to my colleague, it took moments to change and run for the exit, but my sigh of relief was short-lived as a tall figure stepped into my path.

'Sara? Where are you going?' At the sound of Leszek's voice, a curse escaped my lips as I slid to a stop on the polished hospital floor.

'Fuck.'

'Possibly, but not here, my Firefly.' A mischievous smile teased the corner of his lips, but his eyes remained wary. 'You haven't changed your mind, have you?'

Shoulders sagging as he took my bag, and placing the strap over his shoulder, I sighed, taking the arm he proffered, giving him what my nurses called my strong side-eye when he put his hand over mine. *Possessive much?* I thought, but clearly, my look wasn't as strong as my team pretended, his expression remaining one of patient expectation while he awaited my answer.

'No, I'm even willing to admit you might be right that it's the best solution if only to prevent you from fattening up my co-workers.' I said, feeling this awkward need to explain myself before he thought I wanted to run away. 'Alright, as silly as it sounds, I wanted to talk with my cat about the move. Scarface deserves a say in his living arrangements, and I'm no one's anything.' As I spoke, I felt the blush warm my cheeks, silently cursing my pale complexion that broadcast my feelings to the world.

'You're being considerate, not silly, and I must say, it's simply adorable. However, having bonded with you, Scarface will only be happy living beside you, so the consideration is unnecessary; most witches wouldn't even think to ask. Now that you're free let us go so I may greet his illustrious personage.'

Leszek was a handsome man, even if his expression was often stern and unforgiving, but when he smiled, he transformed into a work of art, the mischievous glint in his eyes melting more of the wall around my heart, as I imagined sharing a glass of wine, cuddled against his chest in front of a roaring fire. Sneaking a look at his classic profile, I allowed myself to hope a little. *Maybe we'll do that one day,* the idea making my blush worse. The longer I knew the Lord of the Forest, the more he made me feel at ease, and despite my protests, I was tentatively looking forward to spending some time in his company.

We drove lazily through the city, enjoying a little small talk, when agonising pain tore through my body, and I screamed, grasping my ribs and panting. One look in my direction and Leszek pulled over with the screeching of tyres, but I grabbed his shoulder. This pain wasn't mine. It echoed through the newly acquired mental connection I shared with Scarface, but it felt real no matter the source.

'No... house... Please.' I said, panting, close to collapse. Someone was beating the hell out of me... my cat... the lines between my consciousness and his blurred as the pain tore reality apart. Without questioning, Leszek slammed the accelerator to the floor, and even through the haze of pain, I was sure he would kill us in traffic.

When the pain stopped, my relief was replaced by worry. Was he alive? Had they killed my baby? A sob wracked my body as thoughts tumbled through the link. 'Don't come home, danger, attacker.'

'Someone is in my house. I need to tell you...ugh fu... what is...?' I struggled to talk, my breath trapped in my aching chest. 'We had a... patient, burned at docks... he saw me.'

'Tell me later, Sara. Stay here.' The car jerked when he pulled over, Leszek leaping out and rushing upstairs as soon as it came to a halt.

'No, wait... the fu... key.' As I struggled out of the car, I croaked, 'Not staying here....'

The texture of the concrete looked very interesting from this angle, but why could I see it so clearly? My mind registered the sound of a commotion, and the pressure on my chest disappeared, my burning lungs finally dragging precious air into their desperate embrace.

As soon as the effects of mild hypoxia wore off, I was careening toward my apartment, desperate to save Scarface. The wreckage of my door barely registered as the view inside startled me to a standstill.

Leszek stood in the middle of the room, holding a man in the air. I blinked several times, but the scene didn't change. Did gravity cease to exist when I passed out? How was he holding the man in the air at arm's length? And without flinching as his captive struggled, kicking and clawing to escape.

'Who sent you,' His voice was so menacing it was more growl than speech.

'He can't talk. You're crushing his windpipe. Where is my cat, and why the fuck aren't my neighbours here? Did everybody go deaf in the building?'

I felt strangely detached. I recognised this feeling. In any crisis, I set my emotions aside while the practical, logical part of me analysed the situation. *Detachment, my superpower.* I remembered those moments, resuscitating a child or staunching someone's blood as we stitched their torn body, family screaming in the background, moments where recalling vital information without panic was the difference between life and death. That detachment meant I could assess the damage, ask questions and save my cat without collapsing to the floor in tears.

'A spell that suppressed noise kept your neighbours from investigating. The door was intact until I arrived.' Leszek seemed to calm as he spoke, his arm lowering the trespasser to the ground, and the purple colour receded from the captive's face.

'Where is Scarface?' I asked, turning toward the burglar. Cold sweat drenched me when I failed to see his scarred black muzzle in the wreckage. 'Scarface, kitten... please be here.' I called, feeling the first touch of panic.

I have never been so scared in my life. My precious boy was injured, and the thought I might have lost him shattered me. I tried to stay composed, but my strength broke, and like a maniac, I rushed to the kitchen and then to the bedroom, trying to find him. A pitiful meow from the lounge drew me back as he spoke in my mind. *'I failed to stop them to enter. I'm sorry, Sara.'*

I dived under a broken bookshelf to retrieve my friend, cradling his broken body gently as I rescued him from the debris, tears streaming down my face as I saw the blood and his barely moving chest, realising how much damage had been done from the pain I'd felt being inflicted on his small body. I'd happily feel it again if it meant he survived this ordeal, but I could see the telltale signs of death as Scarface struggled to breathe.

'Please, kitten, please don't leave me. Leszek, can you help him? I'll pay any price and won't fight. Just help him, please?'

I sobbed, begging for my cat's life, embracing him while my soul clung to his, holding it in the dying body. It was instinct, a desperate act that drained my strength far too quickly, but I didn't care. He was family, and I would give anything for my baby to survive this latest battle.

I'd found him as a kitten, matted fur wet and bloody, lying in the filth next to a dumpster, clinging to life, the will to survive enabling him to mewl weakly when he sensed my presence. My little fighter, my guardian. I fell in love with his scarred muzzle, and we'd been inseparable ever since. Scarface had seen more of my tears and heard more of my woes than anyone, and now, when he could reply, I was about to lose him.

'Sara...' I look up through a curtain of tears to see Leszek's outstretched hands, the man he'd been holding, abandoned on the floor, his neck twisted obscenely. Gently removing Scarface's body from my hands, he grimaced in pain before closing his eyes.

'You tethered his soul to this world. Now let me take care of his body.'

I clung to this frail thread of hope and focused on the connection to my guide. The pain I felt in the car returned, only to fade away. I could feel it all as earth magic moved through Scarface, a soft, loving touch for such a powerful man.

Leszek's healing washed over my senses, the lack of pain reminding me of the surgery on the werewolf. *Is this incredible man taking the pain into himself as he did back then?* I opened my eyes, about to ask, when the pale cloud of death dissolved, and my cat stirred in Leszek's embrace. Not fully healed, but no longer at death's welcoming door. A weak, tired voice appeared in my mind. *'Sara, those men were here to take you, it wasn't a simple burglary.'*

'Take me where?' I said out loud, and Leszek's head jerked in my direction.

'Your guide has recovered enough to communicate?' He asked, and I noticed how tired he looked. Healing Scarface must have exhausted him, but he did it for me. I reached out and touched Leszek's cheek, glimpsing a strange expression flash across his features before his shoulders slumped, and he leaned against my hand as if it brought him relief. Nothing could have torn me away from this kind, generous man at that moment as I caressed his temple with my thumb.

'Yes, he said, some men came to abduct me, so there wasn't just the one you killed.' It was difficult, but I kept my voice calm as I continued, 'Is it helping? My touch?' I asked, curious about his reaction. Leszek nodded, and I held him a moment longer.

'How is it helping?'

'We can talk about it at home. Your cat should recover now, and I have to make a few phone calls. Please pack what you need and don't worry about the rest. We can buy replacements.' He said, frowning when I shook my head.

'Hush, it's ok. Unless he ripped open my bag, I'm already packed,' I left Scarface in Leszek's arms, scrambling to grab the carrier. The body on the floor stirred as I moved, and then he laughed. The shock at finding him alive awoke something inside me, and brutal, mindless rage took over. Without conscious thought, my foot slammed into the attacker's rib cage.

The man grunted, no longer laughing after his rib cracked, but I wanted him to feel every ounce of pain he'd inflicted on my defenceless cat. About to swing my foot at him again, I felt an arm lift me up, Leszek effortlessly holding me up as he made a call with his other hand.

'Michal, send a clean-up crew to Sara's apartment. Yes, now, and make sure everything is ready for our arrival.' He said, and a moment later, I was engulfed in his embrace.

'I wasn't done with... Where's Scarface?' I shouted, suddenly frantic, but Leszek turned, and there he was, my little warrior, safe and sound in a pile of my torn clothing.

'No, my Firefly. You are done. I allowed you a moment of anger, but I won't let you walk this path. My people will be here soon, and we will take this filth away for proper questioning.' He said, and I couldn't believe my own ears.

'You... allowed me?' I said through clenched teeth, pulling myself from his embrace. *Did he think I was a silly little woman to be allowed to feel anger?* The voice in the back of my mind whispered that Leszek was right, that he healed Scarface, but I was too far gone for any of this to matter. It felt like I'd lost everything.

'Sara, you are not a killer. I promise he will get what he deserves, but I can't let you rage. Believe me, it's for the best.'

'Best for whom?' I said, looking at him, completely astounded. 'Look around you. Can't you see what he did?'

Leszek frowned, holding me even tighter. 'Sara, please, let me handle this; everything will be all right. You are not yourself, and I can't let you do something you'd regret.'

'Let me... Those words again. How I hate you right now. My house is trashed, my cat was almost killed, and some fucker I don't know is after me. All because of you and that idiot bloodsucker who barged into my ER with a knife in his chest. You don't know me, and you don't own me, and nothing gives you the power to let me do anything. This thing between us is just a contract. A good one, and it has its perks, I admit, but none of this is real. Wasn't this supposed to be a three-month fixed contract? You come into my life, fuck everything up, and assume you have the right to think for me?'

I was lashing out, senselessly beating up the person who helped me because his choice of words focused my fear and anger. Since I met him, I'd been as tense as piano wire, and facing Scarface's death broke me. I needed a target for my pain, and if he insisted on stopping me from punishing the culprit, he would bear the brunt of it. I saw Leszek's face pale, his arms falling away as if scalded like he could feel each hateful word burning his flesh. Part of me wondered how someone so powerful could look so vulnerable, brought to the brink by whatever the hell it was I was spouting in my rage.

'Sara, stop. He is right. You would have regretted it later.' Scarface's voice was a sobering slap to my conscience, adding to the rising guilt at seeing Leszek hurt, but when I tried to apologise, he turned away, lifting his phone up to make a call.

'Adam, come with the witch and set wards around the apartment and let me know if you find anything suspicious, then take the scum I incapacitated to our warehouse. I will question him later.' Leszek said, a sharp affirmation loud in the sudden, heavy silence. I swallowed hard when he walked back to me.

'I'm sorry, Sara. You are right, and if we hadn't stumbled upon you in the hospital, our opponent might never have discovered your talent, but with you working as a doctor, he might have found out, anyway. I know you don't like my arrangements, but it is better than being at his mercy, so please accept my apology for my behaviour and the help I will offer without the desire for repayment.' His voice was emotionless but courteous, the icy mask back in place. Gone was the teasing twinkle, replaced by this no-nonsense warrior. I felt my heart twist as I saw the damage my anger caused to his budding feelings.

'Please, I'm sorry, I didn't...' A scarred man strode through the open door, freezing the words in my throat, but Leszek simply nodded, pointing at my suitcase beneath the shattered door. My shoulders slumped at the dismissal implied by his actions, and I gathered Scarface into my arms, silently walking to the car.

Leszek drove carefully, maintaining his silence as I struggled to find the right words to apologise, embarrassed and terrified by my outburst. I made it more difficult by the truth of my accusations. He'd come into my life and changed everything, but while it had become more dangerous, hectic, and insane, he had opened my eyes to magic and a whole new world of knowledge to learn, ripping away the sense of hopelessness slowly eroding my sanity.

The sound of tyres crunching over the gravel of the driveway surprised me from my introspection, the shame at my cowardice for not apologising almost forgotten as I saw a manor house shimmer into life before me. I'd thought we were still on the highway, but looking around, there were only trees as far as my eyes could see.

'What the hell? How did we get here? Weren't we just on the road a moment ago?'

'The route here is bespelled. I can't let anyone wander in here. Don't worry; as soon as I introduce you to the house, you can come and go as you please.' I stared at Leszek's profile, positive I'd misheard. *Introduced to the house? No, he must mean the staff, surely?* However, my host's features were still emotionless, with no hint of a smile, and I realised this must be more of the magic I had yet to learn about.

I turned away, embarrassed and studied the manor house, its hard edges softened by ivy and an old, wizened wisteria, their foliage seeming to highlight the Eighteenth-century stonework. It charmed me utterly, and the sigh I released was envious as I imagined life here, complete with a modern-day, magical gangster.

'It is so beautiful. I wouldn't have resisted so much if I'd known you lived like this. Thank you for bringing me here,' I said, putting as much contrition into my voice as possible, and for the first time since the incident, I saw the corner of Leszek's mouth curl upwards before he straightened his posture and turned to face me.

'You will be safe here. The area is warded, so you may wander as you please. I will set up patrols as an added measure. You can go anywhere in the house, but if you need anything, ask Michal, and he will provide it,' he said before exiting the car. Before I could move Scarface to safely climb from my seat, the door opened, and Leszek held out his hand.

'Come, Sara, we need to be in contact when you enter the house for the wards and spells to recognise you.' He said, and I reached out without hesitation, but instead of his firm, reassuring grip, Leszek simply supported my weight as I eased from the vehicle and walked toward his exquisite home. When I stepped across the threshold, a tingling sensation ran up my spine, and the image of a majestic stag flashed before my eyes, disappearing before it properly registered, but as I turned to ask my host about the vision, Leszek dropped my hand like it burned.

'I will escort you to your room.' As we moved toward the stunning main staircase, Leszek stole a glance before speaking again. 'I know you value your independence, but please let my driver take you wherever you need. I will also have a few men observing the hospital. If you can give Michal your shift roster, it will be easier for him to plan meals that way. Also, I requested help from the local Coven to train you, and they need to schedule lessons. If you have any questions, ask Michal. He will be able to help,' he said as I followed meekly behind. When we reached a spacious room with an ensuite bathroom and an impressive balcony that sported a staircase to the garden, I put Scarface on the bed and turned toward Leszek, who placed my bag on the floor before turning to leave.

'Stay, please, at least for a moment.' I said quietly, and he stilled, one hand on the door handle.

'I'm sorry. I was scared and angry and shouldn't have snapped at you like that. Not after you saved my friend.' I saw his shoulders tighten before they sagged, and Leszek approached me.

'There is nothing to forgive, my Firefly. You may have been angry, but that doesn't make it less true. My disruption of your life has stirred up our emotions, but you're right; we don't know each other, and my running rough-shod over your choices was unforgivable. I've existed for millennia and should know better than to let feelings override common sense. I apologise for the danger I have brought into your life, but I request you allow me to keep you safe, for both our sakes. Once the danger has passed, I will release you from any obligation you may feel toward me. I would also like to assist with your magical training if you have no objection.' I had tears in my eyes by the time he'd finished. Leszek's voice, so stoic and determined, held a depth of sorrow that made me want to gather him into my arms until this shadow disappeared. Instead, I stood there, utterly lost.

I'd wanted this distance, but now that I had it, I found my heart aching, reaching for his. Unable to bear the feeling, I placed my hand on Leszek's chest, his heart beating against my palm.

'Thank you for saving Scarface. As for the rest, I'm sorry, I was overwhelmed, it... doesn't have to be this way.'

I stopped and shook my head. He was being reasonable, holding to our bargain. I was the one overstepping boundaries now, reaching for feelings that would end with heartache. I wanted to lose myself in his embrace, consumed by his devouring kisses, but that would lead to me depending on someone to whom my life was less than the blink of an eye. *Was I falling for him?* I thought, suddenly terrified. *These emotions weren't real. They couldn't be.* I repeated, my mind going into overdrive. I couldn't deny that he wanted me and spoiled me with those little trinkets of affection, but I promised myself to be careful. Because if I let myself believe this thing between us could be real, where would it take me, and how much would it hurt?

Leszek waited, giving me time to gather my thoughts, but when I lowered my head, he hooked his finger under my chin, tilting my head up.

'I know my Firefly. I am sorry, too. Have a rest, I won't disturb you.' He lowered his head, and I stretched upward, expecting another earth-shattering kiss. Instead, I felt a chaste, brief peck on my forehead, and he left the room, quietly closing the door behind him.

I sat on the bed, the disappointment I was feeling utterly baffling. I got what I wanted: a safe space and freedom from Leszek's interest, and yet the sense of losing something precious was crushing my heart, and it had nothing to do with the destruction of my apartment.

'I will fix this Scarface, whatever *this* is.'

'Yes, you will. Whilst I'm all for bringing him down a peg or two, Sara, that was less than ideal. I should have died back there, but Leshy saved me because he knew you loved me, and then he brought us to his home after you screamed how much you hated him. Do you really hate him?'

Trust the arsehole cat to make a guilt trip worse. 'No, and that is part of the problem. We made a deal to act as lovers and live together, and I'm the one refusing to cooperate because I can't help but like him. It's just... I feel like I'm losing control over my life, which terrifies me. So when he said... when he gave permission for me to feel anger like he had control over my feelings too, I exploded.'

'He is an immortal spirit of the forest, the mighty Leshy, Master of Beasts, and you threw a tantrum because he stopped your petty revenge. Oh, Sara. He didn't save my attacker. He prevented a healer, who couldn't abandon a dying kitten, from becoming wracked by guilt and self-hatred because that is what killing a defenceless man would have caused. Once the Leshy interrogates him, that bastard will beg for an easy death.'

'Fine, but what do you suggest I do?' I asked, falling back onto the surprisingly soft bed while Scarface carefully walked over and sat on my chest.

'What do you want to do?'

'I want to make him smile. I want to lay my head on his and gently stroke his cheek until his worries disappear, even for a moment.' I trailed off as my thoughts wandered aimlessly till they caught on a remembered image, and I startled, nearly unseating a now hissing cat from my chest. 'Oh Fuck, I'm so sorry, sweetie. I just remembered the burns victim and my vision. Leszek needs to know what I saw.'

After gently settling Scarface on a pillow, I rushed into the corridor, stumbling to a halt, unsure where to go. Following my instincts, I ended up in a lounge or sitting room full of thick rugs and soft, inviting sofas, the atmosphere one of relaxed sophistication. Unfortunately, it was empty of people, and I silently cursed my instincts until the shadow of a large man filled the doorway.

'Leszek!' I shouted, relieved at finding him so quickly.

'Sorry, madam, but no. My name is Michal. The boss went to question your attacker, and I wouldn't count on him returning today. He was rather angry and may need time to cool off. I'm the housekeeper here, so if you need something, let me know. I am authorised to cater to your every whim.'

'How can I get hold of him? I have important information he needs to know.' I was back to my rational self. He might be right about the age gap and all those impossible cravings that made our interactions so fiery, but it didn't mean we couldn't be partners in solving the current problem, and if this wasn't the best way to gain his trust, nothing was.

Michal looked at me, assessing my importance. Finally, he shook his head. 'We can't reach him now, but I will tell him when he arrives. Rest now. You look like you need it.'

My anxiety spiked, and I called his number a few times, but as he didn't pick up, I gave up. I didn't know how to contact Leszek, leaving me with no option but to follow Michal's advice. Besides, he was right. I needed the rest, so I admitted defeat and returned to my room to sleep.

Chapter Nineteen

I paused on the threshold of the manor, letting its magic surround me, the slumbering house quiet in the early hours of the morning. I could already feel Sara's presence, the spirit accepting her more thoroughly than I'd expected; not even Jurata had been this welcome, the memory reminding me that the Council of Gedania needed an update on the situation here, but I found my motivation to call them sadly lacking. My subconscious clearly agreed as I stood looking at the door to Sara's bedroom and not my office. Despite Sara telling me she hated me and that I'd ruined her life, I could not walk away from her. I felt tethered to her, enthralled by this fierce woman. If I could only fix how she felt about me. If I could make her love me. Her magic enhanced mine, but it was her radiant smile that made me sneak like a thief into my own home just to see her face.

I'd opened the door before I realised and was standing over her like some creep from a horror movie, watching as she slept, her hair luminous in the moonlight, one hand beneath her spirit guide's paw, adorable. Less adorable, however, was the suspicious glare the protective cat was aiming in my direction, and if I hadn't spent half the night torturing and burying his attacker, I would have felt intimidated.

Sara looked so innocent, lying there, lips parted, a faint smile highlighting the dimple on her cheek. My rational mind knew she wasn't some naïve, inexperienced maiden. If her work didn't tell me that, the kisses we shared would place all doubt to rest, but there was more to it. This woman was a paradox I struggled to understand. One moment, calm and composed despite her world falling apart, the other a sobbing, emotional mess begging for her cat's life.

It was her tears that had doused my ardour and made me realise what I was doing. I wanted her more than anything I could remember. Not just her body but her unyielding spirit, and that caused me to lose sight of our reality. An immortal being wanting a human so much that she was now in danger. She was right to hate me for this; even if part of her enjoyed my company, the resentment expressed during her outburst was enough to wake me up to the realisation there was more setting us apart than connecting us.

We both needed space to think, to make the right choices, and likely to part ways when the contract expired. I watched Sara frown in her sleep as if she sensed my mood, and despite the cat's focused stare, I gently brushed my fingers over her cheek, letting my magic soothe her. The frown eased, and her breathing deepened as she drifted into more pleasant dreams. My Firefly, shining with an inner light that never burns your eyes, so beautiful, so ephemeral, her life too short for what I wanted to give her.

'I won't hurt her. I will protect her with my life, and when it is safe, if she wishes to leave, I won't stop her, I promise,' I said to the cat, who blinked once and curled up beside her, closing his yellow eyes.

'Sleep well, my Firefly.' I said, resisting the urge to kiss her.

This attraction, these unrequited feelings I imposed on her, were wrong, so before my desire got the better of me, I went to my office and closed the door. Sara's presence, the faint scent somehow suffusing my home, was enough to give me peace of mind, but it was time to think about my next move. The thug that attacked her home was nothing special, but the information we extracted through some not-so-civilised means might prove valuable.

I wasn't proud that my anger had gotten the better of me. His death had been too easy even if we'd extracted the information. Someone had placed him under a powerful geas, rendering the man almost mute, but Veronica had provided a witch skilled in removing such magic, and the fact it wasn't painless helped the interrogation run much smoother. Still, he was loyal to his master; unfortunately, his shouted pleas to be taken by Czernobog fell on deaf ears.

I smirked, pouring myself a glass of cider, the sharp apple taste washing my tiredness away. *I hope you like the afterlife I've given you*, I thought, recalling the yew tree saplings thrust through his soft flesh, new branches spreading in his veins, gorging on blood, while a black lilac wrapped around his neck, siphoning his soul's essence. The desire for immortality swiftly disappeared as his soul was torn asunder, and it only took moments for the zealot to confess with the promise of a quick death.

'How long will our guest be staying?' Michal stood in the doorway, surprising me with his presence.

Forever if it was my choice, I thought before answering him.

'Why? Has she given you trouble already?'

'No, but I'm not used to having a woman around the house. What do you want me to do with her?' He asked, and I laughed ruefully.

'Nothing. Ensure she is safe and, if possible, happy during her stay. Find a reliable driver and some discrete security. A Warlock of Czernobog is after her. They've identified her as a Soul Shepherd, and although this island is warded, I don't want to leave anything to chance,' I said, rubbing the bridge of my nose as I finished.

'And you invited her into the house? For fuck's sake, boss. We still have Czernobog's dagger in the safe. What if she's an assassin, or they bespelled her?' Michal's outburst was understandable, if a little insulting, but I owed him an explanation.

'She is not an assassin. She doesn't even know how much power she can exercise over the gods or spirits and certainly doesn't know she can kill me. Luckily, for now, she doesn't want to. I don't know how my enemy found out about her, but Sara is in danger. The thug we captured was one of several sent after her, and his orders were to take her alive.'

'Why? Did you find what they want or do here?' In an unusual for him manner, Michal sat by me, pouring himself some alcohol.

'All I discovered was that the man we captured called him the Warlock or Master and that he was an upstart mage, exiled by the brotherhood when he became too difficult to handle. After disappearing for several years, he returned as a Prophet of Czernobog, collaborating with the Russian military to kill the elder races. That's apparently who's backing him, but the best tidbit I found? The men who came with him? Each one is a convert, following their leader like a fucking cult.'

'So the Russian brotherhood survived communism and Glasnost but couldn't handle this arsehole?' Michal emptied his glass in one go, and I shrugged.

'I don't think handle is the right word, but I will dig up more. I heard about some problems the eastern Covens had a few years back. A prophecy of the new dawn of the gods or some similar nonsense, but each time we offered assistance, they brushed us off, and it didn't take long for everyone to lose interest.'

'What do your kin think about it?'

'If by my kin, you mean Gedania's Council? I haven't asked, and as long as they're safe in their little haven, I doubt they'd care. As you know, we do not have the best working relationship,' I said, observing him over the rim of my glass.

Michal knew the history. When magic faded with the twilight of the old gods, they created the Nether, escaping through the Gates. I and a few others stayed behind, our magic stripped away to power the spells anchoring the other realm, but despite this, I thrived, able to access a tiny portion of the magical energy from the anchors.

'You should tell them. With so many attacks on the gate, let them decide if they want to support you or ignore the problem till it blows up in their faces.' Michal didn't seem satisfied with my explanation.

'No, my friend, I will protect the Gates from this side. As for the rest, I will fix it. He targeted Sara, planning to use her against me. I can't let it slide.' I said, noticing the hint of a smile on his face. I didn't know why the Warlock and his people attacked the Gates, but there were enough beings in the Nether to ensure the Gates were never breached.

'You like her.' Michal stated judiciously.

'Yes.'

There was no sense in denying it. Within a short period, Sara had become a bright light to my lonely existence, but I wasn't a savage to force myself on a woman who hated me, especially if there was a possibility the attraction we felt was caused by her magic.

'So why….' I didn't let Michal finish before raising my hand to cut him off.

'I misread the situation. Sara repeatedly wished for me to not contact her and disappear from her life, but I took it as a challenge because of the desire I saw in her eyes and how we responded to each other's touch. I forgot that attraction doesn't mean consent, and when she shared how being close to me wrecked her life, I understood that even if her magic complements mine, she would never consciously choose me. The irony is that the more time I spend with her, the more I want her and the more she pushes me away.' I said, hating the defeat in my voice.

'So why is she here?'

'Because I can't let her go. The thought of losing her drives me insane, and I feel guilty. Sara was right, I have placed her in danger, and to atone for this, I will protect her until she can defend herself, feelings be damned,' I said. The sarcastic grunt Michal gave as he stood made me sigh. 'As long as we don't spend time together, there shouldn't be an issue.'

'I will adjust your schedule so you can avoid any unnecessary entanglements. Is there anything specific that will help?'

'Prepare my apartment in the city. I will stay there until it's time to reconnect with the grove or help Sara with her magic.' I thought some more, guilt pricking my conscience at leaving Sara alone in a strange new environment before continuing. 'Come up with a plausible excuse to bring that wolf pup, Jarek, here to stay. I think that will make our guest feel more comfortable.' With that, Michal nodded, muttering something about thinking and heads, leaving before I could ask what he meant.

As I leaned back, the reassuring creak of my chair eased some of the tension in my shoulders, but I couldn't stop thinking about the beautiful woman asleep upstairs. *Will you return to my side if I set you free, my Firefly?*. Maybe I can try again when this ends, and chaos and mayhem no longer disrupt her life? If she could see the man behind the mask, not the mobster or forgotten forest god, would her heart beat with the same intensity as mine?

The sun rose as I sipped the now-warm cider. The house was still quiet, and knowing Adam would be home by now, I called the grumpy vampire, his annoyed tone instantly improving my mood.

'What the hell do you want? I was getting ready for bed,' he snapped, and I imagined him debating whether to throw the phone against the wall.

'Meet me at the office in an hour and ask Tomasz to come, too. I have a plan, but I need you both on board before I go to Nadolny.'

'Leszek, this could have waited till the evening.' His voice grated through the connection.

'No, it couldn't. I also want an update on the new clinic and the situation at the docks.'

'What is wrong with you? You can't sleep or what? Oh... that's right, the good doctor is there. Fine, give me a moment. I fucking knew I'd be the one suffering thanks to her.'

'Adam? Just be there,' I answered, ending the call and getting ready. Before I left the house, I stood in the hallway, closing my eyes and reaching out with my senses. The forest around my home provided a constant flow of energy, directly linking me to the remains of my magic. That connection seemed stronger somehow, and I wondered if Sara's presence was the reason for that change, the errant thought making my desire to stay challenging to overcome.

Adam was already in my office when I arrived, and Tomasz joined us shortly after. They'd both been present while I extracted the confession from our Russian friend, and although both men were used to the violence, the ferocity I displayed as I drove the living wood into the hoodlum's body made them treat me warily.

'What's the plan?' Adam spoke first, looking at me for an explanation. However, it was Tomasz who answered.

'We need to find where they are first. My wolves checked out the Naval dockyard in Gdynia after that damn fool you captured insisted they were there, and while we discovered signs of recent activity, there's nothing left except week-old scents and beer bottles, so if anyone was there, they're long gone. One of the lads insisted he smelled something in the old armoury, but it was emptier than a politician's heart.' The werewolf Alpha sounded angry at such a waste of time, but I felt we were missing something vital, the clues buried deep in my subconscious.

'Did you learn anything about our captive and his prophet from the SWW?'

'The man you so graciously allowed to die was Petr Vladislavovich Sedov, dishonourably discharged from Russian Naval Special Reconnaissance four years ago, alongside his entire squad. The official version was *exceeding operational parameters*. However, there are several notes on the looting of archaeological sites and torture of civilians, along with a highly redacted file on an experimental weapon that went missing from the area of his last posting. I suspect the missing weapon found its way into our people's bodies. After discharge, Petr joined a mercenary group called the Black Horse Brigade, whose ranks are filled by the worst Russian Spetsnaz has to offer before he resurfaced here.' Adam had very little time to dig for information. That he'd already talked with the Polish secret service, or SWW as they were known, and found a link between the thug and the bullets Sara removed from Jarek's body was surprising.

As I mulled over the connection, I absent-mindedly continued. 'I'm impressed, Adam. Did you have any issues dumping the scumbag in the river?' It had been an unusual request, but I wanted this bastard found, wanted the world to know what happened to those who attacked my woman.

Once again, it was Tomasz who spoke first, though this time carefully. 'I told the boys to bury him in the usual spot. You weren't entirely yourself when you issued the order. I thought this would be for the best....'

The Alpha's words made sense, even if it was frustrating that the shifter changed my order. However, I would not berate him for thinking about the safety of his team, so I let the subject drop. I saw Adam roll his eyes, smirking as he watched Tomasz squirm.

'Apart from the overly grandiose name of the mercenary group, is there anything that ties this to Czernobog?' My question made him wince as if he hadn't made the connection between the dark god's avatar and the mercenaries. If a vampire could blush, I wouldn't be surprised to see his cheek glowing at that moment.

'I barely had time to explore this issue, but fine, I will share what I found. I messaged the Moscow seethe, but they were unwilling to help. Thankfully, I called in a favour, and they revealed some information on a scandal there a few years back, one the government was keen to sweep under the carpet.' Adam paused, and I nodded for him to continue.

'I might have the wrong man, but the Warlock our informer mentioned was going by the name Nicolai Borisovich Rostov, and he was expelled after he was caught practising the Dark Arcana. He was particularly keen to explore thaumaturgy, temporal magic, and, of course, summoning. According to my source, this man had an ego even bigger than yours.' The vampire couldn't restrain his smirk again, but I shook my head, annoyed at his attitude.

'Don't tease me today. So why is he still alive? Even in Moscow, they rarely tolerate involvement with the Dark Arcana.'

'He was expelled from the Elitana Brotherhood, but after digging a little, I found out our informant was right, and he worked for some shadowy government agency, often against and betraying the elder races, and they managed to keep him alive.'

'Elitana?' That name rang the bell, but I couldn't think why.

'Yes, those bastards. Remember, just before the last war? They tried to oust Stalin by using necromancy to raise Lenin? Luckily, they failed, but our man must have done something truly appalling to be expelled. That's all I discovered in the little time you gave me. I might have brought a dossier of the wrong man, but it's too big a coincidence, and nothing explains what he's up to.'

I sighed, mulling over Adam's findings. I agreed about the coincidence, and if one was unlikely, then two were unbelievable, and that meant this Warlock was attacking the Gates to the Nether, but why here? Why not any of the Gates in Russia, where his gods were seeded and he had government support?

‘Maybe it is about the number of the Gates. With the emergence of the Gates near Sopot and Gdynia, we now have three of them. For whatever reason, something is influencing our connection to the Nether, and I’ll bet whatever it is drew our friend to the region,’ I said finally. Both men looked at me in confusion. ‘Dark Arcana requires a tremendous amount of magic. With the appearance of two new Gates and the abundance of amber, I’m betting that the Warlock has found access to more power. The magical properties of the living gem helped Gdansk thrive through the centuries. If he is planning something big, he would need both. That’s likely the reason he’s focused on me. I guard the Gates and control the amber trade.’

‘Sure, but why attack Nadolny? He has no magic and no amber.’ Adam asked.

‘Divide and conquer. We already assumed the other party was guilty of the attacks, and if we didn’t have a reasonable association, we would already be at war. Besides, until he has control over the Gates or destroys them, returning true magic to the world, he needs sacrifices to power his spells, and where else would you find a steady stream of victims if not a tourist city and its shady nightclubs and brothels?’

I stood up and walked toward the map, studying it. With its jagged shoreline, Pomerania was easily accessible from Kaliningrad, but it didn’t strike me as a likely place for our Warlock to hide out. No, he’d want to be close to the action. The main

Gates to Gedania were at the Gdansk docks, with one of the lesser Gates between Sopot and the Kashubian forest and the other in the Baltic, close to Hel. While the sirens had been used to entrap victims, I doubted they would help access their gate, especially with its instability after Jurata's departure, but assumptions cost lives.

'Let's base our planning on your assumption, Adam. We know your Warlock wants access to the Gates, and his recent use and torture of the sirens could point toward their gate, but at least it would be the easiest to secure. I will begin negotiations with the merfolk. Since Jurata abandoned them, I might be able to offer them an agreement that will secure our shores and close access to the gate in the Baltic.'

'What about the other gates? Are you not worried about them?' Tomasz pointed out, and I smiled.

'No, the gate near the forest is within an ancient grove, and while the trees are long gone, it is surrounded by nature and under my control. However, I intend to strengthen the wards during the autumn equinox to ensure its security. With the recent attacks, I think focusing on the gate in the dockyard is our best bet. With it surrounded by steel and concrete, my powers are weakest there, and our adversary would be a fool not to take advantage of that. Tomasz, I'll leave that to you and your wolves. Work with Nadolny's men, and be careful. We've lost enough people already, and now that we know Dark Arcana is involved, it is imperative to keep them safe.' I kept the concern from my expression even as I worried.

The Alpha bared his teeth at the mention of the gangster. 'Did Nadolny agree to this?' He asked, but I shrugged off his concern.

'Not yet, but he will. Rostov made the mistake of pitting us against each other, giving us an unexpected ally. I think that's all we can do for now. Thank you for your time; I'll leave the rest to you, gentlemen.' With a nod to punctuate my dismissal, I sat down to consider my next steps.

Once I was alone, the ley lines on the map caught my attention. Whilst the magic running through them paled in comparison to the raging torrents of the past, they still held enough to influence the mortal world, and here in the Tricity area, we had several loci that, because of their magic, attracted trouble and constantly needed to be cleansed of dark energy.

Dozhynki, the harvest celebration, was next week, and I'd need to use that time of transition to help cleanse the loci and strengthen the wards of the second gate to the Nether. I wondered if I should ask Sara to join me as I performed the ancient rites. After my magic's reaction to her presence, it might even help. *I'll have to check with Michal to see if she is working*, I thought, before dismissing the idea when I realised it would draw her further into my world, potentially endangering her life.

I felt calmer after devising a plan of action and indulged myself thinking about how to make this Roskov suffer once I had him within my grasp.

Now that I knew what to search for, the presence of Czernobog was everywhere, his influence affecting the local populace despite my wards, and with no access to my full power, I would have no way to combat him if he fully manifested.

No, I needed to find this bloody Warlock before he did something stupid and plunged my domain into darkness, or everything was lost.

Chapter Twenty

(One month later)

I'd once heard an angry English tourist shout a saying in the ER, 'I'm at the end of my tether,' and it has stuck with me ever since. Well, right now, the end of my tether was so far behind me I'd need a telescope to see it.

With the quintessential manners of a gentleman, Leszek, my host and now apparent candidate for sainthood, had avoided being alone with me for one day short of a month. Not that I'd been counting the days, of course, but with a schedule as regimented as mine had become, lessons, followed by work, followed by sleep, you found amusement where you could. Mine came in the form of asking, once a day, every day, whether Leszek wanted to join me for a stroll in the forest, then counting the seconds till he suddenly remembered an important meeting in town.

This new and improved gentlemanly act was going to end with me either stabbing, fucking, or hiding Leszek's body, possibly all three, if this went on much longer.

Only once had his calm, distant persona slipped. One night, as Scarface was answering the call of nature, I'd had a horrific nightmare, and I must have cried out in my sleep because he'd rushed in and gathered me into his arms. I woke up, thrashing to escape, but the warm, comforting scent of the forest surrounded me; reassuring and loving, softly spoken nonsense soothing me back to sleep as I held my rescuer against my cheek, happy that Leszek had forgiven my hateful words.

However, when I woke up in the morning, it was as if the night hadn't happened, Leszek's gaze lingering only a few seconds longer as he kissed my hand and left for work.

Even though my host left me frustrated and confused, I had to admit that his aide, Michal, made the time at the manor bearable. The regimented schedule had been his brainchild, and when presented with such an organised plan of action, I'd piled on the sarcasm as I asked if the bathroom breaks were just as detailed. With a smug smile, he had simply shrugged, offering to include them if I found it too taxing to make such an onerous decision.

Michal was a sadistic, micromanaging bastard, but his schedule brought an ordered peace to my disorganised life. As much as it pained me to admit that, it did leave me with time to absorb all the new discoveries I made during my lessons on magic.

'Sara, could you please go to the office? Veronica will be here shortly, and we both know she gets prickly when you're late.' The voice startling me belonged to Jarek, my new aide-de-camp, the term still making me laugh even as my feet moved, looking over my shoulder to mock scowl at him.

'If I'd known you'd spend your life sneaking around, I'd have left a bell inside your chest when I operated on you.' My response only made Jarek roll his eyes in that typical fashion all teenagers reserve for grown adults the world over as he followed me. I imagined seeing his tail wagging like a puppy to distract myself from the meeting with Veronica.

Training with the witch always left me wondering why she bothered teaching me. Yes, she was fascinated by my magic, but she also seemed to think it was beneath her to sully her hands with such a mundane activity. I also suspected the attitude had something to do with Leszek because, after the first icy introductions, the troublesome gangster never appeared before her again.

I should be grateful he arranged for me to have lessons, I thought, teeth clenching only slightly at the reminder of our argument. I took a deep breath to regain my composure, admitting that Leszek was only protecting me from the bastard that hurt Scarface and Jarek.

Fuck it! I will talk to him, even if it means acting like a cat in heat. He only had himself to blame after brushing me off so many times, even living in the city five days a week. Well, it wouldn't happen this time. The only thing I was sure about between us was the physical attraction, and stripped of other means, it was time to use it. Jealousy was a wonderful thing if used for the greater good, and after a month of polite conversation, it was time to take the gloves off.

It had taken me a month to decide that not everything was Leszek's fault. The frightening vision in the hospital and the attack in my apartment had dented my confidence, but thanks to Veronica's lessons and Scarface's guidance, I was prepared to take on the world. It was time for the Forest Lord to learn precisely who was living down the hall.

Within moments, I'd hit speed dial, and Nina's phone was ringing.

'Hey girlfriend, guess what?'

'Oh, is that my long lost best friend? The one living the high life deep in the forest? Are you finally ready to leave tall, dark, and yummy's bed and remind yourself what friends look like?' The sarcasm in Nina's voice didn't drip; it hit you in the face with a kipper, and I couldn't be happier. I needed her. Not just her. I needed my entire pack, but tonight, Nina, with her sharp tongue, brazen manner and drunken sailor's charm, would be the perfect companion.

'I love you, too. We're hitting the town tonight, and I can get into the VIP area of the Anchor.' I knew mentioning the VIP area would hook my friend, the gasp I heard giving away her interest, but Nina also knew me well.

'Why?' she asked warily.

'Because I want to check it out and see how they send so many clients to visit us, or maybe I'm feeling adventurous. Besides, we need to talk about what's going on, and I want to have that conversation face-to-face, so what do you say?'

Of course, she was going, and I got an earful for not inviting her earlier, but beneath the sharp tone was the hint of mischief that always appeared before our nights out.

'Ma'am, you can't. It's too dangerous. The Boss would never allow it.' Jarek looked at me with eyes widened in horror as if I'd just proposed cocking my leg next to Leszek's favourite tree.

'First, what did we agree? Call me ma'am again, and you'll clean Scarface's litter for a year. Second, I can and I will. You, however, won't say a word about it to your *Boss* because I am your *Boss,* not Mr I Won't Allow It. Is that clear, or do I need to compel you?'

Yup, I threatened to bespell him, and it was immensely satisfying. Apart from the fear of attack, my training was the only reason I'd put up with Leszek's bullshit for so long. Veronica might resent teaching me, but she was a powerful witch and a brilliant teacher whose patience was helping my skills to flourish. Thanks to her, I'd made tremendous progress in the past month.

I'd learned that to be a Soul Shepherd, one had to be a seer first, similar to how, in order to be a surgeon, you first needed to be a doctor, but with fewer drinking games. That explained the vision I received from the burns victim and my hunches, which I now knew was my subconscious catching glimpses of probable realities and influencing my decisions, aiding my success in complex and unpredictable situations. Once Veronica learned about it, she spent the entire week teaching me to visualise them consciously rather than relying on capricious hints.

'There are many seers. Why aren't there more women with skills like mine?' I asked one day, and she sighed, avoiding looking at me.

'Some legends say that the Soul Shepherd was Dola's gift for a god to calm their weary spirit and connect them with the source. Other books claim only the seer who brushes with death and sees spirits crossing the Veil many times develops the magic that allows them to guide souls to the afterlife. The honest answer is that we don't know, but each time the Soul Shepherd reveals their presence, sooner or later, they become tethered to the powerful spirit. I'm sorry, Sara.'

At some point, we discussed my abilities as a Soul Shepherd and how I could use them in my daily work. She was uncomfortable bringing up the subject, but her explanation gave meaning to another critical part of my life. I could see souls, especially those close to exiting this existence, and I could guide them towards the afterlife or elsewhere. On that matter, Veronica didn't offer any information, moving on to another aspect of my power: the ability to tether spirits to their mortal form as I did with Scarface.

'Your touch balances the physical and metaphysical aspects of the world, giving them harmony. You can help the spirit, but you can also imprison them in physical form.' With that ominous statement, she refused to elaborate further.

Maybe I can make zombies. I thought, chuckling slightly as I entered the office, closely followed by Veronica.

'Ah, good, at least you're here. When you see the Leshy, tell him to stop overdoing it. He should know that better than anyone.' She said, and I wished I knew what she meant.

'Tell him yourself. You know what he's doing better than I, as he's spent all this month avoiding me.' I said, realising too late to bite my tongue.

'Has he?' Veronica finally sat down, and I poured her a glass of water. 'Leszek is not as blind as I thought if he withdrew as soon as he brought home such a threat.'

'Threat? The only thing he's brought here is....Wait, do you mean me?' Veronica's look of irritation baffled me. How could seeing the future or pointing souls to the afterlife harm anyone, let alone Leszek, with his impressive magic?

'Were you not paying attention to your lessons at all, young lady? You are a Soul Shepherd, able to control and tie a spirit to its physical form. Can you imagine what happens to an immortal spirit if it is tied to the physical world when its body is destroyed? Do I need to spell it out for you?'

'Why would I do that? How? I have no bloody idea what I'm doing, and you think I could kill someone I care for?' I stopped as soon as the words escaped my lips, shocked to realise I meant them, and looked away, embarrassed at my outburst, but Veronica took advantage of my silence to drive her point home.

'Why? To kill him, of course, to free yourself from his attention. Your kind has been used to kill gods before. The Leshy is showing a lot of restraint regarding your arrangement. Sara, not all relationships between spirits and Soul Shepherds were voluntary and welcomed by the women. It is all conjecture and guesses as to their reasons for such an act. Only the Leshy might know, but I value my life too much to ask such a question.'

'Veronica, that's fucked up. I wouldn't hurt him. He knows that, right?' The pain I'd felt when I told Leszek I hated him was nothing compared to this feeling. *No surprise that after my outburst, he may think I'll try to kill him*. Guilt nearly overwhelmed me, but one thought kept it at bay. He hadn't killed me, choosing not to remove the threat to his existence. Instead, he protected and educated me in the magic that could destroy him. *Well, I'll take it as a sign.*

It's time I put my big girl panties on and apologise for my outburst properly, even if I have to flirt with every man in the Anchor to get his attention. It was an extreme solution, but only by using his rivalry with Nadolny could I overcome the cool detachment that was his way of avoiding conversation. It was a miracle he'd listened to my vision of the burn victim, but even then, I'd barely finished before he left for work. No, this was my only chance, and I would do whatever was needed.

Veronica studied me for several moments, then gestured for me to take her hand. 'Today, you'll be learning how to ward your mind from outside influence, not that anyone couldn't see what you're thinking from your expression, but at least this way, I'll be saved the lurid images.'

After two hours, she walked out of the office with a self-satisfied smile, hopefully at everything I'd learned and not that I now looked like I'd been ridden hard and put away wet. I'd been through some tough lessons in my life. The medical university was not a kind mistress, but even manual resuscitation paled into insignificance to having a witch rifle through my most embarrassing memories as I tried to eject her from my mind.

Shattered, I looked at the clock. I needed a shower to restore myself before my little adventure, but all I wanted was to collapse and sleep. Still, no pain, no gain, as they say, and if I desired Leszek's attention, I needed to show off in public.

For this visit, there would be nothing understated about my outfit. I'd picked out a formfitting, provocatively short skirt and a bra designed to defy gravity. A hesitant knock interrupted the last of my preparations, and after I gave permission, Jarek sidled inside, looking dapper but incredibly uncomfortable in a dark blue suit.

'I'm going with you, ma... Sara. I can't stop you, but I'm determined to keep you safe.' Even as Jarek's voice trembled, he still looked me in the eye to prove his sincerity.

'I would be delighted to be your escort for the evening.' I addressed him formally instead of asking how he intended to protect me. His boyish face blushed, but he stood taller and offered me his arm. However, before I accepted, I needed to clarify one thing.

'Jarek, I appreciate you wanting to keep me safe, but tonight's about having fun and living a little. We'll be meeting my friend there, and it will look weird if you're acting like a bodyguard, so just have fun, kiddo, and everyone will enjoy themselves.' With that said, I took my escort's arm, and we headed out.

Chapter Twenty-One

Nina was already waiting when we arrived. Her cropped dark hair, faux leather trousers, a Metallica tank top and metal studded jacket made her stand out from the crowd, especially as she was pacing outside the Anchor, which was as busy as every other Saturday evening. The queue stretched around the corner as bouncers filtered through those wishing to gain entry, but at least there was no private party this time.

'Sara! What on earth made you choose this shithole for a night out? It's packed to the brim, and... Are you hoping to get closer to our patients before they start bleeding and cursing?' She said, giving me a hug before checking out Jarek. 'Family?'

'Nope. Meet Jarek, the big bad wolf, come to gobble you up.' I answered. 'He's my bodyguard.' Nina snorted before she could contain herself. I didn't blame her; he looked like a country cousin visiting his cosmopolitan relative in the big city, but she gave him another look when she realised I wasn't joking.

'Come on, Biker Butch, let's go,' I said, heading for the bouncer.

'That's good coming from Slutty Barbie,' Nina muttered as she grabbed my arm.

'It's full.' The bouncer's scowl expressed his thoughts about us jumping the queue, but I wasn't so easily intimidated.

'That may be true, but if you tell Zbyszek that Sara is here, space will miraculously become available.' The nonchalant manner in which I used Nadolny's first name surprised the muscled guardian, but I added a little encouragement to help things along, infusing my voice with magic and compelling him to listen. 'Leszek is always grateful to those that help his Lady.'

After blinking a few times, the bouncer disappeared inside, only to reappear earlier than expected to remove the symbolic rope and let us in, much to the crowd's frustration.

We strolled down the short corridor to the entrance to the dancefloor, but before I could open it, Nina pulled me to one side, hissing in my ear.

'Care to tell me why we were treated as VIPs back there? Sara, what have you gotten involved in?'

The worry in her voice warmed my heart, and I smiled, but Jarek interrupted, growling under his voice as he whispered, 'I don't like it here.'

'I won't keep you in the dark much longer, but let's grab a drink first,' I told her before turning to Jarek. 'You can go home. I told you not to spoil my fun.'

My companions looked at me like two surprised owls, then both muttered their apologies and followed me to the bar. I tried to get the bartender's attention, nearly punching the person who grabbed my elbow, expecting someone's overly amorous advances. When I turned, I had to bite back the curse when I recognised the doorman from my last visit.

'Boss wants to see you, Missy,' he shouted, trying to make himself heard over the music, snapping his fingers at a passing waiter before yelling again. 'Get the alcove ready and escort the Lady's friends there. Make sure they are well looked after, Boss's treat.' The man nodded, approaching Nina, all smiles and hands, to direct her to the VIP corner, but my friend held him back with a straight-armed push to the chest.

'I'm not leaving her alone,' she said, with Jarek standing at her shoulder, nodding fiercely in agreement.

'Just go. I will join you shortly. Trust me, I am safe here.' I said, then shook my head when she stepped forward to argue. 'Please.'

She wasn't happy, but she complied, and when Jarek tried to protest, she simply grabbed him by the collar. 'Heel boy, I'll teach you to sit.' I didn't know if I should laugh or cry. Nina just dominated a werewolf, and he obeyed.

I was escorted by the elbow like an honoured guest or a respected prisoner; I was unsure which, but it didn't take more than a moment to arrive at Nadolny's VVIP alcove. The man himself relaxing with two other guests with several scantily clad women draped over them.

'Sara, what a pleasure to see you again, but alone? Leszek won't be pleased to have missed you.'

'Possibly, but as he is busy with other issues, his Lady must find entertainment in an establishment where she is completely safe but can still find a little excitement, don't you think?' I asked as brazenly as I could. We were playing the game, and I needed to ensure his companions considered me neither prize nor prey.

'Your glowing endorsement gladdens my heart, but please ensure your entertainment remains safe for everyone, not just yourself. After all, Leszek made his views clear the last time you were here.' It was both permission and warning in one. This man was clever, and I must admit, it impressed me.

'Should I ask you to dance with me? You seem to know his desires better than I.' Unable to hold back the sarcasm, I almost forgot who I was talking to, but thankfully, Nadolny saw the funny side.

'Maybe you should; I might even say yes.' Waving me away, he continued. 'Have fun, Sara. I regret we didn't meet earlier. It would have been such a pleasure to tame you,' but his eyes shone with merriment despite the vague threat.

'Oh, I don't know. Many have tried, and each cried out, "Yes, Mistress," by the time I was finished.' *What the fuck am I saying?* I thought the second those words left my mouth, but it was too late. My relief as Nadolny's booming laughter overrode the music left me shaking, and he waved his hand again. 'Go on, Sara, just don't frighten my innocent lambs with your fun. I can do without explaining to your man how his woman got into trouble.'

I nodded, smiling shakily, and returned to my friends, only to be buried under an avalanche of questions from Nina. Jarek initially tried to stop me when he realised how much I was revealing, but Nina deserved the truth. I trusted her with my life and needed to share my new reality. *If she reacts badly to what I am and rejects me, at least I have the means to make her forget.*

I told her everything, with Jarek paling at the description of his surgery, trying his best to stop me, but I ignored his pleas, concentrating on my friend's reaction and gnawing at my bottom lip as her frown grew, worried she'd storm off at the ridiculous story.

I nearly wept when she broke her silence, hope flaring when she stayed in her seat. 'So, you are a seer and this Shepherd thing, and he's a werewolf?' Nina thrust a thumb in Jarek's direction without taking her eyes off me. 'And everything started when we had some vampire in the ER with a dagger in his heart? Which led to you getting involved with the mafia because your boyfriend is the head of some magical criminal syndicate, not to mention an immortal

Guardian thingamabob?' My friend's voice had a worrying edge of panic, but I nodded, hoping I hadn't made a big mistake, even as she started laughing hysterically.

'Fuck Sara, crap on a cracker, this is nuts, but you know what? It makes sense. So many things make sense now.'

'I'm sorry. I'm not supposed to tell you, but it's all true and as crazy as it sounds. See that blonde guy? He will trip in a second, knocking over the poser in the leather jacket. He'll try to stop himself and end up grabbing the arse of the girl in the green dress. She'll slap him, and then, after explaining, they'll both apologise and go home together.' As I spoke, the blonde tripped, and everything happened exactly as I'd predicted. Nina's face grew serious.

'OK, I believe you, but what will you do? Now you have this new magic and all the rest?'

'Recognise, adapt, overcome.' I answered with a mischievous smile.

'Don't you dare to use the emergency mantra with me, I'm serious.' She snapped, and I shrugged.

'What can I do? I was born like this, but until I met Leszek, I was incomplete, untrained, and, to be frank, miserable. For years, I questioned my sanity, worried that you'd have to lock me up for my own good. Now though? I've never felt more alive, and... I'm so curious about all of this.'

'Sara, you should have told me... us, we've been through so much together. I don't know what pisses me off more, that you didn't trust me or that you dragged me to this shithole for the big reveal.'

'I'm sorry, I wanted to, but I really thought I was losing my mind. Then, when I found out the truth, I had to relearn everything. Forgive me? I brought you here because where else can we get drunk watching grown men making fools of themselves?' With a smile, I gestured for the waiter and ordered several rounds of shots to get the party started.

With the shots downed, we hit the dancefloor. I loved to dance. I didn't get out as much as I'd like these days, but I loved it, and tonight, I would dance away all my frustration. It felt so liberating to twirl and gyrate my body, even if the music wasn't exactly to my liking, but who cared? Nina was here, and we danced like teenagers. Jarek insisted on staying sober, watching with wide eyes. A few men approached, and we joined them for a song or two, but they disappeared before we could talk, gently guided away by a bouncer. Once or twice, I caught Nadolny watching, and he smiled with no hint of shame.

It was way past midnight when the DJ slowed the beat, encouraging the dancers to form couples, rubbing their bodies against each other, seduction the primary goal. Nina excused herself, returning to our table while I swayed to the entrancing melody.

'I believe we discussed a dance.' Nadolny's voice woke me from the pleasant daze I'd fallen into, his hands steadying me as I startled. With a firm but chaste grip, he turned me around till I looked up into his smiling eyes, manoeuvring me into a classic waltz as I lost myself in the kindness that shone through them, this older but incredibly vital male leading me around the dancefloor as if no one else existed.

I knew there would be gossip. I felt eyes on me, their scrutiny, the judgement. All evening, I'd been watched, and I was sure it was one of Leszek's bodyguards observing me from the shadows. Now, lost in the moment, I felt that judgement darken into genuine anger, and my senses leapt into high alert.

Nadolny noticed the stiffening of my body, the alarm in my eyes, and looked to one side, nodding once before turning back and leaning in to talk. 'Focus on me, Sara; I wouldn't want to spoil such a wonderful moment by stumbling.'

This man was dangerous to a woman's heart. I'd seen him signal to his men, but to then take a moment to distract me from my fear. I smiled and gave him a gracious nod. 'Thank you for looking after us tonight. I've had a lovely time.'

'Whatever do you mean? I had nothing to do with your... fun,' He said with a mischievous smile, and I rolled my eyes.

'Zbyszek, really. The private table, a waiter, an endless stream of alcohol and snacks and men that treated me like a china doll, not one showing a moment's inappropriate behaviour?' My laugh was indulgent, but my look was reproachful.

'I'm simply a good host, but is there anything else I can do for you? Or are some pleasures reserved for one man only?' He said, but my witty retort remained unsaid as pain erupted inside my head.

The pain worsened as magic smothered my mind, and breathing became so difficult that my legs suddenly failed. In a blind panic, I tried to find the source of the attack, explosions of colour flashing across my vision.

'Sara?' Nadolny's worried voice sounded through the haze of pain. 'Sara, what is wrong?'

'Spell, magic.' That I managed to speak surprised me, but it encouraged me to try again. 'Someone is casting... find them.' I choked on my words, coughing up blood mixed with salty water onto my hand, crumpling to the ground as the gangster tried to shield my body.

Nadolny's eyes widened in fear when he noticed the blood, while all my concentration was focused on forcing air into my lungs past the immense pressure crushing my head and chest, lips moving in a wordless mantra to relieve the pain.

I was scooped up with surprising gentleness, Nadolny carrying me to his alcove. I barely registered his curt orders, snapped out to those surrounding us until we were alone, with Nina staring into my eyes, fingers on my pulse.

'Honey, what is going on? Talk to me, please.' Nina's pale face was streaked with tears as she searched for my vitals with professional efficiency.

I tried to answer, but, unable to breathe, my words remained trapped inside. The metallic taste of blood and darkening vision told me I was slowly dying, crushed by an ocean's worth of pressure on dry land.

Jarek's blurry face swam before me, the sound of sniffing strangely loud over the rushing in my ears. 'She stinks of magic. We need the Boss here now. He'll know what to do.'

The last dim thought as I heard that, my consciousness slipping away, was of Leszek. Well, I wanted his attention....

Pain, blinding with its intensity, dragged me back to consciousness. The pressure around my body receded, allowing the tiniest whisper of breath into my lungs before increasing again, and once more, I fainted. Each time my consciousness resurfaced, I wished to black out again. I wasn't simply being murdered; this was a message, my death used to punish more than just myself, meant to cause the maximum amount of mental and physical pain.

The desperation in Nina's voice, as she used every trick she knew to force breath into my lungs, wrung tears from my eyes. Even through the pain, I could sense the magic being used and knew her efforts were futile.

As soon as I thought that, anger burned through the pain, Nina's actions reminding me I was not the one to give up, to lose hope, and I grasped onto this determination, fighting to live, dragging air through my lips, using my fledgling magic to tie my soul to its dying flesh.

You can do it, Sara, in and out. The air goes in and out. I repeated this like a mantra while a sweet, elusive voice deep inside me whispered, telling me my torment would end if I stopped fighting. *What a way to die, embraced by a gangster in a club with a shady reputation*, I thought, my mind still making jokes till the end. Then something changed, shifted… I was suddenly looking down at my body, listening to Nina's thoughts as she battled to save me.

A loud commotion distracted my friend, and my consciousness crashed back into its own tormented flesh. Before I could register what was happening, my limp form was moving; a different pressure briefly crushing my ribs, eclipsing the magical attack… then loosening, allowing blessed, a whiff of life-sustaining air into my lungs, the scent of oak and elder making me smile as I forced myself to speak.

'Hey, arsehole.' My smile faltered and dropped as the pain returned, but nothing mattered now. Leszek was here; my forest-scented cavalry had come to save the day.

Worry creased his forehead as Leszek stroked my cheek. 'I'm here, darling. Everything will be fine. You are safe now. Just trust me and breathe, my Firefly.' Despite the absurdity of the words, I still found myself obeying, tears falling from my eyes.

He pressed my head to his chest, murmuring something over and over until the pressure disappeared and my chest dragged in its first lungful in what seemed like hours. I sobbed in relief, but as one pain disappeared, another took its place, an agonising burn tearing through my lower back, and I buried my scream in Leszek's firm chest as he murmured, stroking my back, his magic surrounding me with its soothing touch.

'Can you tell me where it hurts, Sara? I can sense someone's touch, but unless you tell me where it is, I can't remove the spell's anchor.' Leszek placed a finger under my chin, making me look up when I shook my head. 'Come now, sweetling, you can do it.'

'My back, it's burning. Oh, fuck, it hurts.' I bit my lip as I finished and swore I would punch whoever did this.

'Nina, check her back,' Leszek said, and I felt my friend open the zip with brusque efficiency, hands running over my spine till they stilled just below my shoulder blades.

'There's something here. The skin is raised like a welt or a burn scar,' she said, anger roughening her voice, and I remembered a boisterous and overly friendly woman slapping me there earlier that evening.

Leszek turned me around gently. His hands slid over the mark, and I heard him suck in a breath, shocked by whatever he found.

'No surprise it is hurting. This is Svarog's rune, born of fire. I'm sorry, Firefly, but it will hurt even more as I remove it.' He said it in the tone that doctors everywhere recognise, and I chewed my lip, expecting the worst.

'Fine, you can kiss it better later,' I said as his touch brought relief and, with it, my sassiness returned, fuelled by alcohol and adrenaline. I was not a child, I was not weak, and I survived despite such frightening circumstances. The pain was still there, but I could breathe and think again, and instantly I turned to Nina, who stood back, watching the scene wide-eyed and shaking.

'Are you alright? I'm sorry for getting you mixed up in all this,' I said, but she only shrugged, carefully brushing a strand of hair from my forehead. When I hissed, sweat beaded on my skin under Leszek's touch. We both ignored the tremor in her fingers and my occasional curses while he kept working on my back.

'I am, and don't you dare to apologise. It was not your fault, but I'm telling you now, whoever did this will get a kick in the balls for hurting my friend. Is this the magic you told me about?' She asked.

'Do you know who did it? I locked down the club as soon as you collapsed. No one can escape while my men secure the building. Just give me a name or description, and I will ensure this person never bothers you again,' Nadolny asked, and I heard Leszek huff in annoyance before replying for me.

'This person is familiar with ancient runes, and they are a master of the Dark Arcana. Your staff wouldn't even see them if they hid. No, open the doors; your patrons' fear is making me uncomfortable, and neither of us wants the publicity.' I felt Leszek's arms tighten as he spoke, pressing my back harder to his chest.

When I felt a shudder run through his body, it dawned on me just how perilous the situation had been, my mind finally willing to face the issue now that the danger had passed. I should have felt embarrassed clinging to Leszek, but it felt like I belonged there, and he showed no inclination to release his hold.

'Thank you,' I said, the word feeling inadequate, so I turned my face toward him to express my sincerity. Words died in my throat as I saw his expression, barely restrained fury raging behind his eyes, his face an inhuman mask. I would have jumped off his lap and fled till I collapsed if not for his hand slowly stroking the small of my back.

'We are going home,' He said, and I could almost hear the grinding of teeth as he spoke, but the change as he turned to Nadolny worried me. 'I'm in your debt. Your timely actions saved my Lady's life; thank you.'

Nadolny shook his head, refusing, knowing the weight of those words. 'I cannot accept your debt. Sara came to harm under my protection. However, I would ask the elder races not to use my premises until this matter is dealt with. The danger to my staff and patrons is too great. I am sorry.'

Leszek closed his eyes, taking a deep, calming breath before answering. 'So be it. I will inform my people as soon as I return home.'

All I'd wanted was a bit of jealousy that would break through his icy demeanour enough for us to talk. I'd made a mistake, putting myself in harm's way, underestimating Leszek's enemy, and now he'd been forced to save my life, then rein back his anger in front of his rivals. It made me feel like an unruly child acting out for attention, and the worst part? It was true. I'd intended to use Leszek's anger but hadn't envisaged fighting for my life. I placed a hand on the floor to stand up, but my saviour tightened his grip.

'No, Sara. No discussion or struggling; we are going home,' he said, standing up effortlessly, holding me against his chest, even as I tried to escape.

'Wait, I can't leave like this. What about Nina and Jarek...?' I tried to argue, but I swear he growled as he ignored me.

Adam appeared at our side as we set off, and Leszek slowed. 'Adam, ensure Nina is safe. She's your responsibility. Jarek? Report to your Alpha, inform him about what happened, and tell him to prepare for a fight, then make yourself scarce. I don't want to see you right now.' The poor werewolf crumbled at the censure in Leszek's voice, shame burning over his cheeks as he bowed.

I wished I could have apologised to Jarek, but we were moving before I could take a breath.

When we got to the car, my feet were lowered gently to the ground as Leszek opened the door, guiding my weak body into the vehicle and reaching across to buckle my seatbelt. I thought he would retreat at that point. Instead, leaning his head against my shoulder, he stood there, lips pressed against the skin, until, feeling unsettled, I reached up to stroke his beard.

'I know you're angry, but we need to talk. I...' He pressed a finger against my lips, gently silencing me.

‘Sara, please, we’ll talk at home.’ The polite tone defeated my need to talk, and we rode back to the manor without speaking.

Chapter Twenty-Two

I understood why Leszek needed this time, but the tension building between us fed the self-pity rising within me, swiftly followed by a growing frustration at being unable to express my feelings. When we stopped in the driveway, I was fuming, promising myself I would finally clear the air. After all, if he'd talked to me like a civilised person, I wouldn't have stooped to such dirty tricks.

I scrambled out of the car before it came to a halt and marched unsteadily to the house.

'Sara, wait!' Leszek's voice angered me further. Yet another order? *Who does he think he is?* I flipped him off, continued inside, slamming the door in his face, and headed to the bedroom.

I increased my pace at the sound of the door slamming again, but it didn't matter, as the infuriating man was already beside me.

'I said wait. For once, could you do what I asked?' Leszek turned, trapping me within the cage of his muscled arms.

'Asked? When have you ever asked for anything? Even now, it's orders, commands you expect to be followed. What next? Roll over for a belly rub like a good little pet? Why do you want me to wait? Why do you care? You left me in this empty house with more questions than answers, then you refused to listen when I asked to talk, and now I have to wait? This is all your fault,' I said, jamming my finger against his chest before wiping away the tears pouring over my cheeks. He didn't stop me. He didn't contradict me, his sorrowful green eyes watching me come apart.

'I have been trying to talk to you for ages, but you, master of avoiding awkward conversations, did everything to show me how much you wanted to stay away from me. I get it; I do, but I never wanted to fucking kill you, alright. You thought you were getting a useful skill, a little future mojo. Turns out I'm nothing but trouble, but do you really hate me so much you can't even sleep under the same roof? Why did you kiss me, make me care if what I am repulses you? Why do I care at all, you infuriating bastard?' By now, I was crying so hard that my vision was blurry, and I couldn't even push the muscle-bound oaf away.

'I don't hate you, my Firefly. I never have. My leaving wasn't a choice but a necessity. Please understand that I'm trying to keep you safe while you're still untrained and vulnerable. I'm trying to give you a choice. Your talent, it's...' The tenderness he displayed wiping away my tears nearly undid me, but I couldn't stop now and needed everything in the open, so I interrupted, determined to continue.

'Yes, I know, I'm a threat to your existence. Veronica explained everything, but guess what, handsome? I can't just hide, waiting for the world to pass me by like a damsel in distress while you ignore me. I know I pushed myself on you, but you should have left me back at my apartment if you didn't want me. I thought we had something, a... a spark. Talk about mixed signals. I am a big girl who can admit to her mistakes, but this world you live in is new to me, and I need someone I can trust. Can't we... can't we at least be friends?'

The confusion on Leszek's face wasn't reassuring, especially when he shook his head, then cupped my cheeks, tilting my face to look at him.

'What are you saying? What friends? I stayed away because you told me I destroyed your life and didn't want to see me again. Do you even know how hard that was? To stay away? It was so difficult that I kept inventing reasons to see you and make you smile. Damn it, woman! I burn for you! I crave your touch, the scent of your hair. I almost crashed the car rushing to your side when Nadolny called, telling me you were dying on the dancefloor. I'm not angry because you wanted to have fun, but because you were hurt and I wasn't there to protect you.' His fist hammered the wall above my head.

'Sara, I don't have a choice, but you do. I want you to live your life, not grow bitter tethered to the god you hate.'

'I don't hate you, I... I want to see you, ok? I like you.'

'But in your apartment, you said...'

'I was hurt and scared. My cat almost died, my life, my privacy was destroyed, and you were behaving like such a man, taking charge and telling me what to do when all I needed was a hug. I lashed out because I needed to release all my anger, my fear and knew you would never hurt me. Are you telling me that was why you avoided me, treating me like a painful spot on your arse? Fuck! How can someone so intelligent be so stupid?'

Leszek's lips crashed into mine, taking my breath away. The kiss was deep and possessive, and I couldn't help responding, matching his hunger, my hands grasping his lapels, pulling him closer. That he'd denied his passion for me broke through the last of my defences, and I opened my mouth for his questing tongue. When his hands stroked down my back, fingernails lightly scratching the skin, I moaned in desire, gasping as he lifted me up. Revelling in the strength of his body, I moulded myself to the firm, muscled torso.

'Tell me to stop,' his voice, rough and dangerous, melted every bone in my spine, his teeth scoring the flesh of my neck. 'Please, tell me to stop, or I'll take you here on the stairs. I'm losing myself to you. Your smile, your magic, your stubbornness when you face adversity. My fierce little warrior, you attract me like a moth to the flame, and I can't stop… I won't stop unless you tell me to.' His body was shaking. Leszek tried to pull away. Instead, his hand slid to my back, embracing me. Pressing my body hard into his chest while trailing his lips over the hollow of my neck. The earthy scent of the forest overpowered the air and I inhaled deeply, exposing my neck.

'Never,' I breathed when he nipped at my skin. The desperation in his voice told me exactly what I wanted. 'I won't stop you. I don't want to. I want you, Leshy. So take me here, in the bedroom or in your office. I don't care as long as I can feel your touch.'

'Fuck, Sara, you don't know what you're asking for. I'm not like other men. If I make you mine, you will be mine forever, and I'll never let you go.' The warning, the certainty, burned itself into my soul, and I held him tight, leaning in to kiss his neck as I spoke.

'You can't scare me away. I made up my mind; I need you, all strings attached, and nothing will change that.'

His response made me scream as he surged forward, crushing me in his embrace, the world blurring as we moved. I hadn't even drawn breath to curse as the bedroom appeared, my body falling backwards when the vicious brute threw me onto the bed, his predatory eyes hypnotic as he stalked toward me, hand reaching for my throat.

I felt Leszek's fingers slide across my neck, sharp nails grazing the skin, lightning coursing through my body, but nothing could make me look away from his burning gaze, even as his grip tightened to the edge of pain.

'Why, Sara, why aren't you cowering in fear? I am a god, little Firefly, an unfeeling immortal, able to snuff out your existence with a thought. I dispense death and suffering, the antithesis of everything you are.'

He held my throat, and despite his tightening grip, I refused to look away, smirking at his pathetic attempt to frighten me, the fire in his eyes raging with desire. No anger or hate could live within that intensity, and I answered from the depths of my soul.

'Do it. If you think I could harm you, do it. I'm not afraid of you. Are you looking for an excuse to reject me? Fine. I won't force you to fuck me, so just say it, and I will walk away. I will find another man to scratch this itch, to take what should be yours, if you...' I said, pushing him away, only to gasp when Leszek grabbed the front of my dress, ripping it apart.

'Reject you? You are mine, little seer. You may not be afraid, but I am. I lived for millennia, alone, in darkness, content and unafraid, but now... now I fear to live a single day without the light of your soul.' Grasping the tattered remnants of my dress, he pulled me forward, claiming my lips in a passionate kiss.

My moan as his tongue invaded my mouth made Leszek shiver, my teeth nipping and goading him into action, but even now, unrestrained, my lover didn't hurt me, his raw ardour fuelling my need.

'Such a tease. You couldn't even bruise my skin with them.' He said, pulling away, and I couldn't help but glance at his sharp teeth. His lips returned to my lips, kissing along my jaw and down my neck, pausing over the rapid pulse, nipping it lightly, worshipping my skin, leaving a warmth that tingled with magic.

Something was bubbling beneath the surface, calling to me. Something powerful, enticing, and magical. Acting on instinct, I slid my hand over Leszek's chest, seeking and coaxing it forward.

Leszek groaned, his eyes burning with emerald fire, and I wasn't sure who was trembling more, our craving driving us beyond endurance.

When his mouth captured my nipple, I cried out in pleasure, arching my body, moaning as my fingers traced over the dark lines that appeared on his body, swirling and burning beneath my touch.

'Again, Sara, bring it back again. Let me feel the power they took from me,' Leszek murmured. Pain and longing coarsened his voice, but oh god, his touch, so exquisite and masterful, drove me wild, and I obeyed, relying on instincts I didn't understand, coaxing the patterns on his skin to life, drawing forth more as I caressed his body, not knowing when he'd removed his shirt or how.

'What is it, this feeling, the patterns?' I asked, unable to ignore the strange phenomenon before another moan took my breath away as his fingers tore away my underwear.

'My magic, my power. Given up to save my kind from humans, the true Guardian of the Forest. I don't know what you did, but where it leads, I will follow.' This possessive, passionate, yet tender kiss left me begging for more, even as Leszek resumed his slow, delicious journey down my body until he lavished his full attention between my thighs.

As his soft beard brushed over my skin, I spread my legs further, hands reaching down, fingers tangling in the dark auburn hair that had fascinated me since I'd first seen it, and taking firm hold, I moaned softly at the pleasure he offered.

'I want to taste you.' He murmured, breath whispering over my naked flesh, as he leaned back, lifted my foot, and trailed his lips from my toes back toward where he'd started while I melted from the pleasure.

'You are overdressed.' I said, looking down, feeling the urge to see him naked, with my leg draped over his shoulder. Leszek laughed, reaching for his belt, before stepping out of his trousers, and a moment later, he was completely naked. He was a work of art, and I couldn't get enough of his chiselled features and glorious muscles, my gaze sliding over his hairy chest down the narrowing line until it disappeared, hidden by my body.

'Oh my god,' I croaked, mouth as dry as any desert as I strained to look lower. His magic, the scent of oak and elder, filled the room, commanding my submission, but I wasn't going down without a fight.

'Yes, your god, my Lady, and I find your impatience very flattering.' He teased, standing slowly. I let my foot trail over his chest slowly before it fell to the bed, and I propped myself onto my elbows.

'I want to see all of you.'

'But of course, how could I deny you?' He said without even trying to hide his smirk. Then he straightened up, exposing himself to me.

My mouth watered. I had seen my share of cocks, big, small, curvy, and damaged; the downside to my work, but Leszek's was simply beautiful... and massive. I gulped loudly.

'I want to taste you, too. Please let me...' My breathy plea goaded him to action.

'Not yet, sweet Lady. I want to lose myself in your pleasure.' My surprised squeak as Leszek grabbed my ankles and pulled me to the end of the bed was answered by the most delicious evil chuckle before his mouth descended between my thighs, the tickling caress of his beard brushing between my folds. I shuddered with pleasure and felt the vibration of my lover's laughter.

'You like my beard, do you? How else can I add to your pleasure?' he asked, repeating the move and sliding a finger against my entrance, making me buck, trying to push it inside, but Leszek held me down, refusing to allow it, and I felt his tongue trail through my parted lips. I moaned and tilted my hips, unable to do anything but wanting, needing more. No longer fighting for control,

I submitted to this delicious debauchery. His tongue circled my clit before he gently kissed it, surrounding the sensitive nub and lightly sucking on it, and I couldn't control my body any longer, panting and thrashing out of control, praying for release.

'My name, sweet lover, scream my name so the entire world knows you belong to the Leshy. Let my name be on your lips as your world dissolves into bliss, Sara.' His words urged me on, and a vision of this magnificent god, antlers alight with emerald fire, muscled body glistening, exploded in my mind as I screamed his name. Waves of pleasure engulfed me, washing away everything except my Leshy, mesmeric magic swirling around him, man and beast united into one glorious whole and with a single whispered 'Leshy,' I wished the vision to be real.

Breathless, with the waves of my orgasm receding, I opened my eyes, blinking at the sight before me, wondering if I was still lost in joy. Leszek was glowing. Confusion overtook my thoughts as my lover moved, standing up, still gleaming, and brushed the tip of his cock against my wet opening. We weren't done, even if I wasn't sure I could survive another orgasm like the last, but after that much ecstasy, I was willing to try.

'Ohh, is it your turn, my lover?' I moaned, rocking my hips.

'I'm sorry, Sara, but I didn't make you scream loud enough, and I'm a man who delivers on a promise.' He said, a wicked, masculine smile on his lips as he slowly pushed inside me. I didn't know whether to laugh at his cockiness or admire his control. Instead, I relaxed, shivering with anticipation. Leszek took his time, possessing my body completely, wiping away coherent thought. I threw back my head, grasping futilely at the sheets, feeling deliciously and completely filled.

'Look at me, Firefly. I want to see your eyes when I ravage you.' Leszek's command, more growl than speech, was issued through clenched teeth. I looked at him, this marvel of a man whose contours shimmered and changed before my eyes. His body became bigger, bulkier, and wilder than I ever thought possible, growing antlers before my eyes. I was being fucked by a man, no, a god, with golden fireflies dancing within his extraordinary crown, but nothing mattered except for him buried inside me.

The urge to whimper made me bite my lip, and as I focused on Leszek's face, the memory of countless dreams emerged. 'Leshy… I dreamt of this moment.'

'Because you are my destiny, little seer. You were and will always be mine.' The finality and absolute certainty in the statement felt irrevocable, and I felt compelled to answer.

'Yes, Leshy. I am yours.' Desire and joy danced in his eyes as he slowly withdrew, poised inside my entrance. With a single push, he drove forward, the exquisite torment driving me wild, and I rocked my hips, determined to take everything he had, matching his passion with my own. Each movement made my muscles tighten, increasing the pressure building inside me.

'Oh god, yes. Fuck me, Leshy, yes!' I cried out, craving his wildness. His eyes changed, burning with the emerald flames of his power, as he gripped my hips with bruising force.

'Until you beg me to stop, Sara!' Leszek snarled, and all hell broke loose. His shaft relentlessly drove into me as I screamed his name over and over, falling apart beneath him.

When he leaned down, teeth grazing my engorged nipple, I grasped his antlers, now solid in my hands, magic so thick I could taste it, my skin too tight, unable to contain my spirit as my climax surged, devastating and total, triggering my lover's passion, Leszek roaring as he came, exploding inside my welcoming body.

'Mine to love,' The words, half heard as I caught my breath, warmed a place in my heart I didn't know was cold. When I opened my eyes, watching this beautiful man as he held himself above me, careful not to crush me with his body, he looked at me as if waiting for my answer, and my heart lurched in response. Leszek was asking for consent to love me.

I didn't hesitate, answering with a single word. 'Always.'

His to love. Just thinking that left me smiling and reaching up to stroke his bearded cheek, using the soft bristles to pull him down for a tender kiss, wanting more than the physical connection of our bodies.

'Did I scream loud enough for my horned god?' I asked, trailing my hand through the hair on his chest, enjoying his shiver of pleasure.

'Sara, it wasn't supposed to be like that... I didn't hurt or scare you, did I? My primal form... was lost to me when they created the Nether.' He said, and I marvelled at how such a powerful man could sound so unsure.

'When we met, the very first time. You looked at me like I was a cockroach, but I saw you, eldritch god, antlers and all. I might not know what I saw, but it was beautiful. You were beautiful, and I'm glad I could return it to you. I have no idea how, but wow it, no, you were amazing. Besides, your antlers are handy. I can guide you like my own naughty reindeer.' I said, and his body shook with laughter. Tentatively, I reached out and stroked his cheek again. Laughing like this, he no longer looked like a heartless Crime Lord, more like a man who'd found peace.

'It wasn't my most stellar moment,' He said, and I shook my head.

'You silly man. Leshy, it was perfect, and... I'm yours to love.' I wanted to reaffirm my feelings in the cold light of day because we both needed to know it wasn't just a moment of passion. His lips were on mine the moment I finished, and the shaft that had softened inside me hardened again.

Before I knew it, we'd moved, and I was sitting astride Leszek's lap, mewling as the movement ignited my desire, my personal god of mischief flashing a radiant smile and slapping my arse.

'You are mine, Sara and I will always be yours. Now show me how well you can ride your naughty reindeer.'

'Oh really, you want your poor, tired woman to do all the work?' I said, rocking my hips and squeezing my muscles.

Leszek's groan was all the encouragement I needed, and leaning forward, I brushed my nipples over the velvety fur covering his impressive chest as I increased the pace. 'What else can you do?' I asked, teasing as I kissed my lover's ear. 'Can you change into a cat?' The amount of body hair beneath my fingertips gave me so many ideas.

'No, not a cat... a wolf... and a bear. Sara, please.' Leszek moaned, grasping my hips when I paused, the tip of his cock held in my entrance. I was trembling, my body yearning to be full, but I wanted to tease him a moment longer.

'Oh, we will have a lot of fun with that. Do you change completely or partially like now?' It was strangely hot to interrogate this powerful man whilst teasing him with my body and looking at Leszek's expression; he was enjoying the role reversal, too.

'Just part... stop teasing me, woman.'

'Hmm, what part? I want more fur. Fuck, I love this.' Shuddering, I couldn't help sliding down his shaft, savouring the slow friction, my nipples still brushing over his chest, sending wicked sparks along my spine. I could feel my climax building with luscious languor, but I wanted to keep questioning him, seeing my man so beautifully undone and at the end of his tether.

'Fur, teeth, anything and everything for you, Sara.' He hissed, bucking under me, the sudden movement breaking my focus, crashing through my body in a powerful wave. I couldn't move any more, my inner walls contracting, milking his shaft as he thrashed under me. His climax hit me, driving my own wave of release, and I collapsed against his chest, too far gone to do anything except drift on the clouds of pleasure while his arms held me tight.

'I can't lose you, Sara. You are my miracle.' I heard him whisper, gently stroking my back as I relaxed into his warm embrace.

Leszek fumbled with the covers, his struggles dislodging his manhood, and a wave of fluid followed, soaking the bed. 'How much did you pump into me?' I murmured in disbelief, and he chuckled, pulling the covers over us.

'All of my longing for you, sweet Firefly. Sleep, darling, you need it. We will worry about the bed tomorrow,' he said with a deep, contented sigh, and I felt my eyes close, mind drifting away in the safety of his arms.

Chapter Twenty-Three

I couldn't tell how long I'd been staring at the ceiling, but with Sara nestled beneath my arm, her head lying on my chest, I wouldn't be moving anytime soon, so using the time to centre myself, my thoughts turned to the unexpected effects of making love with the beautiful seer I held against my heart.

Somehow, Sara had accomplished the impossible, giving me access to the portion of my godhood tied into the Nether's creation and maintenance. Disbelief threatened to overwhelm me when I pondered how she did it. I understood now why Soul Shepherds were so sought after and tethered to the god that found them, willingly or not. I didn't ask for it, and I never would, even if I'd believed it was possible, but Sara's touch led me to the source. It was clearly an instinctive act, and the love that shone within her eyes eased the pressure squeezing my ribs. *She wanted this.* The reminiscence made me smile, washing away the doubts but not my worries.

I didn't like that I couldn't explain the experience. *Was it because we made love?* Love, because I could not call this unearthly experience fucking. *It was love, but did she free the stag because I claimed her or was physical contact enough?* Despite my resistance, I couldn't help it, and she accepted my claim, not just with words, but with her heart. I hadn't planned it; Sara was mortal, and when my resolve crumbled, I begged her to send me away. Now, we were tied by magic older than time, and I had to find a way of keeping her with me forever. *What if she refuses?* The errant thought whispered that my stubborn woman would reject any such gift. Even worse was the worry that someone more powerful than me would try to take her away and force her to use her magic.

The vital energy coursing through my veins, rejuvenating me with every heartbeat, was sweeter than any drug. I worried how I'd feel when it disappeared because this incredible moment couldn't possibly last. It was the hope that undid me. As I looked down, brushing the tousled hair from Sara's face, I studied the living tattoos on my body, their pulse not following the beat of my heart but the woman's I held close. My stubborn little minx who was overjoyed that I now had antlers and was fascinated that I could transform into a wolf.

Naughty reindeer. Only Sara could make such a joke without an ounce of fear. *Should I tell you how much your acceptance means to me?* I thought, trailing my fingers on the soft skin of her back. Maybe I should, but not yet. I didn't want to burden her with the knowledge that she made her decision without knowing all the consequences.

I should have stopped and talked to her before making my claim. Then, I wouldn't feel like such a bastard for tricking her into this situation, but the last month had taken a heavy toll, and my decision-making was erratic at best. My inability to avoid Sara, leading to this moment, was a prime example. One thing was certain, however. Magic or not, she was an exceptional woman that I had learned to cherish, and I would protect and love my Firefly no matter what happened.

Sara accepted me without trying to become the reason for my existence. I'd long since abandoned hope of finding a partner, an equal, someone who could look me in the eye, unafraid of the raging beast. Then Sara entered my life, a tornado of courage and strength, protecting Adam when she stood no chance against me, and I knew my life would never be the same.

Unable to resist, I leaned down, kissing Sara's forehead, smiling as she sighed, still deeply asleep, and carefully eased her to the side, avoiding the evidence of our late-night activities. Another smile graced my lips as I stood up, remembering her embarrassment at the aftermath of our lovemaking, but it swiftly disappeared as I focused on my reason for abandoning my lover's arms. No one could take what's mine. She could leave me if she chose to, but woe betide any poor bastard who thought they could lay a hand on my woman and live. It was time to track down whoever thought they could attack my woman with impunity.

My hands curl into fists as the image of Sara writhing in silent agony flashed before my eyes. Whoever attacked her like that meant for me to see her pain, keeping Sara alive long past the time it would take for the spell to kill her. This was a challenge, a show of power, the reminder they could take her... *Fuck! If I let them!* My hands balled into first when the cruel smile ghosted on my lips because, thanks to the very woman they'd assaulted, I could show them what real power looked like.

I grabbed a pair of sweatpants from the drawer before heading to the kitchen. Michal was already there, frying bacon next to a mound of scrambled eggs.

'Here, something to replenish your energy after last night. I ordered cinnamon rolls for Sara. The delivery should arrive soon. Will you be returning later, or will you be sticking your head back up your arse?' The disapproval in his voice felt almost physical, and if not for the years of service, I would have thought this old shifter was challenging me.

'I'm coming home. Sara and I came to an understanding.'

'Twice from the sounds of it. What sort of understanding?'

'That she is mine, and I will never let her go,' I said, casually putting a piece of the greasy meat in my mouth. Even saying that out loud felt good, and my smile returned as I ate.

'You're mated?' he asked, using the shifter term.

'Yes.' I didn't want to be ambiguous and kept eye contact with Michal as he frowned.

'And she accepted it, knowing what that means?'

Trust him to ask the one question I wished to avoid. My face must have betrayed the answer because my assistant sighed and shook his head.

'Took you long enough, but you should have told her, trusted her with the information. I doubt it would have changed Sara's answer, but when she finds out you hid this?' With a disappointed look, the shifter shook his head. 'You shouldn't have left her in the first place. She was scared, overwhelmed by her new reality, and you just left her running away like a coward. You're better than this, Boss; what's going on?'

I looked at Michal, wondering what had happened to my quiet, loyal assistant for him to question me like this. He must have felt the weight of my displeasure, turning around to busy himself in the kitchen, but I could hear him mutter, 'It just wasn't right.'

Then it hit me. He was protective of Sara, and even though it was shocking, that fact encouraged me to offer an explanation.

'You're right. I know how badly I fucked up, but thankfully, I have you and Sara to tell me. With the claiming, it... again, you are right, but the ability to think rationally went out the window the moment I saw her so close to death. Everything that happened was consensual. I even confessed that I was the biggest idiot for what I'd done before. Sara graciously forgave my stupidity and....'

I stopped momentarily, lowering my eyes as I gathered the courage to admit the next part. 'The only reason I tried staying away was to avoid pulling Sara further into our world, giving her the choice to leave if she wished, but once we'd cleared the air, She chose to be with me, and I could not deny her.'

I could see Michal had more questions, but my phone rang, and, seeing the caller ID, I answered. Adam's voice assaulted my ear with an unusual screech. 'Just tell me your doctor is all right before this harpy rips my head off.'

'What?'

'The woman you told me to protect, Nina. She won't shut up. So tell me Sara is fine, or better yet, tell her yourself, or I'll dump her on your doorstep because you're not paying me enough to handle this. Ouch! What was that for?' I heard the slap and a furious female voice telling him to get Sara on the phone.

'Fine, bring her here. We are having breakfast, so you might as well join us.'

I heard more muffled words than a deep, relieved exhale. 'Perfect, we'll be there in thirty minutes.' Adam said, disconnecting, and I smiled, looking at Michal.

'Would you prepare two more plates? We have guests coming.'

His disgruntled complaining followed me to the bathroom as I dressed, hoping my home and I would be acceptable to Sara's friend.

The sound of tyres ploughing a furrow in my gravel drive announced our guests' arrival, but Michal could not open the door in time to prevent Adam from crashing through it and marching wordlessly into the kitchen.

As I turned back to the door, I flinched, confronted by the scowling face of Sara's friend, Nina, inches from my own.

'Where is Sara?' she asked, and I didn't bother hiding my grin as I answered.

'In my bedroom, resting.'

'Is she injured? Upset or angry? Does she know what happened last night? Come to mention it, why aren't you telling me what happened already?'

'Hold on. Give me a chance to talk, and I'll answer you. At least we know why Adam's pissed off.' Rolling my eyes was probably a mistake, but I couldn't resist. 'Sara is fine, uninjured, but tired from her ordeal. As for last night, someone placed a magical symbol on her back, the rune of Svarog, using it to attack with the Black Arcana, which is forbidden magic.' The frown I expected to transform into concern for Sara darkened into something genuinely fearsome, and I nearly stepped backwards.

'Fuck! How do I combat something like that? Would ice help get rid of that mark? Or should I bleed it out or say abracadabra? How can I save her when you aren't there?' Nina's matter-of-fact approach left me speechless. I looked at Adam, who stood before the coffee machine, pretending to figure out its controls.

'You can't help unless you cut the rune from her skin. You need magic to help effectively.' I said, making Nina frown.

'Then I'll do that if it helps, but how…' she said, stopping when we heard Adam's grumbling.

'I told you. She's impossible and keeps asking pointless questions. The bloody woman even inspected my teeth, asking if they were hollow. I'm a bloody vampire, not a dentist.' He said, shrugging when I sent him a questioning look, knowing Adam didn't let women boss him around.

'You told me she had to be safe, so I kept her safe, even when she pushed her fingers into my mouth, but that ends now. You can beat the shit out of me, but I'm not spending another day in her company.'

'Just because you're too stupid to answer my questions doesn't mean they are pointless or that I'm a troublemaker. I have valid concerns, and you are just an arsehole,' Nina shouted, burning with righteous indignation, making the vampire shrink back in his chair.

'Oh...' That was all I mustered to say before the image of Nina inspecting Adam's teeth for cavities broke me, and I roared, shaking from laughter.

'Why is it so noisy?' Sara was standing at the top of the stairs, dressed only in my shirt, her hair tussled, eyes half closed from a passionate but sleepless night.

'Sara, you all right? I was so worried... oh, damn, Honey, you need to go to the bathroom right now. I guess it's too late to ask if you used protection.' Nina gathered Sara under her wing, looking at me with one eyebrow raised, and I pointed down the corridor.

As she bundled Sara off in the direction I indicated, Nina looked over her shoulder, giving me a stare filled with accusation and disgust, but I kept my silence, even as they entered the bathroom, and she peppered Sara with questions about last night.

'Antlers? What do you mean, antlers?' The nurse's strident screech was audible to everyone in the building, my smile growing wider as Michal and Adam turned to look at me, understanding flashing in their eyes.

Warmth blossomed in my chest. I was proud, but there was more to it than that. That Sara felt comfortable sharing last night's adventures with her friend showed it wasn't just the near death and an adrenaline-fuelled encounter, but she wasn't ashamed of us.

'Adam, make us all coffee once you finish playing with the knobs. I feel like it today,' I said to the vampire, who hadn't stopped staring at me over the industrial-grade coffee maker. I saw him rolling his eyes before he exaggeratedly bowed to me.

'Of course, O' Great Stag of the Primeval Forest, your lowly vampire servant, is happy to serve coffee and babysit whomsoever you send his way,' he answered, and I flicked a simple wind spell from my fingers, smacking him on the forehead, and making him stagger. Adam snarled, his eyes completely black, and I realised how easily I'd manipulated my magic.

'It looks like Sara did more than just coax back the Great Stag.' I said, turning my head to listen to muffled laughs from the bathroom. 'Adam, I want you to keep an eye on Nina. She makes my Sara happy. I know it's a lot to ask, but everyone my Firefly cares about is under threat now. Use your talents to find her family and whoever else she cares for, then make sure our Russian friends can't get to them.'

'Fine, but maybe you should talk to her first. Nina has some strong opinions on how Sara should be treated, and from what I understand, she doesn't like how you've isolated her. I've never seen you bother with women. You've only ever mentioned Jurata, and women have changed since the Romans invaded.' Adam, as usual, couldn't help teasing me, even as he tried to help, and I felt guilty until I remembered how distraught she'd been holding Scarface's broken body in her arms.

'This isn't a permanent arrangement, so for now, keep it discrete, and once we have control of the situation, we will withdraw,'

I said, knowing I could accept her anger if it kept those tears from falling.

'I still say you're making a mistake. Now, will you stop thinking with your cock and focus on the problem? We caught some of his men causing problems around old Hel and Rewa right before the trouble in the club, but they were lowly goons. They were hardly worth the effort, so the probability of them being a diversion for the attack on Sara is quite high. If we could only discover how he's getting around Tricity undetected.'

'Maybe he isn't moving around?' Michal asked before placing two cups of coffee before us from gods knew where. I frowned, thinking about it, but none of my spells or our informers could detect him. Not even the ritual I performed during the Harvest celebration revealed his location.

'That may be what he's using the amber for, and with more shipments missing, it might be worth halting all trade for a while. There must be something else; I just need to find it.' I was frustrated, and while Michal had a point, it also meant there would need to be a hideout near the docks allowing Rostov to slip out and attack.

'You going to ask the Coven for help?' Adam rubbed his stubble, 'We had to halt the collection of amber. Our workers got attacked. Not the humans but the wolves guarding the excavation. They used those funky bullets. We lost three wolves and a Wila. Tomasz is furious.'

'I'll talk to Nadolny. Using his men will help deal with that fucking ammunition and let's invest in a bulk order of bul-let-proof vests. Insist on everyone wearing them; the bullets might not poison the humans, but they are still lethal. Lock down all the amber and explain to our customers that there's an embargo on all sales but that everything will return to normal soon.' It wasn't ideal and would damage our reputation, but cutting off a potential power source to this Warlock was more important.

'So what are we going to do about finding this bastard? There was a report of a fire at the public marina, with a witch confirming the presence of Dark Arcana, and Nadolny sent a text earlier that someone hexed his prostitutes and closed down the premises after reporting them to the health department. Nothing we've done has hinted at their location, so unless you have another idea....' Adam's question left me frustrated, as it felt like I was trying to catch a ghost.

'Let's focus on guarding the amber warehouses and stores. That is the only thing that is consistently attacked. If needed, move it all to one place. I will set up new wards and bolster the witches' detection spells,' I said, wondering how much power I could muster now that Sara had helped me access my avatar.

The women emerged from the bathroom, chatting happily as if my thoughts summoned them.

'I need to go to work, but I promise I will be home for a late dinner unless we have another catastrophe.' Sara spoke casually, but I felt my blood freeze at her plans.

'Maybe you could take some time off. Until I solve our current issue?' I said cautiously, trying not to alarm her, but the last thing I expected was for both women to burst into laughter.

'Now that would take real magic to arrange. You need to give three months' notice, and besides, it wouldn't be fair to the people who'd have to find my replacement or those who would cover my shifts,' Sara replied, pulling Nina toward her bedroom.

'You need to stop her. She is your weakness now. If you paint him into a corner, Rostov will try to kill you, and all he needs is Sara and Czernobog's dagger, both of which are in your possession,' Adam said, barely avoiding the ladle Michal swung in his direction.

'Tell me something I don't know, Adam. Sara is not a captive, and I would never cage her like some dangerous animal, no matter how much I want to keep her safe. Ask Tomasz for extra security and ensure we have someone in the hospital to monitor her while she works.' I said, turning sharply when I heard the front doors opening.

'Have fun, and don't break my coffee machine, vamps. I like it more than you.' Sara threw that comment casually over her shoulder, not giving me enough time to stop her or say goodbye.

With her abrupt exit, my good mood vanished, and I snapped out my orders.

'Phone Tomasz now. I need his men waiting for her in the parking lot. Michal set up a meeting with Nadolny. Inform the witches we need better wards placed over every strategic building we own. Let Veronica know I require her service, but be polite. I will be in my office making a few phone calls. Adam, talk to your seethe. I need them to prevent our Kaliningrad counterparts from filling the temporary void we're creating in the amber market.'

As soon as they left, I locked myself in my office. With Sara exposed, I was on edge. The person who marked her with the rune could be out there, just waiting for my woman to emerge from the protective wards of my island.

Czernobog's dagger and Svarog's rune were old magics that hadn't surfaced in centuries, and what was Rostov's plan? *Is he the leader or just a tool in his god's hands?* I wondered, swallowing hard. All this time, I assumed he was nothing more than a greedy mortal who gained possession of a few artefacts and used his men to muscle into the amber business, but the fact I couldn't find him made me rethink the situation. If he was just a tool, who was pulling the strings?

I needed advice, but only a few would answer my call, none willing to visit a human city. Using the passage to Gedania would garner too much attention as the Gates became unstable without my presence in the mortal world to tether their power, so crossing would raise some questions, exposing my failure, not to mention alerting whoever was involved in this. The secondary gate near the Kashubian forest might reduce the chance of discovery, but there were no guarantees, especially considering my destination. I had only one solution. I needed to persuade Veles to see me, and the old bastard wasn't very welcoming, even to the offspring he liked.

With Michal out running errands, I scribbled a note informing him of my plans in case I was delayed, time in my father's realm being subject to his whim. I wasn't looking forward to this venture, but I would beard the dragon in his home if it meant keeping my people safe.

The drive was over quickly, and after performing my spells on the gate to the Nether, I headed into the forest. An unseen weight lifted from my shoulders, contentment filling my soul as I felt the welcoming presence of the trees and creatures that lived here. I missed this feeling, wishing I could spend the majority of my existence here, untroubled by the affairs of humanity. However, in order to protect my people, I'd had little choice, becoming a pale imitation of the once mighty Lord of the Forest.

I walked until the last path disappeared, the trees crowding in to protect the grove I'd planted after the Christians destroyed the previous one, its location still a well-kept secret. Fog rolled in from every direction, obscuring the surrounding area, but I didn't need sight to reach the epicentre of the powerful nexus.

'Father, I beseech you, grant me entrance to Nawia. I wish to petition for your advice.' I said, studying the mist as I waited for his response. Something shifted in the shadows, and an enormous figure emerged, stopping before me.

'You cannot pass, and you know it. You lost all rights when you turned your back on the world to become the Guardian of that place.' He said, tilting his head, and for a moment, kindness replaced the anger on his face. 'Dola finally forgave you, I see, and wove love back into your life. I can sense your woman's power.' His eyes widened when he trailed a hand over my head, touching my spirit. 'You've regained the stag; now that is a surprise. Maybe I was wrong to dismiss you. Ask your questions, my son.'

'A Warlock has come to Gdansk, threatening the elder races and the Nether; worse than this, he threatens my love, and despite appearing to be nothing more than an ambitious magic user, his whereabouts elude me.'

'I can't help you in the mortal world, child.' Veles' voice trailed its icy fingers along my spine. 'You should know better than to ask for this.'

'I'm not asking for your help that way. I only need information on whether this man has the power to hide from me or if the gods are interfering in the mortal world again. That's not too much to ask, is it?' I winced at how harsh my voice sounded, especially as a supplicant to a greater power. I understood his reason. Stepping into the mortal realm meant not only breaking old gods' accord but also losing a significant amount of energy, the spells that fuelled the Nether's existence draining it away constantly, and only this grove offered protection from that.

My father stilled, his long, unblinking stare giving the impression he wasn't wholly here but in many other places at once, but I stood there knowing it would be worth waiting for his reply.

'Many gods want a return to the old days, yet the existence of the Nether makes that impossible without the sacrifice that most are not ready or willing to commit to, but there is a way. One can create pockets of null-time and either expend more power to create a body or find a willing sacrifice to become their vessel.' The mention of pockets of null-time caught my attention. Could that explain our inability to find him? The lack of time preventing spells from noticing his presence? That certainly made things complicated, but at least I had something to research. Unfortunately, it also pointed toward the old gods' interference.

'Is that why the Warlock is attacking my amber business?'

'Svarog returned once, using some vainglorious monarch's greed, encouraging the human to construct a room of amber and gold, infusing it with magic. He was by no means fully manifested, but even so, his influence caused war and chaos, resulting in an influx of souls to Nawia until we arranged for his room of power to be destroyed, forcing him to retreat. He is still licking his wounds, but others are always ready to repeat his mistakes.'

'So it all depends on my amber. That I can deal with.' I smiled, bowing to Veles, stepping backwards. Now I had my answers.

'They may not need the Amber Room anymore,' My father's words stopped me in my tracks. 'There was a prophecy, some time ago counting in human years. If a god has transferred any part of their being to this world, a Soul Shepherd can tether them to a willing sacrifice, and we both know it's possible to influence a person's actions.'

'I thought Rostov wanted to use her to kill me.' I said, only now realising my mistake. It wasn't about me. Maybe it was never about me or my business. The fog swirled, displaced as I transformed into my avatar.

'Kill you? Maybe, but only so you cannot stop them from achieving their goal. If I hadn't seen the consequences of such idiocy, even I might have been tempted to return.'

'I should return to Gdansk. Thank you, Father,' I said, bowing, and he returned the gesture solemnly.

The trees parted before me as I rushed to the car, fuelled by the fear my Sara could be taken away. It was already evening when I emerged from the forest, still manifesting my avatar, much later than I'd hoped. Dismissing my magic, I leapt into my car, driving home like a maniac, knowing I wouldn't rest until she was safely in my arms.

Chapter Twenty-Four

I regretted my decision to drive almost immediately, as it gave Nina free rein to concentrate on coming up with more questions. I'd been half-asleep when she marched me to the bathroom, and in my surprised state, letting her take charge seemed the best thing to do. Of course, her interrogation started as soon as the door closed, the first question asking if the mess I was in was entirely consensual and not coerced by magic. Once Nina was reassured that I had, in fact, not just consented but been an enthusiastic participant, the questions turned into a performance review, which thankfully became sidetracked as I mentioned Leszek's antlers.

I thought nothing about life, sex or otherwise, could make me blush, but as I shared each gory detail, the memory of his body left me bright red and stuttering. Maybe that's why I rushed out of the house without stopping for a proper farewell.

The inquisition continued in the car, concentrating on my feelings now that we had some privacy, but eventually, Nina's questioning wound to a halt.

'I'm happy for you. It's about time you found someone who cares for you, makes you walk like a cross-eyed duck, and smile so radiantly oncoming vehicles are blinded. Even if it is some mobster that's horny in more than the traditional sense.' Nina never failed to be brutally honest with me, but if she was making jokes, then I had her tentative approval.

'Yeah, trust me to take the weirdest fish in the sea to bed. He is nice, Nina. Well, nice in that weird, burn-the-world-for-your-smile kind of way, but still... I like him.'

'Shouldn't you make sure he likes you too before you jump on his dick?' She said in her usual brazen manner, and I shrugged.

'It would have happened, eventually. The attraction between us was too visceral to be ignored, but I don't know, I can't boss him around, and I... I think I like it.' I said, but my thoughts drifted to my past relationships with men. Leszek was the first to make my heart flutter and didn't abuse me or become a submissive puddle under my feet. 'Maybe I got lucky this time,' I murmured, and Nina laughed.

The road from the island was rarely used but was straight as a rod and very picturesque, with the trees dispersing the light, taking us along the banks of the Motlawa River. I paid little attention to my surroundings, especially since it was only us and a single car on the other side of the road. Suddenly, the vehicle swerved, aimed in a direction that would push us into the water. My vision blurred, the future flashing through my mind, directing my hands. Somehow, with the smell of a burning clutch, I turned the car in time to avoid the collision.

'What the fuck was that?' I asked, looking at Nina, her pale complexion turning an interesting shade of green as I brought the car under control before slamming on the brakes to see what had happened to the other vehicle.

We both stared for a full second. Somehow, the driver had avoided ending up in the river, smashing headlong into a tree and crushing the front of their car. That was all it took for our instincts to kick in, and we leapt out, snatching up my grab bag from the boot and checking the area for danger. As I headed to the crashed vehicle, Nina threw out a warning triangle and called the emergency services. Much to my relief, only one person was inside, so I reached through the broken window to check for signs of life.

'Hello, can you hear me? ' I asked, shaking my head to clear the strange sound I'd been hearing since running over. It faded a notch, and I reached toward the man's face. With no signs of breathing, his head hanging limply, I had to restore his airway, hoping the airbag had prevented any spinal damage as I tilted his head back, relieved when he gasped, dragging in the much-needed breath.

'The song, make it stop,' he pleaded while blood trickled out of his ear, and I worried there was a severe head injury. I registered this, but getting him out of danger was critical, so for now, I ignored it.

'Rescue is on the way, and you forgot to turn off the engine.' Nina commented, reaching past and taking the key out of the ignition, but smoke still rose from the bonnet, and I redoubled my efforts.

'Take the fire extinguisher from my boot and try to smother the flames,' I said, weighing the man's life against the chance of Nina and me being hurt, a decision drilled into every first responder, but one never easy to make. I wasn't sure how much time we had left, so taking a deep breath just as Veronica taught me, I willed my magic to reveal a glimpse of the following minutes, cursing as I saw the explosion and the death of anyone nearby.

'Fuck! Nina, we need him out right now!' I shouted, and hands grabbed me by the shoulders.

'Get away. I'll do it.' My surprise allowed Jarek to pull me away and reach for the door. I didn't know where he came from, but the muscular young wolf had a better chance of getting the driver to safety.

'Hurry,' I said, hearing the sirens of an approaching ambulance, knowing that heralded the flames bursting to life in my vision. Jarek's body transformed into a half-man, half-beast, but before I could say anything, he snarled.

'I'll handle it, so get to safety.' As metal tore, I fell back, watching my assistant carelessly throw the door into the distance. I shook my head at the casual display of strength, watching as he ripped the seat belt from its anchor and dragged the unmoving driver to safety.

I pointed to a place that would be unaffected by the explosion and shouted, 'Put him here, Jarek! Nina, check his pulse while I see if he's still breathing.' We worked as a well-oiled machine, the sound of the ambulance arriving barely registered.

'What the fuck is that? Sara, what the fuck!' I forgot Jarek had shifted, and looking at the faces of Rysiek and Damian, I knew they would never forget the experience.

'Change,' I said to the wolf, fretting about what to do before Nina saved the day.

'Oh, don't be such babies, you two. We'll explain later. This man needs help, so stop standing here like a pair of limp pricks at an orgy and help us.' The team looked at me, and I smiled gently.

'Please,' That was all it took; Nina's swearing and my calm courtesy reassured the paramedics, the years of trust and dealing with all kinds of weirdness overriding any shock or fear. The boys jumped in, and if Nina and I were a well-oiled machine, the four of us were nothing short of miracle workers, not even flinching at the explosion of the car. Within minutes, the driver was stable and loaded into the ambulance.

'We are not done with you. You owe us beer and an explanation, so see you after work. Oh, and just so you know, we are taking him to your hospital.' Damian shouted when they shut the doors, pulling faces at the firefighters as they extinguished the roaring flames behind us. It took several minutes to answer the police, with a promise to give a statement later to escape the scene, and without further trouble, we arrived at the hospital.

The Emergency Department was chaotic as always, and after a brief handover, I took charge while Nina directed her nurses with a mastery of the battle-worn general. I heard our car crash victim was in the neurosurgical ward. Something he said didn't sit well in my mind. Eventually, curiosity got the better of me, so I went to check on him. Still, I could not see him being told his wife had arrived, requesting time alone with her husband.

I stepped into the lift, too lazy to walk down the several flights of stairs, when I heard the crash bell coming from the ward. My hand slammed the button that held open the doors when years of conditioning kicked in, pushing me forward. Someone was dying, and I could help, screamed my instincts, but the sound of someone coughing impatiently broke through the compulsion. *It is not your ward, and you are not the only doctor in this hospital*, I thought before letting the door slide shut, only to be overwhelmed by a sudden sense of foreboding, the lights flickering and going out.

I leapt to the side, pushing my back to the wall, the hollow laugh from my previous position telling me I'd done the right thing. The lights flickered back on, and the man who'd coughed so impatiently looked straight at me, a brown semitransparent globe in his hand, the soft glow it emitted swirling in a slow, hypnotic pattern.

'Sara, it's a pleasure to finally meet you in person. Your lover's wards were difficult to overcome, but as you can see, I have ways to break even the strongest of spells.' The voice was eerily familiar, but I still gasped when he removed his facemask, revealing the face from my vision.

'Who are you?' I asked, and he performed a mocking bow.

'Nikolai Rostov, and, in anticipation of your next question. Yes, I'm here to draw a veil over today's incident and maybe clear the air between us if you're receptive. I would like to apologise for my associate; her actions contradict my plans, and the last thing I want is your animosity. You have piqued my master's curiosity, Soul Shepherd, so I am here to extend a polite invitation.' He said, licking his lips, the action predatory and nauseatingly eager.

I didn't know who this *she* or *his master* were, but I was betting from what Rostov said that they were responsible for my latest near-death experiences.

'Nicely? I think asking nicely doesn't involve attempted murder. Was it you who put that burning rune on my back?' I asked, and he shrugged, gaze darting toward the orb, which was duller now.

'My apologies. The attack on your person was unsanctioned, and a reprimand has already been issued. She was only tasked to find you since our late seer foresaw a Soul Shepherd may be born in this city. It was fascinating to observe how easily you slid into your new life. You surprised me… us. My master wishes to win you to our side with a mutually beneficial arrangement and is willing to enter into negotiations with you. You have two days to think it over, Soul Shepherd. Spill your blood and whisper Czernobog's name if you choose to communicate. He will enter your dreams as he came to mine. Listen to his offer. He will show you who you truly are and why Veles' mongrel clings to your side.' Rostov was nearly spitting his instructions out at the end, a zealot's fervour burning in his eyes. I moved away, but he followed me. 'Two days, Sara. Refuse him, and your loved ones will die to feed Czernobog's power.'

A cracking sound distracted me; it was Rostov's orb splintering and falling to the floor while the lift started moving. Nonchalantly brushing his hands clean, he smiled, unconcerned that his special magic was in pieces, and I wondered what made this seemingly ordinary man so confident. Curious, I tried to assess his power, clumsily directing my ability, then swiftly withdrew, sensing the waves of magic pulsing through the small space. The amount of energy was intimidating, but we were in my domain, and I was damned if some arsehole could come here and threaten my second family.

'Get the fuck out of my hospital and my city, and if you dare threaten my kin, I'll hunt you down and tear your balls off.' My voice had never been this quiet, this icy when I was angry, but I meant every word. Veronica hadn't taught me offensive spells. My magic wasn't meant for combat, but she had shown me one thing I could use it for, and I gathered every ounce of willpower I had, thrusting the energy forward like a dagger into his mind. If I could immobilise him long enough, I could call Leszek and let him deal with the arsehole.

My mind brushed his when I released a mental attack, and I caught horrifying images of the elder races and humans mutilated and buried in peat bogs or marshlands to appease the dark god. Dark Arcana came from suffering, and their pain was transformed into the energy that fuelled dozens of orbs similar to the one he'd held in his hand. Not just the orbs... a room...

Null-time bubble. The name floated to his mind's surface. Polished amber with golden runes etched over the surface. He seemed to cherish it, as if existing outside of time gave him free rein to do as he pleased.

For a few seconds, Rostov looked shocked that I'd dared to invade his mind, and I used this to my advantage. I wished I had something more, but my measly gathered power was already depleted. Still, I wasn't done with him yet. This time, it wasn't magic, but my Krav Maga training, or as Nina called it, that weird fight club, and I launched myself forward to attack. The Warlock was faster, almost anticipating my move, twisting away, so all I could manage was a deep scratch to his neck, blood splashing onto my face as he pushed past me, throwing something to the floor. When it smashed, time slowed, and Rostov escaped through the opening elevator door down an empty corridor leading to the main entrance.

Rostov paused, looking back over his shoulder. 'You are strong and bold, Sara. As I said, I observed you and came prepared. Still, I am pleasantly surprised you went that far.' His smirk made me want to punch him, and that anger helped me fight the effects of his magic.

'I will find you, you arsehole.' I said, my voice distorted by the time dilation.

'Yes, please, Soul Shepherd, but don't worry, we'll see each other soon. With my blood staining your soul, you'll have little choice. Czernobog will be pleased by such a development. Contact my master before the deadline, or we will come for you, killing those you love if they try to stop us,' he said, flinching, eyes widening when he realised I was rushing toward him.

While he was gloating over his superiority, I fought his spell, my mind hammering against the strange feeling holding me tight, imagining it tearing, falling away into dust like his damn orb until I felt it, a break, and I clawed at it, widening the gap, till time snapped, falling back into place. Blood burst from my nose, but I was free and moving at speed, crashing into Rostov like a ton of bricks and falling to the floor, gasping for breath.

'You bloody bitch!' His voice echoed in the still-empty corridor while his fist flew toward my head with furious speed. I raised my arm defensively, blocking the attack, but the force of the blow threw me back against the wall, smacking my head against the solid concrete.

'Hey, what's going on here?' The shouted enquiry helped centre my thoughts, making it easier to focus on Rostov as he turned with a snarl.

'Ungrateful human. I hope you fight, seer. I want to see the light die in your eyes when Czernobog forces your compliance.' With that, he turned on his heel, rushing toward the exit.

Our security guard didn't attempt to chase him, rushing to my side and checking I was safe and sound before helping me stand.

'What happened, doctor? I got comms about a lift malfunction and came to check, but you... what happened? Why are you bleeding?' He asked, pulling a pack of tissues from his pocket.

'It's alright. The elevator got stuck, and I don't like tight, locked-up places.' I said, wiping the streak of blood from my chin.

'Will you be alright? Should I take you to the Emergency Department?' he offered, and I sniggered, patting his shoulder.

'Thank you, but I'm fine. Let me just pick up my things, and I'll be off. Using the stairs this time.' I said, reaching to pick up the pieces of amber, and the guard coughed, trying to ignore what I was gathering up.

'All right then. I'll get the engineers to check the elevator. Be careful, doctor,' he said, and I nodded, forcing a smile, then heading to the staircase.

As soon as I disappeared from the guard's sight, my legs buckled, and I had to sit on the stairs to gather my thoughts. A short, quiet sob was the only sound I allowed myself before reining in my emotions. *Rostov came here hoping to find a Soul Shepherd; talk about fucking luck*. Fear and tension gripped me, but I refused to cry. If someone saw me, they'd want to know why I was sitting on the stairs with a bloody nose, sobbing my heart out.

I felt completely, utterly drained, the need for sleep almost overwhelming, but after a few calming breaths, I dragged myself down to Emergency.

It took an industrial amount of coffee and fussing over from Nina before I could function like a normal human being, or at least pretend to. I put the pieces of the orb and a scrap of fabric I'd somehow torn from Rostov's coat in my bag, making a mental note to show them to Leszek and tell him about the bastard's visit and the threats. Including the one he alluded to, that he's marked me.

It worried me, but I didn't feel any different. There were no burning runes or a desire to go on a killing spree, well, no more than usual when working in the ER, so I shrugged it off, focusing on my patients. Despite the lack of sleep, time flew by, filled with everyday emergencies and minor injuries, a rhythm I welcomed. I didn't notice the time until I found myself changing to go home, with Nina making jokes and pulling faces.

With my head and arms locked in a struggle to tame a jumper I swore used to be bigger, a junior nurse called out from the locker room door.

'Sara, your boys are here to pick you up.' She said, and I frowned.

'My... boys?' My reaction was less than stellar as the jumper fought my efforts to wear it.

Her laugh made everything click, though she took great pleasure in reminding me.

'Damian and Rysiek. They are adamant you owe them a beer. I must admit, they look cute in civilian clothes.'

Right, the accident and the promise we'd made, beer and an explanation. I looked at Nina, and she shrugged.

'It'll do you good. Your head's been in the clouds all day, though you need to get yourself together, or they'll mother hen you till we both scream.' Nina was right, and the dream of laying on Leszek's lap disappeared into the ether as I sighed, and I finally defeated my turtle-neck arch-nemesis, heading out to face the music.

My mood improved at the prospect of drinks with the Dream Team, but I nearly ended up face into the wall when Jarek silently appeared by my side, and when I cast him a questioning glare, he just shrugged.

'Please, Sara, I need to help keep you safe. I couldn't bear it if you get hurt,' he begged, and I instantly felt sorry for him. It wasn't his fault I was attacked, but Leszek made it clear he didn't want Jarek near me and had arranged more competent protection.

'Were you waiting here the whole time?' I asked, and when he nodded, I sighed. Jarek was like an overgrown pup, clumsy and adorable, and I didn't have the heart to dismiss him after he'd spent nine hours waiting.

'I'm going to the pub with friends. If you want, you can come along, but... they will be asking questions. They saw you in werewolf form,' I said, watching his shoulders slump.

'I can't do a single thing right,' he muttered. Nina came to him, placing a hand on his shoulder.

'You helped save man's life today, so stop beating yourself up, kid, and if dumb and dumber saw a bit of fur, who cares?' She said, and Jarek instantly brightened up.

'We love you too, harpy, and yeah, we care, but not because our young friend's different, so shift, get it? Your arse so that Sara can tell us all about it,' Damian snarked. I saw my boys blocking the exit, and it was clear Nina was right; it was time to face the music. My only worry was that the circle of friends who knew about my new life had suddenly grown.

We went to the pub near the hospital, right on the edge of Old Town. It was located in the basement of a medieval townhouse, well known as the watering hole for medical staff, and our group frequented it with a regularity that guaranteed Christmas cards from the owners. I waved to the bartender, and we moved to the darkest corner while Nina placed our order. Jarek sat beside me with the two paramedics opposite, silently waiting until Damian couldn't hold back any longer, and leant forward with a questioning look.

'So, what's going on? I mean, we saw him, he's a werewolf, a fucking werewolf, Sara, and no, I haven't been using the truck's supplies. I know what I saw.' Damian acted like he thought I'd argue, gaslighting them into believing it wasn't real, but I respected my boys too much to lie.

'Jarek is a shifter, a werewolf to be exact, and you saw one of his forms,' I said. Damian and Rysiek glared at Nina as she interrupted, returning with the drinks.

'What she said, besides, our Sara is kind of witchy herself, and her new boyfriend is... what is he exactly, Sara?' She turned to me, and I rolled my eyes at the playfulness I could hear in her voice.

'I wish I knew, but he looks after the elder races and creatures of the Nether. He's kind of well-connected here in Tricity. Leszek runs things in this area, and everyone magical answers to him.' I stumbled over this explanation, unsure how much I could share because I was sure if I mentioned he was some kind of god, my friends, who already were at the end of their tethers, would lose the plot entirely.

Rysiek laughed, surprising me with his reaction. 'Sara, we've always known you were not normal, but this... hell, girlfriend, this is a whole new kind of weird. Let me guess, you wouldn't have told us if we hadn't stumbled on that accident with your young friend donning his haute couture fur.'

'No, I wouldn't. I'm sorry, I didn't know if.' I stopped and took a deep breath before continuing. 'This world, the knowledge of its existence, is dangerous, and I was worried you wouldn't believe or accept the new me.' I was blushing now, but Rysiek leaned over and playfully ruffled my hair.

'It is weird, I admit, and scary, but if you are in it, we are in it, and we will make it work. We're a team through thick and thin. You should have trusted us. Even your harpy knew, and we will hold this against you forever.'

'Will you stop calling me Harpy? It's your turn to buy a round, so stop beating your gums and open your wallet.' Nina knew when the boys were getting too sentimental for me, knowing to split them up when I got close to tears. I sat there stunned that my friends were taking this in their stride, as if meeting a werewolf was as ordinary as ordering a pint. As Nina led Rysiek to the bar, Damian came over, sitting beside me, and I laid my head on his shoulder.

'Thank you, I'm sorry I didn't tell you. I didn't know about this stuff till recently, and I've struggled with coming to terms with it.' The weight I'd been feeling this last month had disappeared with the boy's acceptance, and being able to share my life again with people who were my friends left me with tears slowly escaping my eyes, soaking my friend's jumper. Damian embraced me, kissed my forehead, and rubbed my shoulders playfully before we both jumped at the command snapping out of the shadows.

'Get your hands off my woman.' Leszek's expression was carved from ice, and I sat there, stunned, as he grabbed Damian, pulled him from his seat, and moved in, surrounding me with his arms. 'Sara, we need to go,' he growled, but even as I enjoyed the feeling of his body, my temper flared at his unacceptable behaviour, and I squirmed around to escape.

'Stop acting like a possessive arsehole. Damian is my friend. Jealousy is no excuse for hurting my family,' I said, pausing when I noticed the blood on his suit. 'What happened?'

'My men were targeted with the same damn bullets that hurt Jarek. Please, I need your help.' He said, and my breath hitched. A quick glance at the wolf revealed a face as pale as a ghost. I stood up, grabbing my bag.

'Take me to the hospital. I need to borrow some equipment before I perform surgery. Those tools you had last time were awful. Wait, you said men. How many?' I said, sending an apologetic nod to my friends, but they were already on their feet.

'There's no time for that. I have everything you could need. It was supposed to be a surprise, but I need you to come now. I'm sorry.' The sharpness in Leszek's voice and the tension in his posture told me it was bad.

'We're coming too; she'll need our help, and we work well together.' Rysiek's determination made Leszek frown before he turned to me.

'They know, and he's right; I'll need their help. Please trust me on this,' I said, and he nodded slightly, the hint of a smile expressing his gratitude.

'I will always trust you, Firefly, but please, we need to hurry.'

Chapter Twenty-Five

We all clambered into Leszek's car, packed like sardines, as no one wanted to be left behind, clinging to each other and any part of the interior we could to avoid being hurt as my lover drove like a maniac to the old shipyard. I half expected he would bring me to the same old warehouse where I'd performed Jarek's surgery, but instead, we stopped near a shiny building facing the waterfront. When my brows rose in surprised inquiry, Leszek offered me an apologetic smile.

'It was supposed to be my present to you. The interior still needs work, but it will have to do for now. I promise it will be perfect after we finish,' he said, opening the door.

The noise was the first thing I noticed: the screaming of people at their limits, thrashing about in agony on makeshift stretchers, followed by the metallic scent and blood, which seemed to be everywhere I looked until a man blocked my view, his clothes dishevelled, and desperation etched onto his features.

'About bloody time. They're all dying, and nothing we do is helping. We can't even get close to the wounds without shaking so bad we drop the fucking tools!' He yelled in Leszek's face, hands balled into fists and huge, terrifying teeth bared.

Leszek didn't even flinch, calmly turning to me to explain. 'This is Tomasz. His people got caught in the firefight during a raid on our warehouse.'

I barely acknowledged either man as I pushed past, my team following and spreading out to assess the situation. It was a war zone. Around fifteen people writhed in pain while others tried to stem the bleeding, sweating at the proximity to the poisoned bullets.

'It is a bloody nightmare,' I told myself moments before an elderly woman approached me.

'You are Sara? Yes?' she asked, and when I nodded, she grabbed my hand. 'I am Jora. I can heal the wounds but cannot touch those damn bullets. Dig them out, girl. Alpha and I will do the rest, but hurry; we've already lost one of my boys.'

I exhaled slowly, letting her words sink in when the time slowed around me. I saw a small theatre behind the glass panel, and the room looked well-equipped for surgical procedures. The whole thing looked surprisingly like a military hospital unit, and then it hit me. It was a helluva surprise if Leszek intended to gift me a military-grade medical facility similar to those we had in Kosovo.

'Nina, go to the theatre. Take Jarek with you and prepare it. Guys, triage and stabilise those you can. If you see a bullet hole in a non-lethal place and can dig the metal out, do it. None of the Elder races can touch this shit, but as long as it is gone, they will heal, so don't overthink it.' As soon as the words were out of my mouth, the world snapped back into place. This was my place, my job, and I was going to own it.

Nina was already marching toward the unit, with Jarek following her without complaint, and, to my surprise, Adam joined them. Jora nodded toward a group of women who, swaying from exhaustion, cared for a silent, pale werewolf.

'Take him first. He doesn't have much left. I will point out the sickest to your men for this... triage.' She said before looking at me. 'Save them, and you will have an entire pack in your debt. No one will touch you, not even the Forest Lord. Save our family, please.' She turned, issuing orders. I looked back at the Alpha.

'Tomasz, yes? Go with my paramedics. Make sure they're safe when they work on your people. The last thing I need is a pain-crazed wolf lashing out.' I said, and he nodded, following my guys, who quickly gathered equipment from boxes by the walls.

'Sara... thank you.' I heard Leszek's voice. When I turned, he stood there, hands clenched, and I could see the mixture of anger and concern flashing in his eyes.

'Hey, big man. I got your back. I will do my best, but you need to keep my people safe, and if it's true that fresh meat can help with healing, then please take care of it.' I said, knowing having something to do would help him. He cursed, and I reached out to touch his cheek. 'You are not alone to shoulder the burden. I won't sit back and let your men die.'

I turned, trusting Leszek to do everything I asked and headed to the theatre, pleased that Nina and Adam already had the pale werewolf on the table. Despite my composed exterior, I was anything but calm. I was going to play god, a field surgeon, relying on speed, knowledge and luck to perform life-saving procedures in a half-finished operating theatre, and I had no way to locate the bullets, only the positions of the entry points. In a moment of inspiration, I trailed my hand over the shuddering patient.

'Show me,' I whispered, commanding the gift that inspired my hunches to act by design this time. My magic flared, and the intensifying heat dragged me to knots of corruption inside the male's body, pinpointing the damage.

'Are you sure you can heal him later?' I asked the woman standing beside the wolf, and she nodded.

'His wolf will do most of the work once free from the Dark Arcana and silver. I can encourage the healing process, ensuring he won't die on the spot.' She said, and I gave her a tight smile, reaching for the scalpel. In my mind's eye, I could see the bullet was located deep in his stomach next to the aorta and had nicked one of the kidneys, with blood gushing out each time he shook.

'I hope you're right; otherwise, this poor bastard is fucked. Adam, hold him still if you can. Nina, I will need the forceps and retractor if we have them and be ready to clamp the artery.'

'This is insane. You can't do it without a proper theatre and a vascular surgeon. Sara, what the fuck?' She said, and I looked at her, terrified of doing the wrong thing, just like I'd been when forced to help Jarek.

'You can leave. I know it's frightening, and he might die, but if you trust me...' I said, and she huffed in annoyance.

'The fuck? I won't leave you alone in this mess. Just so you know, I will tell your boyfriend where he can shove his antlers when we're done,' she said, readying the equipment. I raised my head, catching a glimpse of Leszek. He was directing the able-bodied, helping the injured and overseeing the whole mess with a calmness I wish I felt.

'You can tell him whatever you want as long as you help save this man.' I said, cutting through the skin, and despite Adam's firm grip, he thrashed, howling in pain.

I felt like a monster mercilessly digging into his flesh, guided by my uncanny magical imaging until I found the bullet, two others quickly following. My patient's screaming faded as I continued, a worrying sign given the amount of blood he was losing, but as soon as I dug the last one out, tossing it into a nearby bowl, relief washed over his face. I heard Nina gasp in reaction to the movement of the tissue she held as it knitted itself together, stopping the bleeding under the wolf healer's touch.

'Good, let me take care of the rest.' The healer gestured to someone outside and started chanting. My patient's face relaxed completely, serenity overtaking his features, his body hanging limply as his comrade picked him off the table, open abdomen and all. Nina tried to protest, but I shook my head. Shifter powers were so beyond my understanding that I had to trust their healers, but I learned one thing from my previous experience. These ridiculously robust shifters could survive anything if something didn't kill them instantly unless foul magic or silver prevented them from healing.

I didn't have time to explain it to Nina because as soon as the table was empty and the blood wiped from its surface, another body was carried in, and I started the procedure again. This one was quicker, albeit more traumatic. The bullet was embedded in his neck close enough to his trachea that bleeding created a bulging sac that narrowed his airways.

'Nina, we need front-of-the-neck access first.' I said, and she assembled the kit.

'Nothing will ever surprise me again, you know. Nothing, Buzz Lightyear in the rectum, fine, scissors in the head, normal, an ordinary day in the ER, but the depth of weirdness here beats anything I've seen.' She muttered as we fell into our working rhythm.

I'd been exhausted before we started, but I was on my knees after butchering the seventh body on my table. An accident, a long shift at work, and dealing with the Rostov took a toll on me. Nina was unusually quiet, the clearest indication that she was just as exhausted. I looked across the room as, according to my count, we should still have eight more to go, but I saw only two people on the stretchers. The rest seemed to be in various stages of shifting or consuming industrial amounts of red meat.

'I think Damian and Rysiek dealt with the easier cases, but we still have two more to go.' I said, and Nina grunted in response.

'I will sleep for a week after this.' She said, making me smile.

'We both will.' I said, willing my body to keep moving.

When we'd finished with the last one, Adam, who'd been reasonably helpful holding down the convulsing patients, grasped Nina's hand.

'Nina, I ...' he stuttered before shaking his head, 'what I just witnessed was exceptional, but you must rest now. I'm taking you home.' I blinked, hearing the caring tone of his voice. My friend tried to protest, but I raised a finger.

'No, he's right. Go home, and I'll handle whatever's left,' I said in a firm tone before turning to Adam. 'Look after her, or I swear I'll find a way to end you, Vampire.' His laughter at my empty threat made me raise an eyebrow. Still, after I spoke, he scooped up the swaying Nina, who embraced his neck without argument and carried her to the exit. As soon as she was out of sight, I wobbled, catching the table's edge to stabilise myself.

'You should take your own advice, doctor.' I looked up at the voice, trying to smile, and Jora gestured to a box in the corner. 'You worked a miracle here today. Words can never express my gratitude for saving our people. The pack will protect you, Sara, from anything or anyone; remember that.'

'I swore an oath to save lives, Jora. There is no debt to repay,' I said, as the very idea of having a pack of shifters bound to me was unsettling, but the healer shook her head.

'That wasn't an offer.' She said, leaving the room. I saw Damian and Rysiek, surrounded by pack members, all patting the paramedics on their backs while what I assumed was a crate of beer was passed around. It looked like I wasn't the only one the pack decided they owed. The men I operated on were recuperating in a quieter corner, cared for by the healers and their Alpha. Tomasz walked between the stretchers, stopping and talking to the injured.

I envied Nina as my legs felt like jelly, not to mention I was dog tired, hungry and probably dehydrated as my heart was pounding, adding to my unsteadiness. Leszek directed the clean-up while talking furiously on the phone. I wanted to go home, and the only way I could do that was to ask him or one of the able-bodied people rushing around. Or I could catch the tram and sleep in my own apartment. That sounded like an excellent idea, and I hoped to sneak away unnoticed to have a few hours of solitude in the privacy of my own home.

Taking a deep breath, I grabbed my bag from the corner I'd thrown it in earlier and walked toward the exit. The wolves were busy with their people, only Jora noticing my escape, her frown deepening when I gestured for her to remain silent. Not that I minded Leszek's company. In fact, I would welcome a nap in his arms, but he was busy, and judging by the severity of the situation, he wouldn't be free anytime soon, and I didn't want to be another burden he had to deal with. Besides, Rostov promised me two days to think, and I was a grown woman in desperate need of sleep who could care for herself.

My breath became ragged before I could even reach the front door. That alone was concerning, as I shouldn't feel so bad, even after an eventful night and busy day. Still, I felt like I had run a marathon, and now I was on the verge of passing out.

'Sara! Where are you going?' Leszek's voice announced to everyone I was about to sneak away, and, slowly exhaling to combat a wave of nausea, I turned... and someone turned out the lights.

Chapter Twenty-Six

Voices raised in anger dragged me from my slumber, but I couldn't open my eyes. 'What did you think you were doing, exploiting her like that? She's barely learned what her gift is and isn't a seasoned witch who knows her power's limits. She drained herself so much her heart almost stopped! And how could you touch the Dark Arcana? I thought you knew better than to use dark magic... my Lord. Everyone will think you have the same ambitions as Czernobog.'

'How many times do I have to repeat myself? I have not used the Dark Arcana. As for the healing, do you think I'd put her in this situation if I had a choice? I didn't know how much it cost her. Sara said nothing, and I assumed ... Fuck! I didn't notice because I was trying to sort this mess out.'

I heard a heavy crash and a long pause before he resumed in a much calmer tone.

'They tried to breach the amber storage. If my suspicions are correct, someone's using the living gem to break the Nether's magic. The Council reported several attacks on the Gates, but none were successful, including one last night during the warehouse raid.' Leszek exclaimed, his anger clear as he argued with Veronica. With curiosity getting the better of me, I opened my eyes and started searching for something to cover what I quickly realised was my very naked body.

I was in Leszek's bedroom. Not that I remembered getting back here or being stripped and put to bed. *Someone clearly had fun*, I thought, noticing I at least had my panties on. I grabbed Leszek's shirt and a soft cashmere blanket, enjoying the touch of luxury while wrapping it around me before I stumbled downstairs into the kitchen.

'What happened and what Gates?' I asked, confronted by the image of Veronica and Leszek facing each other aggressively.

'You fainted, or I should say, according to my witness, you went pale as a ghost, then collapsed like a felled tree with a thud that still gives them chills. Our glorious leader here claims he didn't use Dark Arcana, but I clearly sense traces of its taint on you and the residue of temporal magic. Please tell me you weren't stupid enough to meddle with anything that dangerous.' Veronica said, watching me like a hawk, while Leszek seemed stunned by my sudden appearance.

'No, I didn't, but I bet I know who did, and it's the same man whose blood splashed on me. I injured a guy called Nikolai Rostov when he cornered me in a hospital lift using a weird-looking orb. I don't know if it was that or whatever he smashed on the floor that messed with time, but the nasty shit seemed overly pleased I got his blood on my face.' I said, marching toward the fridge.

'Do we have anything to drink? I'm parched.'

'He did what?!' Leszek's roar and the sound of broken granite made me jump and involuntarily step back when he approached. 'What did that bastard do to you?' He demanded, grasping my arms. Veronica's pale face told me she was also terrified by this sudden burst of rage.

'Nothing, I swear. I scratched him after he threatened my family, and it splashed on my face. Please don't tell me I did wrong because he was nasty and threatening.' I said, swallowing hard. 'I'm sorry, but this is not my fault. One moment I was visiting a patient, the next, he was inviting me to meet his boss and making shitty threats. I did my best to stop him. His orb thing disintegrated, but I grabbed the pieces after he ran off. I'm sorry. I didn't know he would attack your stash to replace the amber that broke... Leszek, please, you're hurting me.' I tried to stay calm, but I was at a loss for what he expected me to do, especially when his grip on my arm tightened, becoming painful.

The pleading tone in my voice broke through Leszek's rage, and he fell back, releasing my arms before diving forward again, gathering me up in a bear hug. 'I'm sorry, my Firefly. I'm so sorry. I'm not mad at you, but the thought I could have lost you. This bastard attacked you for the second time in less than two days. I'm not mad at you... Please don't be afraid. You should never be afraid of me, darling.'

'Actually, I think it might be the third time. There was a car crash on my way to work...' I said and gasped, trying to pull away when he roared.

'I'll fucking kill him. I will rip his guts out and hang him by them from a tree.' His words were a barbaric pledge fuelled by roaring anger, but there was desperation and the need to protect a loved one beneath it. I stroked his chest, feeling his trembling hands against my back, pressing me to him with fierce need. *That is extreme, even for Leszek. When did I become the centre of his world for him to react that way*? I thought, my heart filling with a warm glow I shouldn't be feeling.

'I'm fine. I didn't even realise it was an attack until Rostov showed up where the driver was being cared for. You should thank Veronica. It might have ended differently if she hadn't taught me so well.' I said, pulling his beard and forcing him to look at me. His soft hair tickled my hand when he tilted his head, the mossy green colour of his eyes drawing me in. 'I'm fine. I promise.' I said, and he kissed my forehead. His hands never left my skin like he feared I could crumble and fall any moment.

I looked at Veronica, who observed this display of affection with tightly knitted brows, and for the first time since I knew her, I saw uncertainty flashing in her expression.

'My Lord, you might have a bigger problem. A human that can influence time and a Soul Shepherd bonding to a guardian? I'm sorry, but you must face facts; the Council will insist on seeing her. You should beat them to the punch and take Sara to Gedania before they force the issue.' She said, and Leszek slowly turned in her direction.

'Force me? Those who could force me can't leave Gedania; the others, I'd like them to try. Sara is mine, and she will remain with me.' He said with a snarl, and the air surrounding us shimmered, making Veronica step back, gasping when the wave of power touched her skin. Leszek had felt so volatile since I woke up that it made me worry about his state of mind.

'Stop it! Just stop it! She only warned you about this Council. What the fuck is going on here? What are Gedania and the Gates, and why are you acting like a psycho as soon as Veronica mentioned them?' I tried to pull away, but he held me tight.

'I'm not giving you up. Even if they demand it.' After a deep, calming breath, he continued. 'Your magic... it is a temptation for us. Veronica's suggestions were misplaced. Even if you are a Soul Shepherd with enough magic to tie a god's soul to a living being, you still belong here with me. I found you, Sara. Even disregarding how I feel about you, this alone makes you mine. You may say our

Lady Fate, Dola, put you in my path.' He was calmer but so fixated on this one issue I couldn't get a coherent answer. I sent a pleading look to Veronica.

'Well... about that. Rostov said he came here to find the Soul Shepherd, that his associate was searching for me here. Maybe if I leave...'

Leszek didn't let me finish. His eyes glowed yellow while a menacing growl rumbled in his throat. 'You're going nowhere.' Before he wrapped his arms around me as tight as he could without hurting me.

'Please explain this to me in simple language. A few weeks ago, I didn't know magic existed. Now I'm being chased by a psycho, and this one seems to have gained an overprotective trait and turned it up to eleven. On top of that, something called Gedania wants me?' I asked.

My words brought a hint of a smile to Veronica's face. 'You triggered Leszek's transformation into a wolf when you fainted, and it's left him a little unstable, or so I'm told. Balancing this energy will take the Forest Lord some time, but he will calm down. Still, I don't envy you having to deal with an Alpha wolf in a mating frenzy.' She answered, and I sighed slightly, turning back to look at my lover.

Looking slightly abashed and agitated, Leszek mumbled. 'I thought you'd died. When you collapsed, I thought I'd lost you. That triggered the shift.'

'And the appearance of the Great Wolf triggered the entire pack, escalating an already tense situation, but on the plus side, having the supreme Alpha with his divine power show up accelerated the healing process. The wolves were as good as new within a few hours. So except for our Lord being slightly unhinged, you did a great job.'

'Are my friends alright?'

'Yes, darling. They even became a part of the pack somehow.' Leszek said, smiling for the first time, and I exhaled, relieved that the worst-case scenario I had in my head was avoided. Still, I had more questions, and I looked at Veronica.

'Tell me about Gedania?' I asked the witch before patting Leszek's hand. 'I'm here, Wolfie. In your arms, safe and sound, but I need a drink, and I'm starving. Could you please let me go so I can make some food while Veronica answers my question?'

'No, you sit here, and I will do it.' He said, lifting me onto a stool and marching toward the fridge.

'Wolfie?' Veronica mouthed silently, trying to restrain budding laughter while I shrugged, sharing her merriment and mouthing back, *'It fits.'*

While Leszek valiantly fought with the coffee machine and prepared sandwiches, she told me about the creation of the Nether and its separation from the mortal realm, creating an alternate plane of existence. The place called Gedania was, in essence, a magical Gdansk existing in the Nether with three Gates that allowed the magical races passage back and forth, but because of the very nature of the magic, the old races and augmented humans could visit and meet but couldn't live in each other's world.

Leszek placed a coffee and a plate of colourful sandwiches before me, and I stroked his forearm. 'How come you are here? You are part of the old races, yes?'

'I'm more than that, my Firefly. I am the Lord of the Forest. I was worshipped as the Leshy by those who lived in harmony with nature. To stay here, I had to give up almost all of my power and live as a magically talented human, stronger than most, but nothing extraordinary. A few of us stayed behind, but many could not endure the loss of power and ultimately left to live in the Nether. I could claim that my intentions were noble, that I chose to protect those touched by magic, but it would be a lie. I stayed because I couldn't live apart from my forest, and I like this life.'

'That's... well, enlightening, but what does it have to do with me and the attacks? Oh, and before I forget, I have the pieces of that amber orb in my bag. You grabbed my bag, didn't you?' I asked, turning toward Leszek, who shook his head.

'I had something more important to carry, but Jarek delivered it earlier. You've acquired a loyal Guardian who also claims he wants to become a paramedic now.' The more time he spent in my company, the more relaxed Leszek became, and I was grateful for this small mercy because I wasn't sure how long I could put up with his Alpha-male-wolf craziness.

'The man who attacked you serves Czernobog, who always was against separating the worlds. I thought he chose Gdansk because of the abundance of amber and because this land is much closer to the Nether, but it looks like he came here to find one of your kind. If what he told you was the truth. The sphere you saw probably created something called null-time, which does exactly what you think. A room built of amber with that spell embedded could house a god safely in this world, allowing them to use the full might of their magic. That room isn't the only means for a god to live in the mortal realm... a Soul Shepherd can also provide that.' Leszek said, and I felt a sense of uneasiness grow.

'So you say I am the means of bringing a god to the human realm, and that's why this man attacked me? What about the woman he mentioned?' I said before realising, overwhelmed by the recent events, I hadn't told him about this part yet. 'Rostov said she was tasked to find me, and that attack was her own doing,' I asked, and Leszek shrugged.

'You are powerful, Sara. Even if your power is not active, the fact that your presence allows a god to exist in the mortal realm makes you a target of any god. Any; even I couldn't resist the temptation, although it was only partially about your magic and mostly about this wonderful, amazing woman coming into my life,' he said, stroking my cheek before his lips tilted in a mischievous grin, and he continued.

'You must have heard the legends of maidens seduced and kidnapped by the gods of old. They all have one thing in common: your abilities. With the stag and wolf's energy coursing through my body, I feel more like my old self than ever before. However, you are the only one of your kind, and the Nether is full of those who would like to taste the mortal world again while walking in their full glory.' He bent, kissing my temple, while I listened, stunned by this information. Veronica told me some of those, but having Leszek disclose it all was a revelation.

'Having your spirit tethered to mortal flesh is dangerous, but many would take this risk. What I'm feeling, it's amazing, and you did it. Czernobog wants you because you can release him from the Nether. The Council of Gedania will want to keep you within their grasp for the same reason, and I just want you safe, here with me, because I'm a selfish bastard.'

Leszek said it all with a hint of sadness, and I felt cracks appear in the facade of my new life. 'Well, I'm tired. I will go to my room and have a nap. If you need the remains of the sphere, it is in my bag. Wherever my bag is. Veronica, can we continue my lessons as soon as we can? I need to learn some offensive magic and how to defend myself. I was left weak as a baby with a nosebleed fighting the null-time spell.' I asked, and she grabbed her bag from the table.

'Just call me when you're ready, Sara. I know we didn't get off to a good start, but you have potential, and if you are to remain here, we must ensure you can look after yourself, not just others.' She said, giving Leszek a pointed look before heading toward the door. Leszek escorted her, and I used the moment to escape to my room, locking the door behind me.

You are sad. Why are you sad? Are you injured? Scarface's voice in my head was as concerned as a cat could be. I picked him up, burying my face in his soft fur.

'That's what happens when you realise you are but a pawn in a game of chess.' I said, sitting at the edge of the bed.

We all are, but why is this making you sad?

'Because I fell for Leszek. I thought there was a spark between us. Something real. I wanted nothing to do with him when I met him, but I learned he's funny, smart, and cares for his people and this place. I thought he had some feelings for me, and I'm sure he has, just not the kind I want.'

And what feelings do you want?

'I want him to love me. Me, Sara Wilska. Not the Soul Shepherd and gateway to his powers. Just me. But I am who I am, and he can't help that my magic has drawn him like a moth to the flame. Now I'll never know if he'd even look at me twice if not for my god-binding power. So I have to decide if being his pocket battery and booty call is enough for me.' I felt tears pooling in my eyes, but how could I explain to my cat that it hurt to know Leszek wouldn't love or even notice me if not for my gift?

The knock on the door and rattling handle startled me.

'Sara? Why are you locked in your room? Have I said something wrong? I promise Rostov will never approach you again. Sara, please, talk to me, darling.' Leszek's voice was strained, and I heard him pacing outside.

'We will talk, but not now, please; I'm tired.' Whatever he heard in my voice made him break into my room, the door bursting inwards, and before I knew it, I was in his arms, trying to blink my tears away. It was clearly the wrong day to reject the big bad wolf.

'Please, my love. What can I do to make it better? What... Sara, what have I done to make you cry?' He said, looking so lost as his thumb wiped my tears away.

'You made me fall in love with you, and I don't even know if you really care.'

Chapter Twenty-Seven

Sara was crying, and although I didn't know why, I knew it was my fault. It helps no one to self-flagellate, but I saw her flinch in fear each time my emotions overwhelmed me. I am supposed to protect her, make her feel happy and safe, not run away, too scared to face me.

I was still on the edge after she collapsed in front of me. Much to my shame, I didn't even catch her, unable to move as a surge of magic and panic caused my transformation, not into the stag, but into my wolf. I didn't hesitate once I had changed, dragging the healers to care for Sara, my form less of a hindrance than expected as everyone's concern for my Firefly cut through any misunderstandings.

Once Sara was safely inside and cared for, I'd finally calmed down enough to change back and call Veronica, meeting her at the manor a few hours later. That's when everything truly went to shit. After examining Sara and performing several spells, the witch had grown angrier with each passing word. She finished her work and turned on me in a furious outburst, accusing me of the most heinous crimes. To say I didn't react well is an understatement, and my Firefly had walked in during our stand-off, witnessing my disgusting behaviour.

I understood why she ran away to her bedroom but was unable to stop myself from following, only to discover I had no idea what Sara was thinking, her confession of love flooring me. The next thing I knew, I was holding my lover tenderly against my chest.

As I looked down, her shoulders shaking as she cried, I knew leaving my feelings unsaid would destroy this fledgling relationship, so I gathered my courage and spoke. 'Why do you think my feelings aren't real? I can't live without you or think straight if we're apart, and that was all before anything happened with my magic. I was in love with you from the moment you tried to kick me out of the ER; I just didn't know it, but when I realised? I was worried my feelings would scare you away. I love you, my Firefly.' I stroked her hair to reassure her about my affection, but Sara stiffened at my words and pulled away. She cupped my face, and although she smiled, it didn't reach her eyes. My woman radiated sadness and resignation, yet she tried to make me feel better.

'I know, Wolfie. I understand now you couldn't help it, and I'm fine. It's not that I mind being the beacon of power for a Guardian god, but it was a lot to take in, and I'll need time to come to terms with everything, so don't worry; nothing's changed between us. I just need a moment.' She kissed me gently, and I let it slide despite knowing she was lying.

'So you bought me a military mobile med unit then? No one's ever given me such a thoughtful gift. I promise I will put it to good use.' She said, and while there was amusement in her voice, she pulled away again. I reached up, holding the hand resting on my cheek, and leaned into it, but Sara avoided my eyes. I felt claws piercing the fabric of my trousers and glanced down. Her familiar looked distressed, and even I flinched under the cat's unblinking stare.

'I like the nickname you used.' I said, hoping that some cheerfulness and intimacy would help her relax. Even if this forever ruined my standing among the shifters, it didn't matter as Sara smiled, leaning toward me.

'It fits you. Even when I saw you with antlers, you looked predatory, and while you may be a big bad wolf for the rest of the world, for me, you are my Wolfie.' She said, placing her head on my shoulder. Fuck, it felt so good to hold her like this that I wouldn't object if she called me Puppy and insisted on playing fetch. Whatever her objections were, the moment I saw her falling was my undoing and whatever doubts were gnawing at her heart, I would discover and dispel them before Sara decided I wasn't good enough for her.

'It is still unfinished, the unit, but I hope you like the concept of this hospital. I wanted you to feel free to practice medicine without worrying about inadequate equipment. You won't have to quit your job, as I know you love it. I wanted to give you freedom from worry while creating something to help my people.'

'I know. Well, now I have a team that I can work with, so we can help set everything up, and this healer, Jora, I want her to work there. She is impressive, and I like how quickly she makes decisions.' Sara patted my forearm before pointing toward the door. 'Let me sleep now. We can go through the details later. I have a shift tomorrow, and I'm still tired.'

Sara made a shooing gesture, dismissing me, but I couldn't let it happen. 'It will be as you wish. I will ask Tomasz if Jora want to work with you. After all, she is his mate. If you need anything else, just tell me.' I said, lifting her up despite her protests and returning to my bedroom.

'You are sleeping in my bed. With me, every night.' I said, looking at her expecting her to challenge me.

'I know.' That was not the answer I expected, and her submission worried me more than her silent tears.

I still had to make phone calls and organise security around the Gates. I had my amber enterprise to run, but it all felt less important than her, and I felt torn between the need to protect my people and worry over Sara. She must have noticed my struggle because she kissed my cheek.

'Go. I promise I will still be sleeping in your bed when you return. Although I don't promise I will be alone.' She said, pointing to the cat who had followed and now stared at me, ready to take my place as soon as I vacated it.

'Our bed, and I don't mind sharing with Scarface, as long as he knows when to defer to the master of the house.'

Sara looked at the cat before she burst out laughing, and knowing how she communicated with her familiar, I had a suspicion his comments had been less than complimentary, but as long as she smiled, I was happy to be the butt of their jokes, and in the spirit of the moment reached down to scratch the cat's chin.

'Look after her, my friend.' I said, and he blinked at me before trotting over to Sara and curling beside her. It took all of my willpower to leave, and as soon as I was out of earshot, Michal appeared, giving me a questioning look.

'Why did you break her doors, Sir?' His overly formal tone didn't bode well for me. He cared for Sara and was ready to give me a hard time.

'She was crying, and I was at a loss for what to do. This evening has been difficult for her, and Veronica wasn't helpful.'

Michal nodded before walking to the kitchen, and I heard him muttering. 'Were you also at a loss for what to do here as well?'

The mess from my food preparation must have bothered him, but feeding Sara satisfied my wolf, and I regretted nothing.

I went to my office, noticing a few unanswered phone calls, one from Tomasz and three others from Adam. After a quick debate, I decided my favourite bloodsucker could wait and scrolled to find Tomasz's number. The whole pack dynamic shifted when I turned into an auburn beast of a wolf and howled my distress in front of them.

The wolves had answered, unthinking, and I was soon surrounded by shifters in their animal form, all pressing closer to ease my suffering. If Sara's friends hadn't been there to take charge, I don't know what might have happened, their no-nonsense attitude turning a disaster into a minor difficulty.

Something I now had to face was the very real chance that my final avatar, the bear, would soon follow if I remained beside Sara. If that happened, I would be living proof that the old gods could walk the earth again with their powers intact. I was sure the Council wouldn't like it, especially if the magic maintaining the Nether was stripped away, returning to those it was initially taken from. Their worries over a few elder races crossing over for brief visits would be nothing compared to the return of magic to the mortal realm at the expense of their home.

Tomasz picked up after the third ring.

'My Lord, my... Alpha, thank you for calling back. The pack has been unsettled since the Great Wolf returned, calling for a challenge. I would like to know how you wish to proceed.' His voice was reverent but full of hesitance and submission I had never heard before.

'I'm not going to challenge you for command of your family. Not now, not ever. The stag, the wolf and the bear are part of who I was, and despite their return, this is the twenty-first century. I am no longer a god and don't need to be worshipped or obeyed. We have a good working relationship, no, a friendship that I wish to continue, if possible.'

I heard a choking sound on the other side of the call before he spoke.

'Thank you, Sir, you have both my loyalty and the packs. I was wrong about your woman. She is a great asset, and... my mate thinks I was an idiot for questioning your decision,' he said.

'Tell Jora she is a sage woman, and Sara would love to work with her again. If she wishes, of course. With this new facility, there will be a lot to organise, but if anything, last night's events showed me it was essential.' I said without bothering to rein in my amusement. A powerful Alpha chastised by his mate, who'd taken a liking to my little Firefly, what wasn't there to love about it?

'I will ask her, but I already know the answer. Jora will be there tomorrow, coordinating the renovations.'

'Perfect, have a good night Tomasz and remember, I have your back as long as you have mine.'

It was true. I didn't want things to change, enhanced power or not. I was, first and foremost, their leader, not their ruler. Having the shifter pack unchanged left me in a good mood that perished when I contacted Adam.

'We have a problem.' He said as soon as he picked up the phone. 'Nadolny sent footage from his surveillance cameras catching some unusual activity near the gateway to Gedania. He posted men there to deter any casual bystanders, but instead, they encountered people spoiling for a fight. I compared the timing to the Council's reports of attacks on the Gates. Whenever these men cause trouble, there's an attack at the other Gates.' Adam paused, letting me absorb the information.

'Go on, I feel there is more to it.'

'Once Nadolny's men are distracted, the cameras pick up a person leaving the gate's vicinity, one that didn't arrive. Add that to the amount of amber stolen during the recent attack.... I'd say we have trouble,' he said before pausing again. The next question I expected, but instead of the usual mockery, I heard genuine concern in the vampire's voice. 'I also heard you shifted into a wolf when Sara fainted. Is she alright? I haven't told Nina yet. Otherwise, you'd already have her knocking down your door, and I'd like to avoid her being upset; it irks me.'

'Are you involved with Nina?' I asked, and he grunted, which was as close to yes as I'd ever get. It was so unusual for Adam to form attachments to anyone, let alone a living, breathing person, that I accepted his answer.

'Sara was accosted in the hospital. She escaped Rostov's temporal distortion, and an amber sphere was destroyed during the encounter. The bastard threatened the lives of her friends, so be careful.' I said.

'She broke through a null-time bubble? Fuck, that means she's powerful enough to cross the Veil and rescue your soul, others too.' He asked, biting back a curse before huffing, 'Gedania won't like it. This will disturb the status quo, and Jurata, you can have her back.'

'Jurata left this place when, despite hoarding amber, she couldn't regain her full power. Her title and magic meant more than the people she swore to protect. It meant more than me. What I do now is for our people and none of her concern.'

'I'm not contesting that, but I know women, and judging by Gedania's attitude so far, they will see Sara in two ways. As someone to exploit or a threat to their existence. I suspect the latter as someone already tried to kill her.' Adam was playing Mister Obvious, explaining what I already knew. Not that there was anyone there strong enough to face me now. The old gods' power, whilst still immense, had faded alongside the human desire to worship them, but they were still a threat, as were their followers.

'I will deal with them when the time comes. Guard Nina. I will ask Nadolny to send more people to the Gates, and we'll reinforce our position, too. This time, tell them I'll personally eviscerate anyone not wearing a bulletproof vest. We need to find Rostov's mercenaries individually; fighting them is too messy when magic is involved. They're human, so I want eyes in every brothel, watering hole, pub, and nightclub in Tricity. Anyone with a Russian accent throwing cash around is to be tailed. We also need press coverage. Make sure you give them something creative.' I said, and Adam burst into laughter.

'I love it when you get all evil overlord on me. Consider it done.' He said, ending the call.

I sat in my chair, pondering the situation. Ideally, I would send a messenger and visit Gedania tomorrow, as it looked like someone there supported Rostov. They already knew about Sara, and it was time to stake my claim to the Soul Shepherd. She wouldn't like it, but the only way to keep her safe was to ensure everyone in the Nether knew she belonged to me. *How will she react if I create a blood tie to her?* I wondered whether to tell her about it but decided against it, not yet, at least.I knew I was ready to share my immortality, but Sara might not want this burden. *I will face this challenge when I come to it*, I decided before quickly showering and joining Sara in bed.

As promised, she was sleeping, her mouth slightly open, puffy eyes a sign she'd continued crying secretly to not upset me. If I could understand what was wrong, I would do anything to fix it. When I slid under the covers, she wriggled, tossing and turning before laying her head on my chest and embracing me with a soft whimper. Fierce protectiveness surged through my body. Sara had become a target of power-hungry maniacs and forgotten gods because of me. I couldn't even promise her a peaceful future, but there was one thing I could swear. I will love no other but her, my brave Firefly, the light of my soul, the woman who agreed to be mine forever.

I awoke to the sun peeking through the curtains and soft kisses trailing down my chest, the desire they awoke chasing away my lethargy. Sara's hands trailed over my naked skin, her featherlight touch making me groan. When I stirred, pushing my hips up, eager for her hand to move lower, I heard her soft chuckle before teeth nipped at the skin of my stomach.

'Endure,' she said, and I barely restrained the need to grab her hair and drag her to my lips for a kiss. Instead, I tore at the sheets, securing my grip, willing myself to be still while my woman took liberties with my body. Liberties I very much enjoyed.

'Don't test me, beloved. I may have no strength to resist.'

My breath came with shallow rasps when her lips trailed over my shaft so close I felt her warm breath but not quite touching. My manhood twitched, a drop of lubrication glistening on the top as she tortured me with her slow, soft caress.

When Sara's nails scratched the inside of my thighs, my hips jerked involuntarily and, taking pity on my torment, Sara grasped my cock. Her fingers applied just the right amount of pressure to make me shiver. She was perfect, my spirited, delightful miracle, the mass of her honey-blond hair flowing down in gentle spell-binding waves.

Sara looked up, still holding me tight and drawing her fist slowly upwards, and when our gaze met, she swiped her tongue beneath the flared dome of my shaft. My mind went blank. Desire shot through me, wiping any reasonable thought, and I moaned, buckling into her hand. My manhood slid into her eager mouth as she lowered her head. Sara started pumping, sucking and hollowing her cheeks to take me deeper till the tip hit the back of her throat.

'You will be the end of me, woman,' I rasped. A moan tore from me as I lost control, and unable to stop myself, I placed my hand on her head, pushing her down. I know I shouldn't have, but the need to dominate burned in my veins. Before I reached my climax, Sara pulled away, leaving me panting and confused.

'Sara?'

'No, my Wolfie, I want to ride you,' she said, sliding over my body and straddling my hips. I was more than eager to oblige. The head breached her entrance, and I hissed when the pain of my strained muscles mixed with pleasure. Sara was tight, so tight I could barely breathe. It felt impossibly good to feel her taking me with the bliss blossoming on her face. I grasped her hips, pulling her down slowly onto my hard cock until she moaned, then thrusting upwards, driving my shaft up to the hilt. Sara gasped at the intense pleasure, leaning forward until her nipples trailed over my chest.

'You feel so good,' she breathed, and I started moving.

Nothing else mattered but the tightness of her body that wrapped around me like a sleeve, sending me into a frenzy. Whether she intended to ride me or not, we both thrust our hips, seeking ecstasy together, the wildness of our passion echoing around the room. Even as control slipped my grasp, I fought to hold back, wanting to feel Sara's climax before my own, but when I saw her pupils widen, head falling back as her scream of delight signalled the pulsing of her bliss, I roared at my own release, ecstasy wiping away thought.

The sounds of our passion could have woken the dead, but I didn't care. Sex with Sara was overwhelming. My body convulsed as I came, her own spasms prolonging my ecstasy. She fell onto my chest with my cock still inside her, and I stroked her back, marvelling at the happiness I felt.

'Take me to Gedania. Just like Veronica advised. I want to see it, and I want to help you. I'm not a pawn to protect, and I'm done with being afraid.' She said, and instinctively, I embraced her harder.

'No, Gedania is not a place for you. Especially being as magically gifted as you are. As for helping me, you are already doing more than I dreamed possible. You saved my shifters. I couldn't have done it without you.' I said, wondering what prompted her requests.

'That's not enough. I want to find the men who shot the wolves and their arsehole of a leader. I have an idea and resources you may not have. I know you think I'm weak, that I'm just a human with passive magic, ready to be exploited, so I understand, but before you say no again, please hear me out.'

The perils of loving an intelligent, passionate woman always appear at the most unusual moments, like now, with Sara wanting to discuss her plans with my cock still buried deep inside her.

'Can't it wait a bit? I'm not sure my brain is working right now.' I said, trying to delay the inevitable, but Sara laughed.

'I have you pinned down. There is no better moment than now. You met my friends. What impression did they give you?'

'Who? Nina and those men, the paramedics?'

'Yes, Nina, Rysiek and Damian. I'm asking because if you can trust me, the four of us have a network wide enough to catch anything abnormal happening in Gdansk. If you give me free rein, I promise to catch those trigger-happy Russians for you.'

'Sara, this really isn't the time....'

'It is the time. Before we met, I was something more than...a helpless princess waiting to be rescued. I used to lead people. I'm not stupid or defenceless and definitely not a damsel in distress. I want to help, so I will, and I'll prove to you, to everyone, that I'm not just the Forest Lord's pet. Please, don't make me beg.'

Why Sara thought anyone saw her as helpless was beyond me, but I suspected her outburst was connected to yesterday's sadness, and, stripped of choice, I answered, my fingers stroking her cheek.

'You don't need to prove anything, Sara, but I understand. I'm just worried everyone will see how little I deserve you and steal you away.' I made light of my concerns, but her radiant smile washed away my worries. Seeing Sara so happy made me want to do anything to keep her smiling. The downside was her jumping off my hips, leaving us both messy from the aftermath of our enthusiastic morning, then giggling as she ran to the bathroom for a shower that included several reminders of eighties pop music.

I waited my turn to get clean, knowing what would happen if I didn't, and by the time I'd finished, joining her in the kitchen, Sara was prowling the room on the phone, coffee in hand.

'I hate doing it, but I'll call in sick at work, Nina and the boys, too.' Turning to me, Sara covered the mouthpiece of the phone, asking. 'Can I use the facility from yesterday, or will we have to squeeze in here?'

'You can use the clinic. Sara? What are you planning?' I asked, but she was already back on the phone.

'Yes, the clinic is good. Tell the others we'll meet there, and I'll bring Jarek to prove our story. No, it's fine.' She said, grabbing the sweet roll Michal left for her.

'Sara?' This time, my voice carried a warning. I loved seeing her happy again, but her enthusiasm for engaging humans in my affairs worried me.

'Trust me, love. I know what I'm doing. Just give me a lift, please?' She said, kissing my cheek, and I closed my eyes, inhaling slowly.

'I have a better idea. I'll help, and if things don't go as planned, I can always make whoever you bring to the table forget that they ever learned about the elder races.'

Sara frowned, not liking this, and for a moment, I thought she would argue, but instead, she smiled and nodded.

'I guess that's reasonable, and it's a suitable solution as long as it doesn't hurt or damage their minds. I promise it will work, though. I'm good at what I do and can be useful even without magic,' she said before placing the cup in the sink and heading to her room.

'I'll be ready in five.' She shouted, and I grabbed my favourite tea leaves for a drink. Sara's attitude and the sudden need to prove herself, despite already being the best thing to happen to me in centuries, must have stemmed from yesterday. I had a feeling it would be a tough day, but if proving herself was going to keep her tears away, I was ready to bespell the entire population of Gdansk to forget once she was done with them.

Chapter Twenty-Eight

Last night was a revelation, mainly about my emotions and what I wanted for my future. So many things became clearer. The way he'd avoided me, how he asked me to stop him and reject his claim. He'd tried so hard to not tie me to him, and I was the one who pushed him over the edge. I knew Leszek loved me, but did he love me or my ability to return the lost pieces of his soul? Did he even know me? Did I let him know me?

These questions hurt because I realised I had fallen in love with him. Not the mighty Forest Lord or wealthy syndicate boss, but the man who brought me cinnamon rolls and cared enough to take the kid's pain away to let me heal him. My strange, maimed god, who'd given away his powers to create a haven for the elder races, stayed behind to protect the ones too human to escape. My accidental criminal overload ruling over those augmented by magic, or rather letting them govern themselves, only insisting on their help to safeguard their own existence. Leszek was unique in many ways, but for me, he was the only one in the long stream of boyfriends to put my needs above his own, and I wanted us to have a fighting chance.

The month I'd been left to fend for myself, any free time had been taken up by learning about magic or, more often, the various races still living in, as they called it, the mortal realm. Michal and Jarek were my primary sources of information, but I met with Ilona, and Veronica had talked to me after her initial reticence. During this time, I also learned about the being that stood apart, protecting those left behind, the man I'd slowly come to understand, and with understanding came love.

He was stern, regal and compassionate, and his violence always came with a justifiable motive and at great personal cost. This was the man I loved, but to him, I was a delicate Firefly to be sheltered and pampered and fed sugary baked goods. He couldn't be more wrong.

I was a woman who could face a maniac with an axe to protect her staff. I was the woman who negotiated with` deserters when they threatened our field hospital in Kosovo. I defended and fought beside those I cared for and was not afraid to face this challenging new life. I wanted Leszek to know the real Sara and love her. I wanted him to love the woman eager to fight, not hide on a warded island, letting others die in her place.

Knowing Jarek and now Jora helped me reach a decision. These were my people, my patients, shot down like beasts by a man who wanted to use me as a gateway for his god. I'd had enough of it, and whoever messed with them would face my wrath, but first, I had to ensure Leszek knew the woman he belonged to.

Our morning encounter, incredible as it was, didn't go exactly to plan. Part of me was delighted that I couldn't dominate him in bed. If anything, our lovemaking was more like riding a bucking bronco than the slow, teasing pleasure I intended, and I adored every moment.

I sat beside him when he quietly drove the car through the bustling city. I knew I would do whatever it took to make him love me. What might have started as a desire for the Soul Shepherd would end with him loving the real me. His partner, his woman and someone determined to make life better for those forced to hide in the shadows.

'You're very quiet, Sara. What are you thinking about?' He asked, a wariness in his eyes like he was waiting for me to cry again.

'You. I was thinking about you.'

'And what conclusion did you come to?' He enquired casually, but I noticed his knuckles whitening on the steering wheel.

'That you pass muster,' I said, chuckling slightly when he snapped an incredulous look toward me. 'I may, however, need more things from my apartment if my stay is to last any longer.'

'We will move your belongings tomorrow. Tell Michal if you need anything extra, and he will buy it. This is your home now, Sara. You can change whatever you want. Just... please be happy.' His last words, though whispered, coincided with our arrival, and I heard every word.

The warehouse looked more like an office in the daylight, its facade slightly intimidating. The row of windows almost looked like one solid glass panel reflecting the light and overlooking Gdansk Bay. Somehow, the landscaping around the building was well maintained, leaving a large, open space at the front entrance. That created a little green oasis in this otherwise industrial district.

Once inside, I saw Nina was already there with her new shadow, Adam. The vampire looked grumpy and lethargic, tucked in the darkest corner.

'Sara, care to explain your cryptic messages and why you rushed everyone here?' She said, waving to Leszek, who nodded in return and went to talk to Adam. I nodded at the porter, whose shadow gave the impression of a larger creature than his size indicated.

'Can you lead me to the office, please, and bring up whoever arrives looking for Sara.' When the man nodded, guiding me upstairs, Nina grabbed my elbow.

'What is going on, hun? Something to do with yesterday?' She asked, and I nodded.

'Yes, I've had enough of being someone's prey. It is time to become the hunter, but I need my pack to help me.'

'Your... pack? You speaking wolf, or do you mean dumb and dumber?' she said, and I rolled my eyes. The nicknames Nina gave to people were rarely flattering, but I hoped one day she would stop using that one for Damian and Rysiek.

'Yes, them, Kris and... Kamil too.'

'You called your ex? The motorbike riding, possessive as all hell, undercover policeman, ex?' Nina's eyes were round with surprise, and I didn't blame her. Kamil was... well, if he hadn't ended up in the police, he would probably be in charge of Nadolny's racketeering business or even the new boss. He loved the adrenaline and the opportunity for violence. We had a high-voltage fling in Kosovo and a few weeks afterwards, but I realised nothing connected us except great sex and the adrenaline rush. Still, we parted as friends and chatted occasionally, even if I didn't tell Nina about it.

'Yes, that Kamil. Try to be nice. I need his help.'

A moment later, the boys waltzed in, dressed like commandoes, led by a puffed-up Jarek, his pride at being included shining through.

Kris was the first to react. Big, burly, and the oldest in the group, he was my shoulder to cry on, the big brother I'd always wished to have. I met him when I was still at uni. He carried me home after a particularly boozy night and then held my hair while I emptied my stomach into the bushes. An experience like this instantly cemented his position as family. Much later, he told me he saw a guy spiking my drink and couldn't ignore it and allow someone to get hurt.

'Hi sweety, what's the problem?' He asked as I was engulfed by a bear hug that always felt like home. *If this works, maybe I can have the best of both worlds*, I thought before seeing Leszek's eyes flash dangerously over Kris' shoulder.

'Have a seat, and I will tell you everything. Nina and the guys already know some of the truth. I ask that you keep an open mind because I need your help.' I said, then explained the complexity of the Nether and the world that existed under their noses yet was so well hidden.

I had to admit I was afraid of Kamil's reaction. My ex had always been unpredictable, borderline psychotic, really, but he took the information onboard with hardly any response. When I mentioned Jarek was a shifter, he looked at him strangely before ordering.

'Show me.'

I nodded, and Jarek complied, making Kris push his chair away, which hit the floor with a loud thud, but Kamil only smiled.

'Well, that explains the family stories. So how can I help, my lovely? Maybe after we're finished here, we could go for a drink and rekindle our friendship?'

Here we go again, I thought, half expecting him to pull this stunt. Kamil firmly believed in friends with benefits, and giving him a chance to show off in front of other men? I would have laughed it off any other time, but he always had to pick the worst time. Leszek moved behind me in a blur, placing a hand on my shoulder.

'I'm willing to forgive you for ordering my people around in the interests of a better understanding, but make no mistake, Sara is mine.' Nina snorted, quickly covering it up with an unconvincing cough while I patted Leszek's forearm.

'I think they got the message, love.' I said, equally embarrassed and happy at his eagerness to stake his claim.

Kris walked toward us, his posture radiating challenge, and I frowned, never having seen him do this before. My gentle giant stood before Leszek, beginning a staring contest before he said.

'Only if Sara wishes. Make her unhappy, and I'll bring the whole firefighter squad to kick your arse.'

I couldn't believe it. We had a job to do, and here they were, prancing around like peacocks. I freed myself from Leszek's arm and slammed my hands on the table.

'Oi. Calm your bollocks. I need you to focus, not engage in a pissing contest. We have half a fecking army out there shooting shifters and a weird Warlock who wants to; well, I'm not sure what he wants, but he's a creepy shit. We can't trace the Warlock because of some temporal magic, but I want you to help me find his men. Between us all, we should be able to locate some Russian soldiers with too much money and saying weird shit about amber and Gates.'

That seemed to sober them up.

'Fine. I will check with immigration and the border police. They have a register for all visas. How far back do you want me to dig? Would the last three months be enough?' Kamil was already pulling out his phone when I grabbed the map from my bag, catching Leszek's nod and confirming the timing.

'Perfect. Nina, you have the number for your crush in search and rescue, yes? See if they've had any reports of unusual activity near Hel, both the town and the peninsula. Damian, is your military friend still in the Border Force?' I asked, and when he nodded, I pointed to the Kaliningrad border. 'If they entered the country illegally, that's the most likely spot. So check the records for any sightings, arrests, etcetera. Rysiek, they've stolen a lot of amber, so probably need trucks or some heavy transport. Your job will be to phone the car dealers and rentals. If you can, sweet-talk transportation services to see if they've had an increase in freight citations as well. I will call the local hospitals to check for people injured in animal attacks and check the rumour mill for any stories. Kris and Adam, analyse the data and see what you can connect.' I said, taking a deep breath and looking at Leszek. 'I need a white-board, food and if you could ask the Coven if they know a way of detecting temporal magic? Also, if we can include Nadolny in this, we could eliminate their operations from our results.'

He looked at me, eyebrows raised and blinking in disbelief before he caught sight of the gathered faces. The mischievous smile that lit his face made my heart stutter, especially when this impossible man sent me a mocking salute.

'Yes, ma'am.' He snapped out, but before he left to fulfil my wishes, he bent down, kissing my temple gently. 'You are incredible. I am fortunate to have you by my side.'

His words warmed the depths of my heart. My first step to merging both of my worlds was done, and looking at my friends chatting with their contacts, it felt like I had made an excellent decision.

By the end of the day, I wasn't so sure of my decision, as tempers had shortened and our initial progress ground to a halt. Still, the whiteboard was full of clues, accidental encounters, and reports. Much to the joy of Damian's border control colleague, we located a few cigarette smugglers and an underage prostitution ring. We also helped Leszek's business when we discovered a fake amber factory. Each problem we solved seemed to help everyone but us.

Kamil even went so far as organising a teleconference between all involved parties, then shamelessly lied to Interpol, asking for extradition warrants from the Russian Federation, claiming it was part of an undercover investigation.

I felt something elusive teasing the edges of my understanding, which irritated me to the core.

'You tried, my love. It is not a failure to eliminate other possibilities. Each negative result narrows down the field and saves time later. I've been looking for over a month, so it's alright if we continue tomorrow.' Leszek tried to cheer me up, but I was angry. So many hours, pins on the board and telephone calls that led nowhere. I even called the tax office because... death and taxes, but I only surprised the poor clerk with my demands.

'I thought I could give you answers. I feel so useless!' In my outburst, I hit the board with the map and carefully pinned notes, screaming shortly when one of the pin's plastic caps broke, and the metal sank into my skin. 'Fuck! Now what?'

I tried to pull back my hand, but a vision overwhelmed my senses. The sight of an old fort, abandoned except for an archaeological exhibition, blossomed in my mind. The image twisted, moving inside to show a stone table encrusted with shards of amber and covered with the blood of several bodies that were discarded to the side like garbage. When I saw men carrying large unpolished blocks of amber, I knew I was seeing current events.

When the vision faded, I found myself held in Leszek's arms while the rest of my team looked at the board with stunned expressions. The papers, so carefully pinned into place on the map, with all their important information, were now ripped and covered in blood, all except for one location.

'The hill?' I queried, frowning as not a single note pointed to this place, but Leszek ignored my confusion, grabbing my hand and turning it over to check the wound.

Nina was the first to react, her usual brusque manner only slightly shaken. 'We have a suture kit downstairs. Damian, you know where they are.' she said, and my friend obediently ran to fetch one.

'I don't have time for this. Look at the map. I know where to find them and why you couldn't sense Rostov.'

'No. I need to make sure you are alright first. Then we will see to the map.' He said, holding me firmly, earning himself an appreciative grunt from Kris while, with a sigh and roll of my eyes, I allowed Leszek to be overprotective, giving myself permission to enjoy it.

'Well, that's new. Congratulations. Sara never listened to me,' Kamil said, and I wondered if he'd developed a death wish over the years because even he should know goading Leszek wasn't the wisest choice. Before I could open my mouth to shut him down, my lover answered.

'Thank you. Open communication is important in a successful relationship. Otherwise, you wouldn't be here. You'd be in a ditch, unable to even remember your name. Sara is wise, only fighting battles she can win.' He said before leaning down and kissing the top of my head, whispering in my ear loud enough for everybody to hear it. 'Can I hex this one, just a little? He is getting on my nerves.'

His teasing made my lips twitch, especially since I wasn't entirely sure if he was joking, but Damian saved the day, returning with a suture kit and together with Nina, they patched me up, fussing more than I was comfortable with.

'Have you finished? Can I talk now?' I asked, irritated at two seasoned emergency practitioners fretting over a minor wound before Nina pointed to the board with an offended expression.

'If you're finished spraying blood around like you cut an artery. Adam said blood magic is powerful and can give you control over the victim.'

'Since when did you become close enough to share educational pillow talk with the vampire?' I asked, only now noticing she was wearing a turtleneck jumper.

'Since you saddled me with him, and he refused to leave.' Nina snapped, and I reached out, pulling the edge of her collar down.

'Oh, that motherfucker! I'm going to kill him!'

Two puncture marks stood out against Nina's pale skin, evidence that my failure had exposed her to the vampire's influence.

'Too late. I'm already dead.' Adam stood in the doorframe, smirking, and I grabbed the nearest object, hurling it in his direction. Nina sighed when the cup smashed above his head, raining porcelain onto his head.

'It was consensual. I was curious, and he was hungry. Can you stop overreacting, please?' she said, and I felt scolded, like a child having a tantrum. I was still shaking from worry, but her calm was infectious. I rubbed the bridge of my nose before pointing to the map.

My blood was everywhere, tiny splashes dotting the terrain except, at one point, almost in the centre of old Gdansk, an ancient military fortification unused for centuries.

'They are in the old fort of Gradowa Mountain.' I pointed my finger to the centre before looking at Leszek. 'You couldn't sense him because they have amber everywhere, and I think... I think they are killing people to sustain the spell.'

Leszek bit back a curse before turning to Adam. 'Gather the men. Tell Tomasz we need his help, and call Nadolny, let him know where we're heading. I need the place cleared of civilians.' He stopped when Kris coughed to gain his attention.

'I have a better idea if you'll let me. Sara, tell your man he can trust me.' He flashed me a bright smile when Leszek looked in my direction.

'What is your idea?'

'Give me till tomorrow afternoon. We can run a terrorist evac drill there. I'll call in a favour or two, put a local politician outside, extolling our readiness for any threat and bingo, empty fort. Anyone left will be a hostile, and no one will be surprised by the sound of gunfire,' Kris said, and Kamil nodded with appreciation.

'I can ask guys from transit control to restrict access to the surrounding roads. The only problem will be how you get there.' He said, and it was Leszek's time to smirk.

'That won't be a problem, and that is an excellent idea. Thank you both.' He said before he stroked my cheek. 'I want you ...'

'To come with you and help break through the temporal distortion if those fuckers still have it,' I finished for him, pretending not to see his eyebrows knit together.

'No.'

'Yes, and the more you argue, the more likely you will sleep alone tonight.' I said with a grin that provoked Rysiek's laughter.

'In that case, we're going too. Just in case something happens to Sara, and everyone freaks out, like last time. We'll tag along with the wolves, as we're already familiar with them.' He said, and I nodded, happy to have my team as backup.

'Jarek, you stay with me. We'll finish preparing this place for the casualties that will surely occur after whatever trouble Sara starts.' Nina said, clearly not forgiving me for smashing the cup over Adam's head.

Before we walked out, Leszek grabbed my shoulders and turned me toward him.

'Tomorrow, you will stay close to me. No matter what, you are not to engage in any fighting, and if you need to use magic, ensure I am within reach.' He said everything so sternly that it sent shivers down my spine, clearly unhappy with me going, but to his credit, he didn't try to stop me either. In fact, he was indulging and supporting my decisions today, and I felt he deserved a compromise from me.

'I will be as close as I can reasonably manage and promise I won't put myself in danger. Has anyone else you know dealt with this temporal spell before?'

'One of the older witches from the Coven, but no one's ever broken it. Sara, thank you for today. I've treated humans as enemies for so long that I forget why they were such effective opponents. What you did today made me realise I was wrong to ignore them, and you, my Firefly, were the key to unlocking this possibility,' He said, embracing me.

We were already alone in the room when he pressed me back against the wall, leaning down to shower my neck with kisses, nipping lightly at the skin when excitement made us both moan. He stopped momentarily, and I felt his teeth hovering over my collarbone again.

'When we return home tonight, I want you to wear this pretty green scrap of fabric I saw in your drawer, then I'm going to spend the night driving out any hint of sadness in your eyes, replacing it with pleasure and love. I will give you anything you want for a single smile.' Leszek's voice had started as a barely heard whisper, but the word love was a growl that sent shivers down my spine, making my knees buckle, my body falling helpless into his arms.

'What if I want your heart?'

'I cannot give what you already own, my love.' He said, sending me into a meltdown. I pulled his beard down, kissing him with all the passion that burned inside. The sincerity in that one statement setting my world alight, but more than this. Today made me feel like a partner, an equal if not in power, then in the skills I possessed that made an ancient spirit re-evaluate his outlook on the world.

My blouse was halfway off my shoulders, Leszek's shirt in similar disarray, when the sound of a car's horn interrupted our antics. I laughed with embarrassment, trying to straighten my clothes, whilst my magical lover, with a simple wave of the hand, made his outfit pristine, not a wrinkle in sight.

'Come, my love, we will finish this in the comfort of our home and tomorrow, I will show you the true extent of my power. I want you to see what your ability has returned to me. Remember your promise, though, Firefly. I can lose this city, but I cannot lose you.'.'

Chapter Twenty-Nine

Leszek was insatiable. I barely slept as he made love to me at every opportunity and afterwards held me tight, as if afraid I would vanish if he let go of me. Not that I would ever complain. I think my magic terrified him. Maybe not the magic itself, but the fact it was coveted by every deity on both sides of the Gates, making our future a daunting prospect.

'I would trade everything I have for this time with you, Sara, money, magic, everything. Eternity is worthless if I have to live without you.' He whispered when he thought I was asleep, curling his body around me.

We slept through most of the morning, then stayed in bed a little longer, cuddling beneath fluffy blankets while Leszek told me stories from old Gdansk, and I reciprocated with outrageous tales from the Emergency Department. It felt like the outside world didn't exist. It was only my Wolfie and I cuddling together. The sun illuminated the bedroom and Leszek's auburn hair with a soft glow, making my man look like the King of Autumn. If I remembered the old legends about Leshy correctly, it was even one of his titles. Now, I could see how accurate it was.

Afternoon arrived with enough aches and pains to remind me of Leszek's prowess and stamina, but at the beeping of several horns, any opportunity to revisit those memories was ruined. Well, not all; my lover's dexterous fingers teasing an orgasm from me as we showered. Unfortunately, we had to admit defeat at the banging on the bedroom door and swiftly got ready, meeting an impatient Adam outside.

My gasp at the menacing crew assembled in three large vans made everyone smirk and a few to flex their muscles as they tried to catch my eye, but I ignored the wannabe lotharios, studying the men that looked suspiciously like Adam, with a slender predatory elegance and pale complexion. Still three vans?

'You should buy a bus next time.' I blurted out, and Leszek's lips twitched before he leaned down, whispering into my ear.

'Whatever my Lady desires, I will buy as many buses as you like.'

He was such an impossible tease, and if we weren't about to ride into battle like some weird hippy version of medieval cavalry, I would order him back to bed so I could finish what he started in the shower.

As I caught Leszek smiling when he tried sneaking a look down my top, I realised how relaxed he'd been, as if a weight had been removed from his shoulders after I'd located Rostov's base.

Leszek stood beside me in the doorway, with this mischievous look in his eyes, pressing me tight to his firm body as he continued enjoying how my lycra workout clothes clung to my curves, only looking away when Michal cleared his throat and threw a black duffel at his chest. After Leszek caught the bag and donned the tactical gear, Michal turned to me, holding out a very rigid vest, nodding toward my now incredibly intimidating lover.

'Boss's orders.' When I refused to move, attempting to catch the assistant's eye, Adam leaned out of the lead van and shouted.

'Nina already knows and said if you don't wear it, she won't pull any bullets out of your Barbie bonanzas.'

Face flaming red as the men in the vans started hooting, I snatched the bulletproof vest to struggle into its tight confines, grumbling and cursing. When my gymnastics were finished, I strolled toward the wolf pack, where Damian and Rysiek seemed to be thriving under the male attention. I waved to them, and Jarek slipped from the crowd with the biggest boyish grin on his face.

'Sara, my Alpha is allowing me to be a paramedic. He said it is a useful skill for the pack. Damian will help me enrol in the school, and Jora will teach me shifter's healing.' He said with unbridled enthusiasm, and I couldn't help but ruffle his hair.

This youngster had grown on me. He was loyal honest, and, despite being stuck to me like a barnacle most of the time, didn't annoy me too much.

'You will be great. I'm sure of it. I can't wait till you bring me your first patient. Listen to Damian and Rysiek; there's a reason they're called the Dream Team,' I said, and he laughed, running a hand through his hair before rushing to another, smaller car I hadn't noticed. I saw Jora smiling and nodding to me while my young friend turned around, sending me another one of his boyish grins.

'And you listen to the boss. He'll keep you safe when I'm not there,' he said, and I heard a familiar baritone laughing softly behind me.

'Jarek, stop flirting with my woman, but you are right. I will keep Sara safe. I could never disappoint such trust.'

I turned to face him, and my knees buckled. I'd been intimidated when he'd been close, but now, the impact of the entire outfit nearly made me purr. Leszek was always immaculately dressed, his suits used like a weapon to impress and dominate, but this. *The man dirties up well,* I thought. It was difficult keeping my panties on when he looked like a gentleman, now, with all the muscles accented by military gear... I swallowed hard.

'Oh, you are keeping this outfit for the bedroom, Wolfie.' I said, enjoying the stunned look on his face at my statement.

The snickers and wolf whistles behind me told me every shifter and vampire had heard my comment, making me blush again.

Adam walked over, lips pressed together, holding in his laughter. 'Come on... Wolfie. We need to get going since Kris and Kamil only arranged a few hours of unrestricted access.' He said, pointing to the radio.

Leszek nodded, heading toward the vehicle. It was my time to snicker when he slapped Adam on the back of his head while passing in a casual, almost tender gesture that knocked Adam a few steps forward.

'Only Sara can call me that,' he said, holding the car door open for me.

We parked on the street below the steep incline of Gradowa Mountain, and before we set off, Leszek called everyone close to check everyone's gear and remind them of the dangers we were facing. I looked away, only half listening to the army jargon, staring at the old fort. The so-called mountain was really a hill that had been heavily fortified over hundreds of years. With its panoramic view over the city, it had seen plenty of battles and was rumoured to be an important geomantic point of the Gulf of Gdansk, a place where positive energy is concentrated. I wondered if that had anything to do with magic, though it had always been a place

I avoided, where reality was distorted and the shadow creatures more palpable.

Tomasz issued an order, and I startled as the men under his and Adam's command swiftly divided, heading up the hill from opposite directions. Leszek and I were left with a small unit comprising two very uncomfortable witches and the three biggest, meanest shifters I had ever seen. Those men were killing machines, yet they felt insignificant compared to Leszek. He turned toward the city before he drew something in the air that blazed with emerald fire, and the air shimmered like a mirage.

'Veles, save us,' whispered one of the witches when the curtain of power appeared, muffling the city noise, and Leszek turned toward her.

'Veles? Really? It is just a cloaking spell to help keep this operation as low-key as possible,' he said, the annoyed tone in his voice making the woman flinch, and I had to bite my lip to prevent myself from laughing nervously.

As soon as we passed the gate, I heard a gentle song that made me feel completely at ease, filling my heart with contentment. I shook my head, looking around to find its source, but everything seemed different. The ruins of the fort were still there, but the walls were superimposed by the hints of other structures, grander, more fanciful buildings.

A tall building of pale stone and polished wood shimmered before me, its sides covered with intricate runes and carvings of mythical creatures, with dragons crowning the roof. Yet when I tried to touch it, my hand passed through the mirage, an unnatural coldness travelling over my skin.

I walked like a blind woman, unsure if I could trust my sight, letting the melody guide me, watching as Leszek paused several times, dismantling traps and spells that had already claimed the lives of several people. I briefly wondered why I felt no fear at the sight of the dead men, the logical part of me knowing something was wrong, but even my questioning thoughts slipped away at the tranquillity suffusing my body.

As I started smiling, a feeling of death and pain overpowered my contentment, its icy fingers brushing the nape of my neck when my hand touched the fortifications, but the melody strengthened, pulling me in.

'Here, we need to go here.' I said, but no one heard me over the sound of gunfire and screaming, everyone focusing on the bitter fighting.

'Report!' Leszek's voice cut through the cacophony echoing from the surrounding walls, and the witch behind him moved her hands, eyes turning completely white before she began describing the fight between a group of shifters and several gunmen. More shots followed, and he gestured for us to go uphill.

'We need to head to the main building,' he shouted, rushing forward. Leszek's hand slipped from mine as he created a shield to protect us. I tried to call out, falling behind the group, unable to keep pace with these warriors.

A pain in my chest left me stumbling, the song becoming urgent, pulling me away, begging me to help, and I realised the melody was a soul trapped and desperate to be free. *Help me, free me. It hurts so much.* When those words came to me, the image that accompanied them tore at my heart. The vision of a man tied to an amber altar, blood soaking into its surface as he breathed his last, and, instead of following Leszek and keeping my promise, I turned and headed into the darkness of the fort's tunnels.

A short incantation later, definitely not a curse at having the wrong type of magic, I pulled my phone, letting its torch light the way in. I would stop and marvel at my skills if not for the irresistible call I felt building in my core.

The sound of automatic weapons and injured people faded the further I delved into the underbelly of the fort. The renovated section, its walls scraped clean of moss and grime, gave way to medieval architecture that looked so unstable I gasped each time I had to squeeze myself under the decrepit beams.

'You can do it, Sara. You can do it.' I murmured. The more I walked, the more I noticed an improvement in my surroundings, the blurry visions from earlier returning, but more clearly, as if the darkness encouraged my belief in them. As my thoughts tried to pick apart the unusual phenomenon, my ears popped, and the alluring melody suddenly stopped. I stumbled, grasping the wall to steady myself, worrying as my mind focused and the reality of the situation came crashing down. *What the fuck have I done? And where the hell am I?*

'Welcome, Soul Shepherd. The Council is expecting you.' Surprised at hearing a voice, even one as dry as dust, I gasped, turning to escape, only to bounce off the newly solid wall behind me.

'What the fuck! Who are you? I have to go back, please. I will return some other time, I promise.' I panicked. The song that lured me here had nothing to do with Nikolai Rostov, and it felt like I was heading to my execution.

The sound of ripping flesh, moist, terror-inducing, stole my reason, my fingers clawing at the stone barrier as I tried to escape the repugnant noise, but I had to turn in the end, fear giving way to a fatalistic acceptance, wanting to face my demise. A spindly creature waited patiently, feeding on the carcass of a massive eel, before tossing it casually aside, shaking her beak clean of blood and meat. She looked at me, and I flinched at seeing an eagle's head with a human face and a beak. It was as fascinating as it was nauseating.

'Come, little seer. No harm will befall you whilst under my care, but I've had to inform the Council of your arrival before others learn about it. You have enemies within Gedania, so hurry.'

'But Leszek...'

'Leshy is fighting his own battle. He did wrong hiding you from them. Greedy, greedy one, he knew who you were but hid you, and they are unhappy.' She said, and with no other choice, I followed her.

'Why have I been summoned like this?' I asked, trying to prepare myself mentally for what was to come.

'I do not know, but there is much debate about your future. You shouldn't have helped the Leshy the way you did. Now Gedania is in uproar, with many wanting a return to the old ways, living and being worshipped in the mortal realm,' she said, and I felt my heartbeat speed up.

'I don't even know what I did, so how can I be expected to recreate a fluke?'

'You will do what you are told. A mortal cannot defy the gods. They want your willing participation, but be under no illusion; they will never accept your refusal. What do you think the melody you heard earlier was? A goddess gets what a goddess wants.' The last sentence wasn't meant for my ears, more thought than spoken word, but I still understood. This was the work of someone with more than magical power.

As I was led from the tunnel, I stopped, blinking against the bright sunlight, gaping at the reality of my mirage from the fort, the stunning edifice of smoky stone and polished wood, the runes and mythical creatures on its surface no longer carvings but animated effigies that danced and frolicked wherever the mood took them.

My companion made a clicking noise with her beak, grabbing my elbow as a wave of magic rolled over us; the mental command, *Hurry, he is forcing the Gates*, echoing through my mind.

'Who is forcing the Gates?' I asked when she forced me to run, but the creature made more distressed noises until we burst through the doors into a circular room, stopping in front of a group of people on stone benches. Their heads turned in my direction with the whole gamut of expressions, from polite friendliness to outright hatred.

'Welcome, child. I didn't expect to see you here so early.' A plump old woman with a crown of golden hair welcomed me with a smile, and I felt warmth spread through my soul like a mother's embrace.

'The Council hasn't offered an official invitation to the Soul Shepherd, yet she broke through the veil, clearly with nefarious intentions if Leszek is fighting for control of the Gates.' A beautiful woman with wavy sea-green hair and a pale complexion looked at me with pure malice in her eyes, though I had no idea why when I didn't even know who she was.

'Then give her to me, Jurata. Even though the Leshy tried to erase it, I can still feel my mark on her soul. I can punish her to your satisfaction.' The person who spoke up was dressed in an opulent robe covered in various gemstones, though I noticed most were the colour of amber. The scorching heat that emanated from his body reminded me of summer days right before the storm when cloudless skies prostrated the unwary with heatstroke. I tried stepping back as he approached, but before I could move, he touched my cheek, and my back spasmed, making me hiss in pain through clenched teeth.

'A seer and a Soul Shepherd with healing magic. Interesting combination. Tell me, little seer, how could you not know about your gifts? You must have seen things no other could see, yet here you stand, your mind defenceless, burning under my touch.' He said, slowly trailing his fingers along my cheek, turning this inspection into a lover's caress, but worse still, I saw the hunger in his eyes, and it sickened me.

'Can you please stop touching me... Sir, I wouldn't want to stain your bathrobe with my vomit. Is there a point to your question? Yes, I could see things, but no one could teach me about them.' I flinched, pulling away from his touch before looking at the blonde matron. 'Is this touchy-feely thing normal here, or is he trying to flirt with me?' I asked with all the bravado I could muster. The snorts and covert laughter upset my antagonist, and I hissed when the heat intensified. I was sure he'd burned me, yet after the laughter, I felt that standing up for myself was the only way out of this situation.

'Leave her, brother and tone down your power. She is a seer. She belongs to me by law, and I introduced her to my son for a reason.' The stern reprimand came from a corner where a man clad in darkness sat motionlessly with the unblinking stare of an ancient reptile.

'Thank you, Sir, though I'd like to point out that I belong to no one. Magic doesn't change the fact that it's the twenty-first century, especially when being passed around like an unwanted gift, but I appreciate your concern regarding the heat and integrity of my skin.' If they were going to kill me, I had nothing to lose, but I toned down my words when I saw the smile teasing on his lips. 'May I know your names? I feel like the only one without the faintest idea what's happening.'

'I like her. She has the spirit of a warrior,' that came from an old man on the right. I struggled to see his face as his shape blurred and changed, rippling like a windswept meadow. 'I'm Stribog. The one who defended you is Veles, the father of the Leshy. The man who tried to ignite your clothes is Svarog, who should know better than to try it on a mortal.' He said, and I acknowledged it with a smile. 'Our mother, Mokosh, who welcomed you here and lastly, there's Jurata, who, I was told, sent the Obra to greet you.' He added, and the green-haired woman sent him a murderous look.

'Obra?' I asked, and the man nodded.

'Yes, the creature that lured you here with its song. The voice doesn't exactly match the visage, but my servant dealt with it before anything untoward could happen.'

'You're talking about the ugly eel thing?' My face twisted in disgust, but it was useful putting names to the faces of those weighing my future, and just to upset Jurata a little for her machinations, I bowed deeply to Stribog. 'Thank you, my Lord, your kindness and protection is appreciated.'

Even though Stribog nodded in reply, it was Veles who spoke first. 'So you can behave? Tell me, how did you return my son's avatars to him?' The questions were deceptively calm, but I could feel the tension in the room ramp up.

'I can behave if no one is trying, or threatening, to kill me, my Lord.' I said, looking at Svarog before I moved my attention back to Veles. 'As for the rest, he didn't ask me, and I don't know what happened. We just had sex, and he grew antlers. A useful talent, I admit, but that was it, I promise.'

'Then lay with me, woman. I promise to be gentle, even considerate, coating you with warmth and attention.' Svarog puffed out his chest, flexing the muscles, and before I realised, the comment was leaving my lips.

'No, thank you. You're not my type.'

More sniggering followed, and the fire god approached me, menace burnt into the angles of his face. Is he going to rape me? I swallowed hard, turning to Stribog, but he was looking at Makosz, so with no other choice, I addressed her. 'Is that why I'm here, my Lady? To have sex with this idi... man, I mean god?'

'No, you are here to die,' Jurata answered, smirking. 'Your kind disturbs the balance, and I won't let you enthral those who stayed behind.'

My lack of understanding must have been evident as Veles once again spoke up. 'Enthral? If my son could be enthralled, I suspect Sara wouldn't be the one to blame, but if you all are so concerned about her presence beside Leszek, she can stay here.' The statement was harsh, words cutting through the tension, but he looked at me compassionately. 'I can protect you here, child, but despite her personal feelings, Jurata has a point...' his words were cut short by a commotion outside, and some of the gods stood, gathering magic in preparation.

I saw Stribog gesturing to me and scurried over. 'Come here, little witch. He wouldn't want you injured.'

Not that I trusted him, but he appeared helpful, and I moved behind Stribog's strangely fluid body, gasping as a whirlwind surrounded me. The doors burst inward, revealing a terrifyingly magnificent beast, his resplendent body covered in blood. I blinked, trying to comprehend the sight, but the half-man, half-beast roared, his gaze locked on mine even through the dust and wind.

'Release her, or I will tear this place apart till only the foundations remain.' His roar was deafening, but instead of fear, I felt disbelief. This was Leszek, no, the Leshy, his naked, obscenely hairy torso covered in sweat and blood, decorated only with a golden torque and swirling tattoos. His antlers no longer hosted a swarm of fireflies. Now they were strewn with some unidentified scraps of tissue, and he had claws, massive, lethal claws.

'Hey Wolfie, you came to rescue me?' I said, a little breathless, gesturing for Stribog to stop the wind. Leszek's eyes widened when I approached him, as if he couldn't believe I was free. I used the moment of confusion to put my hands on his shoulders.

As soon as my hands touched his skin, Leszek crushed me to his body, and I felt him trembling when he held me tight in desperation.

'Sara, are you alright? They didn't hurt you, did they?' his voice was tense and full of concern, but he wasn't looking at me. His eyes slid over the gathered faces, challenging each with this stare.

'I'm fine, despite the green hair bitch trying to kill me on the quiet.'

'Seeing how you charged in here breaking all the rules, you wonder at our concerns? And for whom? A seer, a human. Killing her would be a mercy.' Jurata said, looking at him with a longing that tightened my grip on his arms. He was mine, even if he wasn't looking at me, his gaze fixed on those sea-green eyes.

'You will pay for this,' he said finally, and she paled before her eyes shifted to me. If I thought she hated me before, now it looked like she wanted to dance to the sound of my last breath as she strangled me. Leszek must have seen it, too, because he shifted me behind him, hiding me from her stare, and a growl rumbled in his throat.

I grabbed a handful of the fur on his back, coughing at a distracting thought before speaking. 'No, leave her be. Just take me home, please.'

'You need to remain, child. My son would understand this if he could think clearly.' Veles said, and before I knew it, dark shadows started crawling in Leszek's direction. He growled louder, stepping away, but the shadows lashed out, forcing him to kneel on the floor.

'No, take it all, take my magic, but let Sara leave.' He said, struggling against the shadowy chains.

'Don't fight it, lover. Stay here with me now that you have reclaimed your heritage.' Jurata stood up and approached him.

'You left. You abandoned your people, forcing them to fend for themselves and didn't help, even when a madman tortured them. I can't believe I thought I loved you, but no more. My eyes have finally been opened.' He sneered, turning his face from her outstretched hand, and instinctively I stepped between them.

'Learn to take a no for an answer.' I said, swatting her hand away before her power filled my throat with salty water, and I gagged, fighting for breath.

Svarog's laughter contended with Leszek's roar and a command that felt so final, like death itself.

'Enough!'

The air returned to my lungs. 'I will stay. Please unchain him.' I coughed, begging, my gaze on Veles.

'You can't, Sara. There's good reason humans don't live here. The Nether changes you, corrupts your emotions and memories, destroying your identity. I cannot allow that. I love you, my Firefly. I love your fierce spirit and gentle heart. I love your wit and humour and how everyone you meet is immediately ready to offer you their loyalty. I can't let all those wonderful things fade away in the streams of time.' His voice was so quiet it was almost a whisper full of regret and desperation, and I did the only thing I could. I kissed him while pouring my soul into the connection. *Be free, be free, my love.*

I gasped when his arms wrapped around me, no longer bound in shadowy chains. I broke the kiss, and my gaze drifted to Veles, whose shocked, dark face was several shades paler.

'The Soul Shepherd will stay with the Lord of the Forest. That is their destiny. They will live or die together.' A pocket-size grandma stepped out of the shadows. Everyone surrounding us collectively held their breaths and bowed their heads, and I dived on my knees in front of her. Whoever this wrinkled ancestor was, she was my chance.

'My Lady, please intercede for us.' I placed my hand over my heart, banging my head on the floor so hard I almost saw stars. These people were the old powers, and I hoped the ridiculous amount of historical movies I'd watched accurately covered appropriate behaviour.

'You can't, she endangers us all.' Jurata, the vengeful bitch, screeched, desperate to keep me away from Leszek.

'Are you telling the Weaver of Fate what she can or cannot do?' The elderly woman turned to the sea goddess, and Jurata fell back. 'Change is coming to the world whether or not you like it, and the Guardian of the Land needs his companion,' she said, the finality of her words sealing the mouth of even the most vigorous opposition.

'Come, Sara, we must go now,' Leszek pulled me toward destroyed doors, but before I left, I nodded to Stribog, mouthing a thank you, and the deity of wind acknowledged my words with a nod and smile.

Chapter Thirty

Sara was gone. One moment, we're hand in hand; the next, all hell breaks loose, and she's nowhere to be found, with no one noticing her departure.

'Sara!' I bellowed, but the only replies were the sounds of gunshots and the screams of the injured, reminding me why we'd rushed forward in the first place. 'Sara.' I whispered, and dread washed through me. It could be Rostov with his temporal distortion spell, but I remembered this place from before there were fortifications. There used to be a sacred glade here, with idols of the gods that ruled over these lands. I could even point to the spot my own statue stood.

'Where is she?' I turned to the shifters, but both men shook their heads.

'The melody, I remember hearing a strange melody...'

Jurata? We were far from the waterfront, but I only saw shifters confused like this when my former flame decided they were fair game for her amusement.

With a roar of fury tearing from my throat, my body grew, changing as fear for Sara overtook me. I had to go to her. This world be damned if they took the light in my soul from me.

'Find her. If you cannot do that, find the place she disappeared. If you cannot do that, then don't bother coming back alive,' I said to the witch, who looked at me fearfully, her hands shaking as she tried to form a spell. 'Just find her.' I said before rushing up the hill when shots blasted out more frequently.

I scanned the area, picking out Adam and his team, pinned down on the left, the shifters creeping from cover to the right as Adam's men drew fire. The strategy was sound, but my Firefly was in danger, and these bastards were in my way. The ground shook when I poured my power into the land. I felt it shudder in protest, but I didn't care. My oath to protect the land, the people bound to it? None of that controlled me now that my powers were returning, and I would destroy it all for Sara.

I felt every twig, every root, every worm digging in the ground beneath my feet and every heartbeat that fought on this hill. A stray bullet hit my shoulder, burning through my flesh when the alloy lodged itself close to the bone. I reached up and dug it out with my claws, sneering when corrupted blood poured from the wound before it sealed itself. More bullets followed, and I heard Adam shouting at me to take cover, but it was too late for this; too late for me. The bloodlust that boiled in my veins demanded a sacrifice, a painful, bloody sacrifice. I would take revenge on those who hurt my men, took my Sara, dared to step foot on my land, and when I was finished here, I would find Czernobog and shove the dagger that started it all deep in his rotten heart.

'Come to me,' I said, letting the wind carry my command.

Shifters. Rostov had shifters working for him. I recognised their slow heartbeats between the others. The fluttering of the human heart and the void where the vampires stood and between them, the steady, slow beat of the shifter's heart. 'Come to your Lord and Master.'

Master of Beasts, Lord of the Forest, the trickster, and the devil, meaningless titles used to describe the power that pulled the strings of their essence, forcing the menacing soldiers to step forth, guns and rifles hanging limply from slack hands. Mercenaries, deserters from the Russian army, whoever they had been, now they were reduced to puppets whose strings I pulled.

I prowled to the first one, swiping out with one clawed hand, knocking the sniper rifle he held to the ground.

'Where is Sara?' I asked, and the battle-worn man paled. 'Where. Is. Sara?' I repeated, but his blank stare told me he knew nothing, and in a fit of anger, I snapped his neck like a twig.

'Where is Sara?' I asked the next one, and the mercenary with a face marred with scars wet himself, trembling like a leaf. I looked at the puddle of waste growing around him, grimacing in disgust. My claws sliced through his throat, opening his arteries, and fresh blood sprayed over me, overpowering the stench of urine. I licked my lips before spitting on the ground. It tasted of nothing but fear, but fear was only helpful when it led to answers.

I turned to look at the twenty helpless soldiers, my power holding them in its thrall, their minds still intact for now.

'Soldiers, brave men. The best and brightest of your country's army used to torture pups and sirens or burn humans unlucky enough to be in the wrong place.' I stalked back and forth, searching for the leader, someone, anyone who might have some answers. 'Where is my Sara?' I roared, on the verge of tearing them limb from limb.

The thunderous bellow had even my own men falling back in fear, my captives falling to the ground in abject terror.

'Leshy, my Lord. They may not know Sara's name,' Adam's voice broke through the haze, and I saw the vampire cautiously approaching me, holding his hands up to prove he wasn't my enemy.

I looked at the row of people, then closed my eyes to maintain the last thread of sanity. 'Where is Rostov? Where is that bastard?' I said, fighting the urge to rip them apart.

'Not here. Lady Jurata ordered us to secure this place, Rostov... he didn't want to split our forces but didn't dare contradict her.' The man who spoke looked me in the eye. Rivulets of sweat flow down his face, his gaze trailing over my hands, his focus on my claws.

'Jurata? What does she want from this place?' I asked, trailing the tip of my claw along his jugular, smirking when a thin red line appeared on his skin.

'I don't know, my Lord, I swear I don't know. She comes this way, and we must keep the amber gate open. Rostov fears her but keeps bringing victims to fuel the gate. He came today and said the time was up and took the other team with him... you, you surprised us.' He said, and a chill crept under my skin. If Jurata opened a gate here, and Sara stumbled through... I needed to go to Gedania before they hurt her, before Jurata could hurt her.

I looked at Tomasz and his wolves, heads bowed in submission before I turned to Adam. 'Check the compound. Any human who liaises with that bastard is fair game.' I saw a cruel smile on his face. Adam loved the hunt but obeyed the rules I'd forced him to follow centuries before, forbidding vampires to take lives whilst feeding. They could only live off, as he called them, charitable donations. Today, I gave him free rein.

Before I knew it, he took off, and his people followed, rushing into the corridors and passages of the fort like a wave of darkness.

I shook my head, trying to focus. I needed to find their Gate and go to Gedania.

Tomasz approached me slowly, his head bowed when he avoided looking me in the eye, fearing it would be taken as a challenge.

'What?' I said harshly, and he flinched, 'Raise your head and tell me. I won't challenge you over the pack. You are all mine anyway.' I wasn't even malicious. It was simply a matter of fact. Shifters were mine. They were born from Veles' blood but were mine to rule.

'What about your captives, my Lord?' he tilted his head, pointing toward Rostov's soldiers.

Maybe in different circumstances, I would hesitate or show them mercy, but their treatment of the shifters, of the sirens, left no room in my heart for leniency and without Sara there to brighten my darkness, I took great satisfaction in giving Tomasz a measure of justice.

'Show them the same grace they offered your fallen comrades, and get rid of the bodies, except for the one willing to speak up. He will show me the way to the gate,' I said, grabbing the poor fool and leaving the soldiers to Tomasz and his men.

With the mercenary on his toes, nearly dangling from my fierce grip, I headed back toward the last place I saw Sara, but the soldier began pointing the way without prompting, realising his fate with fatalistic acceptance.

'My Lord!' The witch I'd sent to find Sara rushed up, and I smiled, her pale countenance showing how frightening my visage was. 'My Lord, I found something, a message on the wind.'

The wind? I frowned, looking at the woman, only now realising the rising breeze kept tugging my mane. 'Thank you, now go, death treads on my heels this day,' I said, giving the witch my warning in gratitude and then ignoring her, closing my eyes to concentrate on the breeze pressing against my senses.

She is in the old temple. Hurry!

Yes, I could decipher this message. The whisper of the wind, the words, and Stribog's voice urging me to come. The old temple meant my father and Makosz would be there, and who knew how many more? The gods and guardians, so much more powerful than myself, even now when I was nearly whole, had Sara, and they might not let me take her back.

'The gate, now!' I snarled, and the mercenary led me to a room glowing with magic and amber tainted with the blood of innocent victims.

I ignored the scraps of flesh and bone crudely spread over the altar's surface, dashing into the darkness behind it, trying to sense the Nether. The passage meandered and branched several times, but I pushed forward, unaware of the walls tightening around me, the rock scraping my skin. The doors were closing, but I still detected the lingering feminine scent. Sara, my Sara, was here. I hit the wall in frustration.

'Damn it!' I hit the wall again, my knuckles scraping over the stone, sparks flashing at the contact with my blood. Jurata's spell was fading, the ground closing in around me, but I pushed my magic outwards, determined to prevent the enchantment from failing, roots and stones becoming fluid, bending to my will and creating intricate runes that formed a misshapen doorframe. I tore jaggedly into my forearm, hissing as blood flowed and, muttering a quiet incantation, smeared the fresh blood into the writing.

The stone shone with an eerie light, and I pushed forward, the light exploding into bright sunlight that blinded me. Fresh, clean air filled my lungs with pure, life-giving energy. Shouts and orders followed, and I noticed several doors bursting open to disgorge warriors of the Nether, half-crazed humans driven mad by their existence in the magical realm, sent to battle a god of the old world who wielded power as easily as breathing.

Now, they served Gedania and were determined to prevent my unannounced passage. I looked up at the old temple, still proudly standing on the top of the hill, and roared before leaping forward, claws lashing out indiscriminately. Death was a mercy for those lost to the corruption of magic, releasing their souls to Nawia to end their suffering.

I felt no remorse for my brutality, using every weapon in my arsenal, clawed hands and feet, antlers that impaled, tossing bodies away like toys. These remnants were between me and my destiny, my love, and nothing would keep me from her side.

It was a never-ending tide of death and destruction, but I drew closer to the temple step by step, leaving a trail of blood and gore in my wake. My roar as I smashed through the doors was answered with silence, the tide of crazed warriors disappearing as I stalked forward, searching for Sara. When I finally saw her body surrounded by Stribog's magic, I nearly attacked again until sense returned, and I remembered his message.

I glanced at Stribog. He sent the message and was protecting her. That was a debt I may never be able to repay. Sara stepped toward me, calling me by that silly pet name. Her mind and body were intact, and only now, hearing her voice, did I worry about her seeing me like this. I was bloody and covered in lumps of flesh. Gone was the sophisticated man I wanted the world to see. Instead, in front of her stood the savage beast humans still see in their nightmares. *What if she rejects this part of me*? I thought but still reached for her, trembling when she flew into my arms, pressing her body to mine. Finally, the world snapped back into place, and I could think again.

I searched her for injuries but, to my relief, found none. Sara's hand on my chest grounded me. Even after learning that Jurata wanted Sara's death, I kept my rage at bay, but my calm and focus cost me dearly. My father's chains pinned me down, and I could only watch helplessly as the bitch I once loved choked the life out of my woman. I fought against my restraints, shadows biting my flesh. My father stopped Jurata, but it was Sara who freed me.

Sara looked at me and then surrendered herself to free me. She loved her life and her work, but this beautiful soul didn't hesitate to pledge herself to such a terrible fate. I'd never known such soul-searing love, and with that feeling came real freedom as the chains fell away, crumbling into nothingness.

I glanced at Veles, who seemed as surprised as I, but before he could react, Dola, the weaver of fate, wielder of the scissors that could end any being's destiny, entered the chamber. Older than time, the unyielding Guardian of the Cosmic Order rarely visited the Council, yet here she was.

Everyone bowed except for Sara, who dived to her knees, prostrating herself, pleading for us, and even knowing it wouldn't change anything, I was proud she was willing to fight till the end. Just when I thought all was lost, the Weaver of Fate spoke in our favour, and I didn't wait. I grabbed Sara and ran from the wretched place as fast as possible. She'd asked me to take her home, and that's precisely what I would do.

We burst through the gateway near the docks. I cradled Sara in my arms, happy to breathe the grimy fog of the port. I hastily threw a glamour over us, making sure no one saw my shifted body. I was shaking, unable to believe my luck. Dola's judgement was final, and neither Veles nor Svarog could contradict her. Sara was mine, and as soon as we sorted out the issue with Rostov, I would tell her what this meant for us.

'Are you alright?' She asked, stroking my hair when I pushed my nose into the crook of her neck, inhaling deeply. Sara's smell, a mixture of coffee and cinnamon bun, calmed my senses.

'I thought I'd lost you, and it broke me.' I said, realising I had to call Adam and Tomasz and shift back to my human form, then wash off all the blood and grime that coated my body.

'We can't let that happen, now can we, Wolfie? I'm good, but I can't mend broken hearts. I promise I'll always return to you, even if it's only for a free caramel latte.' She jested, and I rolled my eyes before putting her feet on the ground.

'Stag or wolf?' I asked, observing with amusement how her eyebrows drew closer. 'What mode of transport would my Lady wish to ride on her way home? The Stag or the Wolf?' I said with a mischievous smile.

'I think it will be a brief ride if someone notices me galloping toward the sunset on the back of a stag, and then we'll both end up in a mental institution. You for claiming to be god and me for claiming to ride a god.'

'No one will see us, my love, the perks of having Divine Power. So, decide, or I will choose because I must go home and wash this blood off before it dries.'

'So the perks don't include dry cleaning for the pelt?' Sara asked, and I roared with laughter. 'Stag, I want to ride the stag.' It took me a split second to transform before kneeling for my Firefly to mount.

'That is so bloody bizarre. What should I hold on to? Your neck? Your antlers?' She asked, and I arched toward her, waiting till she figured it out before I bounded toward my island.

With my strength renewed by Sara's magic and the visit to the Nether, it didn't take me long to get home, even with her hands wrapped so tight around my neck that she almost choked me. When we stopped, Sara slid off, crouching on the driveway and taking long, slow breaths.

'We are not doing that again. I love you, and you are amazing, but I will never ride on your back again. You jerk, wobble, your spine nearly cut me in two, and it felt like I was riding a rabbit, not bloody Bambi.'

That, I had to admit, wounded my pride. How often had my avatar been called magnificent and powerful? It was so powerful, in fact, that we'd arrived much quicker than any human transport could travel. 'Take a rest. I will have a quick shower and join you in a moment.' I said, transforming as I stood. Sara gasped, seeing me naked, but I laughed off her shocked expression and wandered into the house. The hot water felt divine on my skin, washing away the evidence of my bestial fury, but I regretted nothing. We'd discovered the corruption in Gedania and decimated Rostov's forces, but the one part that still made me smile was Dola's judgment, which meant I had the chance to offer Sara an incredible opportunity.

Unfortunately, I didn't have time to share it. When I went to the kitchen to share my thoughts, my Firefly was typing furiously on her phone, her concerned expression becoming more pensive as time passed.

'I can't get hold of Nina or Jarek. Do you think they need me in the hospital?' She asked, and I instantly went to the office to retrieve my phone. Twenty messages stared at me, unopened. Twenty in the past five hours.

The first few were the standard reports from Adam and Tomasz informing me they cleared the compound and our enemies had been swiftly dealt with. The next was in a similar tone. Adam cleared the amber-layered room, caring for the human and non-human corpses that served as sacrifices.

A message from Nadolny stated suspicious individuals were spotted next to our clinic, and he was sending his men to deal with it. I didn't get to the others because Sara, pale as a ghost, entered the office.

'We need to go. Now. I saw... There was blood everywhere.... It's past the deadline, and he came for them. We need to go to the hospital, please.'

The woman who had faced down the old powers of the Nether without as much as flinching now looked at me, terrified, with tears in her eyes.

'What deadline?' I asked, wrapping my arms around her.

'Rostov. When I met him in the elevator, he gave me two days to call Czernobog, threatening to hurt my friends if I refused. Please, we need to go now.'

Once in the car, I drove like a madman, but she didn't chastise me, clenching her fists in silence. I called Adam, asking him to send a few men and meet me at the docks. His answer raised the hair on my neck.

'They are on the way, boss. The hospital was attacked. There are casualties.' I bit back a curse and risked a glance at Sara, but her gaze was fixed on the road, and I only heard her whisper.

'Please, don't be dead.'

Chapter Thirty-One

It was carnage. Sirens blared in the distance as we stepped out of the car, and two grey vans screeched to a stop behind us, with Adam, then his men, spilling out, surrounded by the smoke from the burning tyres. They still wore their tactical gear as they glanced warily at Leszek, then promptly secured the perimeter, acting on orders from the vampire.

I felt Leszek gently stroking my back, distracting me for a moment. 'Wait. Let them make sure it's safe inside. Besides, we need a distraction at the docks. I don't want the authorities here.'

His eyes lost focus, and his expression stilled. Before I could ask what was happening, I felt a wave of primordial power pulsing out of Leszek, heightening with each heartbeat, searching for purchase. My head snapped around as flames exploded into the sky, the sight disappearing when Leszek pressed my face to his chest, turning around and sheltering me from the shock wave.

'Leszek. What have you done?' I whispered.

The explosion was far enough away not to hurt us but close enough to redirect the emergency response to the more immediate crisis. Still looking at his unyielding expression, I knew Leszek was not done. Droplets of sweat marred his forehead as he exhaled, and I felt ghostly fingers brushing over the surface of my mind. He was wiping the memories of any human being in this area; I was sure of it.

'Adam, ensure all footage is wiped from the official database and plant the story of an accident at the docks. Hack whatever you need, but this incident must disappear from any official records.' He said, and I barely recognised the man who was nothing but gentle and caring with me.

'What... have... you... done?' I said through clenched teeth, jerking from his grasp.

'What I had to.'

I looked at his haughty expression, feeling nothing but heartache. It was mere luck and the hint of magic that I wasn't one of those unfortunate people so easily manipulated by Leszek's ancient magic. *Did he kill anyone?* I knew he would do anything to protect the Nether and its creations, but ordinary humans? Those seemed to be expendable. I didn't want to think about it, but I had to when my blissful denial was confronted by the roaring pillar of fire that set the sky alight.

'Kris and the firefighters, the paramedics. They will be risking their lives.' I said, feeling my fear turned into anger. He looked at me, almost like he saw me for the first time, and touched my cheek.

'I was careful only to damage an empty warehouse, but I have to protect what's mine. Look around. How long would we stay in the shadows if humans discovered this?'

He pointed to the blood on the street, and I swallowed hard when it reminded me of the reason we rushed here.

'Nina!'

Leszek called out when I bolted toward the entrance, but it was too late to stop me. I didn't care if it was safe anymore. I leapt up the stairs, bursting through the smashed doors of the foyer. The space was trashed and filled with the lingering metallic hint of magic.

'Nina!' my voice echoed between the blood-splattered walls while my heart raced in panic. I couldn't see her. My eyes darted from one corner to another, searching for a familiar figure, but all I could see were corpses.

Shifters and humans were scattered randomly around the room, hunched over the furniture where bullets and magic had hit them. I should have been here, not going with Leszek or explaining myself to those arsehole gods. I should have been here protecting my friend. It was clear that when we went to attack Rostov's nest, he'd come here with the same plan.

A moan of pain and scraping sounds caught my attention, and I turned toward it, ready to strike.

'Sara... he took her, I tried. I really tried...' A weak voice, barely a whisper, made me turn my head, and the view shattered the last string of my self-control.

Jarek tried crawling toward me, leaving behind a trail of bright red blood, and the next thing I knew, I was kneeling beside him, tearing away clothing to examine him, holding back the sob as I saw the gaping hole in his stomach. Mangled tissue and pulsing blood flow told me the artery was damaged, and I had nothing, not even a scrap of bandage, to stop the bleeding.

His life was leaking on the floor in a bright red stream that was getting weaker with every passing moment, but I wasn't ready to give up on him.

'I'm sorry.' I said, pushing my hand into the gaping hole. If I'd only come sooner, he wouldn't be in shock. Even now, if I could plug whatever torn artery was bleeding so profusely, I could buy us time. Jarek screamed and thrashed when my fingers roamed over his organs while my magic tried to locate the bleeding site. And I found it. The alloy bullet, deadly to the creatures of the Nether, pierced his aorta. If I removed it, without the shifter healer's presence, the death would be instantaneous, but he would slowly bleed to death in my embrace if I didn't. *Maybe not so slowly*, I thought, looking at his pale face.

Jarek's hand landed on mine. 'It's alright.' He said, red bubbles foaming at the corner of his mouth. 'I'm not afraid. I fought them, Sara, but there were too many, and they tricked us.' He stopped to catch his breath, and I felt Leszek silently behind me.

'I know you did your best. It is my fault they came here. You fought bravely and with honour. I'm proud of you; your Alpha is proud.' I said, brushing a stray hair from Jarek's cheek with my free hand, and he smiled faintly, his eyes drifting in and out of focus.

'But I still failed... He took her. He took Nina... said you have to come for her. She f...fought, but he knocked her out a...and shot me when I tried to help. I'm sorry, Sara, I'm so sorry.... The boss was right. I was just in the way.' A grimace of pain twisted his face, but I could barely see it, tears blurring my vision when I bent, kissing his forehead.

'You were never in the way. You always protected and cared for me. I couldn't choose a better guardian. Please hold on a little longer. I can fix it... I can't ... I can't let you go.' My voice stuttered.

My tears fell on his face, and I shook as my sobs broke free of my control, knowing there was nothing I could do to save him. It felt so wrong; he couldn't die here, not like this. This remarkable man who helped make my transition bearable, whose company I'd learned to cherish. The wolf who wanted to be a paramedic to help not just his own people now lay here bleeding, and I could not help.

He smiled sadly, reaching for my hand and pulling it from his stomach. 'I'm done, Sara... I...I know it. I'd stay for you..., my new friends, but... it hurts so much. Please..., will you remember me?'

I couldn't breathe. Pain tore through my chest as I watched my hand slide from his body, the horror of knowing what the sickening wet sound meant, breaking something inside me. Blood gushed everywhere, and I turned to Leszek. His eyes were dark, like two pools of stagnant water, but he didn't move when he met my gaze.

'Do something! For fuck's sake, do something!' I shouted, reaching for him. My magic burst out, tethering Jarek's spirit to his body, while I stared in disbelief at Leszek, shaking his head.

'I cannot,'

Those words were final, an admittance that not even our combined magic could bring one deserving boy back from the edge of death. The world around me fractured, and I screamed, unwilling to let go. Time slowed, freezing everyone in place, and when I looked at Jarek's face, he looked so peaceful. His pupils widened, covering the hazelnut rim of his iris, and his lips curled in a fading smile while I held his hand in mine.

'Free his spirit, child. He suffers more with his spirit tied to a body tainted with death.' Dola approached me with her scissors. Her wrinkled hand stroked my hair in a motherly gesture, bringing more tears.

'You know what you must do. Even a Soul Shepherd can't fight fate. It is his time to go. Give it back to him, Sara, this moment of peace, his last breath. Give him back his honourable death.' She said, and I looked down. Covered in blood and clenched in my fist, between the whitened knuckles, was the golden thread of Jarek's life.

I slowly relaxed my hand, watching the thread, as delicate as an autumn spider's web, lying over my palm as the weaver leaned over and cleaved it in two. Just like that, his breath rattled and stilled, the shadow of his spirit moving away, looking back briefly to offer his boyish smile to me one last time before fading into the aether and, with him, Dola, but not before I felt her touch, the faintest of whispers in my ear.

'At the moment of his death, he was not alone. That is more than most mortals can wish for....'

Dola's consolation didn't ease my pain. If anything, she made it worse as it filled with grief and worry. I had to find Nina before I lost her, too. The mere thought hurt so much that I quickly tore apart the frozen bubble in time, crashing back into reality. In anguish, I fell into Leszek's embrace, torn apart by my grief.

'Sara, if I could, I would give all my magic to spare you this, but even I can't fight fate.' My fists made no impression as I railed against the injustice and mourned my friend, even as powerful hands gently stroked my hair until I could shoulder the pain and struggle on, knowing there was more to do.

I lifted my head, looking at Adam, 'Search the place. Tell the men to tear the place apart if needed. Rostov wouldn't rely on one dying shifter to pass on his message. He wanted me, so there's no way he wouldn't ensure I received the information.'

A rough baritone rumbled from the entrance. 'He did.'

Nadolny walked in. His face, with a deep gash across his cheek, was twisted in rage. Gone was the refined philanthropist, and I realised I looked at the true face of the Gdansk underworld, raging and unforgiving. He passed Leszek a piece of parchment, the dark ink covering its surface smudged and blotchy, written in haste by an uncaring hand.

Temple of Jurata, Old Hel, at midnight of Forefathers. Come earlier or fail to appear, and she will die.

That was all it said. I had a week, but why did Rostov want to wait? I looked at Leszek, who exchanged a look with Nadolny.

'I came wanting to blame you, but I can see you have suffered your own losses. Still, three of my girls are dead, and two are gone. All of them were the sirens that chose to stay rather than return to their brethren. Can you at least tell me who it is? His men came from the shadows, tearing through my bodyguards like paper, shooting at those who fought back. As soon as they dropped this at my office, they disappeared. I will help you kill him, but I demand honesty.' He said, and, after gently stroking Jarek's head one last time, I slowly stood up.

'I don't know how much you know, but it's some arsehole called Rostov who took your sirens, my friend, too. He wants me, so he will get me, and we will settle a score that ends with him dead.' I said calmly, voice an emotionless monotone. Jarek's death broke the part of me that was soft and forgiving. Now, all I wanted was vengeance.

Leszek's head snapped toward me. 'No, out of the question. Can't you see what he did here? I will not put you in danger again. No, Sara, just no.'

'I'm not asking for your permission, but I would be grateful for your and Veronica's help. I need to learn as much as possible about time-altering spells,' I said.

Leszek's body tensed. He looked at me through narrowed eyes, and I wished I could spare him this worry, but the void in me didn't want to close. I needed to be there to ensure Nikolai Rostov would never walk this earth again. I'd fought to preserve life all my life, but I needed to end this one, to right the wrongs and ensure no one else would suffer at his hands.

'No, Sara. You know it's a trap. I'm sorry darling, but I won't allow this,' He said, and I felt a wave of magic enfold me. Coercing me to give up? Really? I almost felt the doors of a gilded cage closing on me before I stepped away from Leszek's outstretched hand.

'You don't own me,' I whispered, too tired to cry again. I know why he did it, but it didn't lessen the feeling of betrayal. After everything we'd been through, he still tried to control me with his magic. He had good reason, an excellent reason born from love, but it didn't change the fact that in stripping me of my choice, he behaved like one of those assholes from my past.

I needed to get out of there. It was too much. The pressure in my chest intensified with each passing moment, my emotions threatening to choke me, and I couldn't even turn to Leszek because, for him, the world could burn if it meant I was safe. I looked around, but there were no wounded to help. Rostov ensured everyone was dead except for Jarek, who, I guessed, was left alive to deliver the message. There was nothing for me to do, and I needed to feel the salty wind on my face, blasting the traces of my tears away. I needed to feel free.

I turned and walked toward the exit. The little dream I'd had lasted such a short time. My hospital was in ruins before we could even open it. Kris and Kamil were risking their lives fighting fires in the dockyard to cover up for this slaughter. Rysiek and Damian, with haunted looks, were helping grief-stricken wolves mourning their brethren. Jarek was dead, and Nina...

My world had fallen to smaller and smaller pieces since the day I met Leszek, and the man I loved couldn't accept my decision, acting like my life was more important than those I cared about.

'Sara, stop. We need to talk.' He called behind me, but I kept walking, hoping the fresh evening air would ease the pain in my chest.

'Stop!' He roared, power reverberating through the air, and my steps faltered. I heard Leszek's footsteps approaching but couldn't face another argument. I needed to be alone, so I closed my eyes, imagining my apartment. My safe haven before the Nether came into my life, wrecking it completely.

Magic shimmered in me, resisting Leszek's command. The lingering aftermath of my anguish burned through my body, and with a stumbling twist of reality, time slowed again, and I broke free of my lover's power. I walked through the deserted dockyard, feeling increasingly drained by the temporal distortion, with one thought driving my steps. I wanted to go home. My home. It didn't take long before my body rebelled against the spell, and I found myself panting near the main street with barely enough energy to call for a taxi. I wasn't sure how long the drive was, but the next thing I remember was the blissful darkness of my living room before I fell face-first on the carpet.

I woke up feeling like I'd been beaten with plastic pipes, and the rough fibres of the carpet irritated my skin. Lifting my head slowly, I fought a wave of nausea. The constant buzz of my phone didn't help, but at least I was in my apartment. I'd recognise the coffee stain under the sofa anywhere. Slowly, I rolled onto my back and looked at my phone. Leszek's number repeatedly flashed when I turned down the volume before throwing it on the sofa.

I knew losing so many of his men affected him. Leszek hadn't been himself from the moment he saw the bodies. It didn't excuse him for trying to force my hand, but I knew I had overreacted. We both needed time and right now, I felt broken and selfish, unable to deal with his feelings and attitude before I sorted out my own.

I didn't know how long I lay there staring at the ceiling, but eventually, I got up and went to the bathroom. A hot shower helped me gather my thoughts. Calmer, I phoned Veronica, but she spoke before I could say a word.

'Come to the Coven tomorrow, and I'll teach you all I know, what little knowledge I have, at least. Those who tamper with time and death don't usually live long enough to pass on the knowledge. What you did today skirted close to being Dark Arcana, Sara. I hardly dare to ask if you knew you were using the death of those shifters when you created your temporal distortion.'

'How did you know what I was going to ask? Death... No, I just wanted to go home.'

'I know, and the tiredness in your voice tells me you tethered the spell to yourself. Tampering with time can be dangerous, but nothing is more dangerous than an untrained witch willing to burn up her life force just because she wants to go home.' I heard a heavy sigh on the other side before Veronica continued.

'Still, I can't deny you are a rare talent. That you manipulated time like that with no preparation or knowledge? I haven't heard of anyone doing that before. Our gracious leader thought Rostov had stolen you away, which gave me a bit of satisfaction despite him blowing up my phone, demanding a city-wise search and the promise I would tell him immediately if you showed up on our doorstep. If that wasn't enough, he left one of his wolves here to ensure I followed his orders.'

'I'm sorry.' I managed before Veronica cut me off.

'No, you don't. There's nothing to apologise for. Knowing him, he did something male and upset you, so we, the Coven, that is, decided to shield you until you're ready to face him. Fighting the will of the Forest Lord is draining, and you should get some rest,' she said, and only now did I realise no one was hammering on my doors carrying coffee and chocolate.

He must be worried senseless. I thought, sighing softly.

Leszek may have shown his ruthless, commanding side, disregarding my wishes and opinions, but I hadn't acted any better. Grieving after Jarek and worrying myself senseless about Nina, I almost did something unforgivable, and I didn't even have the whole Nether to protect. We both messed up, but this time, it was my responsibility to fix it before our misunderstanding caused even more damage.

'No, drop the shield. Let him find me.' My quiet words seemed to surprise her.

'Are you sure? He is unhinged. Maybe wait till morning?'

'He would never hurt me. I may not be thinking clearly today, but this is one thing I'm sure of. Lift the shield, please. Let him find me. I will come to the Coven tomorrow.'

When the call ended, I phoned the hospital, leaving a message for HR that Nina and I would be unavailable for a few weeks because of family issues. They would most likely blow up my phone tomorrow, but I needed time and space, and I hadn't taken an absence for ages, so they had no reason not to suck it up.

Half an hour after my phone conversation with Veronica, I heard a quiet rapping on my door. I knew it was him, but I didn't expect him to knock, maybe barge in, but not politely knock. Biting my lip, I went to answer the door.

Leszek stood there, wet and miserable, his eyes two pools of darkness as he looked at me.

'May I come in, please?'

I gestured him inside.

'What happened to you? You're soaking wet....'

'It's raining, and I ran...' He reached up to stroke my cheek before his fingers clenched in a fist, and he lowered his hand. 'I'm sorry. For what it's worth, I'm sorry. I would never hurt you. When you disappeared, I... forgive me, my Firefly.'

My heart ached. What had I done to that proud, haughty male? I stepped toward him, and this time, it was me reaching out, his breath hitching as my fingers tangled in his beard to pull him down to my lips. He was cold, but I wasn't sure if the shiver that ran through him was from the chill or in reaction to my touch. Leszek pulled back, and I swallowed hard, looking at his face. Hope flashed in his eyes, and then his lips crashed into mine again, his kiss ravenous, consuming me.

I was swaying as he paused, his voice full of yearning as he spoke. 'Sara, I can give up my power, money, and responsibility. I'd even let the Nether burn as long as you stay beside me. If I could erase this day, I would. I fucked everything up...' Leszek whispered, forehead pressed to mine.

I kissed him to stop his recriminations. 'Stop it. I'm angry, worried, and... I feel guilty because, simply by existing, I've brought Rostov here and painted a target on my friends' backs. I shouldn't have run, but I had no choice when you tried to force my hand with your magic.'

I saw his shoulder drop, and he closed his eyes, mouthing, 'I'm sorry.' He moved to pull away, but I didn't let him; this new dynamic empowering me to express my feelings.

'I love you, and I hope you love me, too. Me, not my power or my usefulness, but me. I don't want to be a fling or the magical conduit that connects you with your powers. I want to be your partner. I may never be your equal, but I want to be someone whose opinion you value. I won't leave you. I can't. You, with your bloody coffee, cinnamon rolls, and antlers, made me fall in love with you so hard it would break me if I'm nothing but a pawn in your game.'

I blushed at revealing everything I felt, while he was mostly silent, but when our eyes met, the glimmer of hope I'd seen earlier blossomed, lighting his face with happiness, the scent of oak and elder washing over me as Leszek seemed to grow, the weight on his shoulders disappearing. A mischievous smile ghosted over his lips, his finger stroking across my lips, teasing sparks of desire from my body.

'You are everything to me. I will never again make the mistake of underestimating or trying to control you. Your power is... sought over by the gods and men, but if it was only about your power, I would lock you away and use you whenever I choose.' I couldn't help but shiver at that thought, my breathing suddenly unsteady. 'You are beautiful, little Firefly, but if you think a pretty face can turn my head, you underestimate me. Your spirit shines so brightly that it blinds the unwary with its magnificence. The generous heart that cried over the wolf you knew for so short a time, the courage as you stood before millennia-old gods and defied them and the passion that burns away my control. That is what I love, Sara, not your power, you. My Firefly, who makes every day a new dawn.' As he finished, I was unsure if it was my legs or Leszek holding me up, but I couldn't help teasing him as I mouthed *Lothario* at the end of his speech. Still, his words made this dreadful day a little better.

'So you have a basement with chains, interesting. I'll have to remember this. Once Nina is safe, I may want to visit it.' I said, rubbing the bridge of my nose. 'Do you think she is safe? I want to search for her, but I don't know where, and it makes me feel so helpless.'

'She will be. Rostov wants you, and the only way he can make you cooperate is to threaten her life. He won't harm his bargaining chip, especially knowing your talents. He shot Jarek to send the message, but he will keep Nina safe and sound because that gives him power over you, and he knows powerful emotion can trigger a seer's abilities.' His words calmed me down a little before I had another question.

'Why Forefathers Day? I know it is the time spirits roam freely, but why meet then?'

'It's no coincidence he chose that time. Humans have chosen this day to celebrate their ancestors' spirits for a reason. During Forefathers' day, from midnight till dawn, even the old gods may safely roam the earth, and old Hel had a temple for Czernobog and Jurata. I think he wants to use you to anchor his god in the mortal plane.' He said, stroking my hair, and I felt like drifting into sleep.

'I need the dagger.' I said, and he chuckled in my hair.

'My bloodthirsty seer, I love you so much, and I promise we will find Nina even if we have to tear Tricity apart to do it.'

Chapter Thirty-Two

The next few days were a whirlwind of activity. It felt like every soul in the Tricity underworld was trying to teach me whatever skills they considered essential for my survival. I spent most of the day learning how to disrupt temporal magic, counter-spells, protection spells and defend myself from someone invading my mind. Leszek went as far as teaching me about the Dark Arcana, and although I saw how much it cost him, I now understood why the carnage in the hospital allowed me to manipulate time.

I was mentally battered, bruised, and on the verge of complete exhaustion. If I'd considered Veronica a harsh taskmaster before, it was nothing compared to now. She stopped only when my nose bled or I passed out, but she sneered as soon as my head lifted from the table.

Again! She would shout, and the torturous lessons resumed. Veronica forced me to repeat each spell until it burned into my memory, and I could perform them without conscious thought. The only thing that kept me going was knowing that if I failed, Nina would pay the price.

When I was not being beaten into submission by Veronica's lessons, Adam trained me in hand-to-hand combat, teaching me evasion tactics and dirty tricks, as my opponents would all be experienced fighters. I still felt pride when he complimented me on my skills, my Krav Maga training, or, as Nina called it, my *weird fight club*, coming out as I channelled my frustrations and fears into the kicks, punches and bites. I used it all on the vampire, trying my dirtiest techniques, earning his silent approval. Little did he know that, after Kosovo, my reason for training wasn't exercise, grades, or competition but fear of suffering through what those poor women endured.

On the last night before the deadline, I collapsed in bed sometime past midnight. I felt Leszek's hands sliding gently over my body, and the intoxicating scent of the forest soothed my tense muscles. 'Let me help you,' he murmured in my ear. Tingles of magic stroked over my body, further relaxing my sore tendons, and my mind drifted into a deep, dreamless sleep, only to be awakened three hours later for the next training session.

Whatever Leszek did to help me sleep had worked wonders, and I greeted Michal's pancakes with a smile of gratitude, wolfing them down with gusto. After that, it was off to Veronica's, with my Wolfie again teaching me the topography of old Hel.

'Is this really needed? You will be there, yes?' I asked, rubbing my temples.

'Yes, in fact, I intend to have a small army accompany you, but as we saw at Gradowa, sometimes circumstances can disrupt our plans, so I want you to know the land and where to find support if we're separated.' Leszek gripped the steering wheel, and I watched him swallow his worry.

'It will be alright. I know not to create distortion, and Veronica's beaten the knowledge of how to break them into my thick skull. I promise not to take any unnecessary risks, but we both know I need to be there, if only as a distraction for your attack.'

Leszek's eyes darkened before he took a deep breath and spoke. 'I'm not worried about your abilities, love. I'm terrified because, despite our pretence of enlightenment, the gods, myself included, are selfish, powerful beasts that destroy more than they ever create. Make no mistake, Sara, nothing will survive my fury if anything were to happen to you. I have found respect for humanity since you became my tether to the mortal realm, but I am still an old god.'

I didn't have a response to this confession, but I understood his feelings, their weight a heavy burden. I placed my hand on his thigh as he drove through the slowly wakening city, its people blissfully unaware of the dangers that stalked their streets. When we stopped, I tried to lighten the mood.

'See you later, Wolfie. Please don't worry, I'm a tough cookie, but after we sort out this mess, I demand a few days off. Just you, me... no clothes, maybe you show me your dungeon, I mean basement.' I said, kissing his cheek, enjoying that flash of hunger that, for a moment, replaced the worry. Leszek waited until I entered a heavily warded building before he drove off, and I started another gruelling session with the Mistress of the Coven.

By the end of training, I was covered with sweat, my head was pounding, and I felt utterly depleted. Maybe that's why Veronica's question took me by surprise.

'What will you do when you meet with the Dark God?'

'What? I don't intend to. The entire plan is to prevent him from crossing into this realm.' I looked at her, shocked by her words. Veronica sighed, and a gust of wind scattered my notes everywhere.

'It could still happen. You are confronting a madman near the flooded gate to the Nether at midnight on Forefather's night in his desecrated grove. While he may be a madman, Rostov has also been planning this for a long time, and you only learned of your powers recently. Sara, I won't lie to you; even if you trained for years, you'd be unlikely to survive a confrontation with Czernobog. Not on his land when he is at his strongest. It's not like you could kill a god.'

I looked at her for a long time. I knew I wasn't ready, not even close. A few week's magic lessons with an intensive crash course over the last week and my Krav Maga training, combined with

Adam's self-defence lessons, didn't make me a warrior. I would happily skip this part, letting Leszek handle anything related to the gods, but I didn't have a choice.

I remembered a conversation between Veronica and Leszek. That a god could be killed once their soul was anchored to mortal flesh by someone with my power. Of course, they would still have their magic, but we had an ace up our sleeves. We had Czernobog's dagger, and I was willing to use any means necessary to save those I loved.

I smiled at my teacher. 'Teach me how to tie a spirit to mortal flesh. Teach me how to kill a god.' I said, and Veronica paled.

'Sara, that knowledge was lost with the last Soul Shepherd, and even if you succeed, the Council will ensure you follow the previous Godkiller into the afterlife.'

'They kidnapped Nina, and they've already hurt so many. Do you think Czernobog will be a benevolent god once he returns? No, even if I die, it is one life for many. Besides, it may never come to that. I just... I want a fighting chance. That's all I'm asking.'

Veronica may not have known the exact way to anchor a god's soul, but she had her theories, and after working on each of them, I struggled to see straight, so I texted Leszek, asking him to pick me up. My body was a mess, traces of crusted blood still filling my nostrils and ears, and I hoped the drive would give me an hour of rest before I had to face whatever Rostov had prepared for me.

Veronica stood up, and I saw her pondering before she sent me a sad, tired smile.

'For what it's worth, you shall take the blessing of the Coven with you. Even though you weren't officially initiated, we still consider you our sister.' She said, and as if on command, two other women entered the room and positioned themselves around me. They looked so severe, softly chanting with a slow, hypnotic rhythm before raising their hands to bless me. I felt like I was watching a B-rated movie.

'Maiden, protect you,' said the youngest, touching my left shoulder.

'Mother, heal you,' said the other, her hand on the right.

'Crone, guide you. Go with the blessing of the Coven, little sister, and call upon us in the time of need.'

This was Veronica. A jolt of energy flowed through my body as she kissed my forehead, and I felt them and their magic, embracing the physical elements of the world. Their spirits entwined, elevating each other and now me. We were women, bound by magic, the threads of our lives interwoven into one, stronger rope, burning within us, weaving me into the sisterhood of the Tricity Coven.

'I–thank you.' I said, embracing Veronica. I didn't understand the ritual, but deep inside, I knew they'd given me something precious. A connection that was already strengthening my magic.

Leszek cupped my face in his hands, inhaling slowly before he cursed and threw an accusative glare at Veronica. He must have smelled the blood despite me vigorously washing my face, but I grabbed his forearm before he could say anything.

'I learned what I needed. That's all that matters.' I said, and he bundled me into the car, his anger filling the space between us.

'You came here to learn, not kill yourself,' he said, not even looking at me, but his hand rested on my thigh, and unless he had to change gear, it stayed there until my headache and tiredness slowly faded.

When we walked into the manor house. It was quieter than usual. While Leszek dressed in his combat gear, I used the opportunity to sneak Czernobog's dagger into a scabbard on my cargo trousers. When I walked to the kitchen, Leszek played with the butcher's knife, and his expression turned stony.

'I need you to do something for me. I know you won't like it, but I ask you to trust me,' he started, turning toward me.

'What? And don't ask me to stay home,' I said. My eyebrows rose when he approached me, still holding the blade.

'No, but I want you to drink my blood,' he declared, jaw clenched, and before I knew it, he'd lifted the knife, slicing the skin of his forearm. Blood poured from the cut, the red liquid almost glowing as it flowed onto the floor between us. 'My blood will protect you, and as it is a part of me, I will be able to find you even if you disappear from the flow of time. I know it is extreme, but I need you safe.'

'You are not turning me into a vampire?' I asked, and he shook his head. 'Fine, but if I grow antlers, we'll be having a long and boisterous discussion,' I said, rolling my eyes as I leaned over and pressed my lips to his skin. The metallic quality of Leszek's blood was strangely pleasant, and I lapped at his skin. I couldn't help smiling at his groan before my lover uttered an incantation in a language I recognised but couldn't understand. When Leszek's magic coursed through my body, I jerked backwards to escape, but he placed a hand on my neck, holding me in place.

'Not yet.' The commanding tone of his voice sent a shiver down my spine, and this time, it was my turn to moan as I obeyed, taking another swallow of his life's blood. Leszek's power suffused my body, filling me with his essence, rising and falling with my heartbeat.

My stomach roiled, but as he released me, I couldn't resist licking his skin one last time before looking up, intending to tease him about his strange new kink, but the words died on my lips at the darkness in Leszek's eyes.

'I'm sorry. I will explain it later, but it was necessary.' I didn't know what he was apologising for, but I didn't push him for answers, trusting my lover with something so obviously important.

The wound on his arm was already healing when he nodded toward the door. 'Let's go. I need that bastard's blood on my hands.'

No one accompanied us on this journey, Leszek explaining that his forces had spent the day infiltrating the area covertly. He was quiet and deep in his thoughts, and I used the time to rest and prepare myself. Once we reached the Hel peninsula, we left the car in a car park and walked down a gravel path deep into a pine forest. The chill November evening made the night feel confining, and the moisture in the air hinted at a budding storm, the sound of waves in the distance adding to the moment's intensity. It wasn't long until it became too dark for me to see, but Leszek took my hand and guided me to help me avoid tripping.

'Just in case things go wrong, I want you to know I love you, and despite our problems, I wouldn't change anything. The last few weeks, I mean... they were good, great, and I regret nothing. Even if I die tonight, I regret nothing.' I said, hoping that whatever happened, my words would give him some consolation. Instead, a low rumble ran through the woods, the tree shaking in the silent protest, showering us with the evening's dew.

'You won't die, Sara. I already took care of it,' he muttered, and I wondered how many people he'd brought for this fight, but we emerged from the forest before I could ask him. The dark wall of the forest gave way to a meadow, although it looked more like an ancient graveyard in the pale moonlight, its gentle slope descending to the beach.

There was a building in the distance, the only place with any light, with blazing fire pits surrounding it and a crowd of people moving in the flickering flames. Despite the darkness, I could see rifles carried on their shoulders, and the building itself gave me pause. There was something wrong with it. I focused on the slight shimmer before the view made me gasp.

The building was glowing, and not just from the firelight, and I blinked several times before my eyes made out the source of the strange light. It looked like a jewellery box encrusted with gemstones that glowed like fire. Amber. It was amber. The powerful, magical stone and armed guards didn't bode well for me, even in the company of the Forest Lord.

'Where are others?' I whispered when we moved forward, and Leszek pointed toward the beach. I had to strain my eyes, but I saw the movement in the water.

'Merfolk,' he whispered, then gestured toward the forest border, and after a moment, I caught sight of a reflection, quickly covered. 'Shifters.' Finally, he tapped his watch. It flashed a few times with a dim light, and several others on the ground around us responded with the same sequence. 'Adam and Nadolny with their crews.'

Leszek turned toward me, his calloused hand gently stroking my cheek. 'I used this time well, my love. I'm prepared, as much as I can be. Adam and Nadolny will create a distraction. The merfolk and shifters will attack whoever leaves the protective ward around the building; the rest, sweet Firefly, are ours to deal with. That bastard Rostov created a door, or rather, a chamber where even the high gods can exist with their power intact. Unfortunately, that means I also have no way of seeing through the enchantments fused into the amber.' The frustration in Leszek's expression made me smile, and I nodded to let him know I understood.

'Let's go. It is time to kick some arse. Also, remind me not to cross you. Not if this is what happens when you're angry,' I said, feeling the dagger digging into my thigh. Whatever happened, I hoped my preparations were just as impressive.

He grimly nodded, almost smiling, and we walked toward the temple. Leszek used his magic to glamour himself so well that even I couldn't see him, and only his warm hand holding mine reassured me he was still there.

'Hey, arseholes, tell your master I'm here!' I shouted when we got close. Several faces turned in my direction.

A whisper in my ear made me shiver as Leszek released my hand. 'I will be right behind you. Grab Nina and run to the forest. My men will handle the rest.'

'Come along, princess, Nicolai is expecting you.' The man who answered me had a thick Russian accent but didn't look unfriendly. More disinterested and after joining him, I asked.

'So, what does Nicolai want from me?' I asked, trying to give Leszek information about Rostov's plans.

'That I don't know, but he's waiting for you. I suggest you cooperate. You wouldn't want to know what he does to those who oppose his orders.'

'Did you ever oppose?'

'He wouldn't dare after witnessing what I can do to him, his men, and you, Sara. You've made me wait for long eno...' Rostov came out of nowhere and looked at me before he sneered. 'I told you to come alone.'

He was either insanely fast, or he played with time again because one moment, he held me by my arm, and the next, I was standing in the temple with its doors slamming shut behind me.

His actions were the catalyst to pandemonium. Shots burst from the darkness, followed by the shouting of men and howling of wolves, but the most terrifying sound came from the doors that bent and cracked when something massive and powerful slammed into them.

'Sara!'

Leszek's voice was nearly incomprehensible, a roar that shook the small room's walls, but I focused on the man gripping my arm. His ashen white hair and colourless eyes starkly contrasted with his dark clothing. He could even be handsome if not for this lack of colour, almost like he detested all joy in life, opting for the monochrome palette.

'Your lover is exerting his power against my wards, but we will be finished before he breaks them. Come, my priestess, it is time to fulfil your duty to humanity and return our Lord Czernobog to his rightful place. Don't worry, I'm sure he'll grant you a boon for your service, maybe even letting you keep your beast,' he said, laughing when the pounding stopped at the sound of an alluring voice. 'Or maybe not. It looks like the Lady Jurata has come for her betrothed.'

My heart almost stopped as I recognised the name of the green-haired sea goddess with eyes the colour of stormy seas who was hellbent on seeing me dead. Now I knew why.

'I trust him and didn't come here to listen to your lies.' I let my disdain for his games show, looking down at where his hand still rested on my arm. 'Where is the woman you took from the shifter's hospital?' My eyebrow lifted, and he released me with a shrug.

'Come with me, and you will see her, but do not attempt to escape. This place is locked down by the spells even your lover can't breach. If you even so much as twitch in the wrong direction, I'll rip you so far from time's embrace you'll wander eternity alone.'

My mind savoured images of Rostov's demise, but it was more important to free Nina, so I followed him, praying she was alive. We walked from the antechamber to what I could only assume was the main prayer room. The interior was much bigger than I'd expected, and I couldn't help but be impressed by the pillars of black oak until my eyes stopped at the sight of a roughly hewn stone table. *No, not a table, an altar,* I thought, grinding my teeth at seeing Nina laid out, spreadeagled and restrained on its surface, wracked by the pain of struggling to escape from such an awkward position.

I rushed toward her, but Rostov snapped his fingers, and my face collided with an invisible wall.

'You motherfucker! What have you done to her?' I turned to him, but he had already stepped forward, laughing at me from the other side of his barrier.

'Ensured her compliance and, with it, yours. Isn't it clever? With your friend secured here, I can use her to fuel my wards, and as the spells drain her life force, you cannot delay if you wish for her survival,' he said, smirking, reaching down to stroke the back of one hand over her pale cheek, unsheathing a dagger with the other.

'Tell me, Sara. How much do you value your brave nurse? Should I use her for our ritual, carving out her still-beating heart and offering it to our master? Will her death be enough for his freedom, or should I forgo this pleasure so that you may call Czernobog with your power, saving her life? I will even spare those who are attacking my temple.'

'Your temple? Really? Because I don't remember Czernobog being one to share.' I smirked, but he looked at me, rolling his eyes as if he faced an uneducated child.

'A god must have a vessel, ignorant child, and Czernobog chose me. With his essence filling me, we will be immortal. I will breach the prison they call the Nether and free the power locked away for millennia. You and I, Sara, we can bring real magic back to this world.'

'You are fucking insane.' My eyes widened when the dagger dropped a few centimetres.

'Choose Sara. Deep down, you know it is your destiny. The seer foretold the appearance of Soul Sheperd in the Amber City, and I came here for you and you alone. Why degrade yourself next to that beast when you could be a consort of the Dark One himself? Call upon Czernobog to unite us, and nobody has to die.'

I looked into Nina's eyes. She was in pain but still shook her head, telling me to refuse. I couldn't, though, not with a dagger aimed at her chest.

'Fine, I will do it, but let her go.' I said, and Rostov smiled.

'I knew you are a reasonable woman, but I want an oath, a blood oath.' He said. I didn't have the faintest idea what a blood oath was, but on impulse, I bit my lip, smearing blood on my finger, and then touched the barrier.

'You have my word. I will return your god to the world if you release and heal Nina immediately.' I kept it as ambiguous as possible, promising him to draw Czernobog here but nothing more. The barrier shimmered, ripples of power spreading from the bloody fingerprint before it shattered, and Nina raised her head, weak and dazed.

Rostov pushed her off the altar, and I rushed toward my friend, who landed on the hard floor with a heavy thud.

'Sara, you can't do it. This bastard is a monster. He killed so many just to keep this place running.' She murmured, looking around, her dazed eyes slowly regaining focus, but Rostov laughed.

'She swore a blood oath, fool. If she runs, her soul will face unimaginable torture.' He unbuttoned his shirt, gesturing toward me. 'Come, my dear, it is time to fulfil your part of the bargain.'

I studied Rostov as he drew a sigil on the black stone before repeating the gesture on his chest. When I approached, he lay on the altar and grabbed my hand, placing it in the centre of his chest. I could sense his spirit throbbing at the core of his existence. Weak and tainted, but full of greed and desperation. With a boom, the building shook under the pressure of an external force, and Rostov hissed before he started an incantation. The grating melody of his voice gave me goosebumps, but I could easily understand the words and the intent behind them.

Come to me, answer my call, come to me and accept your servant's sacrifice. Darkness condensed around Rostov's body, and he smiled in ecstasy.

Yes, come to him, fill him, and when nothing is left of you in the Nether, let me bind you to this mortal body before I kill you. I thought, sensing another presence in the room. Coiling darkness reached for me, wrapping its tendrils along my hand, still connected to Rostov's chest.

'I can feel him, his power. Guide him, Sara. That's what you were born for. Guide him home, Soul Shepherd.'

'Doer lu'quanth nindol rothe xuil dosst yorn.'

The strange words came from the depths of my soul, but I knew their meaning. *I give you this body to rule, to use, to destroy. I bind thy soul.* I didn't just let Czernobog possess him, instead forcing the old god into the very fibre of Rostov's being, remaking the Warlock's existence.

Rostov's body jerked, his pupils widening in shock, and I felt his heart flutter in his chest like a caged bird before it stuttered to a halt, and he died. The man who'd hurt and killed so many was gone, even as his body was filled with energy.

'Sara! What have you done?' Leszek's roar was filled with fear, but I didn't regret my actions. I owed Jarek and those killed to fuel the Warlock's obsession, this moment of revenge. Rostov was dead; now it was his master's turn. I looked at the body before me, eyes filled with swirling darkness as it slowly sat up, my hand still pressed against its chest. I tried to snatch it back, but Czernobog was faster, securing my wrist and refusing to let go.

'Ah, little witch, I saw you in my thoughts, his thoughts. I'm glad we could meet again.' His voice, low and sensual, with the hint of a hiss, threatened to overwhelm my mind. His hand lazily trailed over my cheek, and like a deer in the headlights, I trembled under a crashing amount of power. His finger slid lower, touching my bloodied lip, and he raised it to his mouth to taste it. Suddenly, his face contorted in fury, and he spat to the side.

'Leshy! He is sorely mistaken if he thinks the gift of his blood will stop me from claiming you. You are mine now,' he snarled.

And then the Dark God bit me.

Chapter Thirty-Three

Venom coursed through my veins, making my thoughts sluggish. I knew I was still in Czernobog's grip as his mouth was against the hollow of my neck, his fangs puncturing my skin. The agony I felt as his teeth tore into my flesh was slowly replaced by a strange, euphoric lethargy, leaving me hanging limply in his embrace.

I watched with detached interest as Nina picked herself off the floor and looked around. As our eyes met, hers widened in terror before she grabbed a tall candlestick, toppling its burning candle to the floor as she brandished her improvised weapon in Czernobog's direction; its spiked end reflecting the flickering light in my eyes as she prepared to do something stupid.

I tried to speak, to stop her, but my mouth wouldn't obey me, and I could only watch as Nina stabbed Czernobog in the back. The only reaction from the old god was laughter, his teeth ripping away from my neck as he expressed his disdain for my friend's attack. Czernobog lowered me gently to the ground, turning his attention to Nina, who still stood there wielding her weapon.

The confusion on her face told me she didn't feel the immense power surrounding her opponent's body, and I tried to warn her, but once again, my body failed me as Czernobog gestured with one hand, his power throwing her against the wall.

I crawled, slowly dragging myself along the floor to get to her. I felt Czernobog's stare on me as he observed my efforts with a lazy smile, but all I saw, all that pushed me forward was my friend, unconscious by the wall, and the need to get to her.

The building shook, and I sprawled flat on the floor, arms trembling weakly. I took a moment to gather my wits, only for another thunderous boom to deafen me. This time, the doors to the inner temple bowed inwards, two massive paws thrusting through a widening gap until they burst apart, smashing explosively against the walls to reveal the monstrous creature that could only be my Leszek.

Wow, is that? Is that what he really looks like? My thoughts were a jumble as I stared. With his antlers brushing the ceiling, he stepped into the dim light of the glowing amber, and my jaw dropped. Leszek's already muscular physique had grown so massively that only tattered remnants of his combat gear were hanging from his gloriously furry torso and arms. I took in the pelt over his shoulders and head, at a loss as to where he'd found a wolf's hide from or the golden torque gleaming at his throat. However, it was his hands, sporting three-inch claws big enough to crush my skull, that kept capturing my attention as they flexed into fists, blood dripping from the darkened fur.

Just like my vision, I realised, but there was no love in his gaze, only death as he surveyed the wreckage of the room. I savoured the image of my wild, elder god in all his glory until my arm was roughly grabbed and my body lifted from the ground. Leszek stepped forward in reaction.

'Don't fucking dare touch her!' he roared, and my head slumped to the side when Czernobog held me before him, showcasing the damage to my flesh as I sagged. 'What have you done to her?'

Leszek charged. My enraged beast rushed forward, body blurring as he sped toward us, but Czernobog simply smirked, and Leszek's body slammed into an invisible barrier, my ears popping as magic flared, and we shifted outside of time. It felt like the world was duplicated, two images not fully aligned. The god who held me created a temporal distortion, and now we were locked in a bubble of time.

The bubble distorted as Leszek raged, crashing into it repeatedly, refusing to accept defeat, making the world ripple as I stared, amazed he could even do that much, but as the magic solidified, his form slowed until he stilled. Anger raged within me, burning through my lethargy, and my body reacted to its stimulus, clearing my muddled thoughts. I needed to break this spell and free us from this temporal cage so that Leszek could deal with this powerful threat. *If I could only reach for the dagger, or move at all, for that matter,* I thought, running scenarios through my head. I couldn't fight, at least not now. I couldn't even cast a spell. I needed something to help me regain control. My eyes drifted to Nina, the woman who was a sister to me in all but name, but she was lying unconscious like a broken doll. Sister… the Coven….

Maiden protect me, Mother heal me, Crone guide me. Help me, please. Veronica, I need you. I directed my thoughts to the witches, trying to find the life-giving tether that connected me with them. I kept repeating the blessing, and when their response came, it was filled with magic so different from Czernobog's deathly embrace that it allowed me to breathe.

We are here. Take what you need, and be brave, little sister; fight back, fight back, fight back.

The chorus of voices in my head urged me to break through the torpor affecting me. Supportive, invisible hands filling me with their wild, feminine power and giving me the strength to act. Czernobog didn't even look at me, clearly dismissing me, solely focusing on Leszek… Leshy.

A hand stroked over my cheek, and I nearly cursed as it continued to the still sluggishly bleeding bite marks. The Dark God was taunting my lover. I looked at Leszek, and somehow, his eyes moved, our gazes meeting. Love and sorrow mixed in the rich green eyes, and I lost myself momentarily, smiling at him to give us both courage before I mouthed, *Buy me some time.*

The touch of a viper's tongue slithered over my skin, making me shudder. 'She tastes delicious filled with my venom, Leshy. Soon, the taint of your blood will be gone, and she will be only mine,' Czernobog said, releasing his grip and whispering. 'Stay here, sweetheart. I will see to you later.' With that, the old god walked close to the barrier and stretched like he was trying to adjust to his new body, the powerful spirit not entirely fitting in his new form.

With a casual wave of Czernobog's hand, the bubble shimmered. 'Join me, Forest Lord. Join me, and we can share in the bounty that is your lover. I am even willing to allow you dominion over your wild and free spaces.'

'Why did you come here?' Leszek's voice, distorted by his frighteningly large canines, was intimidating, but the look he shared with me seemed softer, and I nodded, confident he'd received my message. Relief washed through me, but I didn't have much time, even with Leszek keeping Czernobog occupied.

'Why? For her, for my freedom. Are you not tired of hiding? Of living in the shadows? Nicolai saw what you were trying to do. You want a better future for our people, but this is the wrong way to do it. Freedom must be taken, not scraped off the floor like scavenging dogs, and you, with your politics, hospitals, agreements and alliances, are just a slave to the humans. Once feared and respected, the noble Forest Lord reduced to the role of guard dog for a mere scrap of land. How far you have fallen, my brother, and those idiots in Gedania support this. I can give you the freedom to hunt, to rule. We can tear down the Nether and return magic to the world.' His fervent speech was met with Leszek's icy stare.

'To hunt? To rule? Do you really not remember why we created the Nether in the first place? We were being hunted, mortal bodies killed over and over again, weakening our spirits with each rebirth and with what? With bows and fucking swords. We are immortal. We can survive this, but what about the lesser spirits, magical beings, and hybrids? Do you think humans, with their guns, tanks and planes, would allow a few upstart gods to take control? Even Rostov knew the truth of human technology, killing dozens of our people with bullets he helped create, and how long till they develop worse weapons? Weapons strong enough to kill the gods? I succeeded in this realm because I never underestimated humans, but now they have changed, too. While they have better ways to kill, they have also grown more accepting. We can find freedom in this world, but not through tyranny. The times of ruling through fear and magic are over, but if you crave power, there are plenty of ways to gain it.'

I tuned out their conversation while attempting to unravel the temporal spell, tracing each of the symbols Veronica taught me, one by one in the air, my finger leaving an afterglow in its wake that made me work slowly to avoid being seen. I saw more people spilling through the broken door, spreading out around the room's edges in disjointed stops and starts, the distortion of the Dark God's spell creating the odd effect. Only Adam came closer, his eyes fixed on Nina before he stopped at the barrier.

'You want me to be satisfied with being a husk of what I was? Kowtowing to my inferiors so they don't kill me? I see you, Forest Lord, the power you have gained thanks to the Soul Shepherd, but those women are rare and hidden well by Dola. You're telling me you'd give it up to live as you were? Living on the fringes of a society that uses your image to scare children? Or is the real reason that you want this for yourself? Unlimited power and the freedom to reign unrestricted?'

I paused when Czernobog turned his regard toward me, a frown forming when he realised I was much closer than before.

'No, I cannot stay locked in that gilded cage, filled with power and unable to use it freely. I will ask one last time: join me as Jurata did or face destruction as I take this world for my own.' Czernobog's ultimatum came as I completed the rite and pulled the dagger from its sheath. As the blade trailed over my forearm, it sliced through the flesh effortlessly, blood welling from the wound and trickling into my palm.

Leszek sneered in answer to the Dark God's demands. 'You just want war with humans, your own kind, or anyone that dares challenge your words. Do you really think you can win?' That question was my cue, and I cast my blood at the barrier, my mind focused on the magic boiling inside me as I shouted.

'Restore!'

I assumed the bubble would collapse. Instead, the spell sent shock waves across its surface, a frost expanding and obscuring the outside world as Czernobog turned, grabbing me by the throat.

'You insolent bitch. He won't get you, and once I'm done with him, I will make you regret that,' He spat, his face so close I could smell his breath. *Something had gone wrong. Had I made a mistake? Was I not strong enough?* My thoughts turned frantic as the grip on my throat constricted, darkness creeping into my vision.

'Sara!' I heard Leszek's voice and held on to it as my anchor. I was running out of time, the pressure on my neck stealing my consciousness, entirely in the old god's power. I tried kicking and punching, all to no avail, my eyes scanning the area, desperately seeking a solution even as they caught sight of the frost nearly completely covering my prison. If I could only hold out.

I felt the heaviness of the dagger in my hand, unsure of how it got there. Before today, I'd never killed anyone, not even when I witnessed the horrors of the Balkan War, and we'd been attacked by marauders, but this time I couldn't hesitate. Jarek's mutilated body flashed before my eyes, strengthening my resolve. God or not, he had to die. I stopped thrashing and placed my hand on Czernobog's chest. The Dark God looked back through Nikolai Rostov's eyes. His face changed by its possession, black veins beneath its white skin, and I knew I would see this scene in nightmares for the rest of my life. Bracing myself, I stared, sinking into his gaze, relying on my intuition to determine the right path. Vision blurring, I felt the answer reveal itself.

The grin I let spread across my lips made Czernobog frown, but it was too late, as I was already at work binding the darkness, the nightmares, pain, menace and sorrow that defined his existence into the flesh beneath my hand.

'I hate you,' I whispered, barely louder than a sigh.

'Everybody does,' he answered, his eyes widening when I moved. Not a mindless trashing this time, but a last-ditch effort using a move taught to me by Adam. I arched my body and kicked so hard I felt it in my bones. It gave me a little space, and I struck. He was fast, so fast that the dagger almost missed the mark, catching the rib, but I pushed hard until, with a sickening crack, the blade found its target.

'What have you done? You cannot kill the darkness. You can't... just... kill me,' He rasped. We dropped to the ground, and that gave me another advantage. I pushed him down, my hand still on his chest, holding his spirit in place while blood gushed from the wound. If I'd hit the heart, he would be already dead. Instead, Czernobog kept bucking, and I knew if I let go if I allowed this essence to escape to the Nether, he would return to exact his revenge, so I held on. Pain and darkness engulfed me, choking all light, his claws digging into me. His bite mark radiated with sharp, agonising pain while his poison burned through my veins. Czernobog was using his venom somehow, trying to kill me, but I was going to kill him first.

'I've got you, my love.' The sob that escaped my lips when I heard this was ragged and uncontrollable, but nothing else mattered as Leszek's calloused hands wrapped around mine, adding strength and magic. My Wolfie was here. He'd broken through that damned barrier and come for me. So I clenched my teeth, unwilling to reveal the hellfire destroying my body, weakening me with each breath.

As Czernobog's hands fell from my body, I leaned in close.

'Can you feel death coming, you bastard? For everything you've taken away from me, I will hold you to this body as it bleeds and dies, and you along with it.' A disturbed laugh rose from inside me. I would be a Godkiller, but even if I died, it would mean something.

'Your soul is facing eternity in the void unless I convince my Lady to release you.' Leszek's voice startled me, and I gasped, unsure of what was happening and why he wanted to release this monster.

'What do you want?'

'A blood oath, an eternal promise. You will never return to the mortal world and never seek revenge on Sara or those she holds dear. That is the price for your freedom.'

'He has to die.' I said through clenched teeth, and my words earned me a quick glance from the fallen god, his fear evident as he spoke.

'Usstan swariy pholor l'vlos lu'athiyk ulu neitar xta'rl dos xor dossta.'

He said it so quickly, the words reverberating from the depths of time and reaching into my mind. I knew their meaning. Czernobog had sworn on his blood and power to never enter this realm or hurt me. The magic in me recognised the bargain and demanded his release. We had defeated him, but I felt robbed of my revenge, of my last dying wish.

'Let his spirit go, my love.' Leszek entwined his hands with mine, pausing when he felt my resistance. 'Please, there is no light without darkness, and his death would shatter the world. Let him go.'

Rage, pure unbridled rage, flashed in Czernobog's eyes when he realised Leszek wouldn't let me kill him in fear that the act would condemn the world to chaos.

'You think you've won? She will die. If I can't have her, no one will. My poison is in her blood. Look at her. See how she burns....' He said, hatred dribbling off his words, and I took my hand away, ripping apart the tethers that held Czernobog's spirit to mortal flesh. His voice faded into silence with the death of his host.

'Farewell, nutjob.' I said, staring at the blank expression to check for signs of life. The man who dreamed of becoming a god lay there, broken, with arms splayed to the sides. The Coven's voices faded from my mind, and I looked around. Adam was with Nina. He scooped her off the floor, cradling her while my friend tenderly lay her head on his shoulder. She sent me a faint smile as he carried her out, and I smiled back, rising slowly. I wanted to face my destiny standing.

The room spun, and bitter laughter rose in my throat. *Will my dignity be taken from me, as well?* I looked around, dazed, sweating as I overheated, and shivered simultaneously. I'd lost all feeling in my shoulder some time ago. Now, there was only pain.

'I wish we had more time,' I said, touching Leszek's face, and I swear his skin was paling before my eyes.

'Can you create a temporal distortion? We need time to get to Gdansk. I need my island, our home, to extract the poison from your bloodstream.' He said, searching my face for confirmation, but I shook my head.

'I know how to dismantle such a spell but not how to make it. It always happened by accident, and don't forget, it's a big no-no.'

A delirious giggle escaped my lips, and before I knew it, I was in Leszek's arms, travelling at speed out of the temple. The field was full of corpses, but far more people were standing and walking around. I recognised shifters and a few vampires, but some regular humans stood with Nadolny, guarding the remnants of Rostov's little army.

'I'm taking her to the healer,' Leszek said to Nadolny, who nodded.

'Then go. I will clean up here and let your men know if I find anything worth your attention.' I would admire how effortlessly those two men cooperated if I hadn't felt so sick. I clung to Leszek's body tighter when he carried me away, my tears falling as soon as we were out of sight.

'Nina, will she be alright? Promise you will look after her.'

'Adam will. He seems to be fond of your outrageous friend,' he said, bundling me into the car, pausing as he touched my face. 'Don't you dare to give up, Sara. I need you and forbid you to give up. I promise you will live, my brave Firefly, but please fight for me, my love,' he said, cursing when my head lolled back.

'I'll... try.' I whispered, and he jumped into the car. The screeching of tires was the last thing I remembered.

Pain exploded through my body and filled my existence. No sight, sound, or smell existed in this hell of agony. I screamed but heard nothing, then something else appeared in my awareness, a coolness laid against my forehead, then sound. I was still screaming, but someone else was speaking, offering soothing words that further pushed back the pain. I don't know how much time had passed, waves of torment cresting and falling, taking my consciousness along for the ride. Finally, it faded enough for me to hear him, my Wolfie, with his cheek against mine, whispering to me.

'I know it hurts, love, but it will end soon. You are strong and brave. I never met a woman like you, and it humbles me you chose to be mine. Just hold on a little longer, Sara. Please, I cannot live without you.' The anguished plea reached through the haze, but I couldn't answer. Instead, my hand slid over the covers, reaching for his.

The moment I moved, he held my hand with desperate gentleness and lifted it to his lips. 'Sara?'

'Water,' I croaked. My lips were dry and peeling, but I felt his arm slide under me, and I was lifted off the pillows and placed on his lap. The cold glass rim touched my lips, and I sighed when cool liquid flowed down my parched throat.

'Here, take small sips,' another fluid touched my lips. This time, it was bitter with an aftertaste of lemon and magic. I coughed when it tingled on my tongue, but I felt better and strong enough to open my eyes. Faces, faces were everywhere. Veronica stood closest to me, still holding a vial. Michal was right behind her. When I focused, I could see Tomasz and Adam, and much to my surprise, my boys, leaning against the wall.

'What the fuck?' I coughed out, looking around. I was in Leszek's bedroom. I vaguely remembered he wanted to take me home, but why did they all come here?

'You almost died, my love. We were worried.'

I laid my hand on his chest and turned to look at him. His face looked haunted, gaunt and sickly. Even his eyes had lost their usual lustre.

'You said I was dying, but you're the one who looks like a week-old corpse.' I said, wondering what kind of liquid Veronica gave me because I continued to improve. My eyes went to her, and she snorted.

'The Leshy fought through the night to keep you alive. I wouldn't dare to tell the man who made you immortal that he looks like shit, but whatever rocks your boat. Still, hearing someone telling off the Forest Lord is always a pleasure,' she said, shrugging as I sat there blinking.

'Immortal?' I looked at him, but he turned away to avoid looking at me.

'Everybody out. I need to talk with Sara in private.' He said, and our friends left the room without a word of protest.

'Immortal?' I repeated.

'The blood I gave you came at a price. I should have asked you, but I was afraid you would refuse, and there was no time to explain how much I wanted you to stay by my side. I will beg on my knees for your forgiveness, but I refuse to regret my actions. If not for the gift of my blood and power, you would have perished from Czernobog's venom.'

'Hmm, I didn't have a chance from the start, did I? You just decided I would belong to you.' The situation, already beyond bizarre, left me spinning. Being alive surprised me, but being woken in a room full of people, only to be told I was now immortal? That took the biscuit. Not forgetting, of course, that Leszek, despite his promise, had unilaterally imposed his will on my life. I was happy to be alive, but being immortal was never something I'd wanted. I looked at the man who held me in his arms, watching him become increasingly nervous.

'I couldn't help it. I love you, Sara. The way you face adversity, your passion, and your zest for life have changed how I live and treat others. If anyone didn't stand a chance, it was me. You are my light, my beautiful Firefly.' Leszek took another breath to continue, but I raised my hand, stopping him.

'Where is Nina?' My unexpected question startled him, and I watched Leszek's eyes darken, his muscles tensing beneath me.

'She is safe, resting at home. She was here earlier, but Adam took her back. She was still tired after her ordeal.'

'The shifters and the people who fought for us?'

'They are fine. Sara, why are you changing the subject?'

Leszek touched my chin, tilting it up, and I felt guilty looking at his ravaged face. Whatever this healing and immortality cost him, it was a hefty price. 'Will you be alright?'

'Yes, I just need a few day's rest. What is going on, my Firefly? Are you angry with me? I swear if there was any other way to protect you, I would have taken it.'

'I know, and I'm not angry, just... I'm tired. I need to sleep and think. This is a tremendous change. Do you think you could leave for a moment?' I asked, and a grimace of pain ran across his face.

'Take all the time you need. I will be outside if you need me. I will always be here for you.' He left the room, and Scarface used the moment to sneak in and jump on the bed.

What have you done to the Beast Lord? He looks like you broke his heart. Trust my cat to sink his claws into my aching soul.

'Maybe I did. I just don't have the answer he wants to hear. He made me immortal, and I think he wants more than I'm ready to give.'

Well, that surprised me, you don't love him? Or are you just scared and overwhelmed? Leszek is a wild, passionate spirit and loves with all his soul. You know he nearly died saving you? I heard him arguing with the other man over his decision. It almost came to blows, then your witch friend arrived, and they locked me in your bedroom. There's no such thing as a cat allergy if you ask me. Did they think I'd stop them? Idiots. Scarface sniffed, his disdain clear, then curled up next to me. *So? What are you going to do?*

'I don't know. I just don't know anymore. Can this immortality thing be undone?'

No, he gave you a part of his soul. Do you really not want this, not want him? What are you afraid of?

'Eternity. We haven't known each other long, and the circumstances...? Eternity with one man when everyone else you love fades and dies is a very long time.'

Chapter Thirty-Four

The distress I saw in Sara's eyes shattered my heart, even if I'd expected such a reaction. It didn't change how I felt, though. Not for a second did I regret my decision. It would have happened eventually. Our connection and love had already grown so strong that she would have joined with me voluntarily, given time and the chance to court her.

I should have asked for her permission, but with such a powerful foe to face, my fear won out, and I decided to keep her safe, no matter what. I couldn't let her die. I couldn't lose her in a temporal distortion or watch Czernobog's venom destroy her. Knowing it was wrong, I made my choice and was willing to face the consequences of my actions.

With her sharp tongue and gentle heart, this human had become my soulmate. I found her after hope of finding a companion had long since turned to dust. I'd dedicated myself to protecting my people and living a loveless but satisfying life. Sara was everything I never knew I wanted: brave, bold, passionate and dedicated, genuinely caring for those she loved, and these qualities made her unique.

Jurata had never cared. She was fierce and bold, but under her fire and brass was emptiness. Where Sara was ready to sacrifice herself, Jurata would ally with the enemy for one iota of power. My former lover and sea goddess offered nothing but a void that almost consumed us.

'Is Sara alright? Where are you going?' Michal's question made me look up, and I stared at my assistant without a word. Whatever he saw in my face made him launch into another pep talk. 'Don't you dare blame yourself. We almost lost her, so it was the right thing to do, Boss. She'll come to terms with it. Sara is a reasonable woman, and with a good rest, I'm sure she'll look at things more positively.'

'I hope you are right.' I said, feeling defeated.

'I'll bring Nina over tomorrow. After they talk, she will feel better. Not that I could stop my... that crazy woman, anyway.' Adam offered, and I couldn't help but smile. My rakish vampire was on the quick route to being domesticated by one outspoken nurse.

'Make sure she eats. She forgets to eat when she's upset.' Damian said, and Michal immediately went to the fridge.

'Don't try explaining it to her. Sara can forgive a lot but hates being manhandled and will need time. For what it's worth, she loves you, so instead of giving us this beaten pup look, have a rest and be ready to win her back.' My new paramedic friend finished before he turned to the rest of the company. 'Let's go, give them some space. We still need to clean up the mess; there's only so long before the environmentalists investigate our mysterious spillage.'

Tomasz rolled his eyes, but the wolf Alpha dragged himself from the chair just as Veronica emerged from my bedroom. She stopped beside me, and I saw compassion in Coven Mistress's face for the first time.

'Whatever happens next, you did the right thing, my Lord. I will return in a few days. I think we should talk about our working relationship, and I hope this will change many things for the better.'

Things have already changed for the better. I had united Tricity, not just my people but the Coven, the humans and the merfolk. Even the Council of Gedania had sent me a message of appreciation, with mention of dire consequences for Jurata's antics.

I bade everyone farewell, sat in my office, and poured myself a good measure of whisky. I needed the gently sharp taste on my tongue to clear my mind and its warm afterglow to soothe my heart.

'What if they are wrong and she won't forgive me,' I said out loud, rolling the glass in my hand, but the question I wanted to ask was, would she still love me now? But I dared not allow that to pass my lips. Playing with the glass rim, I focused on the battle's reports. In the cold light of day, it was an unmitigated success. Not only did the combined teams defeat Rostov's mercenaries, but they also did so with minimal casualties. Even the merfolk didn't disappoint me, despite the surprise of Jurata's appearance.

My former lover used the eve of Forefather's Day to exit the Nether, coming to Czernobog's aid. I cursed silently at the memory, reliving that awful moment.

When the song came, I'd been battering the heavily warded door, its magic bowing beneath my fists. With the melody came words of a love that spanned centuries, never truly ending even as we lived apart. However, if I stopped fighting and held my heart's desire in my arms again, we could live as the gods we were born to be in this brand new world. Jurata's dainty hands stroked down my spine, even as my fists crashed into Rostov's wards, soothing my rage. She had smiled when I turned toward her. She had told me how she'd dreamed of living together, ruling together, the union of the sea and forest as it was meant to be. She'd told me she never stopped loving me.

I'd listened, a part of me still wanting to believe she cared. My body sagged, mellowing under the sea goddess's touch. I'd fought hard not to despair when she betrayed me, and the power of Jurata's song reminded me of those days, promising a return of the love I'd felt. A lover, a companion, a woman I could cherish.

I felt myself succumbing to the seductive lies, Jurata's magic using my fear of losing love again to cloud my mind, when a discordant scream tore the illusion apart. I looked up to see a lone siren striding from the sea, singing with enough strength to disrupt the magic of her goddess.

When her purposeful steps brought her closer, I recognised the tortured siren from the dockyard, and now I could hear the words inside the agonised tune. I turned to look at Jurata as she listened to the song of betrayal and abandonment and a people cast adrift to suffer until someone worthy found them and offered their protection. The fury that distorted the sea goddess' face showed her true disdain, and as she raised a hand to punish her subject, I hit her with the full power of the forest. Vines grew so fast they shot upwards, encasing Jurata's body and gagging her. The sea raged, a storm gathering offshore, but the land was my domain, and I held back her fury easily before turning away to face the temple doors. In a flash of inspiration, I forced my vines to grow thorns, piercing the skin of the helpless goddess, stripping away her power to the point her spirit fled to Gedania, and I used the stolen energy to destroy Rostov's wards.

From that moment, everything went downhill fast. A second, stronger ward slowed my progress until something within me snapped, and I grew, a berserker's fury erupting from within as I tore at the doorway, my hands sprouting massive bear claws that shredded both magic and door, allowing me access to the terrifying sight of Sara dangling helplessly from Czernobog's grasp, his fangs embedded in her neck, and I gave in to the bear's fury, charging head first into the wall of another spell.

I tore away at the magic, lost to reason for what seemed forever, until the spell weakened, and I saw Czernobog, still holding my lover but this time looking at me, taunting my helplessness. I didn't care; my eyes focused solely on Sara, and she proved he hadn't broken her yet, mouthing her instructions to me. I nodded, knowing I needed her help, but the acceptance in her eyes terrified me, and I knew I had to stop her before she became a Godkiller. If she succeeded, Czernobog's power would consume her, remaking the dark one in her image, or god's forbid, the world would break if the transformation failed.

I'd felt the depths of the betrayal Sara felt when I stopped her, but she accepted my explanation even as the dark god's venom left her helpless.

Tears continually blurred my vision as I rushed Sara home, calling everyone I knew, paramedics, healers and witches, telling them to meet me at the manor, desperate to save her life.

I watched them working on her, trying to lower the fever, injecting antivenom, chanting spells, and filling her with healing energy. Everyone was fighting for my love and their friend, but despite their efforts, her breath grew shallow, and the heart that beat in her chest slowed down and stuttered. Her face was so pale, like a funeral mask framed in her honey-gold tresses.

'Move,' I'd said, taking back her hand, pressing it over my heart as I laid my free hand over hers.

Magic poured from me. I'd already given her my blood, but what I intended to do now would need so much more. I'd always known I would sacrifice everything for Sara, and now I would prove it, happy to pay the price. I forced my will into my essence, using every ounce of power Sara had returned to me, and slowly, painfully slowly, my spirit splintered. A kernel of my being, a mere splinter of a god's essence, drifted toward her, called by my blood before embedding itself in her soul, sealing her fate forever. I heard a gasp from behind, Veronica's reaction as she recognised what I'd done.

I looked at Sara, colour returning to her face despite her battle against Czernobog's venom, but I couldn't face it, her agonised screams tearing me apart. I could burn the sickness out and restore myself later. I looked at my woman's face. Sara was still human, though now her body wouldn't age, sustained by my spirit for as long as I lived, but if fate took her away, I too would die.

I shook my head, dispelling the dark memories. I was selfish, but I was tired of walking alone through the endless path of life. Sara showed me what love could be, and I wanted this to last or die with her, only now, the woman I gave myself to wouldn't even look at me, and I couldn't blame her.

I poured another glass of whisky just as the doors opened, and Michal walked in.

'Sara is leaving. She packed her bags and asked me to call a taxi to drive her back to her apartment.'

A humourless laugh escaped my lips, and I shook my head. I'd expected this after seeing the haunted look in her eyes. This was the answer to my unspoken question, but stopping her now would once more force my will upon her choices, making my dreadful situation even worse.

'What did the healer say? Is it safe for her?' I asked, noticing Michal's frown.

'Yes, but...'

'I can't force her to stay with me, but make sure someone trustworthy drives her and carries the luggage. Phone our men in town. I want them to stock her apartment with food and ask Adam to inform Nina. I need someone she trusts to let me know if she encounters any trouble, but don't disturb her life in any other way.'

'Leszek, you love her. How can you let her go?' The condemnation in Michal's words goaded my anger, and I slammed the whisky tumbler on the table, shattering the glass and embedding a sizable chunk in my hand.

'What do you want me to do? Lock her up here like a bird with clipped wings and watch her waste away? I love her so much that it terrifies me. I did something unspeakable to keep her alive, so she is right to be angry. Maybe she will come to terms with it, but I have to consider that she won't. Even so, I want her to be happy, Michal. If living her life far away from me will give her peace and happiness… I can deal with my pain.'

'I still think you are making a mistake, but I will shut up if you let me remove that glass from your hand.'

He left after roughly pulling the shard from my palm, and I watched the wound close. I meant every word I'd said, but that didn't mean there wasn't a large part of me wanting to run upstairs and beg Sara to stay, and if it wouldn't make things worse, I would already be there on my knees. Instead, I sat there like a fool when I felt her presence sweep through the building as she left.

I couldn't think straight, but sitting there in my home, suddenly stripped of her presence, I knew it would consume me. It was too much. A sense of abandonment tore away the polished, civilised facade I showed to the world, and I ripped off my restrictive clothing, escaping to the forest. Here, in the shade of the trees, I fell onto the moss and dirt, roaring my grief to the sky.

'SARA!'

I'd lost her, my mate, my Firefly, and now I had to face eternity living without her.

The following month was a blur. I followed the well-worn path of a wealthy man working and publicly helping the community, a role I had played for years without caring. I ate to regenerate my strength after saving Sara, going through the motions of life, and agreeing with everything my advisors suggested without questioning them. All trade routes were restored. Thanks to the disruption, our amber was selling at a premium, and I now harvested the benefits.

The temple and the altar chamber on the hill provided plentiful materials at minimal cost, and I split the profits between the pack soldiers. We'd won with total, unquestionable success. The enemy shifters were dealt with by Tomasz, who declared them rabid and executed them in an unknown location, while the humans had their minds wiped and were arrested for whatever crimes the local police wanted to charge them with.

Nadolny visited me a few days after the battle. It was an informal meeting, without pressure and posturing, and I found it strangely comforting to share my thoughts with a man who, in the human world, was my equal. We agreed to continue cooperating. Sharing warehouses and patrols, ensuring that Tricity was secure and no further incidents like this could happen. After all, we both had our businesses and people to protect. At the end of the meeting, he looked at me, and I saw understanding etched into his expression.

'I heard Sara is back in her apartment. No matter how strong we are, women always have the last word in these matters. She is remarkable, and I want you to know none of my people will touch her. I will ensure her safety. Wherever she goes, she will be safe. If I can offer you a little advice man-to-man, it would be to talk to her somewhere she feels strong, then apologise - even if you have done nothing wrong. Don't let someone you care for walk out of your life,' he said.

There was a quality to Nadolny's advice that was more than platitudes, as if he had faced a similar situation and was still regretting his decision. So, instead of ignoring him, I stood and shook his hand, replying.

'Thank you for the advice. I promise to give it serious consideration.'

After this conversation, business in Tricity slowly returned to normal. I spent every hour improving the lives of the elder races, merfolk included, each night talking to Adam, who was keeping a close eye on Nina and, by association, Sara.

I wasn't the only one returning to their routine, as Sara seemed to throw herself into her work; the number of shifts she worked more than usual which made me concerned she was struggling. Only one thing was unusual: Sara returned to the dockyard hospital's ruins and spent some time there. The guard who reported to Adam mentioned that when she walked out, she looked sad and asked him if the owners intended to open it again.

When I heard this, I grasped onto it like a drowning man holding a rope and instantly grabbed my phone.

'Adam, I need the dockyard hospital open. Hire an architect to make it the best money can buy, and call in that favour with the Health Minister; I want the place licensed. Don't tell Nina, but ask Damian or Rysiek for advice. I want it to be perfect,' I said.

'Nina will be happy. She said the four of them discussed working there. Making it a place where everybody would feel welcome, and beings of the Nether wouldn't be afraid to visit.'

'I don't care about Nina...' I started, but then it hit me, the realisation I could have a glimpse into my mate's thoughts. 'Adam, I shouldn't ask, but... what else did she say?'

'That Sara is sad and doesn't know what to make of it. She thinks you were happy for her to be gone, especially since you're enjoying single life and haven't tried to contact her. Nina said Sara would never make the first move. She also told me that if you ever ask about Sara, I should tell you to shift your sorry arse and do something before she walks into your office to drag you out by the scruff of your neck.'

I was silent for a moment, letting the words sink in. *Sara thinks I'm happy because I didn't go to her? Was I wrong all this time?* My thoughts were racing. I'd wanted to go to her so many times. Go to her, demand to be let in, then kiss her till she agreed to return home, but I was capable of learning from my mistakes and knew I couldn't demand anything, so I'd given her time, waiting for the first glimmer of interest before I made my move.

'I am not happy, I'm not enjoying my life, and you, out of everyone, should have told me about this sooner.' I said, trying to keep a snarl out of my voice. Adam gave me a moment to calm down before he spoke. The mask of the playful rake slipped, revealing a concerned, caring face.

'She is part of your soul. I wish I had someone like that, so don't blow it, Boss.'

'I thought you and Nina...' I said, trying to divert my racing thoughts, and he grunted, a strange emotion in his voice.

'It's complicated.'

We finished our conversation, clearing any urgent business and ended the call, but I felt too unsettled to stay in the office and took the car to drive around the city. I knew Sara would be home by now, likely reading and relaxing with Scarface, two of her favourite pastimes. I smashed my hand on the steering wheel, cracking the wood veneer. *Enough! That's enough. I want to see you, even if it ends with the door slammed in my face; you'll know I'm not enjoying life alone.*

I turned sharply, the screech of tyres and horns ignored as I hit the accelerator, speeding toward her home. I briefly considered buying Sara some flowers and her favourite treats but decided against it. I didn't want to pressure her to let me in, but I couldn't prevent the desperation and longing from clawing at my guts. When I found myself looking at her front door, uncertainty freezing my feet to the spot, I reached up to stroke the protective symbol

I had placed there so many weeks ago. She was mine. Even when I didn't know her well, I'd felt it. The bond that whispered to my soul. I knocked hesitantly.

'Oh, just come in, and I hope you brought pizza. I'm hungry.' When I heard her voice, so inviting and casual, anger flared inside me. She was waiting for someone who could just walk in, and it wasn't me. I knew Nina was working, as Adam had been very vocal about it. Someone else was due to visit her this late in the evening.

I pushed on the handle and entered. The view took my breath away. Sara was more beautiful than ever, her blonde hair almost glowing with health, and as I imagined, she sat in her chair, book on her lap and cat curled beside her.

'I don't have pizza, and whoever you are waiting for can go fuck themselves because you and I have to talk.' I said more angrily than I intended to. Her head snapped toward me, and the book tumbled on the floor when she gracefully rose from her armchair. In a few brief steps, I was beside her. She was dressed in simple house clothes, dark leggings and an oversized T-shirt, but for me, she looked stunning, and it hurt even more to think she'd moved on.

'I missed you. Whatever you heard, I was not enjoying myself. Please tell me you are not seeing someone else? Let me explain first before you give up on us.'

'I'm not seeing anyone, you jealous freak.'

'But the invitation and pizza? Who were you waiting for?'

'Me,' answered the burly figure in the door. I recognised the man as one of Sara's friends. Kris, the firefighter. He casually strolled to her kitchen, leaving a large box on the table before he headed to the doors. 'About bloody time, mate. I was going to drag you here myself,' he said, leaving her apartment, and I stared after him, wondering if everyone had an opinion on my lack of action.

'I'm sorry. Please let me explain. It's been torture without you, and I can't do it any longer. I know you need space to think, but can we talk?' I lifted my hand to stroke her cheek but pulled it back, desperately fighting my desire to hold her.

Sara smiled, biting her lip when my hand fell to my side, then moved closer. My heart stuttered as hope flooded my soul, and I closed my eyes, unable to watch. When the gentle touch of her fingers caressed my beard, I moaned, almost missing her question.

'Would you like some coffee?'

Chapter Thirty-Five

I settled into my chair and tried to read as I waited for Kris to arrive, with Scarface dutifully curled up beside me, but I couldn't focus on my book; the story of two star-crossed lovers was not suitable for my current state of mind. I missed Leszek and his touch, even his occasionally overbearing manner. I missed the man who looked at me like nothing else mattered.

My sigh was deep as once more I mulled over my feelings for the impossible Forest Lord, wondering if these feelings of love and loss were nothing more than infatuation and regret. As usual, whenever I thought about my Wolfie, it reminded me of the changes that he'd made to my life, not just my feelings, but the whole *living for eternity* thing.

When I discovered this shocking revelation, I hadn't been at my best; I knew this. Unfortunately, surrounded by all my friends, each worrying about me, I couldn't process the monumental weight of this change, and the situation was soon circling the drain, taking me with it. So after he left me in bed, I fought with my racing thoughts, the muffled conversation from the other room, and my fears. Surrounded by Leszek's oak and elder scent, its fragrance, which had always felt like a soft, warm blanket, now suffocated me with its implication of forever, forcing me to flee its embrace.

I'd looked at Scarface, packed my bags, and waited for Michal to call me a cab. I knew he would tell Leszek of my leaving, and deep down, I hoped that the mighty Forest Lord would emerge from his office, give me an exasperated glance and say he would pick me up in a day or two because this was my home now. He never came out, though, not even to say goodbye.

It had been so long since I'd seen him, and even now, it was a struggle. Damian and Rysiek became so friendly with the wolves that they were considered a part of the pack and often came to me with news from Leszek's world. After what seemed to be an argument about his boss's attitude, Nina had kicked Adam out of her apartment - but not from her life - and each time we worked together, she huffed and cursed, regaling me with anecdotes of the idiot vampire's behaviour. Even if, despite her harsh words, there was an undertone of satisfaction that he'd refused to be driven from her life.

All their stories painted the picture of a man who continued his life as if I'd never existed. It felt like all we'd been through was a random encounter, easily forgotten by the mighty Forest Lord, and the longer it went on, the harder it was to summon the courage to call him.

Only Kris and Kamil felt safe to spend time around; nothing in their lives reminded me of Leszek and his soft, auburn beard. I was grateful for their company when I felt particularly lonely. Not that I had much time for that feeling anymore.

I doubled my hours in the Emergency Department, much to the relief of the other doctors who had fewer shifts to cover. When I wasn't working, I was learning magic in Sopot at the Coven's Villa. I was grateful for their help, as they took me in like a lost sheep, training me mercilessly until I could control the visions and shadows I saw daily.

So many times I tried to put pen to paper and write to Leszek, asking him to meet me, explaining that I hadn't run away and was scared of my new future; I just needed the time to think, only to realise how much I loved him. Several times, I gathered the nerve to contact him, but as more news of his busy schedule appeared, the more discouraged I was, and in the end, I gave up. Maybe it was better this way.

This was the second time I'd run away, hiding in my apartment, but he didn't come to collect me this time. After so much time with no sign of him, I had the feeling he had given up on us. So, when I heard the knock, I assumed it was Kris, as he'd promised to pop in with some food. Instead, I got a boiling cauldron of jealousy bursting into my home, demanding answers, but I was so overjoyed at his presence that nothing else mattered.

'Do you want coffee?' I asked as he pressed his bearded cheek to my palm, exhaling slowly as if my touch soothed some deep, gnawing pain. I wanted to take it slow and talk through the issues that tore us apart, but some mischievous spark in my soul encouraged me to add, 'Or are we going straight to bed?'

'Sara...' Leszek groaned, the gravelly timbre sending shivers down my spine, his arms surrounding me, crushing me against his chest. His chin rested on my head, and I felt a gentle tremor running through his body, contours blurring, and, for a moment, the image of an impeccable businessman was replaced by the savage god of the forest. When the tremor receded, he scooped me in his arms and, without hesitation, headed straight to my bedroom.

The snort of laughter as my lover saw my small double bed earned him a slap on his very firm chest, but that didn't stop him from leaning in for a soft, tender kiss as he lowered my feet to the ground, holding me close as he spoke.

'I am truly sorry, Sara. I have lived alone for so long, making decisions for my people's survival, that I forget to seek permission. That is unforgivable. If you agree to help me, I know it is possible to change. So if you give me a chance, I will do everything in my power to make you happy, I...' He spoke until I placed a finger on his lips.

'You are in my bedroom, and I definitely remember inviting you. Do you think I'm still mad at you? I never was. You saved my life, for fuck's sake; I almost died that day. I was scared, and that heaped another issue onto my already full plate. I didn't want to die, but this immortality thing? I don't like it. I don't want to watch my friends wither and die while I'm still youthful and thriving. Frankly, it scares me, but we can't do much about it now, can we? So, I will take it as it goes, one step at a time. I'm sorry, too. When I'm scared or overwhelmed, I run and hide, and I can't promise it won't happen again.'

Leszek smiled, his head dipping to my neck as he kissed it slowly. His lips trailed along my collarbone, then higher, teeth grazing against my pulse. Goosebumps covered my skin by the time he reached my ear, the soft breath caressing my earlobe when he spoke.

'You can run and hide, but I will always find you. I belong to you, Sara, and I will make it my life's goal to make you happy.' His hands cupped my face when he gazed at me. Leszek's face brightened with a dazzling smile before he leaned in, kissing the tip of my nose.

'I don't think you need to worry too much about your friends. Damian and Rysiek get on so well with the pack Tomasz is considering turning them. If they want to join the shifters, of course. It won't grant them immortality, but their life span would be much longer. As for Nina? Adam seemed smitten by your scary friend, so you never know what will happen there.'

My hands ventured to his shirt, and I unbuttoned it, eager to touch him. Leszek's breath sped up, and he grasped my hands, placing them flat against his chest. I saw the hesitation in his eyes before he tucked a strand of hair behind my ear.

'I love you. I won't force you to do anything you don't choose.'

'Like eternal commitment?' I asked. His eyes darkened, and I saw the flash of pain.

'Yes, like eternal commitment. As much as I want you to live with me and share my life, I will love you as you choose. However, I won't let you run away again.' So that was it; he gave me the freedom to choose our path, but in my heart, I already knew the answer. Still, it didn't mean this hero would get the girl quite so easily.

'About that...' My hands moved, sliding down to his stomach, fingers tracing over firm muscles that tensed under my touch. 'I can't commit because we have never been on a date, and I am an old-fashioned woman who needs to be courted, so... if you want to have a second chance, I want a proper courting, my knight in shining armour on his white charger,' I said, chuckling, amused by my own request.

Leszek looked at me like he didn't believe his luck or my words. His face was so happy and so vulnerable. 'You will have it all, my Firefly. I will throw the world at your feet together with my heart. My little seer, I don't care how long it takes, so be prepared for a wooing from the pages of legend because nothing is more important than seeing your dazzling smile.' The conviction in his voice raised goosebumps on my arms, and when he finished, his lips fell on mine, devouring me with sensuous passion.

My knees buckled, but he held me tight against him, peeling off the layers of my clothes with reverence, worshipping each part of my body that he exposed until I was naked before him. We didn't turn on the light when he carried me to the bed. Only the pale glow of the moon highlighted our bodies. Leszek snapped his fingers, and my decorative candles burst into flame, adding a warm golden glow to the scenery. I tugged at his shirt, and he tore it off in one powerful move before stepping out of his trousers. My throat ran dry. He was already as hard as steel and bigger than I remembered. Leszek noticed my hesitation and stopped instantly, fingers tenderly stroking across my cheek.

'Sara?'

That was my undoing. Leszek, the undying spirit of the forest, ready to stop at the merest hint of hesitation, caring more about my comfort than his pleasure. My hand drifted to the silken-covered steel of his cock, and I teased its length with my nails, enjoying the shudder travelling through his body. A barely audible moan escaped his mouth while a bead of fluid escaped the tip.

'You looked bigger than I remember, so I may struggle a little,' I said while my hand continued to tease and stroke. Leszek arched under my touch like a giant cat before reaching to stop me.

'My self-control is not the best now. I missed you far too much,' he panted, hands closing into fists when he tried to restrain himself. I welcomed this challenge. My lover wasn't the only one to have missed this, and I was more than ready to be ravaged by my wolf.

'Leshy, I don't want your control. You will give yourself to me because you are mine. Now stop worrying and help me accommodate you.'

'Sara...'

His eyes lost focus, and he growled like an animal when I pointed to the floor, demanding his obedience. The feral beast didn't hesitate, dropping to his knees before me. He grabbed my hips, fingers digging into soft flesh while his mouth pressed to my mound. His tongue darted between my folds, and I moaned, enjoying the masterful strokes of his tongue.

'Just like that... show me you miss me, Wolfie,' I moaned, my back arching when he sucked on my clit, my hand trailing through his hair, silky strands tussled when I tightened my grip and pressed him to my body.

My eyes fluttered open when I felt Leszek pull back, the coarse hairs of his beard brushing over tender flesh. 'You taste divine. I could feast on you the whole night.' He muttered, devouring me, and far too quickly, every nerve in my body screamed for release. I pushed him away, and he stumbled, sitting on his heels, observing me as I backed away, shuddering and trying to control my limbs.

Looking down, I made the mistake of looking into Leszek's eyes, his predatory gaze feasting on my body as I fell back, drawing a finger up between my folds in teasing invitation, moaning as his need drove my own.

'All yours to take,' I crooned, crooking my finger, inviting my beast to take his prize. I could barely think, gasping from pleasure, but his eyes held me enthralled. 'Don't make me beg, Wolfie. I need you. Please, do your worst.'

The ravenous hunger on his face made me almost regret my request. When he dived between my legs, tongue lapping between my folds, curling over my clit before sucking it. I cried out in pleasure, the sensation so great I tried to move away, but he held me tight.

'Mine!' he growled. Sharp nails scratched my thighs when I tried to close them. 'You are mine, Sara.' The wildness in his eyes demanded my response, even as my body bucked, seeking his tongue, and I nearly sobbed as I answered.

'Yes, yours, only yours.' I'd wanted to unleash the beast and got more than I bargained for, and it was driving me just as wild, but I didn't want to climax, not yet. I wanted him to fill me before giving in to my bliss. I fought, attempting to push him away, but the more I resisted, the more feral he became.

'I want you inside me,' I panted, thrashing against his hold, but Leszek raised his head to capture my gaze, his eyes yellow and shining like lanterns in the dark room.

'No, you will cum for me now,' he growled. I had no choice. His tongue lashing inside me, drinking me down, was like a tether that didn't allow me to break free; pleasure building at the back of my spine until, like a spring twisted too tight, it exploded, sending me into ecstasy.

My body was still shaking when he flipped me onto my stomach, plunging inside me with one brutal stroke, forcing a scream of pain and pleasure from my throat as Leszek withdrew and thrust again, grabbing my hips and controlling me completely. He moved hard and fast, taking me with unrestrained passion. I hadn't recovered from the first climax when the second built inside me. This time, it felt more profound. I wasn't fighting it this time; I wanted this more than anything in the world, giving myself entirely to my Forest Lord, letting his spirit surround me. His nails felt like claws on my skin as his driving hips rammed his cock inside me, up to the hilt, and I whimpered, letting him take my body as it pleased him.

'You are mine. I cannot sleep, cannot eat, cannot exist without you.' He growled into my ear with each powerful thrust, and I revelled in his ardent words, giving me precisely what I needed. The pressure built again, faster and harder, when he pistoned into me with feral snarls. I was balancing on the edge, bliss threatening to overwhelm my senses, when I heard his plea.

'Sara!'

'I love you.' That was all I could say before I fell apart in a world-shattering climax. Leszek roared, his shaft pulsing, shooting his seed deep inside me, wave after wave, and all I could think of was how much I needed this. How deep I'd fallen for him. My mob boss, my protector, and my perfect gentleman, all contained in the beast I cherished. He was everything I needed. Tears filled my eyes when I realised how close I'd come to losing him. Before I knew it, I was sobbing in his arms, and he turned me gently to face him, kissing away my tears. Leszek was mercifully quiet, and I was grateful he didn't ask why my heart chose this moment to shatter. I had no words to express my feelings; I finally felt whole, my painful past closing its doors, and I was ready to start anew with him by my side.

It didn't take long to calm down, but he still held me tightly pressed to his chest, and when the last tear fell, he spoke, whispering in my ear.

'I will court you properly tomorrow, my Firefly. Today... I missed you too much to wait.' He said, his voice hoarse and emotional. He carefully withdrew before collapsing beside me with a heavy sigh.

The bed, made with a modern pine frame, was not used to such heavy pounding, and when my lover's massive body dropped onto the mattress, it creaked, cracked, and fell apart, sending us crashing to the floor.

I yelped, and Leszek instinctively grabbed me, pulling me onto his body to lessen the impact. It took me a moment to realise what had happened before I laughed. Seeing Leszek's expression of utter embarrassment was the perfect ending to the best sex ever. I didn't care about the destruction or that I'd have to buy a new bed. The moment was perfect, and laughing next to him after this minor mishap felt like the most natural thing ever. He bit his lip, holding back his laughter before smiling back.

'I will buy you a new one, or we can go shopping together, and you can choose whatever you want. As for tonight ... maybe you could consider coming home. Your room is ready, and Michal would be delighted to cook for you again.'

'Nah, you are not escaping the role of suitor, or maybe that's why you broke my bed? I can sleep on the mattress, and we have pizza. Cold, but still good.'

'Be careful, woman, doubt my honour, and I will court you so thoroughly you'll beg to marry me,' he stated, humour sparkling in his beautiful mossy green eyes.

'Oh really? I am positive that would never happen,' I said with a smirk, escaping the bed and swaying my hips as I walked to the kitchen to retrieve the cold pizza, shivering when I heard him growl.

'Challenge accepted.'

Chapter Thirty-Six

(A year and four weeks later)

Snow blanketed the streets of Gdansk, and I enjoyed the chill air filling my lungs on the way out of the hospital. Leszek, as usual, was already there waiting at the entrance to my department. He hadn't missed a single day picking me up from work, a steaming cup of caramel latte in his hand, and I rushed toward him, bouncing on my tiptoes to kiss him.

He was impossibly handsome. His dark auburn hair, sprinkled with snowflakes, sparkled in the weak sunlight, his green eyes shining brightly when he looked at me, immaculately dressed in a charcoal three-piece suit.

'Hello beautiful, how was your day?' he asked, handing me my coffee when I wrapped my arm around his forearm. I launched into a rant about the system, bureaucracy, and stupid people chopping off their fingers. It was all part of our new routine; he listened, and I felt lighter, the burden and stress of my day dissolving in his presence.

Leszek kissed my temple. 'I have something to show you today.' He said, and I moaned.

'Can't we go home? It was a tough day. You don't need to date me today. All I want is a bath and to snuggle under a blanket.'

'That sounds perfect, but I swear what I'm about to show you is worth a little detour. Once we're done, I will run you a hot bath and massage your feet. We can even order pizza if you wish, although I would prefer to take you to a fancy restaurant.'

'No, no restaurants.' I answered quickly, and he chuckled. True to his word, he'd dated the hell out of me for the entire year. Clubs, restaurants, galleries, theatres, I visited them all. We danced, drank and watched performances, then ate in the fanciest restaurants Tricity had to offer before he took me home and removed the mask of cultured refinement till I screamed his name loud enough to scare the wildlife. I was still living in my apartment, even if Leszek spent more time there than I did, practically living with me. So when he nodded, opened the car door for me and agreed to no fine dining, I sighed with relief.

The snow swirled past as we drove, creating an ethereal tunnel lit only by the streetlights, and I allowed the effect to enchant me. The holidays were just around the corner, so I'd taken leave for the first time in a very long time. I wanted to spend Yule with my friends and Leszek, well, mostly him, especially since he finally promised to take me to Gedania for a brief recreational trip.

It took me a moment to realise we were driving toward the docks, and I looked at him, raising an eyebrow.

'You will see,' he said, answering my unspoken question, and I felt dread sliding down my spine at the thought of visiting the one destination I wanted to avoid. I'd only visited the clinic once since Jarek's death, and it had triggered nightmares. My mind had replayed the moment I watched him dying in my arms, feeling helpless as Dola's scissors cut through his fate, knowing I couldn't help.

'Maybe it is time to face my fear,' I whispered as Leszek pulled over.

The building was full of light. The broken windows and doors had been replaced, and as we walked closer, I saw people moving around inside with soft music playing in the background, muffling the clinking of glasses. We walked in, and I paused, unable to comprehend what was happening, my eyes transfixed by the pristine medical centre with a large reception and waiting room so well furnished it looked like a decadent private clinic.

This relaxed but elegant interior was filled with people, my people. Shifters, witches, and even Nadolny, with his entourage surrounding the buffet table. All were dressed to impress, and I felt woefully underdressed in my jeans, jumper, and thick winter coat.

My hand tightened on Leszek's forearm when the crowd turned in our direction at our entrance.

Nina's voice broke through my trance as she greeted me in her own inimitable style. 'Finally, I thought you'd never arrive. Do you know how hard it is to keep mobsters from a table of food? And damn, you won't believe what they have here. It's a marvel, but we'll need more people working here to make it effective.' It felt like everybody except me knew what was happening because I still stood there, completely shocked.

'You're opening the clinic?' I asked, still blinking like an owl. Leszek took my hand, bringing it to his lips in an old-fashioned gesture of respect and admiration.

'Happy Solstice, Sara. This is for you, a safe place where *all* of your talents will be allowed to flourish,' he said, emphasising the word *all* with a mischievous smile, and my mouth dropped open. I'd expected jewellery or maybe a book as a solstice gift, but not a whole freaking hospital.

'Pull the ribbon,' he said, pointing to the covered sign above the reception, and I absentmindedly grabbed the piece of fabric, jerking it hard.

'Jarek Roch Urgent Treatment Centre,' it read the words carved into a large wooden plaque, and I gasped, choking on a sob. My unfortunate Guardian, who'd helped me so much in the transition to this world. My gentle, caring Jarek who only wanted to be remembered. I hoped his spirit, wherever he was, looked at this with a smile.

'Thank you,' I said quietly, fighting my tears, and like a guardian angel, Nina appeared and grabbed my other hand, dragging me away.

'Come on, you have to see the theatre. You can do so many things here, and so much is automated; it's a nurse's wet dream. It's going to be blissful working here. You know I'm coming with you, don't you? I know some other nurses who wouldn't mind working on patients that are a little more hairy if they get paid decent wages.'

Her enthusiasm was infectious, but I couldn't help stealing coy glances at Leszek, who approached Nadolny, the men clasping forearms, which made me smile. Since they'd started working together, there had been a sharp dip in violence-related attendance statistics in the ER, giving us the best year ever.

Before I knew it, Nina had dragged me through the corridors, offices, lab, examination rooms and finally, the theatre. I couldn't help but stand there gaping in awe at all the equipment.

'Do you like it, my love?' Leszek asked as he wrapped his arms around me.

'I don't know what to say. It's awesome, but I'm not sure I can manage it.' I stuttered slightly, but I liked the idea of having my own space. A practice where I could focus on helping everyone appealed to my sense of integrity.

'No, you are more than good enough. You are perfect for this role, and I will support any decision you make, but can we discuss this tomorrow? Tonight, we should celebrate.'

It was well past midnight by the time everyone went home, and I admitted my man was right. This detour had been well worth it, and I already had so many plans running through my mind. While Leszek had the final say regarding security, a few slightly illegal weapons caches included, everything else was under my purview. That my extraordinary man had found a way to obtain a slew of licences for the facility, all dedicated to Jarek's name, had once more left me slack-jawed, but Leszek cured that with a few well-placed kisses that left me blushing.

I approached the waterfront, staring out across the port, its lights giving the night a surreal beauty while waves lazily broke over the concrete steps leading down to the water.

As I stood beneath the canopy of a dormant willow, its long branches swayed in the chill breeze, their whispers almost hypnotic, snowflakes alighting on my eyelashes to further soften the view; I could feel the magic of the moment. When I felt Leszek's arms sliding around my body, I leaned back, melting against his fierce warmth.

'Thank you, Leszek, you've made me a very happy woman,' I said.

When he didn't reply, I looked up, catching him as he gnawed pensively at his lip, and I started worrying when his arms slid away so that he could move in front of me. It was my turn to bite my lip, but just as I took a breath to speak, Leszek dropped to one knee, and my breath hitched as I wondered if this was the moment.

'Sara, my sweet Firefly, from the first moment we met, you have never once left my thoughts, and the more I learned, the more smitten I became. You are brave, loyal, and loving. For millennia, I was alone, a broken god, a broken man, waiting for a love I didn't know I needed, and I will spend millennia making you the happiest woman in existence if you agree to be my wife.'

I looked at him and the little box with a beautiful pillow-cut sapphire.

'Yes, Leshy, I love you, the true you, and I want to be with you. If it is eternity, so be it. We will experience each moment together,' I said.

Leszek didn't drop his gaze when he put the ring on my finger, kissing my hand with tender passion as he slowly stood, gathering me into his arms, pressing my body to his before our lips met with gentle, confident and teasing pressure; but I wanted my wolf and his passion, so I grabbed his beard and deepened the kiss before I broke away gasping.

'Take me home, Wolfie, our home, on the island, and never let me go.'

Would you like an extra story about Sara and her dream team?

Read

Moonlight Shift,

a free short story available upon sign-up to our newsletter.

About Author

Olena Nikitin is the pen name of a writing power couple who share a love of fantasy, paranormal romance, rich, vivid worlds and exciting storylines. In their books and out, they love down-to-earth humour, a visceral approach to life, striving to write realistic romances filled with the passion and steam people always dream of experiencing. Meet the two halves of this Truro UK-based dynamic duo!

Olga, a Polish woman, has a wicked sense of humour with a dash of Slavic pessimism. She's been writing since she was a small child, but life led her to work as an emergency physician. While this work means she always has stories to share, it often means she's too busy to actually write. She's proud to be a crazy cat lady, and together with Mark, they have five cats.

Mark, a typical English gentleman, radiates charm, sophistication, and an undeniable sex appeal. At least, he's reasonably certain that's what convinced Olga to fly across the sea into his arms.

He's an incredibly intelligent man with a knack for fixing things, including Polish syntax in English writing. If you give him good whiskey, he might even regale you with his Gulf War story of how he got shot.

Olena Nikitin loves hearing from their fans and critics alike and welcomes communication via any platform!

- ALL-IN -ONE Social Link
- NEWSLETTER Please sign up if you wish to recieve free books, updates and giveaways
- WEBSITE
- Also consider following us on Amazon to be notified about new releases, discounts and more.

ALSO BY

When fate tips the world towards destruction, the gods step forth to name their champion.

Peasants proverb

Chaos knows no peace or mercy, but even this primordial power is challenged by a woman willing to defy kings, gods and magic itself, fighting for what is right. When her past returns to haunt her, saddling her with an ill-tempered warrior and death lurking in the sewers of Osterad, Inanuan must face the truth of her birthright and embrace the magic that threatens to destroy her. As she fights for her freedom and to save the kingdom, she must also confront the knowledge that the man she yearns for may never learn to trust her.

What will it take to convince Marcach she is not his enemy, especially when his eyes burn golden each time he looks at her?

"When a Chaos mage fights, only blood and scorched earth remain."
Mage War Chronicles

Some victories are more costly than others, and Ina was the one that paid the price. Determined to rescue her dragon, the newly appointed royal witch embarks on a gruelling journey through the wintery Grey Mountains. The weather is not her only obstacle, as the enemy forces gathered in the kobold mines have only one goal. To capture the Chaos mage and deliver her to the heart of the mountain. With the help of Sa'Ren, Ina arrives at Castle Liath almost unscathed, but her joy is short-lived, as its granite walls hide a shocking revelation. With blossoming love shattered by a possessive dragon's claim and an impossible mission to fulfil, will the mysterious Blessing of the Mountain help or hinder her efforts to protect Cornovii?

"Chaos and the wicked soul know no rest."

(Old folk proverb)

Ina has no time to enjoy domestic life with Mar. As soon as life settles down after the Winter War, King Rewan calls his Royal Witch to give her a new task.

Southern rebellion, crops dying, and an endless stream of assassins attacking the king, leaving a trail that backs to a neighbouring kingdom. To make matters worse, an ancient cult has emerged from the shadows offering sacrifices to Winter's Death.

One fateful letter and Ina is back on the road with an unlikely companion. But what can one Chaos mage do against so many enemies and the power of the Old Gods?

Behold the monster that will shatter the world. Bear witness to her power in awe and despair. Saga of the Last Empress

With their bond gone, Mar is determined to find Ina, even if he has to challenge the Gods to steal her back. With an unparalleled enemy threatening Cornovii, Ina must restore her ability to use magic, or the country she fought so hard to save will fall under the axes of a merciless foe. He would destroy the world for her. She would sacrifice her life to save it. Can the realm survive their love?

Made in the USA
Columbia, SC
26 April 2024

34907604R00309